CEDAR CREEK

DAVID A. WEISS

This book is a work of fiction. The events and characters are a product of the author's imagination, and any resemblance to actual incidents or persons, living or dead, is purely coincidental.

"Cedar Creek" by David A. Weiss. ISBN 978-1-60264-253-9.

Published 2008 by Virtualbookworm.com Publishing Inc., P.O. Box 9949, College Station, TX, 77842, US. ©2008 David A. Weiss. All rights reserved. No part of this publication may be reproduced, stored in a retrieval system, or transmitted in any form or by any means, electronic, mechanical, recording or otherwise, without the prior permission of David A. Weiss.

Manufactured in the United States of America.

To my mother, Diana S. Weiss, who, at ninety-five, having circled the globe eighteen times, continues to display the courage, integrity and humanity that make her a paradigm of the way life should be lived.

I gratefully acknowledge those who helped me in this endeavor: the members of the Schenectady Fiction Writers' Club (Robert Conahan, David Hitchcock, Joyce McCormick and Betty Pieper) who for a decade have provided sage and thoughtful criticism of my writing; my daughter, Lori A. Weiss (B.A., Brandeis University; Ed.M., Harvard University) for creating the cover of this book; and my dear and lovely wife Joyce who is a constant source of encouragement, inspiration and joy.

PREFACE

Midway between the *Leave It to Beaver* era of the 1950's and the early stages of the twenty-first century, the past and future, standard-bearers of the never-ending struggle between tradition and change, converged in 1983 at Cedar Creek. For two hundred years, ever since the founding of America, white males had dominated the country. With the advent of the Civil Rights movement the nation had been forced to re-examine itself. A century after slavery had been abolished, its progeny, segregation and racism, thrived. So too did discrimination based upon sex. By 1983 feminism had begun to redefine the roles and relationships of men and women, but male bastions remained strong as women struggled to break through the glass ceiling. The challenges to long-standing beliefs and customs opened the door for others to step forward with issues of sexual preference and identification.

Cedar Creek invites one to step back into the era of Ronald Reagan and the cold war and the dilemmas confronting those at the vanguard of change. Join with Lauren Worthington, liberal reporter for a rural, South Carolina newspaper, as she struggles against forces steeped in southern tradition. Raised in a plantation mansion once served by slaves, she is caught in a tug-of-war between her conservative father and her black, activist-attorney boyfriend. Her father objects to her love relationship, while her boyfriend is the principal opponent of her father's plan to build a shopping mall. Lauren's professional life is equally complicated. Pressure from her male-chauvinist boss, a pragmatist who puts the newspaper's bottom line ahead of objectivity, tests her journalistic integrity.

Unlike the late 1960's when the unpopular Vietnam War and military draft led many young people to activism and rebellion, the early 1980's, racked by recession and double-digit inflation, spurred heightened focus on personal economic opportunity. All the while the country continued the long process of digesting its era of social upheaval. It is with this backdrop, a blurred snapshot of the complex and ever-changing landscape of America, that young professionals like Lauren Worthington mapped their lives.

Chapter I

Lauren Worthington squirmed in her seat. When Jerry Baker had first invited her to appear on his radio talk show, she jumped at the opportunity. Sound judgment never had a chance. Ego succumbed to the flattering offer. But with airtime only moments away, good sense was kicking in. The conservative Baker's cutting tongue, coupled with his right-wing audience, was likely to turn deaf ears to her moderate views, fiscally conservative, but socially liberal. Of course, by Cedar Creek standards she was simply a liberal.

Unlike the *Chronicle*, where she could always revise what she wrote before it appeared in print, a radio interview offered no second chances. To make matters worse, when it came to the new mall, the primary subject of the evening's discussion, she was in the middle of a maelstrom with her father on one side and her boyfriend, the other. Just as the *On-the-Air* sign flashed, Baker, about forty, rocked back his intimidating, six-foot four, two-hundred-fifty pound physique in his big leather chair. With a forehead that protruded over beady eyes seemingly bored into his huge skull, Cro-Magnons had perhaps found their link to modern-day man. Lauren shifted her gaze to a shelf that sported an autographed football and a photograph of the 1968 Baltimore Colts championship team. The fifteen-year-old picture was too far away to tell whether Baker might be among the players.

"Evening to all you folks in western South Carolina." Baker's kahlúa-smooth southern drawl grew more pronounced

1

the instant he hit the airwaves. "Tonight I have as my guest, the lovely Lauren Worthington, reporter with the *Cedar Creek Chronicle*. And may I speculate that if John F. Kennedy were still alive, he'd give her the presidential stamp of approval. She has Jackie's class, plus other feminine charms the former President certainly would have appreciated. Anyway, she's here to discuss the controversy surrounding her father's plans to construct a new shopping mall out by the interstate. But before we get to that, a brief comment on the news. Today the Soviet Union announced it would boycott this summer's Los Angeles Olympics. The *Evil Empire*, oppressor of the brave resistance in Afghanistan, has again displayed its hypocritical colors." Baker turned to Lauren. "I could hazard a guess at your views on the subject. But relax. We'll save President Reagan and the cold war for another show."

Lauren did a slow burn. Even before she had uttered a word, Baker had painted her with the Kremlin's red brush. Given the audience, her credibility would be no better than if Senator Joseph McCarthy, back when he was alive, had labeled her a communist.

"Let's go straight to tonight's topic," said Baker. "Tell us, Ms. Worthington, where do you stand, for or against the construction of the mall?"

She drew in a deep breath. With the *Chronicle* yet to take an editorial position on the project, the trap was obvious. "The mall has its pros and cons. On the one hand, Cedar Creek needs new businesses, as well as the jobs it would generate. On the other, it threatens our finest green space, the park and the lake that adjoin the proposed site. It also threatens the business district on Broad Street where vacancies continue to mount. A mall outside of town would — "

"Excuse me," said Baker. "Are you suggesting that an entrepreneur should be foreclosed from opening a new business, in this case a mall, because it would compete with existing businesses?"

His glower underscored he was not playing touch football. She hesitated, aware that she was between the proverbial rock and hard place. "It's . . . uh . . . " Her mind conjured an unwelcome image from her high school Latin textbook

2

depicting a scene from mythology that helped give rise to the rock and hard place proverb — a pen and ink drawing of Jason and the Argonauts trying to negotiate the narrow strait between the rock that was home to Scylla, the six-headed monster, and Charybdis, the devouring whirlpool.

Baker extended an arm toward her. His fingers, like the snarling heads of Scylla, communicated impatience.

Lauren tried to refocus but drew a blank.

"Ms. Worthington," said Baker, "your father is confident the mall would benefit Cedar Creek. True?"

Walking into a possible ambush was foolhardy, but tongue-tied silence, worse. "Yes," she said.

"And your boyfriend, Jordan Jackson, a member of the Village Board, is the project's staunchest opponent. Correct?"

"Well . . . uh . . . there are other opponents who may feel just as strongly."

"But none as vocal."

"Uh . . . I suppose." She broke eye contact the instant Baker, with arms folded across his massive midsection, shot her a menacing stare. She had assumed a radio interview would be easier than television. Her host's non-verbal antics, invisible to listeners, were altering that assumption.

"Ms. Worthington, earlier you seemed to imply the Constitution shields existing businesses from competition."

"I . . . I'm not a lawyer." She glanced at the glass walls of the tiny studio. It was as if they were closing in. "But we . . . uh . . . need to strike a balance. The environment and increased traffic . . . the general well-being of our community are proper matters for consideration when granting approvals of new construction."

"Sounds like a copout," said Baker. "But for the moment, we'll let it pass. Let's take a call from a listener." He pressed a button. "You're on the air with Baker."

"Hi, this is Joe, and I wanna say that this town is dyin'. It's cretins like Lauren Worthington that's killin' it. And if she wuz datin' her own kind, she wouldn't be sidin' with the likes of Jordan Jackson. Don't get me wrong. I ain't got nuttin' against colored, but rabble-rousers like Jackson are the reason Cedar Creek is headed for the big dumper."

3

Lauren's jaw clenched. An instant later Baker leered at her chest, his lecherous ogle reaching beyond her trim, brown suit. With a slight nod, he seemingly complimented the curves he had mentally undressed. Given his reputation as a womanizer, his boorishness was no surprise. Regardless, it offended Lauren no less. She was about to lash out, but Baker was quicker. He said, "Joe, can you be more specific as to how Jackson is harming Cedar Creek?"

"Sure. He was behind the housing project on River Street. That place breeds nuttin' but crime. And cause it's cheap, it draws out-of-town riffraff. Thanks to Jackson, you got more guys fightin' for fewer jobs. And most of them jobs is payin' less. It's one of them — Whatd'ya call — visual circles."

"You mean vicious cycles?" Baker waited several seconds. "Apparently our caller has hung up." He turned to Lauren. "Ms. Worthington, does Joe have a valid point?"

"Absolutely not." Her fingers were squeezing the arms of her chair. Anger had superseded nerves. "Personal innuendo and racial slurs are a poor excuse for legitimate arguments. Cedar Creek is suffering, but not for the reasons given by your caller."

"Ooh," said Baker. "My guest is becoming feisty."

You would too dealing with a bigot like Joe and a pig like you. If they weren't on the air, she would have told him exactly what she was thinking.

"Would you care to enlighten us why Cedar Creek is suffering?"

She eased her grip on the chair. "For years this was a one-horse town. Half our workers were employed at Piedland Mills. When Piedland began its layoffs two decades ago, the town began to decline. Then Piedland closed. That was the knockout punch. As for Jordan Jackson, he's one of Cedar Creek's best assets. He's endeavored to attract new businesses. It's outrageous that he and the other members of the Village Board who oppose the mall have received threats."

"In your opinion do the threats need to be taken seriously?"

"Without doubt." Lauren pointed at Baker. "You disagree?"

"As a matter of fact — no." He smiled, but the look was laden with daggers. He said, "Perhaps I'm confused. I thought I was the interviewer, the one asking the questions."

You mean the one conducting the inquisition. Lauren hoped her face conveyed the sarcasm. She said, "Threats of violence against any citizen can't be tolerated."

"There are some who believe your father is behind those threats."

"And there are some who believe that you're responsible for those rumors."

"Excuse me," he said, his look as patronizing as his voice. "Me thinks my guest *protestith* too much. Lest she forget, she is hardly the objective journalist. Her relationship with those involved, her father and boyfriend, is more than casual."

Lauren folded her arms. "Well isn't that a sweet bouquet. My charming host labels his guest biased. And pardon me for coming down to your level — referring to you in the third person."

"Now, now. Let's *not* get personal."

The little that she had listened to Baker's show, she knew that was exactly what he wanted. She sat motionless with sealed lips.

"You expect my listeners, especially the good citizens of Cedar Creek, to take your comments at face value?"

"That's up to them." She gestured his way. "As you often point out, this is a free country where citizens are entitled to speak their minds. And unless I'm mistaken, nothing in the Constitution excludes newspaper reporters."

"Ah yes. The price of democracy." His melodramatic tone modulated with the eccentricity of a vaudevillian rescuing a damsel from a villain's clutches. "Like Voltaire, though we loathe your words, we will defend to the death your right to speak them."

Cliché — but his defense of unfettered speech inveigled his audience to stifle hers. She suspected he had used the remark before.

"Ms. Worthington, before rancor diverts our attention from more meaningful matters, let me take another call." He pushed the button. "You're on the air with Baker."

"Hi Jerry. This is Jethro. I wanna tell you. I love your show. You speak my language. Us ordinary folks need a straight talkin' guy like you who sticks up for us."

"I appreciate the kind words. I know . . . "

For a moment Lauren's mind trailed off as she recalled the warm reception the audience at the community college had recently given her. This was a different theater.

"So, tell me Jethro," said Baker, "what's on your mind tonight?"

"My school taxes. A fella down at the foundry where I work told me them politicians in the Statehouse got things fixed with mandates, so we can only vote ten percent of the school budget. That true?"

"I'm not sure your question relates to tonight's topic, the proposed mall, but — "

"Sure it does, Jerry. We need the mall to pay them skyrocketing taxes."

"I see." Baker looked at Lauren. "Ms. Worthington, care to comment on Jethro's question?"

Her gut said argue. Her brain flashed minefield. "Jethro raises legitimate issues, but he's mixing apples with oranges. Education — "

"Hold the phone," said Baker. "Let me separate the issues, so there's no confusion. First, do you disagree that Cedar Creek needs a broadened tax base? And second, shouldn't communities like Cedar Creek be entitled to run their own schools?"

Lauren was fast learning Baker's techniques. Like Houdini, he distracted the audience and then pulled off his illusions. Fortunately, Baker was no Houdini. Lauren said, "No one disagrees that Cedar Creek needs new businesses. But that begs the issue whether the mall would, on balance, be positive for the Village. Let me amplify," she immediately added, sensing that Baker was about to jump in. "Suppose the owner of a vacant storefront on Broad Street wanted to tear it down and put in a waste dump. Who would want that?"

"You're comparing the mall to a waste dump." Baker uttered a loud groan. "And *you* talk about begging the question. Ms. Worthington, please."

6

Lauren reminded herself to stay cool. Speak slowly. Avoid a raised voice. "My point is that each new business must be scrutinized on its own merits."

"What about Jethro's second concern — the right to run our schools?"

Her first point had been ignored, but why beat the dead horse. She said, "Local control of schools is not simple." Another groan from Baker suggested things would only get tougher. "What if a community in the Sunbelt, the majority of whose residents were seniors, voted to cut funding for schools by seventy-five percent. Would we permit the children there to go without education? Of course not. Minimum standards must be imposed. And that's where the state and federal government come in."

"Ms. Worthington, if I recall, earlier you accused our caller of mixing apples and oranges. It seems you've poisoned the fruits. Protect education — *Yes*. But a mandate of ninety percent — you call that minimum standards. Give us a break. Next thing you know, you'll take Jethro's guns as cavalierly as you confiscate his right to vote the budget."

Wait a second. How did we jump from the proposed mall to school taxes and now to guns? She said, "Our fruit basket now stocks guns?"

Baker smiled, but any warmth was fire from a dragon's mouth. He said, "Taxes, taking property as if the Fifth Amendment didn't exist or ignoring the Second Amendment right to bear arms — With you liberals, it's all the same. The Constitution means nothing. What's the word that gay Congressman from New England uses? Flexibility. Well, flexibility my ass. Just another euphemism for emasculating fundamental rights."

Earlier Lauren had sampled Baker's use of familiar patter. Only now did his proficiency exhibit itself. True, he was no Houdini, but when it came to his craft, Baker was a master. The world of radio more closely resembled the world of magic than Lauren had previously surmised. The tongue, especially a glib one, was quicker than the mind.

"Ms. Worthington, let's talk about a subject on which it appears we agree — the threats made to members of our Village Board. "We do agree. Don't we?"

"Uh . . . yes. I think so."

"You sound hesitant."

Much as she abhorred the threats, she feared what the question masked. But anything other than condemnation would open her to an onslaught. She said, "Threats of violence have no place in our community."

"Like your boyfriend, Jordan Jackson, are you convinced the threats are linked to the proposed mall?"

Baker's newest stratagem had all the subtlety of a Times-Square neon sign. She said, "At this point it's premature to draw any conclusions. And keep in mind, he and Steve Ward, the two members of the Board who oppose the mall, weren't the only ones to receive the threats. Medford Laughlin got one too."

"True. But Medford is yet to indicate which way he plans to vote." Baker put his hand to his chin. "A rather strange coincidence that the two members who support the mall received no threats. Wouldn't you say?"

Another leading question. Warning lights again flashed in her brain. "As I said before, it's premature to draw any conclusions."

"Fair enough."

The acquiescence, a pleasant surprise, momentarily mitigated her tension.

"Let's take another call." He pressed the button. "You're on the air with Baker."

"Hi, this is Marsha. I live in Beaulin, but I'm interested in the mall. This area could use a good place to shop. I read Ms. Worthington's article in the *Chronicle*. It was interesting, but it left some loose ends. My question is whether she plans to follow the issue and, ultimately, come down for or against the project."

Baker gestured at Lauren.

She took another deep breath. "First, let me emphasize that the article was exactly that. It was not an editorial. Having said that, I agree there are loose ends, and I hope to tie them up

8

in a future article. As for a recommendation, pro or con on the mall, the editorial staff at the *Chronicle* will have to decide what, if anything, they plan to say. Marsha, I hope that answers your question."

"Yes, thank you."

Baker glanced at the large clock on the wall. "We're just about out of time. But before we conclude, I have a couple more questions for my guest. Tell us — do you really believe you can be objective given that your father and your boyfriend are at opposite ends of the spectrum?"

Lauren hesitated. Had Baker saved a nasty setup for the end? She said, "I think so. I know I'll try. In any event, your listeners and my readers will be able to judge for themselves."

"Tell you what," he said. "You follow the mall, and we'll follow you. And once we all know more, I'll have you back to do this again. Okay?"

Lauren pressed her lips together. Once with Baker was more than enough.

"I believe I saw a nod. I'll take that as a *yes*." He gestured at her. "But be prepared. Cause next time I might be coming on the blitz, the way Big Daddy Lipscomb did in his heyday." He glanced at the clock again. "Till next time, when once again the straight man will deliver more straight talk, this is Jerry Baker wishing you all a very pleasant, good evening." He smiled at Lauren.

She smiled back. *A good evening*? It had been anything but.

Chapter II

Seated in front, Lauren laid her paddle across the gunnels of the canoe. She gazed upward at the starlit sky. The Big Dipper immediately caught her eye. Though stargazing had never been her thing, on a clear night she could always spot the elbow-handled ladle. Before the auto accident that took her mother's life twenty-one years earlier, she had often pointed out the constellation to Lauren. After her mother's death the Big Dipper became her mother's place in heaven. Bridging the trillions of miles that separated earth from the seven stars was easier than the few feet from gravestone to casket. In the cemetery Lauren felt empty. Under the stars her mother's presence was palpable. Seven was Lauren's favorite number.

"Do we have a slacker up front?" said Jordan from his seat in the rear of the canoe.

"You bet."

"Two can play the same game." Jordan pulled his paddle out of the water.

Still spurred by the momentum of earlier strokes, the canoe glided silently through the tranquil waters of Shadow Lake, the centerpiece of Cedar Creek Village Park. Lauren took a deep breath, imbibing the peaceful night air. Apart from the tiny ripples carved by the vessel and the faint sound of crickets chirping on the wooded shore, all was still. Lauren checked the Big Dipper. The double star at the bend of the handle appeared to flicker. Her heart wanted to believe her mother was blessing her relationship with Jordan. Cold, hard logic, plus years of stoic indoctrination, prevented her from buying into the fanciful speculation. When her mother had died, her father had sought to escape heartbreak with silence. So too, Lauren had suppressed her emotions, never able to properly grieve. Issues were never addressed. A single twist of fate had forced her to grow up fast. Painful wounds left lasting scars. Like a tortoise, Lauren developed a tough shell. Crying was for sissies. Emulating her father, Lauren approached life pragmatically. Reason, not feelings, guided her. Strangers remarked that she was mature beyond her years. She fed on their words, her behavior becoming even more adult-like. Her childhood evaporated as she gravitated to friends who were not only older, but also serious.

With sights set on a career in journalism, in college she was highly motivated. Football games, fraternity and sorority parties and frivolous high jinks were for the unambitious. Once she had graduated, her job as a newspaper reporter at the *Chronicle* perpetuated her behavioral patterns. Her boss, Barker Nielsen, Editor of the *Chronicle*, was all business. Facts, indisputable verifications, were the coin of the realm. Hell was the price of inaccuracies. Sentiments were nice, but incontrovertible evidence was everything.

Lauren eyed the Big Dipper again. Light-years away, it was as close as she could come to dealing with the childhood loss of her mother. A slight smile, one consciously forced, came to her lips.

"Hello — anybody home?" said Jordan.

She looked back over her shoulder. "I love you."

"I love you too."

Lauren glanced at the Big Dipper one more time. The past six months since she had begun dating Jordan had been a whirlwind, the high point of her life. Over the years she had dated numerous guys. Many had been interested in her, but the outcome was consistently the same. After a few dates the suitor seemed shallow. The thought of spending a life together with any of them was inconceivable. Such was the pattern until Jordan swept her off her feet. Lauren was smitten. She turned back to him again. Moonlight reflected off his handsome face. His muscular pecks and biceps protruded from his T-shirt. He looked great in a pinstriped suit, but in a tee and jeans he was hot. Eight feet apart, at either end of the canoe, she could feel his arms wrapped around her. Soon enough reality would supplant imagination. Soon enough she would take another trip to the stars. A passionate night with bodies ablaze, the kind they had frequently shared, lay ahead.

———————

Flames — satanic beacons of anomalous splendor — lit the nighttime sky. Scores of onlookers gawked. A dozen or more firefighters poured water onto the inferno as lights flashing from a trio of fire trucks, along with several police and emergency vehicles, compounded the chaos. Lauren raced from her car. Her eyes searching for Jordan frantically surveyed the surrealistic scene. She dashed to her left and then off to her right. She squeezed past a heavyset man. Near the front line she spotted Jordan speaking with a police officer. She curbed the urge to rush to Jordan. Knowing he was okay allayed her worst fears. That comfort would have to suffice; at least for the moment. Her brain darted in another direction as she refocused on the flames. How quickly they were consuming the structure. Just like that, Jordan was becoming homeless. Was it an accident? Might it be the handiwork of the person behind the threats? From the center of the ranch-style house a sudden burst of red and yellow painted the night with a spectacular palette of horror and beauty. Lauren watched as the firefighters aimed two hoses directly at the flare-up. Bent knees and braced legs evidenced the powerful streams with which they sought to quell the blaze. Their courage was undeniable. Their fortitude, manifest. But the battle, man against nature, was a gross mismatch.

Journalistic instincts ever at work, Lauren observed the crowd. Arsonists were known to admire their dirty work. Lots of strangers were roaming around. Jordan came her way. "I'm sorry," she said, embracing him.

"Hey, it's only stuff." He drew back, his focus directed to the conflagration. He sighed. "But that stuff was important to me. Pictures from my childhood; the spoon my great, great grandmother ate with as a child on a plantation in Mississippi;

and the cane . . . " His voice trailed off, as tears welled up in his eyes.

"It appears . . . " Lauren stopped herself. Words, empty words, were meaningless. She ran her hand back and forth across Jordan's back. Her gaze returned to the flames and then to the gawkers, most of whom, their backs to her, were silhouetted between her and the burning house about a hundred yards beyond. Like prurient onlookers at a carnival sideshow, they appeared to revel in the calamity. A man with a camera, snapping a shot, caught her eye. How grotesque. But if this were any other fire and she had her *Minolta*, she would have taken some photos for the *Chronicle*. She turned back to Jordan.

He shook his head. His face was blank. "It's no accident."

The same thought had crossed her mind. The reporter in her, or perhaps the optimist, responded, "You can't be sure."

He looked at her, his anguished face masking any reaction.

"I'm sorry. I didn't mean to debate. That's the last thing you need."

He took hold of her hand. "I understand. Regardless, it's not your fault."

"Do you think whoever is responsible thought you were home?"

"I don't know." He paused. "No, I doubt it. If they wanted me dead, they could have done it in the wee hours when I was likely to be asleep."

"What do the police think?"

Jordan shrugged. "Hard to say. The big jerk, Detective Loggin, talked to me." Jordan glanced in the direction of the police cruiser parked along the curb. "He made me feel like a suspect. First he asked me how much insurance I had. When I told him, he rolled his eyes. Next thing I know, he was asking about my every move."

"Perhaps he was just confirming you weren't at home."

"You think so." Jordan folded his arms. "Then explain this. When I told him I had been hiking the escarpment trails west of Kyberville, why'd he ask if there was anyone who could verify that? I was tempted to tell the lug I had a right to remain silent."

Lauren waited a moment. "What did you say?"

13

"That the fellow from whom I bought the gasoline and matches could corroborate my story."

"You're kidding?" The words no sooner spoken than Lauren kicked herself. She said, "Anytime you're looking to sell the Great Wall of China, Ms. Gullible here will pay a hefty price. For now, tell me what you really said."

"I summarized my day. It went like this. I took a sandwich with me and hiked alone. On the way back I stopped at a little hole in the wall on Route 23 where I bought two slices of pizza and a can of soda. I doubted the woman at the register would remember me since the place was busy. And by the time I got home, the fire was roaring and the police and fire apparatus were already here."

"Did Loggin at least show some concern?"

"You mean because the fire interrupted his snack time or a game of solitaire down at the station?"

Jordan's sarcasm stirred recollections from several months earlier when Lauren had contacted Loggin about a story she was doing involving a break-in at the hardware store. His jaundiced questions made her uncomfortable, and the little information he provided was replete with double talk. She said, "You're right about Loggin. But did the numskull say anything about the fire?"

"Yeah. He told me to be careful. I asked him if that was a threat."

"You didn't?"

Jordan laughed.

Lauren smacked her forehead. "God, there I go again. But you needn't smirk. Loggin has a point. You need to be careful."

Jordan laughed again.

"C'mon. This is no joke." She gestured at the flaming house. "I'm worried."

"Relax. I'll be fine."

The look on Jordan's face hinted his concern exceeded his words. And why not. His views were controversial, and as an influential black man in a town where bigotry had deep roots the possibility that he had been targeted was real. A loud crack followed by another burst of flame drew Lauren's attention. An instant later a portion of the roof caved into the interior of the house.

Jordan bowed his head.

Lauren searched for comforting words. She chose silence. Remote possibilities, if any, that the house would not be a total loss had vanished.

Fire Chief Jim Murray approached. "I've told my men to move back. There's not a lot we can do. I'm sorry."

"I understand," said Jordan. "I know you've done your best."

"We tried, but . . . " The Chief gestured at the inferno. "It spread so fast we never had a chance. Arson is a real possibility, not that I'm drawing any conclusions. Once the ashes have cooled, we'll check for accelerants." He pointed to the homes on either side, each several hundred feet away from the burning structure. "I know it's no consolation, but we're fortunate this wasn't Broad Street. A fire like this could wipe out a string of buildings."

Jordan pressed his lips together. Lauren sensed his frustration. The Chief had mentioned the silver lining to the wrong person.

"We'll do what we can." The Chief patted Jordan on the back and then walked away.

With her eyes fixed on the burning house, Lauren stood silently alongside Jordan. How easily the blaze had transformed the attractive home into rubble. Dark smoke, visible only by virtue of the very flames that had spawned it, billowed forth. The upward flow of the heavy, dark cloud contradicted logic. Then again, the entire scene, its mindless destruction, contradicted logic. Lauren had covered fires before. Dramatic pyrotechnics, their seductive lure, masked the pain that smoldered when at last the illumination had been extinguished. And this time the loss hit much closer to home. She turned to Jordan. "You're welcome to stay at my house tonight."

"I thought you rented that studio apartment we looked at over on Park Street."

"I did, but the lease — it's only month to month — doesn't start until next week." Before she had signed the lease,

Lauren had weighed the possibility of moving in with Jordan, but she had opted for a place of her own. After a lifetime of living at home, she needed a period of independence. Regardless, Jordan and she would be able to spend nights together whenever they wanted. And no longer would she face her father's jaundiced eye or, worse yet, prying when she arrived home late. She said, "Anyway, that little futon I ordered is only big enough for one. But forget my apartment. How about staying at my house?"

"You mean *your father's* house. He'd love that."

"Under the circumstances, he — " She stopped herself. Whatever the circumstances, her father would be cool to Jordan. Their animosity had begun several years earlier when Jordan had first run for the Village Board, long before he and Lauren had started dating. Numerous issues, such as the low-cost housing south of Broad Street, had created the divide. Friction over the mall had pushed it wider. Once Lauren began a relationship with Jordan, it became an abyss. History counseled against her invitation, but Jordan had lost his home. She said, "We've got plenty of room, what with six bedrooms."

"That's not the point. You could have more bedrooms than *Buckingham Palace*, and it wouldn't make a difference. Your father would sooner invite Jack the Ripper than me."

"Well — he's not the one doing the inviting. I am."

Jordan smiled and put an arm over her shoulder. "My dear, I believe you just confirmed my point." He leaned around and looked her in the eye.

She shrugged. "It's not that he has anything against you personally. It's — "

"It's just that he dislikes all people of color."

"C'mon — that's not what I meant. And you know that's not true."

"It may not be what you meant. But true? That's another matter."

Lauren squirmed. She and Jordan were open, but at that moment she found eye contact difficult. She said, "My father isn't the bigot you think him to be." The sight of Jordan's furrowed brow reminded her of the time her late mother had accused her of taking a dozen cookies from a package intended

16

for the *DAR* bake sale. Only seven years old, Lauren protested she had not taken a dozen. Her protest convicted her. She waited, anticipating Jordan would jab her with a sharp comeback. His silence underscored that she had hung herself. She said, "My father's attitude is changing." The wishful thought rang hollow in her ears. Much as her father had come a long way, her relationship with Jordan was another matter. "Unfortunately, when it comes to his own daughter, let's just say, he's not there yet. But as I said, he's doing better."

"So I heard. I understand he treats his slaves quite well."

"C'mon, that's not fair."

"Oh no?" Jordan's tone turned serious. "That pillared mansion up on the hill, the one he calls home, as well as his hefty bank balance, trace back to forefathers who made their fortune on the backs of my ancestors."

Instinct begged an argument. Conscience stilled her tongue. Guilt that her advantaged lifestyle had roots in slavery had surfaced before. But the pangs were small, and their visits brief. The sins of those past generations had always seemed distant. Very distant. For the first time, a black man, one for whom she cared deeply, had confronted her with the injustice she had adroitly avoided. She bowed her head.

"I'm sorry," said Jordan.

The unexpected apology drew her gaze. "You're sorry?"

"That was a low blow." He gestured at his home, where the flames had shrunk to a fraction of their earlier height. "Frustration provoked me."

"Don't apologize." She took his hand. "Your point has merit." The admission, though hardly subtle, made her wonder whether she and Jordan had been as open as she had previously assumed. She said, "How does it make you feel, knowing that my comforts are spawned from your pain?"

He took a deep breath. "It's a . . . " He hesitated several seconds. "Let's leave it for another time when other matters — excuse the bad pun — aren't already on the fire."

The play on words, standard fare from Jordan, ordinarily would have drawn a groan. Circumstances curbed the tendency. She said, "So, you won't stay at my house?"

"It wouldn't work."

She shrugged. "You'll be my guest."

He shook his head. "No offense. But given today's aggravation, Roger Worthington is more than I can handle. The back room at my office will do just fine."

"Well — " She heaved a sigh. "Is there anything I can do?"

He pointed at his home which was fast becoming a water-soaked pile of blackened char. "You have a magic wand?" He chuckled.

She gave him a hug. It was the best she could do. Did she love Jordan? She had no doubts. She had often daydreamed of their life together as if it were a fairy tale. But all too often fairy tales demanded the wand she didn't have. And all too often, dreams went up in smoke.

———————

Seated in her cubicle at the *Chronicle*, Lauren stared blankly at the keyboard of her computer. For more than a hour she had been working on a story how community civic organizations were doing more and more to improve Cedar Creek. Leaders of the organizations, welcoming the chance for favorable publicity, had supplied her with loads of information. Writing the story should have been a breeze. Why then had she cranked out just one paragraph? The rhetorical question ran through her mind, not that the answer was subtle. The image of Jordan's home, along with numerous questions, preoccupied her. Was the fire arson? If so, who was responsible? What was the motive? Was Jordan, not just his home, a target?

The ring of her telephone interrupted her ruminations. She picked up the receiver. "Lauren Worthington speaking."

"Hi Sweetie."

The sound of Jordan's voice was a welcome distraction. "I was just thinking about you."

"Warm thoughts, I hope."

"You might say that." She paused, anticipating her response would evoke a quick comeback. Nothing. She said, "I was pondering the fire, and whether it was an accident."

"No need to rack your brain anymore. Chief Murray just called from the firehouse. He said that several of the rear windows had been smashed and the remains of gasoline-soaked rags lined the floor below the broken panes. They found an empty gas can on the ground outside."

Two thoughts popped into Lauren's head: one, concern for Jordan's safety, and the other, speculation who the culprit might be. She said, "I'm worried."

"That makes two of us."

The concern in his voice magnified hers. She said, "I'm glad you're finally taking the matter seriously."

"Well, threats are one thing. Arson, another. A few weeks back when three of us Board members received the notes, it was like misery. Company softened the blow."

"Have you spoken with the police?"

"I put a call in. They're going to get back to me." Jordan chuckled.

"Unless I'm mistaken, that laugh sounds sardonic."

"They told me who's assigned. Three guesses, and the first two don't count."

"God, not Loggin." Lauren recalled the detective's inane comments and licentious looks the last time she had spoken to him. "He wouldn't know crab grass from that shaggy rug he calls hair."

"You got that right. Plus he's probably applauding the guy with the torch. And for all I know, that applause could be for himself."

"You don't think Loggin's responsible?" She waited a moment. "Do you?"

"Not really. But I haven't excluded him either. Let's face it. He hates me."

The word *hate* seemed strong, but otherwise it was hard to argue. Loggin had no use for Jordan's liberal views. And Loggin had become even more vocal since Jordan had proposed a neighborhood crime watch as an alternative to adding more police.

"You recall the parking ticket he gave me last month. Since when do detectives issue parking tickets? And given that the meter had expired five minutes before I returned to my car,

I'd bet my house — not that it's worth two cents anymore —
that Loggin wrote me up the second my quarter ran out. And
don't tell me it was a coincidence. Loggin knows my Maxima,
as well as my license plate."

The logic, as well as discretion, something Lauren often
ignored, discouraged debate. She said, "Did Chief Murray
indicate whom he suspected?"

"No, but he asked if I had any guesses."

"What did you say?"

"Half the town."

Once again, Jordan's point, though exaggerated, had merit.
His controversial views — calls for affirmative action, support
of community housing, environmental activism, anti-gun
proposals, pro-choice stance, etc. — had earned him many
enemies in the conservative village. She said, "Weren't you
more specific?"

"As a matter of fact, I was."

She waited a few seconds. "So, whom did you say?"

"The *Aryan Alliance* . . . or whatever the skinheads who
belong to that infernal group call themselves."

The thought had already crossed Lauren's mind. And if
the *Alliance* was responsible, Jordan had reason to be alarmed.
Then again, an arsonist, skinhead or not, posed a grave danger.
She said, "Maybe you should ask for police protection."

"Just what I need. They'd probably assign Loggin."

"C'mon, you know that's not true. He's a detective."

"And a crack one at that. Why just last year he suspected a
thug was tailing him. All by himself, Loggin caught the culprit.
His shadow. And if that wasn't enough, he gave it the slip. He
ducked under the awning in front of the bakery."

Lauren suppressed a laugh. "You're making jokes, but this
is serious."

"No fooling. Maybe I should resign from the Village
Board."

"Resign? You wouldn't," she said, though she assumed
hyperbole had invaded his words again.

"Well, it's not a bad idea. Village business takes too much
time from my law practice. Between *pro bono* work — and I'm
not about to give that up — and the damn Board, there's hardly

time to make a living. It's time I earn a few bucks. Otherwise the bank will be foreclosing on this place I call an office."

"C'mon things aren't that bad."

"Easy for you to say. You're debt free. Your father paid for your education. My days in school left me with b_g loans."

Lauren swallowed hard. Too often she assumed that anyone who was a professional or had a good job enjoyed the financial security to which she was accustomed. She said, "Apart from the skinheads, did you mention any other possible suspects to Chief Murray?"

"The listeners of Jerry Baker's talk show. Oh, and one more possibility — your father."

"My what!"

"You heard me."

"How could you?" she said, though the answer was hardly subtle. Her father had never cared for Jordan and his liberal views. Jordan's outspoken opposition to the mall, coupled with his dating her, had magnified the friction. "How could you suggest my father?"

"Wait a second. Chief Murray asked me about possible enemies. There are lots of people who dislike me, but few as much as your father."

Damn. Jordan had made another valid point, and, unlike earlier ones, it was no overstatement. She said, "Whatever my father's feelings, he'd never resort to violence." Anticipated acquiescence was not forthcoming. "You agree, don't you?"

He sighed.

"What's that supposed to mean?"

"Look — I doubt your father's behind last night, but I can't rule him out. Put yourself in my shoes."

Logic had become a persistent thorn. She said, "I don't like it, but — " She glanced at the clock on her desk. "I need to get back to work."

"You're angry, aren't you?"

"No. Just frustrated." The moment she spoke the words, she chided herself. Blaming Jordan, after what he had been though, was unfair. "Why do things have to be so complicated? And, please, don't answer. I'm simply thinking out loud." She waited a moment. "How bad is it living in the back room of your office?"

"Oh — I'd rate it a nine. Maybe even a ten."

An image of the place came to mind. It was fine for a quick siesta or a snack, but home, it wasn't.

"Of course, that rating is on a scale of a hundred. But I thought you need to get back to work."

"I do, but — " Conscience dictated an apology. Ordinarily pride might have prevailed. "I'm sorry," she said. "I shouldn't be giving you — "

"It's okay. I understand." He paused. "Get back to work. And by the way, I love you." He hung up.

The receiver still to her ear, she gazed at his photo on the corner of her desk. "I love you too," she mouthed silently. Intelligence, integrity, patience, seriousness of purpose and a sense of humor were rare in one man. Jordan had all that, plus he was sexy and handsome. He was, indeed, the love of her life.

The sound of the dial tone, like the buzzing gossips on the street, invaded her musing. What right did people have insinuating themselves into her affairs? Elsewhere attitudes were changing. Why was Cedar Creek years behind? Maybe still in the nineteenth century. And, worse yet, why was her father there? Part of her denied it. But only part. A recorded voice told her to hang up if she wished to make a call. She glared at the receiver. No one was going to tell her what to do.

Chapter III

Comfortable April air greeted Lauren on an evening stroll down Broad Street. She loved the season, the rebirth of nature it heralded. Most of all she loved the camellias. By day her eyes marveled at the delicate pink and white blossoms. Even after sunset when darkness hid them from view their fragrance filled the air. She stopped for a moment, closed her eyes and inhaled deeply. She reopened them and gazed at the red and pink and turquoise hues that painted the western sky. Evening's veil eclipsed reality. Broad Street seemed lovely. Vacant storefronts, peeling paint and sidewalk weeds were all but invisible. Widely spaced street lamps provided just enough light to make the old, wood-framed structures, many of them Victorian, appear quaint. As she passed the Village Library, her mind drifted to the large mural depicting the Battle of Shiloh that decorated the lobby. A century earlier when the painting had been done, Cedar Creek was a beautiful place both by day and night. A lost war, followed by a dozen decades of a struggling economy, had changed that. But with the aid of a vivid imagination Lauren resurrected the hamlet's earlier charm.

She continued on her way, wondering when, if ever, the sleepy community would recapture its youth. Her father contended his proposed mall was just the ticket. And yes, it did mean jobs and lots of new businesses, both of which were desperately needed, but the panacea he claimed was another matter. The proposed location, on the outskirts of the village, adjacent to the ramps to and from the interstate, would lure traffic away from Broad Street. Might that seal the fate of the already languishing business district. Might it also mean that Cedar Creek would metamorphose into a cookie-cutter locale of *Anywhere America.*

Concerns and questions — Lauren had many. Answers — few. Most were littered with doubts. As a newspaperwoman, one with integrity, she was determined to explore the issues. And when they grew difficult, and surely they would, she would let the chips fall where they may. At least she thought she would.

As she passed beneath the marquee of the old movie theater, long since converted into *Rutledge Antiques*, the sound of barking voices in the adjacent alley drew her attention. She peeked around the corner of the building. About thirty yards down the narrow way she observed three boys, all around mid-teens.

"Leave me alone," said a short, chubby, white boy, his back to a fence.

Two black youths blocked the white boy's exit from the alley. The shorter said, "Clan boy ain't so tough when he don't got his buddies to protect him."

Lauren hesitated. Judgment encouraged her to walk on by. Conscience favored a different alternative.

"Maybe we should give him a taste of his own medicine," said the second black.

"You mean like him and his buddies done to me over in the park last month." He displayed a clenched fist and laughed.

"It wasn't me," said the white youth.

Lauren glanced up and down the street. Unfortunately, no one else was around. She nervously stepped out into the center of the alley. "Is there . . . a problem?"

The white boy yelled, "Help! They're gonna beat me up."

The taller black spun around. "We never touched the creep."

"Why don't you just go your separate ways?" Lauren inched back as she spoke.

The taller black pointed at the white boy and muttered. His words were hard for Lauren to hear. He looked back at his buddy and motioned for them to go. They walked up the alley in Lauren's direction. She swallowed hard. As they drew close, the taller one said, "We didn't do nuttin' to him. We never planned to. Unlike him and three of his Nazi comrades who kicked my ass last month, we don't fight dirty." He glared at Lauren. "Course, you don't care. The punk is white. Gotta be right. Lady, good night." The duo started down the street. The tall fellow turned back. "No charge for the rap. Don't give me no crap. Ain't got no . . . " His voice trailed off as they continued on their way.

Lauren heaved a sigh. She looked down the alley. The white youth slowly started her way. She watched the two blacks, making sure they continued to depart. Finally, she said, "They've gone." As the white youth drew near, she said, "What was that about?"

"Ah . . . nothin'. They just wanted to kick my butt."

"That's not what they said."

"You gonna believe them?"

Lauren focused on the glow of the street light reflecting from the boy's shaved head. On his arm she observed a large tattoo with the letters *AA*. She knew what it stood for. About her height, 5'5", with a chubby, non-athletic body, he appeared harmless enough apart from his shaved head and tattoo. She said, "The taller fellow claimed that you and your friends beat him up. Is that true?"

"I didn't touch him."

"But your friends did." She waited a moment, but no response. She gestured in the direction in which the two blacks had disappeared. "What do you have against them?"

"If you can't figure it out, that's your problem."

He appeared ready to go on his way. She would have let him had she not already noted his *Aryan Alliance* insignia. What motivated his hatred aroused her curiosity. The fire at Jordan's home loomed in the back of her mind. The possibility, however remote, of information linking the group to the crime was too good to pass up. But the subject had to be cleverly broached and only after she had gained his confidence. "I'd like to hear your side."

"A rich bitch like you don't care."

"Try me."

"I got better ways to kill time." He leaned forward, appearing to study her face. "Say, ain't you that reporter from the *Chronicle*, the one I nailed with a cream pie last fall at the County Fair?"

The question evoked memories of the three hours she had spent as a target raising money for the local homeless shelter. She had been glad to lend her support for the worthy cause. The pies did no damage. Affectionate words often accompanied those thrown by friends and colleagues. Others who paid two dollars for the shot were less kind. Some used the opportunity to denigrate her liberal social views. No doubt this fellow fit the latter category. She said, "I can't say I remember you. Of course, I got hit so many times I lost count."

He shook his head and laughed.

"What's so funny?"

"Knowin' who you are explains why you stuck up for them jerks. You're in bed with . . . " His voice garbled into a muttering stream.

Her jaw clenched as she thought she caught the *N*-word.

"I heard ya on Jerry Baker's show. I even read your stuff in the paper a couple times." He pointed at her. "The only thing worse than a bleedin' heart like you is one with dark skin. Like that boyfriend of yours."

Taut fingers longed to wring his fat neck. Be professional, she told herself. Don't let pride spoil a chance to acquire information. She said, "What do you have against blacks?"

"They're wreckin' the country."

"Just how do you figure that?"

The teenager gestured up and down Broad Street.

"You don't blame them for this, do you?"

"I sure do. They moved in. Whatd'ya get? Too many people chasin' too few jobs."

"So?"

"Folks end up unemployed, less they wanna mop floors at a greasy pit." He pointed at her. "Course a richy rich like you wouldn't know nuttin' about that."

Lauren glared. "Just so happens, I work hard."

He laughed. "Big deal. You wuz born with a silver spoon in your mouth. I know who your father is." He pointed at her again. "Make me shed a few tears. Tell me about your tough childhood."

She gulped. A teenager, worse yet, probably a drop out, was giving her a verbal fencing lesson.

"That boyfriend of yours wuz behind the cheap housing. All it did wuz bring in more of their kind. That's why there ain't no jobs."

"That's garbage." The comment rang in her ears. The snot was drawing her down to his level. She hesitated, just long enough to regain control. "Cedar Creek went downhill because we were dependent on the mill. When it closed in the seventies, lots of workers — about a fifth of the work force — got laid off. People had less to spend. Other businesses, already struggling, began to close. That's why the village spiraled downward."

He sneered. "Save your sob stories for services over there." He pointed several doors down to the little white Baptist Church on the other side of the street.

"You still in school?"

"Nah, I quit last year. What's it to ya anyway?"

"You strike me as smart." The disingenuous compliment, one of the less appealing tools of her trade, rolled off her tongue with surprising ease. "Why swap your future to run with — "

"Yeah, I'm a skinhead." He put his hand on his head. "And I'm proud of it. Damn proud."

"Why did you give up school?"

"Cause it sucked."

"That bad?" The active listening skills she had learned at the employee seminar the preceding summer came in handy. "The teachers? The courses? What was it?"

"The whole nine yards."

"What did you hate most?"

"Why should I tell you?"

The truth — curiosity — wouldn't work. "I'm willing to listen if you give me a try."

He shrugged.

"So, what was the worst?"

"The schmucks that roamed the halls." He looked her in the eye. "How would ya like to be called *Lard Ass, Blubber*

Boy and a whole lot worse. Or maybe you'd like to walk into the shower after gym class with a body like this (he motioned at himself) and have the jocks snap towels at your privates. Course ya wouldn't know nuttin' about that. I'm sure when you wuz in school, you ran with the cool click, the rich assholes in the preppy clothes.

His germ of truth, even if overstated, gave her pause. She recalled the time Orville Fritz had invited her to the sophomore gala. Her comment to her friends that she would sooner shovel manure than go with the smelly farm boy got back to him. Hindsight painted an ugly picture. She said, "Let's assume the in-crowd treated you badly. Why do you blame blacks?"

"They're the reason I was an outsider."

She suspected he had resorted to a scapegoat. But the accusation would make him defensive. She said, "I'm confused."

He hesitated, as he appeared to study her. "Fine. Ya wanna know. Here it is. We weren't rich, but we wuzn't poor neither. Least till the furniture factory over in Greenbrook started with the affirmative action crap. Next thing ya know my dad wuz canned, and we couldn't make ends meet. He fell behind on the mortgage, and right off he gets a letter from the bank threatenin' to foreclose. He went there, and this black guy, an idiot who didn't know crud from a candy bar, wouldn't give him the time of day. Anyway, my dad tried to go higher. Wha'd he get? Some Jew with a fancy title. The money grubbin' bastard wouldn't listen for nuttin'. Not that I'd expect different from slime like them."

Lauren gritted her teeth, debating whether the dialogue justified the ever-mounting price.

He looked her in the eye. "Ya don't like what you're hearin'. That nasty puss gives ya away. Don't bother me none." He folded his arms. "Anyway, the bank took our house. Pretty soon my dad wuz hittin' the bottle, and when he got loaded, that weren't all he hit. My mom and me got it as well. That's when I quit school and looked for a job. Ended up flippin' burgers for forty cents over minimum wage." He pointed in the direction of the housing project. "Welfare pays their kind more for sittin' on their cans."

You bigoted little brat. She would have expressed the thought had she not wanted to explore the fire before parting ways. She said, "Maybe if you finish school, you could find a better job."

"Yeah — sure." He spit into the gutter. "My dad graduated high school, and look what it got him." He pointed at the *AA* tattoo on his arm.

"Your father is a member too?"

"Nah. In his case it's *Alcoholics Anonymous.* Me — I seen enough. I joined my own *AA.*"

She shook her head. "I guess you did."

"Lady. Don't get high and mighty with me cause I heard that shit too many times. Folks like you, all them damn teachers, had tons of advice, but you think they ever listened, let alone help. The guys in Double-A wuz the first who ever made me feel like I belonged. Unlike them jocks, preppies and other scum-suckers at the school, my brothers (he put his hand on his tattoo) treat me like a human being." He looked across the street in the direction of the large clock atop Village Hall. "Time for me to split."

Her plan to use the subtle approach had to be scrapped. "Before you go, any thoughts about the fire at Jackson's house?"

"Yeah — good for whoever done it." He displayed a smirk, the self-satisfied kind, and then immediately started on his way. He turned back for a moment. "I only talked with ya cause what ya done for me earlier." He gestured at the alley. "Thanks." He hurried off.

Lauren watched him until he disappeared around the next corner. The things he stood for turned her stomach. Yet despite his fractured grammar, he was smarter than she had expected. His rage-flawed views, often illogical, explained his gravitation to the *Aryan Alliance.* Had her childhood been a combination of a dysfunctional home and relentless abuse in school, what road might she have traveled to win acceptance? Could she blame him? Yes, but not completely. Society, so-called decent folks, herself included, had helped breed him.

Lauren waited until the last moment, just when the Village Board meeting was about to commence. With her father's proposed mall topping the agenda and Jordan its most outspoken critic, she wanted to stay as far from the fray as possible. The last row in the back, end chair, was the best she could do without remaining outside. Nielsen, her boss, had not assigned her to cover the event. Still she planned to take notes, albeit fewer than if she was doing a story.

As Medford Laughlin, Chairman of the Village Board, banged his gavel calling the meeting to order, Lauren scanned the five members at the front table. Like a tug of war, the two supporters of the mall sat on the right, and the two opponents, on the left. In the center the punctilious Laughlin, who was yet to take a position, acted as referee.

He pounded his gavel again. "We have an extremely important matter to address this evening. May I have order." He waited a moment, furrowed his brow and rambled off into extended discourse. His precise diction, a trademark of his affected speech, drew a silent chuckle from Lauren. A murmur in the audience suggested that others might be laughing as well. The bow-tied headmaster in the three-piece suit prided himself on being an intellectual. Wealth was nice, but membership in the intelligentsia was the epitome; at least according to Laughlin. If only the slim pedagogue with the bony face knew what people said behind his back. Pretentious. Didactic. Pedantic. Adjectives, the kind Laughlin himself used, ran through Lauren's head. Of course, folks in Cedar Creek used more earthy terms to characterize him, but those labels, often laced with four-letter words, were even more derogatory. She chuckled again as she surveyed the other four members of the Board.

Off to Laughlin's left sat Janet Warner and Jack O'Leary, both backers of the proposed mall. Warner was divorced and O'Leary, separated. Generally they voted together on issues. And their togetherness often appeared to extend further. Both were reasonably attractive and of medium build, but with a few extra pounds. They had the look of the high school cheerleader and football player whose best years were fading behind several decades of indulgence. They were remnants of the stereotypical American duo, assuming such a paradigm might be more than an illusion.

Lauren wondered whether her father had courted Janet Warner's support with the huge fees the insurance agent could garner from the project. Even if unmentioned, no doubt Warner had foreseen the opportunity. Lauren's father had bought his insurance from Warner for nearly fifteen years As for O'Leary — *location, location, location*. His tavern nearly adjoined the site of the proposed mall. The multi-million dollar project would not only enhance the value of his property but also increase his traffic. O'Leary, like Warner, had assured his constituents that personal interests would never come before those of Cedar Creek. Even before Lauren had become a newspaper reporter, a vocation that made her more cynical every day, his claims would not have fooled her.

As Laughlin continued to pontificate, Lauren shifted her gaze to the left side of the table. Steve Ward, the owner of the strip mall at the south end of the village, had a vested interest too. His six-store shopping center already had two vacancies. A big, new mall might leave him with four more. And finally, what about Jordan? His legal practice had no apparent link to the proposed mall. But was his opposition genuine? When Jordan and Lauren had first begun dating, Jordan had tried to bridge the gap with her father. Whether it might have been possible under other circumstances, in the face of the budding romance her father reacted with deaf ears and a caustic tongue. The harder Jordan tried, the more intransigent her father grew. Repeatedly rebuffed, Jordan began to respond in kind. Lauren told herself that Jordan was extremely fair-minded, but the very cynicism that made her a good reporter left doubts about Jordan's current stance. Lauren interrupted her ruminations as she refocused on the meeting.

Laughlin cleared his throat. "Matters of housekeeping completed, I wish to move on to a weightier subject. We had intended to debate the merits of the proposed mall, and, if time permits, we may yet do so. However, first we need to address the issue of threats and violence. As everyone knows, Mr. Ward, Mr. Jackson and I have all received threats. Mr. Ward and Mr. Jackson have been outspoken critics of the mall, while I remain undecided. The two Board members who support the project received no threats. This hardly seems a coincidence. The other night, fire burned Mr. Jackson's home. The police have termed it arson. While the threats never mentioned the mall, they warned, and I quote (Laughlin peered down through his narrow bifocals at a small paper): *Opponents of progress — Repent! If not, violence shall strike your homes and families.*" He put the paper back onto the table. "When the threat first came, I assumed it was nothing more. But the fire at Mr. Jackson's home refutes that assumption." Laughlin looked up and down the head table. "I know that I speak for *all* my colleagues, regardless of leaning, when I say that intimidation of any form cannot be tolerated. In that spirit of unanimity, individually and collectively as a Board, we hope that you, our fellow citizens of Cedar Creek, will help us address this matter. With that preface, we invite your comments."

A murmur meandered through the hall. Numerous individuals headed for the microphone that stood off to the side between the audience and the Board. First there was a plump, middle-aged lady in a pastel print dress. Last to join the line was Lauren's father. Lauren wondered what he would say.

"The floor is yours, Mrs. Clay," said Laughlin.

"A group of us were talking after church on Sunday. We want the Board, especially those who support the mall, to know that we're behind you. Facts, not fear, must guide your decision." Her comment drew a smattering of applause.

"We share your concern," said Laughlin. "Do you have any information that might help us?"

The woman shook her head and stepped away from the microphone. One-by-one, as others spoke, Lauren's mind drifted again. The headmaster, Chairman Laughlin, had put himself in an enviable position. The other four members of the Board, their positions firm, had split two and two. Laughlin held the deciding vote. Perhaps he was holding out in order to garner some advantage. For years he had encouraged the Village to build a park with ball fields and tennis courts adjacent to his exclusive private school. Ever the cynic, Lauren was convinced he had an angle. Her musing halted as an elderly black gentleman, neatly attired, approached the microphone.

"Sorry, I don't know your name," said Laughlin.

"Grover Williams." He leaned closer to the microphone. "Jordan Jackson has repeatedly stood up for the disadvantaged people of this community. His courage has earned him enemies. If those enemies are responsible for the arson, the threatening notes could be red herrings, a clever ploy to divert suspicion toward supporters of the mall."

Laughlin furrowed his brow. "Sir, are you suggesting the threats against Mr. Ward and myself should be ignored?"

"No. Just that all possibilities need to be considered."

"I'm sure we will," said Laughlin.

Lauren, who was busy jotting a note, squeezed her pen. Odds were that Laughlin had already dismissed the man's theory.

Several more individuals approached the microphone, but none shed light. The next to last, a chunky fellow with a *Gamecock* baseball cap, stepped forward and said, "I ain't accusin' nobody, but I got ideas. Them skinheads from that *Aryan Alliance* group oughta be looked into and — " He hesitated as he gestured behind himself. "Roger Worthington ain't above suspicion neither."

Lauren bristled. She could only imagine what was going through her father's head. Up at the Board table, Jordan nodded demonstratively. Lauren suspected her father saw the gesture. An instant later he started toward the microphone.

"Mr. Worthington," said Laughlin, "you'll have your turn in a moment."

Laughlin refocused on the man who had been speaking. "Jake, we need to be careful what we say. Do you have any facts to substantiate your insinuation?"

"Yup. I heard Worthington spent over two million buying up land for the mall. If it don't go through, he'll be out a bundle and he'll have to pay the land taxes to boot." He gestured at the microphone as he turned to Lauren's father. "It's all yours."

Six-feet tall, broad shouldered, dark complexioned with thick, brown hair, Roger Worthington stepped forward. "Let's get one thing straight. I didn't threaten anyone, and I had nothing to do with the fire at Jordan Jackson's home. Everyone knows how I feel about him, but I'd be an idiot to torch his house."

The anger that lurked behind her father's words was no surprise. Whether his all-too-familiar short fuse would supersede judgment was another matter.

He turned and glared at Jordan. "I saw you nod a minute ago. You think you're pretty cute. Well, as long as we're tossing suspicions around, you rate a turn." He pointed at Jordan. "And save the indignant look for your courtroom shows. Your house has been on the market for six months with no takers. From what I hear, you had it mortgaged to the hilt. The way things are in Cedar Creek, no buyer would have paid enough to cover what you owe the bank. Maybe you sent the threats and torched your house for the insurance."

Jordan leaped from his seat.

Lauren feared he was about to go after her father. Steve Ward got up and put a calming arm over Jordan's shoulder.

Jordan pointed at the South Carolina flag that stood nearby. "If it weren't desecration, I'd use that pole for more than displaying the state colors."

"I'd love to see you try." Lauren's father folded his arms.

Laughlin pounded his gavel. "Both of you. Stop!"

Please, thought Lauren, knowing the gulf between her boyfriend and father had just widened. Worse yet, the differences may have become irreconcilable.

Laughlin looked at her father. "Mr. Worthington. Kindly return to your seat." He turned to his right and gestured at Jordan's vacant chair. "Please."

Jordan's clenched jaw appeared to ease. "Well — okay." He started to take his seat but stopped. A pensive expression came over his face. "Before we continue, I'd like the record to note that Will Rogers never met Roger Worthington."

Laughter broke out. Laughlin hammered his gavel, again demanding order. The woman seated next to Lauren tapped her on the shoulder. "What does Will Rogers have to do with this?"

Lauren tried to contain the look of exasperation she knew she displayed. She said, "Will Rogers once said that he never — " Laughlin was moving on, and Lauren was determined to listen. She said, "I'll explain it to you later."

"The purpose of this meeting is to unite us," said Laughlin. "Accusations and name-calling are the antithesis of our goal. Unless people have information, not barbs, to exchange, I propose we adjourn until police and fire authorities have had more time to investigate the fire. Any comments from the Board?"

"I concur, Mr. Chairman, and will so move in a moment," said Steve Ward. "First I want to condemn the personal attack on my fellow Board member Jordan Jackson. On the issue of the mall we happen to agree, but, as you all know, on most we don't. That, however, is neither here nor there. As a member of the Board, Mr. Jackson is entitled to respect."

The remark sent Lauren's thoughts adrift. Of all people, Steve Ward had come to Jordan's defense. True, they both opposed the mall, but for very different reasons. Jordan was concerned about traffic, the environment, etc., while Ward feared his Broad Street rental property would end up vacant. On most issues, Jordan, the liberal, and Ward, the conservative, clashed. Jordan had often argued that Ward was a latent bigot. Lauren wondered if Jordan had misjudged Ward.

By the time Lauren refocused on the meeting, Laughlin, with a rap of his gavel, had adjourned it. She hurried out before either her father or Jordan could spot her. She longed for them to make peace. Unfortunately, changing Jordan's attitude appeared impossible, and convincing her father, harder yet.

CHAPTER IV

C *hronicle* — Lauren Worthington here." Lauren clicked *Save* on her new computer as she spoke into the telephone receiver.

"Hi Sweetie," said Jordan. "How's your day going?"

"Pretty good. And yours?"

"No complaints. Say — I missed you last night after the meeting. Where'd you go?"

"Oh . . . " Lauren was glad the question hadn't come face to face. "I had some things to do at home."

"You couldn't spare a few minutes to say hello?"

"Well — I know you Board members like your private *post mortems.*"

"But they're generally brief."

"That's — " Digging a deeper hole was a bad idea. She said, "Sorry, I should have waited."

"So, what'd you think of the sideshow?"

The question — no surprise — was one she preferred to avoid. "Things did get a bit testy. Where do you think the Board will come out?"

"It's hardly the Board's decision. Laughlin has it all to himself, and he knows it."

"But that's only because the rest of you are split."

"You've missed the point."

What point, she wondered. She waited a moment. "Hello?"

"Sorry — I was debating whether to go into it." He hesitated. "What the hell. As long as it's off the record."

"Sounds intriguing."

"Don't sidetrack me. Are we off the record?"

The phrase, one she despised, triggered familiar frustration. Too often it opened the door to tidbits that would make great press. Unfortunately, the promise needed to extract the information kept the story from seeing the light of day. On the other hand, without the promise she got nothing. She said, "Fair enough. It'll be as if you never told me."

"You remember the proposal a year or so ago to improve the sanitation plant?"

"Yes. But what's that got to do with the mall?"

"Nothing."

She pulled the receiver away from her ear and shook her head. She put the receiver back. "Let me guess. Your question about the sanitation plant was a test. You wanted to see if I have Alzheimer's?"

"Of course not. That I know. You're taking your medication, aren't you?"

"Very funny."

"Here. Let me explain. When the sanitation issue arose, Laughlin was coy. In the meantime the rest of the Board split two and two. One day he came to Warner and me, the two who supported the proposal. He asked us for our reasons, but the next thing you know he was talking about the need to pave the dirt road behind that damn school of his and connect it as a secondary access to the main road. Little by little he worked it around so he got his road, and we got the sanitation plant improvements."

"Sneaky, but — " Lauren thought for a moment. "Isn't that the way politics generally works."

"Well — yes and no. And before you react, let me explain how Laughlin puts a different twist on the game. I'm convinced he supported the sanitation improvements all along. But he kept his mouth shut. Once he saw the two-two split, he bargained for something else — something that benefited him personally."

"Let me guess. He's playing the same game now."

"Actually," said Jordan, "he does it all the time. As Chairman of the Board, he claims he should listen to all sides. As soon as he finds a two-two split, he swings into action."

"Why don't you expose him?"

"I may — when the time is right. In the meantime I'm adopting a new tactic. Like him, I plan to play my cards close to the vest. That will make it harder for him to turn his vote into a bargaining chip."

"What about the proposed mall?" Lauren waited. "He's already got the upper hand on that one." She waited again. "If I read between the lines, you might let him play his game."

"I might." Jordan breathed a loud sigh. "That damn mall would be a disaster for Cedar Creek."

Lauren squeezed the receiver curbing her journalistic instincts to question; at least out loud. Was Jordan using the same ploy as Laughlin? Not really. He wasn't looking for personal gain. But to what extent might animosity for her father be playing a part?

"You still there?"

"I guess," she said, halfway between her ruminations and their telephone conversation. "We're meeting at six over at the *Ale House* for dinner. Right?"

"Yes. I made a reservation. By the way, I got a call from Loggin this morning. He said that one of my neighbors reported seeing a stranger, mid-twenties, hanging out on the street shortly before the fire. The guy was tall — six-six or maybe more. That's what drew the neighbor's attention. He said the guy had on a plaid, flannel shirt. And one more thing — he was totally bald. Maybe a skinhead."

"Sounds like a good lead. If . . . " Better judgment slowed her tongue, but only momentarily. "If it pans out, you'll owe some apologies, not the least of which will be to your buddy Loggin."

"Why — because he took a phone message from my neighbor?" Jordan paused. "On second thought, I see your point. Who'd have imagined the dunce could answer the phone, let alone take a message." He paused again. "And who else do I owe an apology?"

"Uh . . . nobody."

"Oh no. You said apologies. Plural."

Lauren preferred to remain silent. The thought reminded her of the advice her mother had given her as a little girl. "Think first. Speak second. When in doubt — Don't!" Experience, the countless times she had ignored the advice, had proved her mother right. At that moment she missed her mother. Losing her to a drunk driver at the age of eight had left a wound; one that had never healed.

"I'm still waiting."

Jordan was not about to let her off the hook, not that she would have done otherwise if the roles were reversed. She said, "If this stranger turns out to be the arsonist, you'll owe my father an apology."

"You're referring to my reaction at the Board meeting suggesting he might be responsible."

"Exactly." A less resolute response might have eased the controversy, but Lauren was a Worthington, and Worthingtons were stubborn.

"You've got things backwards. In case you've forgotten, your father accused me first. Plus you're putting the regrets ahead of the invitation."

"Come again?"

"Your father hasn't been ruled out."

"You really believe my father may have set fire to your house?"

"I'll take the Fifth."

"Not so fast," she said. "What's good for the goose — " Distaste for the hackneyed phrase gave her pause, but only for an instant. "Are you accusing my father?"

"No, but I certainly haven't eliminated him."

Her mother's advice came to mind again, but it had no chance. She said, "Jordan Jackson — You should be ashamed. No way would my father set fire to anyone's home. Yours included."

"Wait a second. I should be ashamed? Your father pointed the finger first."

"Well — just because he behaved like a blockhead doesn't mean you have to. And by the way, after he got home last night, I blasted him. Of course, that probably doesn't interest you."

She waited a moment. "Both of you should be ashamed of yourselves."

"Did your father apologize?"

"No, but you could be a bigger person."

"You've got to be kidding. Someone burns my house down. Your father accuses me. And I'm supposed to apologize to him." Jordan muttered inaudibly and then added, "Dickens had it right. *The world is mad. Mad as Bedlam.*"

Ordinarily Lauren welcomed Jordan's clever literary references. Not at that moment. "Save your cheap ironies. And don't try to change the subject. I want to know. Do you really believe my father could be responsible?"

"In one, very succinct word — *Yes!*"

Her jaw tightened. Candor hinted she was being unfair, but dealing with the issue was too exasperating. "I need to get back to work."

"Okay. But we're having dinner tonight?"

"Well — " She clipped her tongue, aware that frustration was affecting judgment. "Of course."

"Fine. I'll see you at the *Ale House* at six."

As she hung up the telephone, Lauren breathed a heavy sigh. Ordinarily easygoing, she was not herself. For no apparent reason, she was snapping at everyone. Even Jordan. She loathed the behavior, but the stress of being caught in the middle had her on edge. She had become a stranger, one she disliked. Compounding matters were her father's efforts to control her. But she could be as obstinate as Dad. The observation was unsettling. There was even the possibility that she was being pigheaded. The thought angered her. Women had long since ceased to be chattel. She was entitled to chose whom she loved. Jordan was an extraordinary person. That should suffice. Why was the world the way it was? Worse yet — Why was her father that way?

———

As she and Jordan approached the reception stand of the *Ale House*, Lauren eyed the massive timbers that lined the ceiling of the English Tudor structure. Lantern-lit tables and a

planked floor linked simplicity with elegance. The maître d'
disappeared for several minutes with another couple he was
seating. When he returned, he rearranged a stack of menus so
each faced in the same direction. He shuffled some other
papers. Lauren watched impatiently. She suspected Jordan was
equally put out. If so, he didn't show it. Finally the maître d'
looked up. He brushed a trace of lint from the sleeve of his
black tux. "May I help you?"

"We'd like a table," said Jordan. "Out on the verandah,
please."

"You don't have a reservation, do you?"

Jordan shook his head.

"I'm sorry," said the maître d'. "The verandah is limited to
reservations. He pointed to an alcove off to his left. "You can
dine in the Gray Room."

Jordan glanced at Lauren. She knew what he was thinking.
Only moments before a white couple, just ahead of them, with
no reservation, had been escorted to the verandah. She
whispered to Jordan. "Whatever you decide is fine."

He turned back to the maître d'. "A minute ago you gave
the gentleman and lady a table on the verandah. They had no
reservation. I heard them."

"Sir, would you like a table or not?"

"I would, but as I said: *On the verandah.*"

"I've already told — "

"I know what you told me, but before you reiterate
something you might regret, let me set the record straight. If
you decline to seat us on the verandah, my friend and I will
leave, and I will sue this establishment for violating the Civil
Rights Act of 1964. You are aware, I assume, that it is illegal
for restaurants to discriminate based upon race." Jordan
reached into his wallet. "My card, Sir."

The maître d' swallowed hard. "Please accompany me to
the verandah."

As Lauren, along with Jordan, followed the maître d', she
poked her elbow into Jordan's side. She flashed a discrete
smile.

The maître d' pointed. "How is that table, the one by the
rail overlooking the water?"

"Excellent," said Jordan.

Lovely, thought Lauren, as she eyed the string of white lights that ran across the long deck.

The maître d' pulled out Lauren's chair and helped her into her seat. He then assisted Jordan. "Eugene, your waiter, will be with you shortly. If I can be of further service, please let me know. Enjoy your dinner." He walked away.

"I hope you didn't mind," said Jordan.

"Not at all." Her eyes focused on the shimmering ripples of the moonlit lake. "I'm glad you spoke up. It's beautiful out here."

"You're right. But that's not why I pushed." He looked around and spoke in a lowered voice. "It's about responsibility. As a black professional in a society where change comes slowly, I . . . " He turned and stared out at the lake. Several seconds passed. He looked back at Lauren. "It's a long story; one, perhaps, better left for another time."

"I'd like to hear it."

He shook his head. "That's kind. But a candlelight dinner in a romantic setting (he gestured beyond the rail) hardly needs a menu of social injustice."

"I'll risk it," she said, curiosity, more than civility, prompting her words.

"Okay — but remember, you asked for it." He reached for his water and took a drink. "Where should I begin?" His eyes narrowed. "Way back when, I guess." He put his glass down. "When I was a teen, my foster father — he was the man of the house in which I was placed that year — sat me down for what he termed *The Talk*."

"The one about the birds and the bees?"

Jordan chuckled. "That's what I thought he meant. I should have known better. He wasn't like most men of his day; certainly not most black men. Not that any group can be stereotyped." Jordan grew momentarily pensive. "Damn — he was a good man. I wish I could have stayed there longer than a year. But before I digress further, back to *The Talk*. My foster father asked me, 'What is it like to be black?'"

The look in Jordan's eyes hinted that he could read Lauren's mind. Indeed, he had.

"The kind of a question you'd expect a white to ask a black, not a black to another black. That was my reaction too."

"How did you respond?"

"I told him he already knew. Good answer, wasn't it?"

Logical though it seemed, Jordan's mocking tone suggested otherwise. "I guess," said Lauren, uncertain how to respond.

Jordan waited until the busboy finished putting a basket of rolls on the table. "I remember what my foster father said as if it were this morning. He told me he knew what it was like for him to be black, but what it was for me, only I could say. Then he asked me, what, if any, responsibility I had when faced with discrimination. To me, the answer seemed obvious. Since only I knew how I felt, only I could determine the appropriate response."

Once again, Lauren suspected that logic was leading her down an erroneous path. Jordan's knack of inducing false inferences was familiar. "I'll bet your foster father had something else in mind."

"You're quite astute. More than I was; though my foster father didn't press the issue. Instead, he hit me with another question. He asked which black group had best addressed discrimination: our forefathers who said, *Yes, Sir*, and turned the other cheek; Martin Luther King and his followers who engaged in passive resistance; or activists like the Black Panthers who advocated violence." Jordan gestured at Lauren. "Whom would you say?"

Given the pattern, a trap was likely. Still she said, "Martin Luther King."

"Excellent answer. The same one I gave."

"But not the one he was looking for."

Jordan smiled. He reached for his water and took a drink. "Picture this. It's 1937. *Separate but equal*, affirmed by the Supreme Court, is the law of the land. In many southern towns members of the Ku Klux Klan wear sheriffs' badges and judicial robes. Federal civil rights acts are as distant as voyages to the moon. The new Cedar Creek High School has just been built, and sharecropper *I. M. Negro* wants his son and daughter to go there rather than the Negro school out on Lincoln Road.

He marches his children over to Cedar Creek High and demands admittance. Any chance? Of course not. But in the dead of night, a firebomb might take his home and the lives of his wife and children. And the so-called justice system would say they got what they deserved. That's the way it was."

Lauren waited a moment. "So, what should he have done?"

"You tell me."

She shrugged. Her seemingly insipid gesture made her squirm. "There's nothing he could have done given the times."

Jordan nodded. "That was my foster father's point. Mr. Negro, 1937, for the sake of his family, had to compromise his dignity. Under the circumstances that was the right thing to do. Once times had begun to change — the Supreme Court had struck down *Separate but Equal*, and presidents, beginning with Eisenhower, had exhibited a willingness to bring in the National Guard to enforce federal law — resistance, both passive and militant, became a meaningful alternative." Jordan reached for his water again.

Lauren contemplated what he had said. She was about to verify whether she had gleaned the message when the maître d' approached with a bottle in hand.

"Compliments of the house," he said. "Apologies for the earlier inconvenience."

"Apologies accepted," said Jordan. "But since all I ask is to be treated like other patrons — no better or worse — I must decline the wine. Please be assured, however, your gesture is appreciated."

The maître d' nodded, his fingers fidgeting with the bottle. "Is there anything else I can do?"

"We're fine," said Jordan. "On second thought, there is one thing. In the future please avoid favoritism."

"I understand." The maître d' walked away. As he disappeared around the corner, Lauren refocused on her earlier reflection. She had her explanation. The lesson helped define a previously subtle aspect of Jordan's character. So much about him had made him more attractive that any man she had known. Why then did doubts, the kind that constantly recur, simmer? She knew the answer. Indeed, it was self-evident. The old adage, *ignorance is bliss*, came to mind. Folks in Cedar Creek, her father included, were ignorant. Whether their insensitivity brought them happiness, she couldn't say. Regardless, it made her life difficult.

Lauren and Jordan ordered. Course by course, appetizer, salad and entrée, they exchanged small talk. Even as they finished their meal and Eugene brought her a cup of Café Amaretto, concerns lingered. Without tasting it, she dumped an entire packet of *Equal* into the hot beverage. She took a sip and turned her mouth down.

"Do you want to send it back?" said Jordan.

She shrugged and took another drink. The beverage, an *Ale House* specialty, was fine, apart from the fact that it contained too much sweetener. She glanced at the package that had contained the powder. The blue shade matched her mood. The problem, however, extended far beyond the liqueur-flavored coffee. Her eyes moved around the stately inn. They focused on the picture of Jefferson Davis that hung from the sturdy, timbered walls. Local lore claimed that the Confederate President had dined at the *Ale House* during the Civil War. Lauren found it hard to imagine the burdens he must have shouldered. The thought did little to lighten hers. She looked across the table at Jordan. Six months they had been going together, and contrary to early optimism, tension had invaded their relationship. When they had first begun dating, she had convinced herself that the times were changing. Even in provincial Cedar Creek, what had been illegal under prior miscegenation statutes, had begun to occur; though less on the streets than on television. Her father, traditional southern gentleman that he was, had seemingly shown hints of change. No longer did he abhor the concept of interracial marriage. However, embrace it, he hadn't, especially when it came to his own daughter. His rationalization, an old standby, was that children need an identity. As he put it, loving parents would not make their offspring half fish and half fowl. Lauren detested the argument. Still, he was her only living parent, and she loved him. She took another sip of her coffee. Was she having second thoughts about Jordan? Not really. She loved him far too much for that. But guilt, along with angst, could infect even love.

"So, you sending it back?"

Lauren shook her head, her thoughts halfway between two cups, both nearly full, but each lacking full-bodied flavor. "No, the coffee is fine. It's just me." She was not herself, and she knew it. How to address the problem was another matter. Ever since she was young, she had always been easygoing. It was one of her hallmarks. Caught between her father's disapproval of her relationship with Jordan and Jordan's staunch opposition to her father's mall, she was under constant stress. Affability was giving way to impatience. Smiles came less easily. And her tongue had grown sharp. She disliked the person she was becoming. Unfortunately, tension foiled efforts to regain her customary demeanor.

Jordan gave her a funny look, but one she had seen before. He had gotten to know her well and could tell when something was bothering her. However, unlike the usual concerns, a problem with her car or an inaccuracy in one of her articles, this involved him, and she suspected he knew it. Dinner conversation had grown uncommonly sparse, and what there was, had little zest.

"Are you still angry from this morning?"

She shook her head. Why, she wondered, when Jordan was being direct, was she ignoring the overture. Thoughts of her father and the ongoing dispute between the two gave a hint.

"Can we try to discuss it?"

Jordan's willingness reminded her of an article she had written months earlier concerning female frustration with the stereotypical non-communicative male. The recollection, the chiding thoughts it provoked, pushed her to be more responsive. "I can't deal with the conflict between the two people closest to me, especially when I'm in the middle."

"What are you saying?"

"Exactly what I said."

Jordan frowned. "C'mon. I'm trying to understand you."

Her frustration begged to vent. His sincerity demanded better. "I'm sorry. I know you are." She hesitated. "The whole thing is tying me up in knots. I can't deal with it."

"Can't or won't?"

"A bit of both, I suspect."

He nodded. "Let me guess. It's like a vice, with your father and me pressing harder and harder."

"Uh . . . not exactly. It's . . . it's more like you're tugging in opposite directions."

Jordan leaned back and stared at the ceiling. Finally, he looked back her way. His voice somber, he said, "Do you want me to let go?"

She shook her head. "My father would love that. Then he could yank me away." The image stirred anger. She said, "Much as I hate being caught in the middle, a pull only from his direction would be a thousand times worse."

"I'm glad to hear you say that." Jordan smiled.

She smiled back. Despite frustration, no way did she want to lose him. She took a drink of her Café Amaretto. The over-sweetened beverage had cooled to an unsavory level, close to room temperature. Nevertheless, it tasted better than before.

"The Bastard wants to see you," whispered Lucy, the *Chronicle*'s gal Friday.

"So I heard," said Lauren, already on her way to her boss's office. Like everyone at the *Chronicle* she tried to minimize her contact with the browbeating editor. Unfortunately, actions seldom mirrored intentions. She poked her head into the open doorway. "You wanted to see me, Mr. Nielsen?"

"Have a seat." He gestured at the chair on the opposite side of his desk.

A bad sign. If he wanted to discuss mundane matters, a front-page headline or a story that needed follow up, he would have done it with her still in the doorway. A moment later, when he shut the door, he confirmed her suspicion. She tried to fathom the problem as he sauntered to his big leather chair. The last time Nielsen had called her in for a closed-door meeting, almost a year earlier, the source for her story about a drug problem at the middle school had turned out to be an inveterate liar, and the *Chronicle* had to print a soft-shoe follow up. The veiled retraction was better masked than her boss's displeasure.

"I heard your interview the other night on Jerry Baker's show." Nielsen's gaze focused on his impressive, walnut desk.

She watched as the stocky, middle-aged man with the round, bespectacled face adjusted the onyx base of his gold pen set so it perfectly paralleled the edges of his desk. How he managed to maintain such an immaculate office while editing a daily newspaper was beyond her. The man was fastidious.

"You went onto Baker's home turf and held your own."

Were she not familiar with her boss's methods, she would have thanked him for the compliment. But past experience had taught her to anticipate the thorns his roses camouflaged.

"What did you think of the Village Board meeting the night before last?"

She had opinions. She kept them to herself. In the meantime Nielsen looked up at the ceiling and shook his head. "Your boyfriend and your father really went at it. They've put you in a tough spot." He finally turned back to Lauren. "It isn't fair." He waited a few moments. "You agree, don't you?" His voice had grown louder, and his steely eyes demanded a response.

"I guess."

"Hardly an enthusiastic *yes*."

Given his propensity for traps, what did he expect? She said, "I have to admit, it's difficult."

"Good." He nodded repeatedly. "I'm glad we're on the same page."

Lauren breathed a sigh, not one of relief. She could only imagine what horror she had acquiesced in.

He poked his finger into his chest. "I'm on your side. You can count on me."

The ray of hope cast doubt that he had darker intentions. "I appreciate that."

"No problem." He rocked his chair back. "So, I'll tell Ted that he'll be handling matters related to the mall and the fire from now on."

"What!"

"I thought we had agreed that the men in your life had put you in an impossible position."

She fought the urge to go off half-cocked. "Let's keep them out of this," she said. "Anyway, I intend to do my job."

Nielsen lowered his gaze. An instant later his eyes drew within inches of his desk. "Damn," he muttered, as he brushed off what must have been microscopic specks of dust. "Can't the cleaning people do their job?" He looked back at Lauren. "No. It isn't fair to you. I won't let you be a martyr."

You three-dollar bill, pretending you're worried about me. She hesitated, as she formulated a more diplomatic reply. "I appreciate your concern, but I want to stay with the story. As I said on Baker's show, I intend to follow it, wherever it leads."

Nielsen put his hand to his chin and muttered under his breath. Finally, he said, "I don't like it. But you know me. I'm the kind of boss who gives his people slack."

Sure — just enough to make a noose.

"You want the story. You've got it." He pointed at her. His voice grew stern. "Just remember, it's against my better judgment."

"Thank you," she said, her stomach in knots.

"No need to thank me."

She got up from her seat. Just as she reached the door, he said, "One more thing."

She turned back to him.

"A word of warning. This better not turn out like that so-called middle-school drug problem. God, was that a fiasco."

She headed out the door, closing it behind her. Nielsen had her right where he wanted. His *modus operandi*, allowing employees to make their own decisions, was a pellucid ruse. Like her co-workers, Lauren had faced it before. She knew that her decision to pursue the story had left her out on a limb. But had she opted out, Nielsen would have moaned and groaned, and then let her have her way. Of course, that would have been a big favor, one he would not forget — one entitling him to tribute. Lauren shuffled over to her desk and sank down into her chair, a fabric seat, far smaller than Nielsen's sumptuous leather throne. She kicked her desk's masonite modesty panel. Wasn't it enough that she was caught in the middle of a tug of war, her father on one side and Jordan, the other? Did her boss need to add another dimension, changing the linear predicament into a triangle, a scalene one at that, where unequal forces were pulling in oblique directions? She glanced at her computer but then reached for her purse. She needed a *Coke* before finishing the art-show article she had started earlier. She took a dollar bill out of her wallet. The sight of the eye atop the pyramid on the obverse of the bill flashed the image of Jerry Baker into her mind. The talk show host had pledged to keep a watchful eye over her handling of the pending issues. Like the *Cyclops* Baker loomed at the top of the pyramid, his jaundiced eye watching for any misstep and his savage tongue ready to unleash its venom over the airwaves. Lauren heaved an exhausted sigh. Her problems had pyramided into three dimensions, their expansion geometric.

Chapter V

From behind the bar forty-four year old Jack O'Leary, paunchy, but still with hints of a virile youth, looked over at the booth in the far corner where Steve Ward was nursing an *Old Lager*. What did the smooth talker with the slicked-back hair want? Whatever it was, the fact that Steve was looking to talk after closing hours convinced Jack he wouldn't like it.

The usual weekday stragglers stayed right until eleven o'clock. The last of them, Buck Ryder, finally came out of the john. Jack tried to ignore Buck's stagger. Still the image of Buck behind the wheel of his rusted pickup was unsettling. As a tavern owner Jack knew his potential liability. An accident seven years earlier had schooled him in the Dram Shop law. His insurance agent and very close friend, fellow Village Board member Janet Warner, had often warned him, but only a huge jump in premiums following the accident brought the message home. As he locked the front door behind Buck, Jack contemplated why he put up with the lowlife. The answer to the familiar question was no revelation. Buck Ryder and his booze-drinking buddies paid the bills.

Jack headed to the booth where Ward sat waiting. "Can I get you another?"

"Still have half-a-bottle." He gestured toward the door. "How do you tolerate riffraff like him day after day?"

"Buck? He's okay." Jack slipped into the other side of the booth. As a tavern owner more gossip passed his ears than bubbles from his foamy tap. He imbibed the chatter with noncommittal nods and smiles. But repeat it? Never. Hard lessons learned years earlier had taught him how easily such talk drooled from the mouths of inebriated patrons. He said, "So, why the late evening powwow?"

"Thought we might discuss the proposed mall."

"We could have done that at the Board Meeting." Already the wheels were spinning as Jack contemplated why Ward wanted the private tête-à-tête.

"C'mon — Village Hall is no place to talk." Ward took a swig. "This mall thing has really split the Board. It's bad for the community. I was hoping we could find a solution."

Translation — you're looking for me to change my vote and help you kill the mall. Jack feigned a puzzled look.

"What's the matter?"

"Why come to me when you could go to Laughlin? He's the guy on the fence."

"Well — I figured I could talk to you."

Translation — you tried Laughlin, but he shot you down. Jack leaned back and folded his arms. "If you ask me, the mall would be good for the Village."

"You must be kidding. A monstrosity like that overlooking the park. Who wants to fish on the banks of *K-mart*? And the engineer says it might threaten the aquifer." He gestured with his bottle in Jack's direction. "Think of the poor folks who live out this way. The traffic will be awful. And the Village . . . the whole business section on Broad Street will dry up."

At long last, the real reason. Ward is afraid his strip mall, already with two vacant storefronts, will end up empty. "Broad Street is important, but Cedar Creek needds jobs. New businesses, even on the outskirts, are better than nothing."

"You're making a mistake, Jack. Just because you're close to the new mall doesn't mean you'll get more traffic. From what I hear it may include a *Friday's*, as well as a microbrewery. Far be it from me to tell you your business, but Worthington's project could kill yours."

"I appreciate your concern, but the Village needs jobs." Jack breathed a contrived sigh. Like Ward, he could resort to the tactics of a used-car salesman. "I'll have to risk it," he said.

Exasperation showed on Ward's face. "Last year you called Jackson a straight shooter. He opposes the mall. That oughta tell you something."

"Wait a second. I said he was honest, but I also said his views were harebrained. If you ask me, his opinion about the mall is exactly that."

"Damn it, O'Leary. Talking to you is . . . is like talking to my ex-wife."

"Why — because I don't agree with you?"

"That's not what I said." Ward stewed a moment. "Maybe I gave you too much credit. I thought you were too smart to be taken in by Worthington. He and his ancestors got rich off this town. That mansion of his up on the hill, all fifteen or whatever rooms, came from the blood and sweat of slaves."

Jack chuckled, but only to himself. Since when was Steve Ward concerned with social injustice.

Ward took another swig, this time rapping his bottle back down on the oak table. "You know the old saying about the rich get richer. Well — if Roger Worthington gets his mall, chalk up another for the adage. As for Cedar Creek, it'll get a kick in the ass."

"Just a second," said Jack. "You gotta give the Worthington devils their due. More than a century of their philanthropy lines the streets of Cedar Creek: the Village Park, the museum and the hospital, just to name a few."

"Sure, they keep the peons happy. In the meantime, they get their name on everything. Kinda like the Pharaohs. A few slaves go a long way."

Jack debated whether to point out the obvious. Generations had passed since the Worthingtons had owned slaves. However, apart from the technicality, Ward's slant on history had merit. "I've got a question," he said. "You think the threats are linked to the fire at Jackson's home?"

"Unfortunately, I do." Ward's manner turned somber. "As a recipient of one, I'm scared. Damn scared."

"Frankly, if you hadn't told me, I wouldn't have guessed."

Ward shrugged. "Whoever sent the notes is a terrorist. Showing fear plays into his hands. As an elected official, I've got to set an example. Anyway, my grandparents came over from England. It's in my blood. You know, the stiff upper lip."

Jack scratched his head. "And all this time I thought it was botox." The quip, however, masked his thoughts. Ward had far more backbone than Jack had previously imagined. Had the roles been reversed, Jack doubted he would have shown such courage. He said, "Any guesses who sent the threats?"

Ward's eyes narrowed as he reached across the table and aimed a finger squarely into Jack's face.

"You're not serious?"

Ward chuckled. "Of course not. If I thought you were involved, I never would have told you I was frightened."

Jack pointed back, but not in the menacing way his counterpart had done a moment before. "You got me."

Ward laughed and then looked at his watch. "It's getting late. I'm sure you wanna get out of here." He stood up and walked to the door. He glanced back. "By the way, a bit of friendly advice. You need to be careful. Rumor says you served some underage skinheads. Rumor also says that someone — name unmentioned — may notify the Department of Revenue's division of Alcoholic Beverage Licensing." He unlatched the door and headed out to his Cadillac.

Jack stood by the window as the car drove away. Ward knew how to play hardball. His so-called friendly advice could not be taken lightly. Jack locked the door. He looked around his empty establishment. Being a member of the Village Board had lots of advantages. Still, it was far more complicated than he had imagined when first he had decided to run for the seat.

Long-stemmed *Waterford* in hand, Lauren peered down the *Chippendale* table where her father, a full twelve feet away, was adjusting his napkin. The weekly ritual, Tuesday evening dinner, just the two of them, in the dining room at Worthington Hall, had grown increasingly troublesome. She loved her father, but at twenty-nine she longed to be free of his manipulative thumb. She sipped her 1978 *Rothschild* Cabernet Sauvignon. Outside rumbles of thunder grew faint. The thunderstorm that had raged when she had arrived earlier was yielding to brighter skies. Out the window she could see the contrast of sunshine slipping past the remaining dark clouds; the kind of atmospheric conditions that spawned rainbows. The thought reminded her of her mother. Though the recollections were limited, like lilacs that bore the scent of her mother's favorite perfume, rainbows stimulated fond memories. Lauren recalled the warm, sunny days years earlier when she had skipped through rainbows her mother had created with a misting spray from the backyard hose. Her mother had loved the colored crescents. She had adorned the refrigerator with a rainbow-colored magnet. Days earlier when Lauren had moved into her new apartment, the time-worn magnet had accompanied her.

"I'm re-doing your bedroom," said her father. "Wallpaper, carpet, furniture — the whole nine yards. Mary Thompson — she's a terrific decorator — will work with you. Whatever you want, that's the way it'll be."

Lauren's fingers tightened on the delicate crystal. "Dad, please don't start. We've been this route before. I've got my own place now. I'm not moving back home."

"Who said anything about moving home? I'm doing your room over. Is that okay?"

"Fine. Then do it to your tastes. This is your house, and every room in it is yours."

Her father folded his arms and jerked them against his chest. "Damn. Sometimes you're exasperating. And about moving home — since *you* raised the subject — it's beyond me why you rented that one-room dump."

Lauren stemmed the urge to slam her goblet down. "How dare you call my apartment a dump. And I'll have you know it's a one and a-half room studio. Bedroom, kitchen area, plus a bath, and, best of all, it's all mine."

"One . . . one and a-half. What's the difference. The point is — " He stopped when his long-time housekeeper Bessie Walters, an attractive woman in her late forties with high cheek bones, slim waist and impeccable posture, set a shrimp cocktail in front of him. "Bessie, talk some sense into this daughter of mine. Please."

Lauren chuckled to herself as Bessie stepped away pretending not to hear the request. The scene, her father looking to Bessie in the face of father-daughter issues, was familiar. And why not. Bessie enjoyed a rapport with Lauren her father lacked. Bessie had been with them for as long as Lauren could remember, and ever since her mother had died, Bessie had been like a mother. She was the one adult with whom Lauren allowed herself to be a child after her mother's death. In the years following the accident Bessie read to Lauren at bedtime, soothed her fears following a bad dream and later exposed her to good literature. When a thirteen year-old girl who had flunked twice bullied Lauren in fifth grade, Bessie pressed the school to halt the abuse. When Lauren was fourteen and an appealing high school junior stood her up for what was to be their second date, Bessie consoled Lauren's wounded heart. Even into her twenties, Lauren still confided in Bessie.

"There you go, ignoring me again," said Lauren's father. "I could use your help."

The caramel-skinned housekeeper turned to her employer. "Lauren's an adult. Anyway, it's not my job. I serve the dinner, do the dishes and clean the house, but when it comes to your daughter's personal life, you're on your own."

Lauren loved how Bessie bantered with her father. It hadn't always been that way. Back when Lauren's mother was alive, her father was always businesslike with Bessie, and her responses, the model of decorum. That pattern had continued for nearly a decade after Lauren's mother's death. But in recent years there had been a gradual shift. Repartee, laced with subtlety, had replaced formal exchange. What surprised Lauren most was that her father, though seemingly indignant, invited the change. Non-verbal cues belying gruff words hinted at esteem.

"Big help you are," he said.

"What did you expect? After all, Ms. Lauren is a guest, now that she has her own apartment."

"Guest?" He groaned. "And since when did you start calling her Ms. Lauren again. You haven't done that since the days of Lyndon Johnson."

Bessie shrugged. "Old habits rear their head at the strangest times, don't they?"

His eyebrows shot up. "Well — tell Ms. Lauren or whatever you call her how lucky she is to have a home like this."

"Give her a break," said Lauren. "This is between you and me."

Bessie started for the kitchen. "More of this talk, and I'll be serving roasted shoe-leather."

"Just like her. She always takes your side."

"C'mon. She didn't take anyone's side." Lauren knew otherwise.

Her father picked up his fork but then laid it back down. "I really want you to reconsider. That also goes for my offer for you to join the business. And think about it, rather than giving me that irritated look. Instead of making a pittance as a lowly reporter, you'd be a vice-president with a beautiful office and triple the salary."

"Look, I've told you before — I like my job. I have no intention of changing."

He sighed loudly. "It makes no sense. You're putting in sixty hours a week for peanuts when you could be an executive making big bucks while working half the time."

Minor detail, thought Lauren. The impressive title would be in exchange for independence and self-respect. She said, "I thought we settled this months ago." His patronizing look, one Lauren knew all too well, suggested the subject was far from closed.

"C'mon," he said. "This is the first time since Christmas I've mentioned the job. Anyway, I want you to know that the offer still stands. In the meantime, you oughta move back here. It would be a tremendous improvement."

For whom? She said, "Do we have to spoil dinner with an argument?"

"I'm not arguing." He gestured at himself. "Have I raised my voice?"

Not yet, but if the past were a predictor, it would happen soon. "You know what I mean. Can't we talk about something more pleasant?"

"Sure. Once we discuss this."

Lauren took a deep breath. "Look, I'm not moving back."

"You'll have your space. I promise."

"What about my privacy?"

He gestured in all directions. "Of course."

"That's not what I'm referring to. What about Jordan?"

He muttered under his breath and then stared down the length of the table. "How can you put me, your own father, in such a position?" He pointed toward the kitchen door and whispered, "For the moment, forget the matter of race." His voice grew louder. "The fellow accused me of burning his house down."

"And you accused him of burning it down himself."

"He — "

"That's not the point," barked Lauren. "How can the two of you, the two men I care about most, behave so ridiculously. And how can you put *me* in such an impossible position?"

"Terrific. Now you're blaming me."

"You bet I am. And Jordan too."

He stabbed his fork into a shrimp, which he shoved into his mouth. He chewed it and jabbed another.

"Fine. You want to sulk. Be my guest."

"I'm not sulking," he said without looking up. "And as long as you raised the subject, let's talk about your relationship with Jordan."

"What about it!"

He shook his head. "Do I need to spell it out?"

She lowered her voice. "You're referring to the fact that he's black?"

He nodded.

Lauren's jaw tightened. "This is not the nineteenth century. People, at least those who are educated, are moving beyond color."

"Despite what you think, I'm not a bigot. Yes, I grew up in a house where my father and his father before him were prejudiced, but I'm not them. I respect people, regardless of race. But marriage is another matter. You have to think about the children. When they're half this and half that, they're neither here nor there. Chances are, they end up as outsiders.

And don't shush me with your finger. Anyway, Bessie knows my views about interracial marriage. And chances are, she agrees."

"I doubt that," said Lauren. She envisioned the two discussing the issue; her father the pontiff and Bessie, the stoic listener.

"Just because the liberal press and the left-wing writers of TV sitcoms want to embrace racial mixing doesn't make it wonderful. Ask the kids of those relationships how it feels, especially after their parents have split."

"Are you suggesting that interracial marriages have a higher rate of divorce?"

"You bet. And no, I don't have statistics. So, don't ask."

Lauren would have pushed the point, except she feared her father might be right. Sound judgment said check it out first. If his point had merit, let it be. On the other hand, if it turned out wrong, once she had the ammunition, she would blast him. She reached for her wine. One evening a week was more than she could handle. The thought of living there again, returning to her childhood, was inconceivable. Wine and shrimp, fancy china and a stately home were nice, but having a life, ten times better. She sipped her wine, swirling it over her tongue. Time had seasoned it well. Unfortunately, the same could not be said for her relationship with her father. Though she had aged, he was still controlling. Love him? Yes. But like the *Rothschild* he served, a sweeter vintage would never replace his *appellation contrôlée*.

Bessie came through the kitchen door and put a medium-rare slab of prime-rib on his plate. She moved to the other end of the table and gave Lauren one, a bit less red. Bessie looked up and down the table. "I'd better go back and get my carving blade."

Lauren eyed the utensils that adjoined her platter. "I have a steak knife. I'm sure it'll do."

Bessie shook her head. "Not for the beef. The atmosphere. You need a machete to cut it."

He groaned. "We can do without the dramatics."

Bessie smiled and headed for the kitchen. A moment later she re-appeared in the doorway waiving a big, black-handled knife in the pattern of a figure eight.

Lauren burst into laughter as Bessie stepped back into the kitchen and shut the door behind her.

Lauren's father folded his arms and stared in the direction of the door. "God. Her antics."

"You love those antics. And admit it or not, you couldn't get along without her."

He shrugged. His face, however, showed the hint of a smile. He cut a bite and chewed it slowly. "Done to perfection."

"It is indeed," said Lauren. Despite the tasty morsel, she worried that all too soon the usual grisly fare would dominate their menu.

———————

Lauren lamented her decision to leave her brief case in the car. As long as she had to wait, a few paragraphs on her feature about civic pride would have been preferable to counting the squares in the old tin ceiling. When she had first contacted Loggin, the idea of a face-to-face meeting, rather than a telephone conversation, had seemed wise. After sitting in the police station for forty minutes, she was having second thoughts. She was about to ask the desk sergeant to ring Loggin again when the paunchy detective emerged from the inner sanctum. As he approached, she saw his eyes go up and down her, their pause at her chest not at all disguised. A brazen smile stamped his imprimatur on the fruits of his imagination. The ostensible compliment clenched her jaw.

"Did I keep you waitin'?"

Lauren stared up at the big clock on the wall, the minute hand having circumscribed two-thirds of a revolution since the appointed time of their two-o'clock meeting. "Well — I was a few minutes early."

Loggin shook his head. "My late mother, rest her soul, used to make the same mistake."

"Pardon me," said Lauren, his comment a far cry from the apology she had anticipated.

"Doctor's appointment, church, the hair dresser, you name it — Mom was always ten or fifteen minutes early. Add them bits of time up day after day, year after year, and before you know it . . . " He shook his head again. "Time is money. That's what most folks say. But it's more than that. It's . . . it's the only thing we got." He paused just long enough to allow a self-satisfied expression to commend his astute observation. A moment later he continued. "Me — I value time. Waste not. Want not. That's my motto. You won't — "

"Excuse me," said Lauren. She gestured at the clock. "Can we get started?"

Loggin groaned. "You young folks, always in a rush. Relax. Smell them flowers." He inhaled slowly. "In this case, coffee. How 'bout a cup?"

"No, thank you."

"Suit yourself." He inhaled again. "Well — I could do with one. You don't mind," he said, already on his way to the pot. A minute later he returned with a huge mug in hand. He pointed at the large vessel. "Got this at the flea market last year. Holds over twenty ounces."

Lauren pointed at the side of the cup that was decorated with the Georgia state flag, complete with Confederate battle symbol. "Interesting choice."

"Yeah." He looked at the emblem. "Even though I'm a South Carolinian, I was born in Georgia. Some folks lose their roots. I'm a man of tradition — if you know what I mean."

"I suspect I do. But — " She stopped herself. Loggin's attitude was no surprise.

"But what?" He waited a moment. "I saw your look. I know what you're thinkin'. I've read your liberal stuff." He took a drink. "The Constitution isn't just for folks like you. The rest of us are entitled to free speech." He put his free hand on the star-crossed emblem.

Lauren pressed her lips together. Debating politics and social issues was not the purpose of her visit. Regardless, words would never sway Loggin. On the other hand, time, the very commodity he supposedly cherished, might cure the ill.

The addition of better-educated, open-minded, young officers could alter the force. As for Loggin, he was certain to retire in a few years.

Loggin sipped his coffee. "Apples ain't supposed to fall far from the tree." He eyed her with a furrowed brow.

She struggled to maintain an impassive exterior. She said, "You love your old adages, don't you?"

"Those sayings don't get repeated 'less their good. Same thing we talked about before. Tradition. Course, lots of young people, like yourself, think you're smarter than the past generation. Gonna fix the world." He gestured at her with his mug. "Your father's got things right. And you, young lady, could learn a thing or two from him."

Lauren bristled. Being patronized was bad, but of all dolts, Loggin? "I'd like to discuss the arson." She pointed up at the clock whose minute hand had nearly managed a full revolution since her arrival.

"Sure. Let's go into my office."

She followed him through an oak door, then down a dim hallway with granite floor. As she did, it crossed her mind that in recent days conflict-ridden conversations with men had become a staple. Her father, Baker, her boss, Loggin — the pattern was the same. She was at odds with all of them, and she didn't like it. Might the blame lie with her? The thought, her inability to dismiss it, rankled her.

Loggin stepped into a tiny office and seated himself behind an old wooden desk. Lauren took the chair on the opposite side of the messy cubicle. He said, "So, what can I do for you?"

"I was wondering what progress you've made with the arson investigation. Jordan said one of his neighbors saw a tall stranger roaming the area shortly before the fire."

Loggin hesitated. "I can't say too much. But let me put it this way." He moved his hands toward one another until they were less than an inch apart. "I'm this close to an arrest."

"The stranger?"

Loggin looked her in the eye. "We off the record?"

"Absolutely."

"I won't read it in the *Chronicle* tomorrow?"

"You've got my word." She waited, concealing impatience, while he reached for his mug and took a drink.

Finally, he said, "Yup. It's the stranger."

"You know who he is?"

"Let's say I know where to find him. And don't ask." He pointed at his wall calendar. "Today is Wednesday. I'll lay guns to gumballs, by the time the week's out, your arsonist will be rooming in the hotel out back. And he won't have a key."

"You sound sure."

Loggin leaned back. "Twenty-four years I've been on the force. I know when my ducks are in line. And in this case, the fine-feathered quacker, a live one, is dead in my sights." He folded his arms and smiled warmly. "That sweater becomes you. Complements your blue eyes."

"Thanks for your time," said Lauren, her expression as businesslike as her words.

She started to get up.

Loggin hurried around his desk and opened the door. "I'll show you out." He reached over and put a hand across her shoulder as if to guide her.

She jerked away. "I know where to go." She headed out the door and down the hallway, her head ringing from the clatter of her heels against the stone floor; the noise, however, insufficient to drown out the echo of Loggin's confident words. Despite his boorish conduct, shoddy diction, repulsive anatomy, glaring dullness and various other unenviable traits, which, for the moment, slipped her mind, maybe he had a trace of investigative talent. And maybe . . . just maybe . . . he had found the culprit who had set fire to Jordan's home. What scoops, she thought, unsure which was more amazing — the prospect that Loggin had identified the arsonist or the possibility he had a positive attribute.

———————

Arms spread across the top rail of the bench, Lauren leaned back and inhaled the alluring fragrances of Cedar Creek Village Park. Her eyes transfixed on the pink and white azaleas. Much as she loved the fall spectacular, heightened senses confirmed her preference. The herald of warmer days, followed by summer evenings in comfortable pastel outfits, elevated her spirits. The sight of Jordan coming her way boosted them more.

"Hi Sweets." He kissed her. "Shall we take a stroll?"

She gestured him to join her on the seat. "Let's sit awhile first."

He eased down beside her. "How'd your day go?"

"Pretty good." Soon enough she would tell him about her meeting with Loggin. She said, "Were you in court today?"

"Was I ever. The *Bryant* case. My client turned down the insurance company's offer. He wants to go to trial."

"You've got a good case. Right?"

Jordan nodded. "That's not the rub. My client expects a jury to hand him the keys to *Fort Knox*."

"You couldn't get him to change his mind?"

"Nope. I outlined the risks, but — " Jordan shook his head. "By the way, I'm not telling you anything out of school. Judge Graber put the offer, along with my client's rejection, on the record. But enough of me. How'd your day go?"

"I met with Loggin. And you needn't make a face. He provided a fascinating tidbit."

"I can just imagine."

"Well, if you're so enthusiastic, maybe I should keep it to myself." She pressed her lips together pretending to ignore his impatient frown.

"C'mon, my sarcasm was aimed at Loggin, not you."

She might have debated the point if it weren't self-evident. She said, "Not for publication. But remember that stranger your neighbor saw roaming the street the night of the fire. Loggin has the goods on him. He plans to arrest the guy before the week is out."

Jordan's eyes widened. "Loggin?"

She nodded. If she had her *Minolta*, she would have captured Jordan's expression.

"Amazing." He shook his head repeatedly. "So, tell me, who's this stranger?"

"Loggin wouldn't say. Anyway, he made me promise not to print the story until he makes the arrest." Lauren studied

Jordan's face. An opaque expression had replaced his initial reaction. "What do you think?"

"I'll believe it when I see it. For now — " He stopped, his focus directed toward a young fellow who was just approaching. "What do you want?"

"Figured ya might help me out."

Lauren eyed the skinny guy. He was clad in torn jeans and a T-shirt with cutoff sleeves and a skull and crossbones across the chest. Lauren guessed his age at mid-twenties, but anything between eighteen and thirty was possible.

"Can't you see I'm busy?" said Jordan.

"A few quid, and I'm outta here."

Jordan muttered to himself. He reached for his wallet and pulled out three ten-dollar bills. As the guy leaned over and took them, an *AA* tattoo near his shoulder caught Lauren's eye. Why was Jordan giving this guy money? An instant later, a possible explanation clicked.

The guy slipped the cash into his pocket and without a word hurried off.

"What was that about?" said Lauren

"Uh . . . nothing."

"Nothing." She waited a moment. "I've got a suspicion."

Jordan's eyes widened, but he remained silent.

"You were assigned to represent him. Right?"

Jordan drew a deep breath. "Not exactly, but . . . but how about we take that walk?"

Lauren glanced off in the direction where the guy had disappeared. Something seemed amiss. She felt the tug of Jordan's hand. They got up and started along the path that led around the lake.

Jordan gestured at the hill a few hundred yards beyond the water. "Can you imagine what this place would be like if bulldozers turned that hill into a parking lot for your father's mall?" He breathed a heavy sigh. "Unfortunately, it won't be a fair fight. It never is. Not when the environment steps into the ring with a high-priced project. Greenbacks, not grass, deliver knockouts, and Roger Worthington — not that I need to tell you — has fistfuls of the stuff needed to win a tough bout."

"You never know," said Lauren, her interest in his words confined only to greenbacks and fists. Unanswered questions from the scene a minute before still preoccupied her. Why, of all people, would Jordan slip thirty dollars into the fist of a member of the *Aryan Alliance*?

Chapter VI

Two pillows at her back, Lauren sat on her bed with a pair of manila folders in hand: one held a photocopy of her father's Cedar Mall proposal and the other, a pile of documents faxed to her by a Green Party member who had opposed construction of a mall in Charleston. She glared at the folders. What a way to spend a Friday night. On the other hand, it was better than a Saturday, and, regardless, she had put the chore off too long.

An indoor mall raised issues unfamiliar in Cedar Creek where for years new businesses, rare as they were, simply moved into vacant Broad Street storefronts. Like everyone in the Village platitudes had sufficed for Lauren. Even Jordan and Steve Ward, the mall's two most-outspoken opponents, had voiced nebulous objections. Their warnings about traffic, contamination of the aquifer and harm to the adjacent park carried few specifics. Supporters of the mall were equally vague. Apart from a claim of several hundred new jobs, fiscal impact analysis was non-existent.

Lauren took out her father's spiral bound proposal. The glossy document was replete with an artist's sketches of both the interior and exterior of the mall. Set on seventeen acres, the twenty-three store, 240,000 square-foot complex was anchored by a 60,000 square-foot *DarMart*. The impressive plan stood in stark contrast to the dilapidated state of the Broad Street business section. Lauren had to concede that Cedar Creek begged for vision. She focused on the artist's rendering of the mall's centerpiece, a cascading fountain and large domed skylight. She closed her eyes, the afterimage of the seductive picture vivid in her mind. Perhaps her father's proposal could breathe new life into the depressed Village.

She took out the papers on the Charleston Mall. Jargon about a *just and sustainable society*, non-point pollution risks, traffic and infrastructure issues, as well as complicated cost/benefit analysis, boggled her mind. Recollections of the economics course she had taken in college, a nightmare of graphs and formulae, came to mind. Had not she promised herself when she had pulled the all-nighter for the final exam that she would never again study inscrutable information about a subject she so detested. Frustration cajoled her to toss the Byzantine study into the garbage. But what about her vow on Baker's show to see the matter through? And what about the fireworks with her boss? The old *approach-avoidance* dilemma, the kind she had learned about in her survey course in psychology, reared its odious head. Like every such dilemma there was a reward for enduring the ills she wished to avoid. But in this case her reward was little more than reduced criticism for not following through. "Damn," she barked, as pride, like a hammer lock, twisted her arm. Page by page, hour by hour, she waded through the monotonous gobbledygook.

One-thirty in the morning, Lauren laid aside the folders, along with a page of synthesized notes. Answers — she had none. Questions — she had many. Had someone told her five hours earlier that the painstaking efforts would lead only to queries, not conclusions, she would never have wrestled with the monstrous documents. However, much to her surprise, the time had been well spent. No longer were the issues surrounding the proposed mall incomprehensible. She had armed herself with a cadre of questions which, when asked, would define the pros and cons of Cedar Mall, and, when answered, could spawn an intelligent verdict. She faded off to sleep knowing she was ready to wrestle not just with the issues but also an overbearing boss, a sneering talk-show host and anyone else who wished to debate the mall.

The moment Lauren spotted Nielsen coming through the door she got up from her desk and headed him off Had her boss returned an hour earlier, she might have passed up the opportunity, but his two-hour lunch suggested the absence of stress, the kind that often turned him into a beast. "Mr. Nielsen, do you have a few moments?"

"I guess." He gestured toward his office. "C'mon."

Plan of attack already rehearsed, she seated herself across from him.

"So, what's on your mind?" He rocked his chair back.

"I've been researching Cedar Mall, and I'd like to do a follow up."

Eyes narrowed, he folded his arms across his chest. "You're back on that kick?"

"Well . . . " So much for her strategy of catching him in a good mood. "I think some important questions need to be asked before the project is approved."

"Such as?" His tone echoed a disgusted look.

A quick assessment had Lauren altering her plan to dive directly into the complex and controversial realm of taxes. She said, "Concerns about traffic need to be addressed."

"The loop they plan to build around the mall should be adequate. And if the customers don't like it, they'll shop elsewhere."

"The loop isn't the problem. I'm concerned about Cedar Creek Road. The flow off the interstate ramps is overcrowding it already. And it's the only link to Greenbrook. With more and more of our residents working there, tie-ups are commonplace. Just imagine the intersection with Route 178 if the mall were built. Rush hour — " The sight of Nielsen thumbing through his *Rolodex* halted her.

Nielsen jotted a phone number on a slip of paper and then looked back at her. "So, is that about it?"

At least pretend to listen. She let her face voice the frustration. If the balance of power were equal, her tongue would have. She started to get up. Experience indicated if she tried to raise the issue in the future, Nielsen would have none of it. It was now or never. And with time a luxury, she had to focus on the most important aspect. She said, "Given Cedar

Creek's financial health, pre-approval scrutiny of the mall's fiscal impact is a must."

Nielsen's jaw clenched. "Ms. Worthington, I'm a busy man. I don't have time for ivory-towered debates. Cedar Creek has high unemployment and needs jobs. The mall will bring them, be it two, three or four hundred." He started to reach for the telephone.

"That's not the point."

He slammed his hand on his desk. "Jobs are not the point! Then enlighten me, Miss Know-it-All, what is?"

She glanced at the sheet of notes in her lap. The reaction was instinctive, not to refresh her memory. She said, "The Cedar Mall proposal includes fifteen years of costly tax breaks: the first five years, taxes would be paid on only one-quarter of the assessed value; the second five, on one-half; and the third five, on three-fourths."

Nielsen shook his head. "Big deal. Major cities give tax breaks all the time. How do you think football stadiums get built?"

"Politics and influence, not all of which are good for the communities or their taxpayers."

Nielsen scowled.

Ordinarily she might have taken the cue, but not after she had given up a Friday night wading through the arcane issues. She said, "Cedar Mall could turn into a white elephant, one with huge costs for public services — police, fire, sewage, water, road maintenance, etc." For a change he appeared to be listening. What, if any, impact her words were having was another matter. Regardless, this was not the time to stop. "With Cedar Mall paying only a fraction of its share of these costs, the remaining taxpayers will have to bear the expense. Already burdened with rapidly rising taxes, and with many out of work, the added hardship could be a back-breaker."

"So . . . " Nielsen leaned back. "You think we should recommend that the Village Board put the kibosh on the mall."

"That's not what I'm saying."

He jerked forward. "Well, what the hell are you saying?"

"That the Board should require a complete fiscal impact study; one conducted by an independent consultant."

"And who, may I ask, will pay for it?"

"The developer." Lauren avoided mention of her father's name. "If he wants his tax benefits, he should prove his project is good for the Village. That's how it's done in large communities; at least those where the politicians are honest."

Nielsen rocked backed again and gazed up at the ceiling. For the first time she sensed real headway. Additional ammunition, concern about pollution from the mall, had her tongue twitching, but discretion restrained her from gilding the lily.

Finally, Nielsen looked back at her. "If the *Chronicle* were to make a recommendation regarding the mall, it would be an editorial." His voice grew louder. "You're a reporter." He pointed at her. "Since when do *you* make editorial policy?"

His glare erased even the remote possibility his question invited an answer. Nevertheless, Lauren said, "You and the owners of the paper make those decisions, but I would like to think that I can give my input. I work here. I care about the positions we take. And I care about Cedar Creek."

Nielsen scowled. "With caring like yours, the *Chronicle* will be out of business. We need the advertising revenues the new mall is sure to generate. And in case you hadn't noticed, the proposed developer, Roger Worthington, your father, is a major real estate advertiser." Nielsen reached for the telephone but stopped. "Of course, for someone like you — " He shook his head. "Not everyone born rich is an ingrate." He lifted the receiver and began dialing.

Lauren was ready to fire back, but Nielsen swiveled his chair away from her. She got up from her seat. She glared down at the lout, not that he saw it. She stormed out of the office and back to her desk. She plopped down in her chair, her eyes focusing on the picture of a palm-treed Hawaiian beach on the nearby wall calendar. Her mind, however, failed to make the trip. It remained focused on what had just occurred in her boss's office. Over and over she replayed the scene. The more she ruminated, the angrier she grew. A light flashed in her head. She leaned back, conscious of the broad smile that had come over her face. She checked the telephone book and then dialed the number of talk-show host Jerry Baker. If Barker Nielsen thought he could treat her like a spineless jellyfish, he was at best half-right. Spineless, she wasn't. And whether he knew it or not, jellyfish sting.

———————

Seated at the desk of his Broad Street law office, Jordan checked his watch — 4:43. Last appointment on a Friday, and Nicholas Peters, the adjuster from *Rockhill Indemnity and Casualty*, was thirteen minutes late. A few days earlier when Peters had called to arrange the meeting he had seemed eager to satisfy Jordan's claim. But now the possibility loomed that the adjuster might be a no-show. Jordan wondered if the insurance company was giving him the run around. He buzzed his secretary Myrna on the intercom. "Any sign of that Peters fellow?"

"No, but I can call his office to see if he's on the way."

"Nah. That's okay." Jordan clicked off the intercom. He eyed the brief in the *Cowan* appeal that sat front and center on his desk. Saturday or Sunday morning would be soon enough to spell out the challenge to subject matter jurisdiction. He stuffed the papers into the file and headed to the back room. He ran his eyes over the four walls of the eleven-by-twelve cubicle. When he had opened his law office six years earlier, the extra room with convertible couch, refrigerator and microwave was a convenient afterthought; a place to grab a snack or a nap when burning the midnight oil. Little did he imagine that the Spartan quarters would become home for a period of at least three months. Unfortunately, the contractor had indicated it would take that long to rebuild his fire-damaged house. And when that would begin depended upon *Rockhill*. Jordan headed to the refrigerator for a microwave pizza when his intercom drew him back to his office.

"Nick Peters is here to see you."

"Send him right in. And call it a day for yourself. Lock the front door. I'll let him out when I'm done."

"You sure? I'd be glad to stay."

"Don't think of it. Have a great weekend."

A minute later Nicholas Peters, a rotund fellow with a beard, about sixty, clad in a red and white madras sport jacket, stepped into the office.

"Sorry I'm late," he said, as the two shook hands.

"Have a seat. Would you like a cup of coffee?"

"Thanks, but I'd better take a rain check. I'm driving." He gurgled a belly laugh and then drew some papers out of a beat-up brief case. "Sorry about your loss. I stopped at the house today. The place really got fried. Apart from the foundation and chimney, pretty much rubble."

"Chief Murray says accelerants increased the damage." Jordan took several sheets out of his file. "I made a room-by-room list of the furnishings and other personal property, just as you requested." He handed the papers to Peters. "How long until I can expect a check? I'd like to start rebuilding."

Peters scanned the sheets. "You sure you listed everything?"

"Not really, but I did the best I could."

"Well, if you — "

"Excuse me," said Jordan. "You didn't answer my question. When can I expect a check?"

"Uh . . . don't take this wrong, but we gotta wait . . . just until the authorities give you a clean bill of health." He gestured at Jordan. "You're a lawyer. I'm sure you understand, what with arson and all."

Damn, thought Jordan, making no effort to keep the reaction off his face. *Rockhill* was giving him the hard-ass routine. On the other hand, Peters was right. If *Rockhill* were Jordan's client, in the face of arson he would have advised the company to withhold payment. Regardless, he refused to concede the point. He said, "What am I supposed to do in the meantime?"

Peters shrugged. "If I were you, I wouldn't be happy either. But I'm just the messenger. Herb Wakefield, my boss, and Mark Allen, Regional Counsel, made the decision. You're welcome to go over my head. Convince them, and I'll bring you a check."

Jordan pointed at his back room. "That lovely, one-room mansion is where I'm living these days." He glared at the adjuster but squeezed his lips together. Whipping the husky bearer of bad tidings would accomplish nothing. Well — nothing more than the satisfaction of a splenetic vent. And unfortunately, past experience told Jordan that any temporal relief gained from bullying would spawn later guilt. He said, "Any estimate of a time frame?"

Peters shrugged again. "I could hazard a guess, but you know as well as I it depends when and how the facts shake out. On the bright side, I spoke with Detective Loggin, and he claims an arrest is imminent. With a little luck we might be paying you any day. In the meantime, I have a few questions."

Jordan gazed upward and muttered. "Instead of a check, I get questions." He looked back at Peters. "Okay — let's hear them."

"My records show that about six months back . . . " Peters checked his notes. "Here it is. November, 1982, you increased your coverage from $97,000 to $125,000. Why the change?"

Jordan shook his head and smiled.

"What's the matter?"

"You're not subtle."

"Hey, if it were up to me, you'd have your money. But like I told you, the higher-ups are calling the shots."

Sure — the old good-guy routine. He eyed Peters. The purported Santa Claus had come through the front door rather than down the chimney. He was carrying a satchel, but the bag wasn't loaded with goodies. Not even coal. Then again, was it any surprise? Too often a jolly fellow with a beard was nothing more than Scrooge. But this one had a great costume; his whiskers and stomach both genuine. Jordan realized that if he weren't careful, *St. Nick* would pick his pocket. "So, you're here to investigate me."

"No, I wouldn't call it that."

"I'm sure you wouldn't. Not when you can camouflage it."

"You don't trust me?"

Jordan sat motionless, allowing a wry smile to appear on his face. He waited several seconds.

"You didn't answer my question."

"Oh really?" Jordan leaned back. "Unless I'm senile, I could swear that when you called to arrange this meeting you said you wanted to pay my claim."

"I do, but . . . uh . . . first things first." He fumbled with his papers. "You never said why you increased your coverage."

Peters' persistence was no surprise. Jordan had faced it many times in his legal practice. But it felt entirely different now that he was the claimant. He said, "I made some improvements."

"Who'd you hire?"

"I did them myself."

"Almost thirty-thousand dollars worth?"

"No, but I felt that property appreciation justified the increase."

"Interesting," said Peters with a furrowed brow. "Our information indicates that real estate here has been struggling to maintain its value."

Jordan's gut, like a client, was tempted to debate, but his brain, one armed with a legal education, counseled patience.

"Our information also shows that last year you took out an equity loan. The original appraisal when you bought the place hardly supports it."

"Are you insinuating something?"

Surprise appeared on Peters' face.

Jordan suspected the look was bogus. He said, "You have a problem with the loans I've taken out on the property?"

"Problem?" Peters shook his head. "I wouldn't call it that. I . . . I just want to be sure our company doesn't pay more than the property's value." He looked Jordan in the eye. "As an attorney, I'm sure you understand our concern, especially with arson."

Jordan pointed at Peters. "I resent the accusation."

Peters reacted with another bewildered look. Like its predecessor, Jordan suspected it was contrived. Perhaps even rehearsed in front of a mirror. Jordan said, "Just for the record, I had nothing to do with the fire."

Face impassive, Peters glanced at his notes.

Jordan waited a moment. Finally, he said, "How does *Rockhill* plan to proceed?"

"Slowly. We'll let nature take its course. Once the authorities complete their investigation, we'll review the results and go from there."

"In other words," said Jordan, "*Rockhill* won't pay until the police and fire departments give me a clean bill. And even then, there are no promises."

Peters frowned. "You make it sound so harsh."

"No, I call a spade a spade."

A wide-eyed Peters chuckled. "You said it, not me."

"What's so funny?" barked Jordan, aware the irony could have crossed anyone's mind. But only a bigot would have laughed. "This meeting is over." Jordan got up from his seat and marched out of his office through the reception area. He could hear Peters' footsteps behind him. Without looking back, Jordan unlocked the front door. He swung it open allowing Peters to exit.

"We'll be in touch," said Peters. "Okay?"

Jordan, his eyes focused on the handle, shut the door and locked it. *Rockhill* had every right to put coal in his stocking. But Nicholas Peters, his humor colored, could hardly expect milk, cookies or even a kind word when he left.

———————

Lauren ran her eyes down the police blotter. Arrests for vagrancy, criminal mischief and a petit larceny, but no arson. She looked at Jordan. The disappointment on his face reflected her feelings.

"Anything new on the fire?" said Jordan to the desk sergeant.

"Not that I know of, but you'd have to talk to Detective Loggin."

"Is he in?"

"Not yet, but — " The sergeant glanced up at the clock. "He was . . . uh . . . ought to be here any minute."

Jordan turned to Lauren. "Shall we wait?"

She shrugged. "I — "

"Here he comes now." The sergeant pointed to the doorway.

Jordan immediately headed there. "Detective Loggin . . . "

"Morning," he said, hurrying toward the inner sanctum.

Jordan chased after him. "We'd like to speak with you."

He looked back over his shoulder. "Well . . . I suppose." He started back. "What can I do for you? Busy day ahead, you know."

Sure, thought Lauren. You show up late for work, and now you want to dodge us. She said, "I told Jordan you expected to arrest the arsonist before the weekend was out. I was wondering — "

"Damn. Last time I talk to you. Our conversation was off the record."

"I only told Jordan. You said you didn't want to read about it in the *Chronicle*."

"Good. Then let's leave it that way." He started to walk away.

"Wait a second," said Jordan. "You haven't answered the question. Have you made an arrest?"

"Not yet."

"What about the stranger?" said Lauren.

"What about him?"

"You said he was the one."

Loggin started for the coffeepot. He muttered, "Now I know why I don't talk to reporters."

Jordan grabbed Lauren's hand and pulled her along after Loggin.

"You folks are like a bad penny, if you know what I mean." He reached to an overhanging shelf for a mug, the same one he had used during Lauren's previous visit. He filled it with coffee.

The moment he finished adding cream and sugar, Lauren said, "So, what about the stranger?"

"I checked him out. The guy is clean."

"But . . . but you were sure."

Loggin frowned. "You musta misunderstood me. I said he needed to be checked out. I checked him out."

You liar. Lauren hoped her glaring eyes communicated the message. She felt the nudge of Jordan's elbow against her side. Did the jab mean *I told you so*? Or, worse yet, did he think that she, not Loggin, had twisted the facts? Whatever, she needed to move on before Loggin did. She said, "So, who was this stranger, and why was he hanging around the neighborhood?"

"Relax." Loggin sipped his coffee. His mouth turned down. "Needs more sugar." He dumped some in, stirred, and again tasted the brew. "Now *that's* better."

"You haven't answered the question," said Jordan.

Loggin looked at him and then at Lauren. "Damn. I think lawyers may be worse than reporters . . . if that's possible." He put a hand up in Jordan's direction. "Chill."

Lauren felt the urge to dump Loggin's coffee over his head. Jordan's gritted teeth hinted that he preferred something more violent.

"Seems that stranger works for the Village. Just moved here. He was out inspecting the roads for potholes and the like. I went to see him. The guy's okay." Loggin tapped the Confederate flag that adorned his mug. "Strikes me as a decent sort."

Lauren glanced at Jordan. She suspected what he was thinking though his face was less revealing than moments before. She said, "I still don't understand why you thought the stranger set the fire."

Loggin looked at Jordan. "She wants *me* (he pointed at himself) to tell *her* (he gestured at Lauren) why *she* confused what I told her. Damn. Like my pop used to say — *Women*." He turned to Lauren. "Just kidding." He looked back at Jordan. "These days a body has gotta be careful. You know — that politically-correct stuff. Especially with the feminists. They're everywhere. Oh — by the way, I almost forgot. I checked the stranger out on the computer. No criminal record."

"Our crack detective has left no stone unturned."

"Mr. Jackson, are we being *sarcastic*?"

Lauren quickly spelled the word in her head. Eight letters, complete with irony. Loggin had outdone himself.

"Like I told you," said Loggin, "I got a busy day. So, if you folks 'll excuse me."

"Before you go," said Lauren, "do you have any other leads?"

Loggin laughed.

"What's so funny?"

"You." He pointed at Lauren. "You actually think I'd give you the time of day after you misquoted me." He started to walk away but turned back to Jordan. "By the way, you're still on my short list. Arson, like incest, begins in the home." Loggin laughed. "Insurance makes a great motive, doesn't it?" He headed off.

Jordan took hold of Lauren's hand. "Get me out of here." As they walked outside and started down the steps, he said, "Do you believe that son of a bitch? He suggested that I torched my own home."

"He didn't treat me any better. He all but called me a liar." She waited a moment, checking Jordan's face for a reaction. "You don't believe Loggin?"

"Well — "

Lauren stopped in her tracks, just as she reached the bottom of the stairs. She pulled her hand away. "You're taking his word over mine?"

Jordan smacked her lightly on the back. "Can't you tell when I'm kidding?"

She gave him a dirty look. Loggin's antics had killed her sense of humor.

"By the way," said Jordan, "I don't recall you sticking up for me when Loggin suggested that I set fire to my home." He looked her in the eye. "You don't have doubts?"

"Of course not." The response was instinctive. Regardless, deep down Lauren was certain; at least she thought she was.

———

Lauren parked her car adjacent to the lush green lawn that fronted Steve Ward's commodious, side-hall colorial. The unannounced visit made her uncomfortable, but the possibility of greater candor overcame reluctance. With her return engagement on Baker's show but a few days away, anything she could garner regarding the Village Board members' motivations would come in handy. As she climbed the porch stairs, she eyed the baskets of red geraniums that hung above the white wicker coffee table and matching chairs. She made a mental note. Someday when she had a porch of her own, she would decorate in much the same way. She rang the bell. A moment later the door opened.

"Good evening," said Ward, his deep voice resonating with the rich sound of a news anchor. His style, however, more closely resembled a used-car salesman. "What brings you out this way?"

"I was hoping to discuss the proposed mall." Her businesslike manner gave no hint she was checking out his physical attributes. Tall, wavy-haired and dark-complexioned. Some claimed he was the most handsome man in Cedar Creek. Lauren disagreed. In her mind Jordan was even better looking. She said, "I hope I'm not interrupting your dinner."

"We just finished. C'mon in." He led her through the hallway into the kitchen where Mary, his live-in girlfriend, traded greetings with Lauren. Ward gestured Lauren into the family room. She seated herself on the black leather couch, while he took the club chair across the way. "Word travels fast," he said.

She tried to make sense of the comment. "Apparently slower than you think."

"I assume you're here because of the note I received in this afternoon's mail."

"I wasn't even aware of it."

Ward reached for his wallet and pulled out a folded piece of paper that he handed to her. "I gave the original to Detective Loggin a couple of hours ago. This is a photocopy."

Lauren read the printed words:

CEDAR CREEK NEEDS THE NEW MALL. SUPPORT IT OR YOUR HOUSE WILL MEET THE SAME FATE AS JACKSON'S. SLEEP TIGHT. IT MAY HAPPEN AT NIGHT.

P.S. Don't waste your time trying to trace this with fingerprints or other hocus-pocus. I wore gloves and mailed it far from home.

She read it a second time and was still digesting it when Ward said, "Unlike the first threat, the one the three of us got, I have to take this seriously. After what happened to Jordan's house, there's no doubt the guy means business."

"What did Loggin say?"

Ward rolled his eyes.

"You have a point." Lauren silently commended her host for skipping the chance to slam the incompetent sleuth. "I don't suppose there's any chance of tracing it."

"You read the P.S. And it looks like it was printed on one of those IBM ball typewriters or maybe a computer."

"Any idea who sent it?"

He shrugged. "Presumably someone desperate for the mall."

"You're not suggesting my father?"

"Well — given his interest, he hardly rates a free pass."

The point was undeniable. She said, "I know my father. He wouldn't."

Ward gazed off into space and muttered, "Good sense tells me not to go there, but . . . what the heck." He looked back at her. "From what I've heard, the land cost your father a mint. Folks held out for big bucks once they got wind of his plans. Charlie Curran claims to have made a killing when he sold his little plot. Says his lawyer checked the County Clerk's office and saw a pattern. He didn't know why your father wanted the land, just that he did. That was enough. Apparently the whole thing snowballed. Each parcel got more expensive than the one before. Your father got caught in a squeeze. Without the last few pieces he had a jigsaw puzzle with a bunch of holes. To make matters worse, those holes included a cow pasture and a scrap metal heap. A hay field filled with cow patties and rusted junk hardly makes for a shoppers' paradise. The landowners had him right where they wanted, and they knew it." Ward gestured toward Lauren. "You'd know better than I. But rumor has it your father went into hock up to his ears."

The disclosure came as a surprise. Her father had never shared his financial dealings with her. However, the possibility that he had overextended himself might explain his recent volatility. Argumentative, he always was, but lately he had become unreasonable. On the other hand, threats and, worse yet, arson? No way. She said, "I'm sure my father isn't involved."

"Well . . . uh . . . " Ward's eyes nervously drifted toward the adjacent wall.

Lauren's gaze followed in the same direction taking in the mega-sized projection television with multiple speakers, along with other state-of-the-art electronics. Her heart dismissed the possibility her father was behind the arson. Her brain was less cooperative.

"I . . . uh . . . didn't mean to accuse your father," said Ward. "He's not the only one interested in the mall. Certain members of our Village Board have a stake as well."

The two supporters immediately came to mind. "I know Janet Warner expects to bag the insurance business, but it's hard to imagine she'd resort to arson in order to get it. As for O'Leary, his motive is even more remote. The mall may give him more traffic, but it's a two-sided coin. The possibility of a sports' bar there could mean tough competition."

"True, but the value of his property is sure to increase. Anyway, I wasn't thinking of Warner or O'Leary. It's the others."

Jordan? Laughlin? And Ward himself? Lauren grappled with the seeming illogic.

"You look confused."

"That's because I am."

"Well — let me throw this out." He leaned back. "Jordan and I — talk about strange bedfellows — have strong reasons for opposing the mall. Jordan claims it'll be terrible for the town. Traffic, strain on public services, the aquifer, etc. That plus he dislikes your father. Me — I'll feel it in the pocketbook. My strip mall already has a couple of vacancies. An indoor mall will be tough competition."

Lauren ran the scenario through her head again. "Minor detail. Whoever is making the threats wants the mall built. That's hardly you or Jordan. Anyway, if you did, all you'd have to do is throw your vote with Warner and O'Leary. Why would you risk prison?"

Ward shrugged. "I suppose that's true, but I thought I should cover all the bases. That, plus the one I really had in mind is Laughlin."

Ward's intellect, unlike his looks, had never impressed Lauren. But at that moment he was making Loggin seem bright. She said, "If Laughlin wanted the mall, all he'd have to do is get off the fence and become the third affirmative vote. As the only uncommitted, he can have it anyway he wants."

Ward shook his head. "Laughlin doesn't care about the mall."

"Wait a second. You're suggesting Laughlin committed arson and threatened the opponents of the mall to change their votes, all for an issue that makes no difference to him?"

"That's what I'm saying."

With leaders who reason like that, no wonder Cedar Creek languishes. Lauren contained the urge to make the point.

"You think I'm crazy, don't you?" He paused. "I see it on your face."

"Well, you've hardly made a compelling argument."

Ward nodded. "Let me explain." He stretched his legs. "Laughlin's private school has been losing students every year. A few more, and it'll be history. The tuition is simply too expensive, especially when folks have already paid public school taxes. For several years he's been quietly trying to get the Board to approve a voucher program; one which would give the parents of his students a credit against their school taxes for the tuition they pay to his school."

"Makes sense, at least from his standpoint. People would gladly send their kids to private school if the ride were free."

"It wouldn't be free. The credit would be limited to the amount of their school taxes, but, as you know, Laughlin's school is selective. Most of his students come from well-to-do families with nice homes. Their real estate taxes are high. They'd save a lot. From what I've heard, the average would be close to seventy percent of tuition."

"That's quite a deal he's cooked up." As she spoke, Lauren refocused on the issue. "Wait a second. What's that got to do with the mall and the threats?"

"Patience," said Ward. He took a deep breath. "As I said, Laughlin has been fishing around. He's been waiting for the Board to split on an issue big enough that he could exchange his vote for approval of his voucher plan. Your father's mall, the most controversial thing to come down the pike in years, presented the perfect opportunity. I think Warner was ready to deal with him, but no one else would. Unless he can get three votes, he's got nothing."

So what, thought Lauren, still waiting for the link that would tie Laughlin to the arson and the threats.

"It'll make sense in a moment," said Ward, apparently reading her face again. He paused just long enough to move forward in his seat. "Given recent events, Laughlin knows he needs a change in the Board in order to get his voucher program. Along with me, Jordan is the stumbling block. The last time Laughlin's plan came up, Jordan called it perverse. He pointed out that those with expensive homes — high real estate taxes — would be the winners. On the other hand, renters would save nothing. Of course, that's just how Laughlin wants it. His school is for the elite."

Intriguing thought Lauren, reacting no less to her underestimate of Ward than his theory. Still she found it difficult to imagine that the pompous headmaster would resort to violence. She said, "It's an interesting concept, but — "

"Laughlin isn't the type. Is that what you're thinking?"

Lauren nodded. "His tongue may be caustic, but that's a far cry from arson."

"Perhaps," said Ward. "But you might have a different view if you dealt with him on a regular basis, especially behind the scenes. He's quite the fast-shuffling politician. If you doubt me, ask Jordan. And speak of the devil — I won't try to hide my feelings toward him — he says he's fed up with the Board. Might even quit. Just what Laughlin wants."

Lauren recalled that Jordan had recently mentioned the possibility. She had assumed it was an idle vent, but Ward had her wondering. "So, you think Laughlin may have made the threats and set fire to Jordan's home in an effort to get his voucher plan."

Ward jerked back. "Hold the phone. I'm not accusing him. It's strictly a theory. Like your father, another possibility that needs to be explored." Ward hesitated, his expression pensive. "Look — all I know is there's an arsonist in our midst, and he needs to be identified before he kills somebody."

The concern in Ward's voice was palpable. And why not. He had just received a chilling threat. "Did you mention all these theories to Loggin when you gave him the note?"

"Absolutely. I also suggested he check out the skinheads, though I have my doubts about them."

"Why so?"

"Why would they care about the mall. No doubt they hate Jordan, but . . . " He gestured at himself. "Anyway, I've never done anything to antagonize them."

Ward had a point. Most likely his conservative politics appealed to the Aryan group. The observation was better left unsaid. "So, what did Loggin think of all your theories?"

"He told me to relax. He said he had it covered." Ward shook his head.

Lauren sensed he was biting his tongue. She suspected that, like so many others, Loggin had him frustrated. She wondered, however, whether Ward might be withholding other misgivings about the detective. She was about to inquire when her host got up from his seat. As he did, he said, "I must be nuts, running off at the mouth to a reporter. And without an *off-the-record* promise." He shrugged. "What the hell." He glanced at his watch and headed for the door.

She followed his lead. Her visit to Steve Ward had been filled with surprises, but only speculations, not answers. As she headed from the porch to her blue Neon, she made a mental note — a *double-L*. Laughlin and Loggin. Both required follow-up. Once the mnemonic reminder was locked in her brain, her thoughts drifted to her father. Much as she tried, she could not dispel the unsettling concerns Ward had fostered.

Chapter VII

As she and Jordan walked up the stairs of Worthington Hall's white-pillared portico, Lauren checked her watch. "If we stay a half-hour, we'll still have plenty of time to make the movie." She had chosen that particular evening to bring Jordan to the house because her father was out of town. It was the perfect opportunity for Jordan to meet Bessie. Lauren had no doubt they would hit it off.

She reached into her purse for her key but realized it was back in her apartment. She rang the bell.

Moments later Bessie opened the door. "What a pleasant surprise."

"Hi, I'm Jordan."

Bessie shook the hand he extended. "Yes, I know. I've seen you on TV, as well as in the newspaper. All that stuff with the Village Board."

"Apparently my infamous reputation precedes me." Jordan feigned a chagrined look. "I've heard about you too. But all very flattering."

Bessie leaned Lauren's way and with her voice lowered, but still much more than a whisper, said, "He's even more handsome in person."

"I know," said Lauren, "but that's just between the two of us. I wouldn't want him getting a swelled head." She took hold of Jordan's hand and gave it a squeeze.

"Can I fix you both something to eat?"

"No thanks," said Lauren. "We can't stay long. We're going to see *Terms of Endearment* over in Beaulin. It's at the *Strand*."

They headed into the den where Lauren and Jordan seated themselves on the couch. Bessie took one of the easy chairs across the way. "I assume you know your father is out of town."

"That's why we came tonight. I wanted you to meet Jordan without my Dad spinning everything in the wrong direction."

"Now, now. That isn't nice, especially when he's not here to defend himself. You know he has your best interests at heart."

"I guess. But sometimes he has a strange way of showing it." Lauren ignored Bessie's furrowing brow. "He doesn't understand that the world is changing."

"Yes, I suppose it is. But . . . "

Lauren waited several seconds for Bessie to finish the thought. "But what?"

"Nothing." She looked at Jordan. "Can't I at least get you something to drink? I've got a pot of coffee on the stove, or a *Coke* maybe."

"No thanks."

Bessie looked back at Lauren. "I'll bet Jordan would change his mind if you have something."

Lauren might have were she not still focused on Bessie's earlier comment. "What did you mean before when you said *but*?"

"It's not important. Anyway we have company, and I'm sure Jordan would rather discuss something else."

"You'd like to hear Bessie's thoughts, wouldn't you?"

"Uh . . . I guess so."

"Sure — you put him on the spot. What do you expect him to say?"

"No," said Jordan. "I'd love to hear your views."

"There . . . you see," said Lauren. "Now you'll have to tell us."

"Well . . . " There was an inordinately long pause. "If you insist." Bessie hesitated again; this time perhaps to measure her words. "Let me put it this way. If I had a daughter, only her happiness would matter."

"I knew you disagreed with my father."

"Wait a second. That's not what I said."

"Not in so many words. But it was implied." Lauren looked at Jordan. "You're the lawyer . . . the expert in logical reasoning. Am I right? Or . . . am I right?"

Jordan shook his head. "Oh no. You're not dragging me into the middle, especially with a loaded question like that. You, my Sweet, are on your own."

"Thanks a bunch." She turned to Bessie. "You agree that race shouldn't make any difference. True?"

"Yes. But that's not the point."

Such double talk would have been no surprise had it come from her father or Nielsen or Baker, but not Bessie. "Not the point. What do you mean?"

"As I said, my only concern would be my daughter's happiness. And you're right, race shouldn't be an issue. But this is Cedar Creek, South Carolina. People here aren't color blind. Maybe down the road in the year 2000 or 2050, attitudes will change. I'd love to see it. But for now I'd worry about my daughter." She looked at Jordan. "And I'd worry about her boyfriend too."

"I don't believe it," said Lauren, curbing the instinct to raise her voice. She glanced at Jordan. A quick shake of his head confirmed he was staying on the sidelines. She refocused on Bessie. "Of all people I was sure I could count on your support."

"You misunderstand." Bessie looked off into space and muttered to herself, "I had to open my mouth." She heaved a sigh and then looked back at Lauren. "Let me be clear. I have no opposition to your relationship with Jordan. None whatsoever. I simply worry how others will treat you. I can't help it. Good, bad or whatever, that's how I feel." She paused, her gaze drifting into empty space. "Life is tough enough without trying to swim upstream."

"Salmon do it," quipped Lauren spontaneously.

"They do indeed. But most of them never make it."

Lauren swallowed hard. Bessie's upstream comment was nothing more than a cliché; at least until Lauren had taken the bait. More important, she realized Bessie had a point. Many Cedar Creek residents, both black and white, were unwilling to accept an interracial couple. Others, such as members of the Aryan Alliance, would make things harder yet. And there was always the issue of children. But this wasn't some backward country of a bygone era. It was America. 1983. Lauren loved Jordan. Of that she had no doubt. She also had no doubt that Bessie was genuinely concerned for her happiness. And Bessie was right. There were *buts*, and to simply ignore them would be foolhardy. Unlike love, free to be blind and guided by emotion alone, marriage, a lifelong commitment, required open eyes. Before saying *I do*, one had to think. Think carefully.

Jerry Baker sported the same smug face that Lauren had seen when she had appeared on his talk show several weeks earlier. She glanced at the picture of the Baltimore Colts that occupied the shelf behind him. Growing up, she had seen lots of professional football, or at least she had been in the family room while her father, in front of the television, played armchair quarterback and argued with the referees. Lauren had learned the game and its jargon without ever becoming a fan. She looked back at Baker. He was as massive as the Colts' biggest lineman, but a flabby midsection suggested any similarity ended with size. His gaze met hers. Unlike her previous visit, she challenged his stare. For an instant he glanced away; a hint that a chicken might lurk behind the bully with the huge body and over-inflated ego. Sure, he was cocky, and why not. He always enjoyed home-field advantage, played by his own rules, and served as self-appointed referee and scorekeeper. If that weren't enough, the fans, his listeners, always rooted for the home team. But put him on a level playing field and instead of the Colts' blue and white, his true color, yellow, would paint the gridiron.

"I'm glad you decided to accept my offer for a return engagement, even though it'll cost me a steak dinner," said Baker.

If that was an invitation, he could forget it. The mere thought of dining with the boor, even if he was picking up the tab, turned Lauren's stomach.

"Is that a puzzled or a peeved look?" He gestured toward a fellow sitting on the other side of the glass wall of the soundproof chamber. "Last time you were here, I bet my engineer a dinner at the *Gibson House* you wouldn't come back. Have to admit you've got more moxie than I figured. That or Jim bribed you with a sawbuck, just so he could win the bet."

Lauren smiled. If Baker thought he could seize the upper hand, she'd make him think twice. "Damn," she said. "Jim told me if I didn't come back you'd ask me out on a date. No offense, but put yourself in my position." She contrived a look of revulsion. She pointed up at the message prompter that showed ten seconds to airtime. "Looks like we're on."

Baker leaned back. He took a couple of deep breaths. "Good evening to all my good American friends out there in the rolling, western South Carolina hills." Per usual, his southern drawl intensified the moment the show began. "As always, I appreciate the invitation into your homes and vehicles, especially those pick-ups sporting a *WURY* bumper sticker. Back again for another ride is *Chronicle* reporter, Lauren Worthington; here to discuss the proposed mall — what some are calling the best thing to hit Cedar Creek since sunshine." He gazed at her. "Ms. Worthington, last time you promised an objective follow up on the pros and cons of the mall. So, tell us, is it thumbs up or thumbs down?"

"Thumbs sideways."

"Wait a second. That's the gibberish you dished us last visit. About time you go out on a limb. Wouldn't you say?"

"What — so you can start sawing?" Armed with her new strategy, right from the kickoff she wanted him to know that she was learning his game. She gestured at her host. "Where do you stand?"

"Aha . . . someone wants to turn the tables. Well, unlike that someone — far be it from me to mention her name — I won't duck the issue." He winked at Lauren. "My listeners want the mall. That's good enough for me."

It was good enough for Lauren as well. Baker had taken a position. He was no longer free to play both ends of the field. She said, "So, you give them what they want. Right?"

Baker offered up one of his condescending looks. "Something wrong with that?"

"No . . . but . . . " Her thoughts hardly mirrored her ostensible hesitation. She said, "Lower taxes. Now, that's something your listeners really want. True?"

"Of course. But before you get carried away, let's not confuse our roles." His face, invisible to his radio audience, bore an icy stare. His voice, however, remained warm. "You're my guest."

"Excellent point," said Lauren. "And gracious host that you are, I'm sure you'll defer."

"Provided you act like a guest and allow me to do the interviewing." Sarcasm had slipped into his tone. "You mentioned taxes. You agree that the mall will be a shot in the arm for Cedar Creek's ailing tax base?"

Armed with her research, she drew a page from her host's playbook. The idea was to fake the straight dive and do an end run. "If I get your point, you support the mall because it will reduce our homeowners' taxes?"

"You catch on fast. Not that it's rocket science. Enlarge the commercial tax base, and you'll cut the homeowners' burden."

She scratched her head, purely for effect. "Apparently, I'm a little slow. I thought if you sell below cost, you don't make money."

"What's that got to do with anything?"

"Just this. When the cost of public services for a new commercial property exceeds the taxes it pays, homeowners have to help make up the difference." She paused, but only long enough to savor his blank expression. "By the way, the proposed mall with all its tax breaks may fit the scenario. But no doubt, you've taken that into account."

Baker's beady eyes widened. "I see we have a caller waiting."

Lauren was tempted to point out that he had ignored the call light when it had flashed a minute earlier. She reminded herself that she was playing by Baker's rules. And she had just learned one. Only the host could call time out. His allotment, unlimited. His guests, none.

"Hello. You're on the air with Baker."

"Hi Jerry. How ya doin'. It's Jake."

"Jake — always good to hear from one of my regulars. What can I do for you?"

"Well — when I dialed, I was gonna tell you why I support the mall. But if it's gonna jack up my taxes, I ain't so sure."

Face smug, Baker rocked back. "Ms. Worthington, it seems you've troubled Jake with the specter of higher taxes. Be kind enough to address his misgivings."

You slime bucket. Pretending you didn't fumble the ball. "Let me try," she said, giving no hint that soon enough instant replay would expose his seemingly slick handoff as a camouflage for his *faux pas*. "Buried in the fine print of the Cedar Mall proposal are huge tax breaks. For the first five years after the mall's completion, taxes would be paid on just one-quarter of the property's assessed value; the second five, on one-half; and the third five, on three-quarters. It's an enormous project and will require huge amounts of public services: sewage facilities, water supply, fire protection, road maintenance, police — "

"We get the point," said Baker. "But let's cut to the chase. What does it mean to a taxpayer like Jake? I assume you have the numbers."

"As a matter of fact, I don't."

Baker rocked back again. "Another Monday morning quarterback. But this one wants to change the play, whether it works or not. Is that how it is, Lauren? You don't mind me calling you Lauren?"

"If it makes you comfortable, Jer." She folded her arms. "Let's go back to your first question. You talked about me second-guessing the play. The mall hasn't been built. The Board hasn't even approved it. The game hasn't been played. What we need is a game plan, one that includes the real costs of Cedar Mall." She pointed at him. "Since you're such a big advocate of the project, you tell me: What's the cost?"

He glared. "My listeners want the mall. I'm trying to give them what they want."

"C'mon, let's not weasel. The folks out there are — just as you said — listeners. You're their coach. They look to you."

Baker reached for his button. "Jake, you still on the line?"

"I'm here, Jerry."

"What do you think?"

"I want the mall, but not if I'm gonna pay through the nose. How do we get them costs?"

"Excellent question." Baker gestured at Lauren. "Let's ask our guest."

Lauren restrained the urge to slam her host for again refusing to take the hit. "The Board should commission a study."

Baker emitted a sigh loud enough to fill the airwaves. "And who's gonna pick up the tab?"

"The mall developer, Roger Worthington."

"Your father?"

"He happens to be my father, but that's irrelevant." She pointed at Baker's picture of the Baltimore Colts. "You're a big football fan. Right Jer?"

"True-blue. Both literally and figuratively. But what's that got to do with the price of pigskins?"

"Well — suppose a team owner was planning to build a new stadium, but only if he got tax incentives. How would a well-run city handle it? And I mean a city that isn't dominated by special interests."

Baker laughed out loud. "You're talking about a fairyland. Things don't work that way."

"Your friend Jake wants them to." She looked Baker in the eye. "Or tell me, Jer, maybe you think Jake doesn't deserve a square deal."

Baker glowered, but for a change he was his own victim. His indignant look broadcasted no further than the walls of his studio.

"Jake," said Lauren. "As a loyal listener, I'm sure Jerry cares about you, as well as Cedar Creek. And just to make sure we all get that fair deal, I believe an independent consultant, chosen by our Village Board, should provide a comprehensive study, fiscal and otherwise."

"Great," said Baker. "Every time a developer has a proposal, we'll make him jump through expensive hoops. Talk about a way to kill progress."

"Excuse me," said Lauren. "I don't recall saying that every developer should be required to pay for a study."

"You're right. You didn't." Baker heaved another sigh. "I get your point. Only if the developer is your *father* should we slap him with the bill." He shook his head. "Damn. I glad you're not *my daughter*."

"Not as happy as I." She flashed him one of his own condescending looks. "And by the way, you've still missed the point. What I've been saying is that only developers who want tax breaks, the kind that could cost good folks like Jake, need to provide fiscal studies."

A momentary silence punctuated her words as Baker looked away just before he resorted to another time out. "Jake, what do you think?"

"Sounds good to me."

"Jake, you're a good man. I appreciate your input. You have a good day." Baker pushed the buttons on his control panel. "Let's hear from another caller. You're on the air with Baker."

"Hi, this is Mary. I'm a first-time caller."

"Round of applause for Mary." Baker's push of another button initiated the sound of applause. "So, tell us, Mary, how do you feel about the proposed mall?"

"Not sure. I live out on Rockwood Road, less than a mile from the planned site. I've had concerns right from the start. I think a study is a good idea."

"Do you agree with my guest that — " Baker checked his light panel. "Appears we've lost our caller." He glanced up at the clock. "And it looks like were running low on time. Before we go, let me ask my guest some final questions. How do you think your father will react to this study idea?"

Lauren swallowed hard.

"You seem hesitant."

"I . . . I can't speak for him. My job is to follow the issues." The remark, fine for a radio audience, echoed in her ears. Her father would be another matter.

"One last question," said Baker. "The recommendation you've made today — No doubt it represents the position of the *Chronicle*."

She swallowed hard again. "I've been speaking for myself, not the newspaper."

"Very interesting," said Baker with a wry smile. "And on that note, we'll call it a wrap. Until next time, when the straight man will deliver more straight talk, this is Jerry Baker wishing you all a very pleasant *good evening*." He swiveled his chair back and peered up over his shoulder in the direction of the shelf where he kept his picture of the Baltimore Colts and his autographed football. "Damn. It would have been fun to watch *Johnny U* throw deep with you defending at free safety." Baker swung back around toward her. "The pigskin is in your hands. My suggestion — run fast and far." He shook his head and then laughed out loud.

Lauren silently got up from her seat and left the studio. She climbed into her car and began driving into the hills outside of town. The road wasn't all that steep, but with men like Baker, Nielsen and her father imposing roadblocks, it seemed insurmountable. Their patronizing pats on the back failed to disguise underlying attitudes. She was a *woman*. And Cedar Creek, even in the 1980's, was still a man's world. Feminism remained unpopular in the sleepy hamlet. And if Baker, Nielsen and her father had their way, change might never come.

Was she right to recommend an independent study? Doubtless. But little good that would do. Nielsen was sure to blast her. And her father, as always, would treat her like a kid. Her gut screamed unfair. But a softer voice, one from her heart, whispered a different message. Sure, her father was wrong, but couldn't she have left it to someone else to play Brutus. She eased her foot off the gas as she passed over the crest of a hill. Her car coasted. The road ahead was smooth; the ride, however, a different story.

Lauren reached for the receiver. "Worthington here."

"I want to see you now."

The telephone clicked even before she could respond. She braced herself and then headed to her boss's office. As she entered, Nielsen, without looking up from his work, gestured toward a chair on the opposite side of his desk.

She seated herself and waited. Finally, he raised his head. He pointed at the door. "Shut it."

Had he said so when she had entered, she would have. She suspected he bounced her up and down intentionally. She did his bidding and returned to her seat.

"You know why I called you in?"

"Not really," she said, despite a strong suspicion.

"Want to hazard a guess?"

Better judgment caused her to shake her head.

"I caught your gig last night."

Nielsen's pause suggested he was looking for a reaction. She remained poker-faced.

"You really went off half-cocked." He waited a moment. "What do you have to say for yourself?"

"For the moment — nothing."

"Is that sarcasm?"

You bet. Though the thought failed to reach her lips, her face may have been less discreet. She said, "I'm not sure why you wanted to see me."

"I hate being ignored." He glared. "I told you not to write an article questioning Cedar Mall."

"I didn't."

Nielsen jerked forward. "Don't get cute with me. You knew full well you were circumventing my instructions when you mouthed off last night."

Lauren was fed up with men telling her what to do, particularly her boss. "Since when are newspaper reporters excluded from the benefits of the First Amendment?"

"Don't get smart with me, young lady. I've seen your type before. Loads of times. Still wet behind the ears, but you think you know it all. Self-righteous and full of bluster." He pointed at her. "Let me give you some advice. Keep it up, and you're out the door."

Losing her job gave her pause, but kowtowing to the little Napoleon was unacceptable. A trump card, one she had never expected to play, allowed anger to grab the upper hand. "Give me one good reason I can't speak my mind on my own time." The startled look on Nielsen's face emboldened her more. "Well . . ."

He folded his arms. "When it comes to the First Amendment, *think* whatever you please."

"As long as I don't say it. Is that what you're telling me?"

"That's not what I said, and you know it. I'm talking about controversial issues like the mall."

"Next time I'll give a disclaimer. How's that?"

"There won't be a next time. Get it? And before you open your mouth, understand that one wrong word and you're history."

The gauntlet he had thrown down, like an irresistible force, drew her trump card. "Do what you have to. But keep in mind, Roger Worthington is the *Chronicle*'s biggest advertiser. He might take offense if the editor fired his daughter. Maybe cancel his business. I wonder how Mr. Decker in the home office would react to that."

Nielsen's jaw clenched, but he said nothing.

Lauren stared at her boss. A part of her was amazed by what she had just said. Another part worried she would regret it. Regardless, she had crossed that skinny excuse for a river known as the Rubicon.

"Are you threatening me?" said Nielsen.

"Such a harsh label. Whatever gave you that idea?"

"What would *you* call it?"

"Well . . . " She hesitated, pretending to think it through. "To use your earlier term — advice. Friendly advice."

Nielsen did a slow burn. "You think you're smart. Well, let me tell you, Miss Hotshot. I'm still your boss, and you haven't heard the last of this."

She started for the door. Bravado, plus unwillingness to give him the last word, turned her around. She said, "What would you do if I called you a tyrannical son of a bitch?"

97

"Try me." His fiery eyes were as daring as his words. "Just try me."

"No, that wouldn't be ladylike." She gave a theatrical scratch of her head as she seemingly confirmed the conclusion. "On the other hand, I'm free to *think* whatever I please. Isn't that what you said?" She looked him in the eye. She continued to stare for several seconds and then marched out the door.

"Detective Loggin speaking," he said, the telephone in one hand, his empty mug, which he was about to refill, in the other. "What can I do for you?"

"It's what I can do for you," said a nasally, muffled voice on the other end.

"Who is this?"

"That don't matter. I — "

"Look here," snapped Loggin, wishing he had ignored the call and allowed his answering machine to free him up to get his caffeine fix. "If this is some kinda joke, you dialed the wrong number."

"This ain't no joke. I got . . . "

Loggin struggled to understand the garbled voice. "Speak more clearly."

"Can't. Gotta disguise my voice."

Enough, thought Loggin, his years of detective work having taught him the difference between a jerk and a caller worthy of attention. "I don't waste time on the likes of you." He slammed the receiver. How, he wondered, did the idiot have the nerve to pull such a stunt. If more pressing matters, his empty mug, didn't await, he might have pushed caller ID and made the wise-ass pay. Loggin got up from his desk. Just as he reached the door of his office, his telephone rang again. He looked back over his shoulder. He shook his head. Whoever it was would do fine with the answering machine. Of course, if he had a secretary, like he had requested years earlier, all his calls would be screened. Mug in hand, he headed out to the coffeepot. Minutes later, after giving the desk sergeant a laugh over the joke about the encyclopedia salesman and the farmer's daughter, and with his coffee cup refilled, he eased back down at his desk. He pushed the button to play his messages. The nasally muffled voice he had heard earlier greeted his ears.

"I know who torched Jackson's place. Five o'clock sharp, I'll call again. Ya better answer cause that's ya last chance. And don't try to trace this, cause it's a pay phone, and the next one ain't gonna be the same."

Loggin got up and shut the door to his office. He replayed the message. The Chief would go ballistic if he knew the potential lead had been blown. Loggin glanced at his watch — 3:17. His shift ended at four, but he would have to wait for the call. An hour of overtime. Could he at least claim his time-and-a-half? If he did, Shumacker, that buttlicker from Human Resources, was sure to verify the reason. Without prior authorization there would be explaining. Loggin couldn't afford that. He kicked his desk's center panel. He reached into the bottom drawer and pulled out his puzzle book. He tore out a crossword. He put it on top of his cemetery vandalism folder. He rocked his chair back obscuring the brainteaser from passersby. No pay. Then no work. Fair was fair. He looked at number one across, a four-letter word for *rabbit*. He wrote in *H-A-I-R*. It crossed his mind that come five o'clock, when the call came, he'd actually be working, and he wouldn't be getting paid. He banged his foot against the panel again. Why was *he* always getting the shaft?

One-by-one he worked the clues. Another trip to the coffeepot killed a few more minutes. He was back at his desk when the Chief poked his head into the doorway of the little cubicle and pointed at his watch. "It's after four."

"I know," said Loggin. "I'm workin' some angles on the cemetery vandalism." He held up his manila folder.

"You're off the clock. Right?"

"Yup. Strictly on my own time."

The Chief gave a thumbs-up. "Dedicated. That's my men."

"Tell it to the Village Board next time our contract comes up." Loggin contained the urge to laugh.

"Don't stay too late."

He watched the Chief disappear down the hall. Little did the boss realize his underling was a step ahead. Then again, that was the mark of a crack detective. He eyed his puzzle. Sixty-three across, a ten-letter word for a football field general. He wrote in *Q-U-A-R-T-E-R-B-A-C-K*, his boldly printed letters overshadowing some wrong ones he had entered earlier. He moved on to sixty-three down, a four-letter word for a witty saying. *JOKE* came to mind. But it had to begin with *Q*. He glared at the puzzle, most of it blank or crossed out. The clues, all of which had been tried, yielded nothing more. His mind began to drift aimlessly. His eyes grew heavy and . . .

"Hey Loggin. Wake up."

He lurched in his seat, too late to catch a glimpse of the passerby. A moment later, he grabbed his bearings. He checked his watch — 5:09. If the telephone had rung, he would have heard it. He checked his messages. Nothing. "Damn," he muttered. "The son of a bitch never called." He slipped the crossword puzzle into the paper shredder next to his desk and stuffed the manila folder back into a drawer. No one knew about the anonymous caller. That was just how Loggin would leave it. If anyone found out, an unlikely scenario, he would argue the tipster had failed to call back as promised. Loggin eyed his dirty mug. Late as it was, he could give it the once over in the morning. What really mattered, his strategy was set.

Chapter VIII

Lauren parked her car in the lot of *Cedar Creek Academy* and headed for the main entrance. In the spot designated *Headmaster* a shiny, black Mercedes, a virtual twin to her father's, caught her eye. She doubted there was a third in Cedar Creek. She also questioned if Laughlin could afford such pricey wheels. Style, not substance, was his hallmark. She went inside the building and rapped on his office door.

"Who's there?"

"Lauren Worthington."

"Be with you shortly."

A check of her watch confirmed she was two minutes early for her scheduled appointment. She seated herself in the hallway on a nearby bench. She began contemplating possible scenarios surrounding the fire. Someone was desperate to have the mall approved — desperate enough to burn down Jordan's home and threaten that Steve Ward's would be next. Might Laughlin be that someone? Ward's remarks regarding the headmaster's voucher program had given Lauren food for thought. But as a journalist she had to keep an open mind. All possibilities needed to be considered. What about Ward? Might he have sent himself the newest threat in order to divert suspicion? Unlikely, given that he opposed the mall. Regardless, if he wanted the project approved, he could simply cast the third affirmative vote. Might the *Aryan Alliance* be responsible? They hated Jordan, but why would they threaten Ward? And why would they care about the mall? Loggin? The detective was a bigot, as well as an idiot, but that was hardly an arsonist. What about her father? The distasteful scenario made her uneasy, but she could not ignore the possibility. No one had a greater interest in the mall. And according to Ward, her father would be in dire financial straits if the Village Board killed his project. What about Jordan? Instincts — or more likely, emotions — instantly dismissed the possibility. The reporter in her balked. Every explanation, however remote, deserved consideration. Jordan opposed the mall. But that hardly amounted to motive. On the other hand, insurance proceeds could. The point had merit but only in the abstract. Lauren knew Jordan. It had to be someone else. But who? She was contemplating the question when Laughlin finally opened his office door.

"Sorry to keep you waiting." He motioned her in and gestured for her to take a seat. "It'll have to be quick. I have a history class to teach in ten minutes. Running a small, private school, one has to wear lots of hats." He eased down behind his desk. "So, what can I do for you?"

"I'm interested in your voucher program. I understand you've been pushing for Village Board approval."

"It's an idea whose time has come. People should be able to choose where their children are educated."

"They can do that now," said Lauren, inviting a baited response.

Laughlin shook his head. "I mean a real choice; one where they don't have to pay twice — school taxes and private tuition."

"There aren't many private schools in Cedar Creek. *Cedar Academy*, all by itself, makes up the list."

"Not so. Mary Bradford has her nursery school."

Lauren would have debated the point were time not at a premium. "I'm surprised you haven't taken a position on the proposed mall yet."

"Why?"

His response with a question rather than an explanation, a reporter's trick, irked her. "Everyone else has."

"Not everyone." He pointed at her. "A certain reporter — her name will remain unmentioned — appeared on Baker's talk show the other night. She said we need an independent consultant's study before making a decision. I thought she made some cogent arguments. What do you think?"

Another question. Lauren's toes tightened within her leather pumps as the headmaster reached for his gold pocket watch and gave the timepiece a conspicuous look. She blurted out. "Are you hoping to trade your vote on the mall for your voucher program?"

"I won't dignify the insinuation with an answer." The tall pedagogue with the bony features got up from his seat and glared. "I have a class to teach." He pointed to a framed copy of the Bill of Rights that decorated the wall. "I instruct my students on the importance of the First Amendment. It's unfortunate that certain members of the press, those who should cherish free speech the most, exploit it to make a buck." His gangly neck fully extended, he peered disdainfully over the top rim of glasses that hung low on his prominent nose. He opened the door to his office and motioned her to leave.

As she got up, she said, "I've noticed that your school has only one African-American. That's hardly representative of our local population."

"Ms. Worthington." He shook his head. "Snide innuendoes will get you nowhere." He ushered her out the door. He shuffled past her as he started down the hall, but then he glanced back and said, "Do you know what Bayard Taylor said about *ignorance* in the first stanza of his poem, *To My Daughter*?" Laughlin disappeared around the corner.

Lauren had never heard of Bayard Taylor, let alone what he had said about ignorance. She headed out of the building. As soon as she stepped outside, she pulled a pad and pen from her pocketbook and jotted down the reference. She looked back at the stone structure with its strange combination of ornate spires and pointed arches. The edifice, which Laughlin had once classified as an exemplary combination of English and French High Gothic architecture, seemed anomalous for Cedar Creek, but no more bizarre than the pedantic headmaster who called it home. She glanced at the note she had written down a moment before. Medford Laughlin had gotten the last word, and chances were his allusion was an insult.

Loggin flipped the calendar pages counting the months. Just eleven more and he would have his twenty-five years and could retire without an early-retirement penalty. He knew South Carolina's statutory formula better than the *Miranda* warnings. He would be entitled to an annuity based upon his own contributions, plus 2.14% of his average final compensation for each year of service. An annual pension only slightly more than 50% of his salary; paltry, given his extraordinary talents. Worse yet, it was insufficient for him to pack it in and lie on a beach the way he wanted. He would have to find another job. Just what remained unclear, but it would be laid back and free of demands on his gray matter. He reached for his calculator to do the exact pension calculation. Even before he finished punching in the numbers, the ring of his telephone interrupted his work. "Damn," he muttered. "Never a moment's peace." He reached for the receiver. "Loggin here."

"Remember me. Your buddy from the other day, the one with the tip on the arsonist."

"Who is this?" said Loggin.

"Call me Mr. Anonymous, and leave it at that."

"Why didn't you call back at five o'clock the way you promised?"

"Whatd'ya expect after ya hung up on me?"

"You're — "

"Even usin' a pay phone, I ain't got time for chitchat. Your arsonist lives in Potterstown. His last name is Boxley. That's *B* like in blaze, *o-x-l-e-y.*"

Loggin jotted the name. "What's his first name?" An instant later, Loggin heard a click. "Hello . . . Hello." The sound of a dial tone caused him to hang up the receiver. He reached into his desk and pulled out a telephone book. He opened to the *B 's* and looked up *Boxley.* There were four: Alice Boxley in Woverton, Clyde Boxley and Orin Boxley, both in Potterstown, and T. Boxley in Cedar Creek. Loggin immediately focused on Clyde and Orin Boxley. He took a fresh sheet of paper and wrote down their names, addresses and telephone numbers. He typed the information into his personal computer and pulled them up. Sure enough, both had rap sheets. Clyde Boxley had spent three years in the big house for grand larceny, plus another six months in the county jail for menacing. Orin Boxley had served a total of five years resulting from convictions for grand larceny, forgery and assault.

Loggin leaned back. His eyes focused on the attendance certificate he had received the summer before from the detectives' conference at Hilton Head. He could teach the young upstarts with their college degrees a thing or two about police work. The green hot shots talked a good game, but it took a shrewd cop like him to develop good leads. He got up from his desk and went into the Chief's office. He filled the boss in on the breakthrough and headed off to Potterstown. A half-hour later he pulled up to the curb at 25 Walden Place, an old, two-family house just across from the railroad tracks. He climbed out of his police cruiser and, after negotiating a couple of garbage cans on the badly cracked sidewalk, ascended the rickety porch. Beneath the doorbell for the lower flat a piece of masking tape bore the handwritten name *Clyde Boxley*. Loggin rang the bell. A minute later a weasel-like figure opened the door.

"If you're sellin' somethin', I don't want none."

"Police business." Loggin displayed his credentials. "You Clyde Boxley?"

"Yeah."

"I'd like to talk to you." Loggin made some mental notes: age, about forty; weight, not much over 130; and height, roughly 5'6".

"What about?"

"An arson in Cedar Creek."

Boxley shrugged. "Talk all ya like. I don't know nothin' about it."

Loggin, his sixth sense like a lie detector, watched for incriminating signs. Shifty eyes, nervous fingers, halting speech — he knew them all. "Where were you on the evening of April 16th?"

"Offhand, I ain't sure." He pointed at Loggin. "Supposin' I asked ya where ya wuz on April 16th. Would ya know?"

"If you don't mind, I'll ask the questions." Silently Loggin conceded Boxley had a point. "Would it make a difference if I told you April 16th was a Friday?"

Boxley stared off into space. "Let's see. That'd be the Friday before last . . . Yeah, I remember. I helped served barbecue to the homeless over in Beaulin. I wuz there all evening."

"Can someone verify that?"

Boxley hesitated. "Yeah, the Reverend. What's his face . . . Miller. That's it. He oughta remember me. Hell, I stood next to him for God knows how long. I slopped on the baked beans after he stuck chicken on the plates." Boxley gestured at Loggin. "Let me tell ya. That chicken wuz good. Like them ads say. Finger lickin' good." Boxley ran his fingers over his tongue.

The sight of dirt-filled fingernails turned Loggin's stomach. "You know this Reverend Miller well?"

"Nah. Just met him that night."

Convenient, thought Loggin. "You belong to his church?"

"Nah."

"So, why'd you help at the barbecue?"

An indignant look came over Boxley's face. "Ain't everyone that's fortunate like me to have a roof over head." He gestured behind him. "Ya know what I mean?"

Loggin ignored the self-serving question. A two-time loser like Boxley was more likely to glom a few bucks from the collection plate than lend a helping hand at a church dinner. "So, what's the name of the Reverend's church?"

"First Baptist or something like that. It's on Hillside Avenue, just beyond the elementary school." Boxley peered at Loggin. "Ya ain't got doubts, do ya?"

You bet I do, thought Loggin. He said, "I have to check out your story. That's my job."

"Hey, I wouldn't want it no other way. Us decent folks need ya to protect us. With all them criminals out there, ya can't be too careful."

"Speaking of criminals, my computer says you have a record."

"Yeah. But I done my time." Boxley folded his arms. "I know. Ya figure, once a jailbird, always a jailbird." He looked away and muttered, "A guy can't get an even break."

Loggin had heard that line from ex-cons too many times. "I'll be in touch," he said, and he headed back to his cruiser. He drove several blocks up the street where he pulled over and jotted some notes. He checked his watch. His shift was only half done. He was about to go to Orin Boxley's place when he recalled there was a great little ice cream stand on the road to Beaulin. He decided to pay a visit to Reverend Miller. that is, assuming the preacher actually existed. A banana split. a large Pepsi and an hour later, he found the First Baptist Church on Hillside Avenue. He went inside where an elderly lady directed him to the Reverend's office. He knocked on the door.

A moment later when it opened, a man about forty, dressed in a dark suit and cleric's collar, greeted him. "How may I help you?"

"I'm Detective Francis Loggin of the Cedar Creek Police Department." He showed his credentials. "I'm investigating an arson in our village. I need to verify the whereabouts of a fella named Boxley on the evening of April 16th."

"Boxley?" The Reverend looked at his calendar. "The 16th. That was the night of the church barbecue. I remember him. A short, skinny fellow."

"Looks kinda like a weasel?"

"Well — not to caste any aspersions, but I . . . uh . . . suppose that describes him."

"You know this Boxley fellow well?" said Loggin, giving no hint that he was testing the credibility of Boxley's earlier answer.

"The barbecue was the first I met him."

"But you're sure you remember him?"

"No doubt. He worked right next to me the whole evening. Every time he put beans on a platter, he said, *Beans and chicken sure is great, lick your fingers and lick your plate.* Said it so many times that I woke up in the middle of the night with the lines running through my brain."

"I take it he got on your nerves."

The Reverend hesitated. "I didn't mean to make it sound that way. Anyway, you can't criticize a fellow who is helping to feed the homeless. Let's just say he was enthusiastic."

Loggin read between the lines. The Reverend was what the Chief would call *diplomatic*. That was fine for someone in the Reverend's line of work, but not for the police force. If only the Chief understood the difference, he might have had a force of men, not cream puffs. Loggin said, "How long did Clyde Boxley work that evening?"

"Clyde . . . So, that's his first name." He looked back at Loggin. "He never mentioned it. He said to call him Boxley."

Loggin was about to repeat his question when the Reverend said, "Oh — sorry, I'm digressing. You asked how long he was here." The Reverend stared into space. "Let's see. We served from six until nine. He arrived well before we started, and he helped clean up afterward. Does that answer your question?"

"Yeah," said Loggin, satisfied that Boxley had a solid alibi. He thanked the Reverend and started back to Potterstown. On the way he stopped again at the Dairy Bar for a chocolate milkshake. Long days of tough investigation demanded a few breaks. He continued on to 107 Briar Way in Potterstown. The dilapidated, two-story, wood-frame building bore a sign, *Rooms for Rent*. What a dump, thought Loggin, as he eyed a boarded-up window on the second floor. He approached the front door and tried it. It opened into a hallway; one with fallen plaster, numerous holes in the walls and a light socket with a single bulb that swung from loose wires two feet below the ceiling. Off to his left he spotted a cardboard list of tenants taped to the wall. He perused the first floor roster and then on to the second. Near the bottom he found *Orin Boxley — Room 9*. Loggin climbed the stairs. With each step the decaying floorboards creaked. How, he wondered, did the rattrap avoid being condemned? Chances were the landlord slipped the local inspector a few shekels. A little grease in the right place cured far more ills than fresh wood and a hammer and nails. From the top of the stairs Loggin headed down the hallway until he reached the last room on the right. A brass 9 adorned the badly marred door. Loggin rapped.

"Who's there?"

"Police."

"Police who?"

"Don't toy with me," muttered Loggin, but he kept the reaction under his breath. He was outside his jurisdiction. He said, "Detective Francis Loggin of the Cedar Creek Police Force."

"Ain't you never heard of *Knock-Knock*?"

Loggin felt his blood start to boil. "What the hell are you talking about?"

"*Knock-Knock* jokes. When I said *Police who*, you were supposed to say *P-lease can I come in*?"

Loggin did a slow burn. What kind of idiot was he dealing with? "You gonna let me in or do I have — "

"Don't get your brain in a brawl." The door opened.

Loggin did a double take. He could swear he was looking at Clyde Boxley.

"You could use a sense of humor. You'll live longer."

"Are you Orin Boxley?" barked Loggin.

"That's what my mother called me."

"What do you call yourself?" snapped Loggin, wondering if Clyde and Orin Boxley were one and the same.

Boxley hesitated. "I . . . I don't generally talk to myself, and when I do, I don't never call myself by name."

Loggin stepped forward into the doorway and glared down at Boxley. Years of practice had enabled Loggin to master the intimidating move. "Are you Clyde Boxley?"

He shook his head. "Why — do I look like him?"

"Don't push me."

Boxley stepped back. "I wouldn't push you." He raised his hand well over his head. "You're . . . you're much bigger than me."

You bet I am, you little weasel. Loggin let his eyes convey the thought. "Do you know Clyde Boxley?"

"Yup."

Loggin waited, anticipating more information. None was forthcoming. "You look just like him."

"Funny, you should say that." Boxley put his hand to his chin. "Maybe . . . maybe it's because me and him is identical twins."

Loggin took a deep breath. Orin Boxley was a smart-ass who thus far was having his fun. But the wise guy with the criminal record was about to discover he had picked the wrong audience for a comedy routine. "I'm investigating an arson that occurred on the night of April 16th in Cedar Creek."

"Yeah, I heard about it. I hope you catch the creep who done it."

Maybe I have, thought Loggin. "Where were you the night of the fire?"

"You ain't arrestin' me, are you? Cause if you is, you better give me my rights."

"No, I'm not arresting you. I just want to ask you some questions."

Boxley reached for the handle of the wide-open door. "I don't have to talk to you. I could shut my door and . . . " He moved it a few inches. "But since I got nuttin' to hide, c'mon in." He motioned Loggin into the one-room studio. He pointed at a chair across from an unmade studio bed.

As Loggin took a seat, his eyes moved around the room. Apart from cracks and peeling green paint, the walls were bare. Several newspapers and an issue of *Rod and Gun* decorated the floor, while an array of dirty dishes filled the sink.

Boxley plopped down onto the bed. "So — shoot with the questions."

Loggin took a deep breath. The smell of cigarette smoke filled his lungs. He said, "You didn't tell me where you were the night of April 16th."

Boxley looked pensively into space. "You're right. I didn't." He shook his head and mumbled, "Can't slip nuttin' past this guy."

Loggin checked his watch. With an hour still remaining on his shift, Boxley was welcome to play his games. "So, where were you on the evening of April 16th?"

Boxley leaned back. "I was over in Beaulin serving chicken and beans to the homeless at the First Baptist Church barbecue."

Loggin's blood began to boil again. Before he could think up another question, Boxley said, "Matter of fact, I was standing next to Reverend Miller the whole time. He piled on the chicken, and then I slapped on the beans. We made a helluva team."

Loggin's brain raced. Twin brothers, both with the same alibi. One was lying, but which. Regardless, with nothing more than an anonymous tip to link them to the fire, he was flying by the seat of his pants. He had to draw upon his vast experience. He needed to be shrewd. He drew a blank.

"Do you do charity work at your church?" said Boxley.

"Do I what!"

"Charity work. You should try it. Good for the soul."

Where does this three-time loser get off telling me what to do? Loggin glared at Boxley. "Save your advice. And if you don't mind, I'll ask the questions."

Boxley shrugged. "My mamma — may she rest in peace — said we can learn from everyone. But if that's the way you want it, you do the askin'."

"You ever been to Hickory Lane in Cedar Creek?"

"Can't say that I have. Is that where the place got torched?"

Loggin pointed at himself. "I'm asking the questions. Remember."

Boxley muttered inaudibly.

"You know your brother has the same alibi as you."

Boxley lurched back. "Ain't that a rooster's crow in a rainstorm." He shook his head. "Funny, I don't recall Clyde at the barbecue. Did he tell you I was there?"

Loggin glared. "You're asking the questions again."

"Damn — you is right again." Boxley slapped one hand across the back of his other wrist. "Can't put nuttin' past you."

"You think you're pretty clever, you and your brother." Loggin watched Boxley like a hawk. The weasel revealed nothing. "The way I figure," said Loggin, "you and that twin of yours planned this caper together. It doesn't matter who baked the beans and who baked the house. You're both gonna fry. It's called conspiracy."

Boxley pointed at Loggin. "Whoa. I owe you an apology. You do got a sense of humor."

Loggin struggled for a quick comeback but drew another blank.

"By the way," said Boxley, "even if you had proof one of us was tied to the fire, and you ain't, how you gonna convince a jury beyond a reasonable doubt that one of us ain't innocent. The fire coulda been a one-man show. The other, me, had nuttin' to do with it. I was dishin' beans. Didn't know nuttin' 'bout no arson. Course Clyde, he claims things wuz the other way around." Boxley laughed.

"You think you're pretty smart, don't you?"

Boxley shook his head. "Nah. I just think you ain't got no case."

"Well — " Loggin got up from his seat. "You haven't heard the last of me." He headed for the door.

Boxley got up. "I'll show you out."

"I'll manage myself." Just as he got to the door, a thought clicked. Loggin glanced back. "By the way, did you tell the Reverend your first name?"

Boxley laughed again.

"What's so funny?"

"With a name like Orin, would you?" He slapped his hand to his mouth. "Oh — I forgot. You the one askin' the questions." He nodded. "I told the Reverend to call me Boxley, and that's what he did."

Loggin stepped out into the hall and closed the door behind him. He started down the dimly lit passage toward the front door. The Boxleys were daring him to make an arrest. Their thinly cloaked scheme obscured little, but Loggin had no clue how to fashion a case against them. No way could he prove that one of them set the fire. Even if he could, he had no idea which one and no way to prove a conspiracy. The single bulb hanging from the hall ceiling flickered. He glanced up at the poorly wired light. *Get me out of this firetrap.* As he stepped outside into the sunshine, he thought back to when he was a youngster. Back then when his dad was on the Cedar Creek police force, they would have gotten the Boxleys to talk. Some friendly encouragement, the kind that brass knuckles provide, would have done the trick. Unfortunately, Chief *Namby-Pamby* had put the kibosh on tried and true techniques; one more reason Loggin was counting the days to his retirement.

———————

Lauren thumbed through the author section of the card catalogue at the Cedar Creek Public Library. The tiny branch, a converted bungalow on Broad Street, had no books by Bayard Taylor. No surprise. What, she wondered, was Laughlin's message when he had referred her to Taylor's words about *ignorance* in the first stanza of the poem *To My Daughter*.

In her mind Lauren reconstructed her conversation that led up to Laughlin's poetic reference. She had insinuated he engaged in discrimination and was trying to trade his vote on the mall for his voucher program. Perhaps his obscure citation was an insult. Maybe it was nothing more than a defensive comeback, the pedant's way to get the last word. But might it be more significant. Even a clue. Lauren wanted an answer. Apparently the Cedar Creek Public Library didn't have it. She was about to leave when she decided to check at the desk. She told the woman there what she was looking for.

"Did you try *Bartlett's Familiar Quotations*?"

Lauren shook her head.

The woman pointed to the adjacent wall. "It's over there in the reference section. I'll get it for you. But let me warn you, our copy is rather old." She stepped around from behind the desk and a minute later brought the book.

Lauren read the back of the title page: *Thirteenth Edition, Published, November, 1955*. Wonderful, she thought, as quick arithmetic confirmed the twenty-eight year old book was printed the year after she was born. She flipped to the index of authors. Sure enough, under the letter *T* was the name *Bayard Taylor*, page 634. She turned to the designated page. She scanned the various verses until she reached the last one. It was, indeed, *Stanza I* of *To My Daughter*. It read:

Learn to live, and live to learn,
Ignorance like a fire doth burn,
Little tasks make large return.

The second line unnerved her. Was Laughlin's reference to the poem a threat? Could he be the arsonist? Perhaps the metaphor was a coincidence. Should she contact Loggin? What — with nothing more than a poetic reference. He would laugh at her. She was meeting Jordan for dinner. She would run it by him and get his reaction. She copied down the verse and headed out of the library. The knot in her stomach served notice her meal would not be well digested.

———————

Lauren perused the menu at the *Broad Street Café*, not that it was necessary. Even before she had joined Jordan at the convenient eatery, just a couple minutes from the *Chronicle*, she had decided upon the lamb gyro. She loved the tzatziki sauce. Once their server had taken their orders, she took the verse from her purse and handed it to Jordan. She said, "I met with Medford Laughlin today. Just before I left, I took a couple swipes at him and his school. With his inimitable flair he asked if I knew what Bayard Taylor had said about ignoranc*e*."

"Pardon *my ignorance* — no pun intended — but who the hell is Barnyard Taylor?"

"Bayard, not Barnyard." Lauren feigned a look of shock. "C'mon — you're kidding? Next thing you'll tell me you've never heard of Abe Lincoln."

Jordan's face grew taut. "You don't have to treat me like an idiot. Just tell me who this Taylor fellow is."

Lauren shrugged. "Got me. I've never heard of him." She pretended to miss the sardonic smile across the table. She said, "Anyway, I went to the library and looked up Laughlin's reference in *Bartlett's*. Here it is." She handed Jordan the verse.

He studied it for the better part of a minute. Finally, he said, "So?"

"Doesn't the second line trouble you?"

"You mean the part about *a fire doth burn*?"

"Exactly."

"That's a — " Jordan halted himself but then shook his head. "Laughlin is a strange bird. No doubt about that. But an arsonist? That's a whole different story."

"So, I'm making an epic out of a verse."

"I don't know." He hesitated. "Earlier you said you took some parting shots at Laughlin just before he referred you to this Taylor fellow. What did you say?"

"I accused him of discrimination, along with trying to swap his vote on the mall for approval of his voucher plan."

Jordan's eyes widened. "You didn't pull any punches. He musta — Wait a second. How'd you know what he was trying to pull?"

"Steve Ward put me on to it. I spoke with him at his house the other night. He suspected Laughlin might be desperate, what with declining enrollment at *Cedar Academy*."

Jordan pressed his index finger to his lips as their server drew near with their food. Once she left, he said, "I knew he wanted vouchers, but I didn't realize his situation was that bad."

"Do you think I should contact Loggin?"

"That moron." Jordan shook his head. "I know. That's no answer. I suppose, though — " He cut himself off again as a skinny guy with a shaved head and a T-shirt bearing the logo *Praise Satan* approached their table. Lauren recognized him as the same fellow who had asked Jordan for money two weeks earlier in the park.

The fellow leaned close to Jordan. "I could use a little, if you get my drift."

"Not a good time," said Jordan in a low voice.

"Forty bucks, and I'm on my way."

Jordan scowled. A moment later he reached for his wallet and pulled out two twenties and handed them to the fellow. "You're pressing your luck."

The fellow stuffed the money into the pocket of his skintight jeans and left without another word.

"What was that about?" said Lauren.

"Uh . . . nothing."

"Not so fast."

Jordan, his expression faltering, reached for his water glass.

"It's twice now that guy has hit you up for money. What's going on?"

"Can't I help someone down on his luck?" Jordan took a quick swig. "So, what were we talking about before the interruption?"

"Don't change the subject." She stared across the table. "And don't give me that look." She folded her arms. "This time I want a straight answer. Who is he?"

"Someone I know."

"No fooling." She waited a moment. "I want an answer."

"You're not getting one."

The refusal, unexpected, left her speechless.

"If you were doing a story involving a confidential source, would you tell me his name?"

"That's different."

"Is it? I'm a lawyer. My work involves confidentiality."

"Are you telling me he's your client?" She looked him in the eye, but he immediately broke eye contact. "And since when does a lawyer pay his client?" She waited. "Do you intend to answer my question?"

He shook his head. "It's personal, and let's leave it at that."

She stared across the table. Jordan was entitled to his privacy, but she didn't have to like it. She ate her gyro. It didn't taste as good as usual. Possible scenarios, some absurd, raced through her head. Perhaps the fellow was a friend? Sure — with an *AA*, Aryan Alliance tattoo. A private investigator? Not likely, given his shiny head and shirt logo. Jordan's offspring from a prior relationship? She was grasping at straws. The fellow was just a few years younger than Jordan, plus he was white.

Conversation grew sparse as they finished their dinners. Jordan paid the check. They left the café. Their goodnight kiss before going their separate ways — he to his temporary home in the room behind his office and she to her studio apartment — was as empty as his answers. Lauren headed to her car. She longed for the romance and passion they had shared in the early months of their relationship. Unfortunately arson, politics and controversy had cast dark shadows. The seeming love of her life had grown complicated. Misgivings bedeviled emotions. Why was Jordan giving the seedy guy money? What was Jordan hiding? She slipped her pocketbook from her shoulder onto the passenger seat. The bag reminded her of the slip of paper it held. Was she being paranoid, or had Medford Laughlin threatened her? She tried to dismiss her concerns. The effort failed. She drove to her apartment — *Home Sweet Home*. In the back of her mind, her father's pressure to move back to Worthington Hall stirred. She worried also that Steve Ward's claims about her father's financial predicament might be true. With Nielsen on the verge of firing her, things were equally bad at work. Lauren walked into her apartment and flopped down onto her bed. Her *posturepedic* and soft pillow cushioned her exhausted body, but their touch, surface only, did nothing to relieve the rack within.

"It's your bid."

"Oh . . . sorry." Lauren looked at her cards and arranged them by suit. She had five spades including the king and the ten, plus several other picture cards and an ace. "One spade."

Across the table her partner Mary shook her head. "Hello?"

"What's the matter?"

Seated to Lauren's right, Leigh Ann said, "Your partner already bid *two* spades."

Lauren pressed her cards to her forehead. Her mind was everywhere but on the game. "I'm sorry. I'm not very good company." She had been playing Bridge on Sunday evenings with her long-time friends for nearly five years. Two hours of cards was always followed by dessert and coffee and lots of light conversation with plenty of laughs. She looked at Mary. "You bid two spades?"

Mary nodded.

Lauren gestured to her left. "What did Jane do?"

"I bid a partridge in a pear tree." Jane let out a groan. "I passed."

"Oh." Lauren eyed her cards again. She and her partner had to be loaded. "Four spades."

"Pass." Leigh Ann pushed her cards together. "How come people who don't give a damn about the game get the good hands?"

"It's one of those fundamental laws of — "

Leigh Ann shot Mary a petulant look. "I can do without an answer. I was merely thinking out loud."

"Oh . . . " Mary studied her cards. "Six spades."

"Pass."

The likelihood the hand had *grand slam* potential crossed Lauren's mind, but it was easier to let the bidding be. "Pass," she said.

"Pass," said Leigh Ann.

Lauren laid her cards face up on the table. She was happy to be the hand's dummy.

"You're not yourself," said Jane.

"I know," said Lauren. "I apologize. I'm ruining the game."

"No," said Leigh Ann. "My cards did that." She laughed.

"Is it the arson?" said Jane.

Lauren nodded. "The arson. The mall. My job. My boss. My father and Jordan." She sighed. "It's everything."

"Can we help?" said Mary.

"You have already. Just being here for me means a lot." Lauren moved her gaze around the table. "I know I haven't been very good company in recent weeks. I appreciate your putting up with me."

"Hey, some of us owe you. Back when Jack — God knows what I saw in the creep — dumped me for that blond slut from Kyberville, you were there for me."

"And how many times did you have me to your house for dinner after my mom died," said Jane.

Lauren heaved another sigh. "Thanks," she said and then pointed at the table. "Go ahead and play the hand. I'm going to get a *Coke.* As she headed for the refrigerator, she glanced back. She was fortunate to have such wonderful friends.

Chapter IX

As he poked his head into Chief Snyder's neat, well-appointed office, a familiar thought popped into Loggin's mind. If he had spacious digs, rather than a cubbyhole, and, more important, a cushy administrative job with peons to do his bidding, his workspace would be impeccable too.

"C'mon over," said the Chief, who was staring out the window. He pointed to a spindly maple that adjoined the sidewalk. "Look right there."

Loggin gazed at the unimpressive tree. *It must be nice having nothing to do but stare out the window. Of course, if he were Chief, the limbs he'd be eyeing would be endowed with shapelier trunks.*

"Out there on the end of that branch, that's a Carolina wren, our state bird. You can tell by the brown plumage and tawny bottom. If you've got any doubts, check the erect tail."

And you're a dodo bird. Loggin pretended to focus on the feathered nothing.

"So, tell me about the arson."

His opening lines rehearsed, Loggin said, "I've got good news and bad news."

"Let's hear it," said the Chief, looking at Loggin for the first time.

"The good news is I know who torched Jackson's house. It's a fellow named Boxley from Potterstown."

"That's great." The Chief patted Loggin on the back. "I knew the guys at the Lodge meeting were off base the other night when they said — " The Chief broke eye contact. "Uh . . .

you know, they're always badmouthing cops. But I defended you."

Sure, thought Loggin. Just like his pal Woody in fifth grade. When the guys began chanting, *Loggin ain't fit to eat lice in a cesspool*, true-blue Woody disagreed.

"Wait a second," said the Chief. "You said you had good news and bad news. What's the bad news?"

"Clyde and Orin Boxley are identical twins. You can't tell them apart. One of them set the fire. Which one — I don't know. The other has an airtight alibi. He was serving beans with Reverend Miller at a church barbecue over in Beaulin. Both claim they were dishing the beans. Once I discovered they were identical twins, I checked back with the Reverend a second time. When I showed him their mug shots — they both have records — the Reverend threw up his hands. He couldn't tell one from the other. Said he never met them before, and the one who dished the beans simply went by Boxley."

The Chief tugged at his chin. "Maybe we could charge them both with conspiracy." A look of disgust came over his face. "Yeah, and have the DA on my ass demanding to know how he's supposed to convince a jury beyond a reasonable doubt that one of them isn't innocent." He pointed at Loggin. "How do you know one of them set the fire?"

"An anonymous tip."

"A what!"

"An anonymous tip."

"I heard you the first time." The Chief rolled his eyes and muttered just loud enough for Loggin to hear, "Maybe the guys at the Lodge deserve more credit."

Loggin's hand clenched, especially his middle finger. He glanced out the window in the direction of the Carolina wren. Mentally he shot the bird at his birdbrained boss.

"What did you say their names were?"

"Clyde and Orin Boxley."

"You sure one of them set the fire?"

"I'd stake my reputation on it." The scowl on the Chief's face had Loggin bristling again. He reminded himself to cross off another day on his retirement countdown the moment he returned to his office.

"So, where do we go from here?"

Loggin shrugged, though he suspected his face communicated his feelings. The Chief had some nerve. Instead of playing John Audubon, for once earn his impressive title and big bucks.

"You've thought about it, haven't you?"

"Yeah, but — " Loggin had all he could do to hold his tongue. If he were Chief, the Boxleys would spill their guts after one meal: a knuckle sandwich loaded with brass. Unfortunately, Chief Snyder lacked the stomach for the job. And to make matters worse, he took his incompetence out on his underlings.

"I've got an idea." The Chief went to his desk and pulled up the Boxleys on his new computer. He spent several minutes. Finally, he said, "Clyde Boxley has a two-inch scar on his right cheek. Call your Reverend friend and see if he knows whether the one who dished the corn — "

"Beans, not corn."

"Beans, smeans . . . whatever," barked the Chief. He pointed at Loggin. "You certainly have a knack for focusing on critical details."

The remark pushed Loggin over the edge. "Those so-called details make or break cases. Some cops — the kind that are for the birds — miss that point." The Chief's glower gave Loggin second thoughts. Prudence dictated that he curb his tongue for another year when he would become a twenty-five year veteran — eligible for the kind of pension that would allow him to turn in his badge on a moment's notice.

The Chief turned and stared out the window. Finally, he said, "Call the Reverend and see if he knows whether the fellow had a scar on his face. And tell him if anyone other than you contacts him, not to discuss the matter."

Loggin immediately dialed the church. As soon as he finished, he said, "The Reverend had no idea. He said whoever dished the beans stayed on his right the whole time. The Reverend doubted he ever saw the fellow's right cheek."

The Chief sighed. "Bring the two slimeballs in for questioning. We'll separate them. Make them think the

Reverend managed to make a positive ID. Good chance one of them will slip up."

Better than nothing, conceded Loggin, though brass knuckles were still his preference. He observed a curious expression on the Chief's face. "Something wrong?"

"I thought you might have a reaction to my strategy."

"Oh — I like it." His middle finger twitching, Loggin added, "Excellent plan, Chief."

Poised before the microphone at the special meeting of the Village Board, Roger Worthington cleared his throat. Quiet settled over the room. "Mr. Chairman, requiring me to furnish an independent consultant's report on the impact of the mall is preposterous. Compounding the absurdity is the range of issues."

Lauren, who had come into the hall just moments before, slipped into her usual seat in the rear. She had intentionally waited outside for the meeting to commence before entering. That way she didn't need to face her father. Friction between them had mounted since her recommendation to hire a consultant had gained momentum. A part of her hoped the Board might reject the idea. That way she could rationalize she had pursued the matter, just as she had promised.

"Mr. Worthington," said Chairman Laughlin, "you challenge the need for an independent consultant's report. You call it unreasonable. Your point is a bald conclusion, buttressed by nothing more than hollow protestations."

Lauren focused on the back of her father's neck. Tightening veins would be a telltale sign his thermometer was rising. Distance prevented the observation, but she knew her father well enough to make the assumption.

"You want evidence," he said. "Walk up and down Broad Street. Take a look at the vacant storefronts." He gestured at the audience behind him. "Talk to these folks, your so-called constituents. Ask them whether Cedar Creek needs the mall." He took hold of the microphone and tilted it close to his mouth. "Mr. Chairman, members of the Board, you can vote to make me jump through hoops. But understand, if you chose that route, I may tell you to take your hoops and shove them. And if I do, don't whine, not to me, about Cedar Creek's depressed economy."

A buzz vibrated through the hall. "Quiet,' barked Laughlin. He waited a moment. "Mr. Worthington, lest there be any confusion, let me make two points unmistakably clear. This Board will do that which serves the interests of Cedar Creek best. Threats of gloom and doom, especially the kind grounded upon theoretical speculations, will not intimidate us."

Worthington glanced at the audience where a smattering of applause mixed with an undercurrent of boos. Lauren cringed, as her father seemed to look her way. He turned back and pointed at Laughlin. "Of all people, you, sitting in your ivory tower, have the nerve to accuse anyone of theoretical speculations. And just to set the record straight, Cedar Creek's eleven-percent unemployment rate is *not* theoretical. Neither are the rising foreclosure statistics." Worthington stormed away from the microphone. He started to take a seat in the front row but stopped. "Like you, Mr. Chairman, I wish to avoid any possible confusion. Let it be known, that if the Board rejects my mall, I intend to sue."

Laughlin laughed.

"You find that humorous?" said Worthington.

"Quite." Laughlin shook his head and then turned his gaze to the side of the audience away from Worthington. "Apparently our petulant applicant has forgotten that his proposal is predicated on this Board granting him tax breaks — generous ones that are *not* a matter of right." He turned back to Worthington. "Sue if you wish, but spare us . . . please spare us your idle threats."

A hush, the kind that speaks louder than a raised voice, draped itself over the room. Though Lauren's view remained obscured, she was certain veins were now protruding.

"We have heard the applicant," said Laughlin. "Now the Board will speak. And keep in mind, we are only deciding whether Mr. Worthington must pay for an independent consultant if he wants us to give his proposal further consideration. As I call for a vote, each member is free to comment." Laughlin looked down to his left. "Mr. O'Leary."

"I vote nay. Cedar Creek needs the mall. A consultant's report, a bunch of mumbo-jumbo, would only muddy the waters. We've dawdled too long already. Let's get on with the project . . . before Cedar Creek becomes a ghost town."

"Ms. Warner."

"For the reasons just expressed — nay."

"Mr. Ward."

"Aye."

"Mr. Jackson."

Jordan pushed back so he sat tall in his seat. "Before going ahead with the mall, we need to assess its impact. Demands on fire and safety services, effects on the water supply and the aquifer, increased traffic and harm to the adjoining park are just a few of the consequences." He looked toward Worthington. "The applicant has requested huge tax breaks. Approving the mall without a consultant's report would be a dereliction of duty. For all we know we might be subsidizing a project that lowers our community's quality of life." He leaned forward and stared down at the far end of the table. "What motivates my colleagues who vote *nay*, I cannot be certain. Perhaps the artist's rendition of a skylight and cascading fountain with lush vegetation amidst bustling shops has taken them in. But cynic that I am, other explanations cross my mind. Personal gain is a distinct possibility. And too, I wonder what role an arsonist's intimidation plays in their position." Jordan hesitated, and then his voice grew softer. "My final comment requires a difficult concession. Over my several years on this Board, I've often criticized Steve Ward. Our differences on political, social and environmental issues are notorious. There are those who would argue that self-preservation, the survival of his Broad Street strip mall, drives his opposition to the current project. Regardless, he deserves kudos for courage as he stands up and defends the future of Cedar Creek in the face of the arsonist's most recent threat, one addressed directly to him." Jordan reached over and shook Ward's hand. Many in the audience applauded.

From her seat in the back Lauren studied the scene. Ever the journalist, her eyes, unlike those around her, observed a fascinating story. Along the byways of Cedar Creek abundant black soil still bore the weight of a few white, pillared mansions. Strong foundations had enabled the contrasting hues of land and structures to remain intact. However, a clasp of hands hinted that different shades might someday paint the landscape. Lauren contemplated the possibility. But reality muted excitement. Write the story, she could, but Nielsen would never print it. Worse yet, perhaps it was pie in the sky. Traditions die hard.

Laughlin, his patience more than usual, allowed the din to wear itself out. He said, "With the vote at two and two, it appears the Chair has the deciding ballot. I have already enunciated my views and, accordingly, will eschew reiteration."

From the back of the room a voice called out, "Do us a favor and *ezchoo* them three-dollar words too."

Laughter filled the hall. Laughlin pounded his gavel. The craggy features of his bony face appeared more pronounced as he removed his glasses and glared at the heckler. "Some of us, those who value education, can articulate without resorting to slang, vulgarities, argot or Ebonics." He reached for his water and took a drink. He rapped the glass down on the table. "Where was I before the philistine interrupted. Ah, yes. My vote." He paused. "Like the gentlemen to my right, I vote *aye*. We need the consultant's report." He folded his arms. "And let the vote of this Board serve notice to the arsonist, whoever you are, that the representatives of Cedar Creek will not shirk from their duty, intimidation notwithstanding."

The audience's applause suggested Chairman Laughlin had garnered support. But Lauren wondered whether it was deserved. Might the headmaster's bombast mask ulterior motives? Was he blocking the mall until, and only until, O'Leary and Warner would give him their votes for his voucher plan? And too, the possibility loomed that Laughlin himself might be the arsonist. If so, his refusal to be intimidated was show; his courage, bogus; and his motive, deceit.

———————

Loggin silently mouthed a chain of expletives as he trailed Detective Marks to the room where Orin Boxley waited. Though the Chief hadn't said it in so many words, Loggin had gotten the message, and he was pissed. Marks, a junior nobody, had been made lead interrogator. The Chief had told Loggin to play the hard-ass. Ordinarily, he preferred that role, but not at the price of his ego. Marks had been designated the nice guy, and, unlike usual, Mr. Nice-Guy was instructed to do most of the talking.

As they entered the room, Orin Boxley got up from a captain's chair. "This is Detective Marks," said Loggin. Marks smiled. He reached out and shook Boxley's hand. Boxley started to sit back down in his seat. Loggin pointed at a narrow hardwood with straight back and no arms. "Over there." He flipped a switch turning on an extra light; one aimed at the corner where Boxley's chair was located.

"Before we begin," said Marks, "I want you to know that you're not under arrest. You can leave whenever you like."

"If you do," said Loggin, "you'll be sorry. We've got you by the short hairs." He folded his arms, flashing his tried and true stare. Without threats of physical harm he could strike fear, especially into a slimy creep like Boxley.

"Would you like some water?" said Marks.

Boxley nodded.

Marks stepped out. A minute later he returned with a cup that he handed to Boxley. "You're headed for a big fall. We know you started the fire. You and your brother's twin routine didn't fool anyone."

Loggin watched Boxley's every move, ready to pounce at the smallest hint. The suspect remained impassive.

"Your brother is no better off than you. He's an accomplice."

"You ain't got nuttin' on us."

Marks shook his head. "We've got you, and you know it. But the way I see it, you've got something we want."

A momentary furrow of Boxley's brow, an inquisitive one, hinted at interest. Loggin would have jumped in, but he had no idea where Marks was going.

"You and your brother," said Marks, "don't live in Cedar Creek. You don't care about its politics. No doubt, a bigger fish hired you. Tell us — come clean with the whole story — and we'll recommend you get a break. Whatd'ya say?"

The sneer on Boxley's face underscored the shake of his head.

Loggin restrained the urge to laugh. What did Marks expect? He was dealing with a professional criminal. The only amateur in the room was the guy asking the questions. Loggin thought about giving his partner some help, but not yet. First let the greenhorn strike out. Only then would the master pinch hit.

Marks got up from his seat. "I'll be back in a few minutes." He walked out the door.

Loggin did a double take. Was the kid so inept that he needed a time out? Did he hope the Chief would give him some suggestions? Perfect, thought Loggin. Let the boss see how raw the college boy was. Loggin got up from his chair so he could stare down at Boxley. "We've got you nailed. With a prior felony you'll be pushin' eighty by the time you get out. My buddy here gave you a chance. Pretty quick we ain't gonna play nice-nice. So you better smarten up fast."

"I can go whenever I want. Right?"

If Marks hadn't said so, Boxley probably would never have asked the question. But little good it did to engage in *ifs*. "Yeah, you can go. Course, then we might decide to arrest you. And make no mistake, if you play hardball, that good word we mentioned is gonna turn sour." Loggin inched closer to Boxley. "If you're smart, you'll talk now."

"Like I told you the other day, I don't know nothin'. I was dishin' beans at the church." He pointed at the light "You mind shuttin' that off."

Loggin ignored the request. "You think you're clever cause my partner treats you with kid gloves. Keep it up, and I'll start asking the questions." Loggin rubbed a fist against an open palm. He was careful to keep his hands close to his stomach so the surveillance camera directly at his back couldn't pick up the gesture. He stepped out of the room. As long as he had to wait for Marks, he might as well enjoy some coffee. Minutes later, mug in hand, he returned and seated himself across from Orin Boxley.

"Can I have a cup?"

Loggin shook his head and then took a sip.

"Nice mug," said Boxley.

Loggin eyed the Confederate flag that adorned his mug. Perhaps Boxley wasn't all bad. Loggin even considered getting Boxley a cup. But not after the way the weasel had jerked him around at their first meeting.

Fifteen minutes passed before Marks finally returned. The junior detective smiled at Boxley. "Orin, my friend, I've got good news." He paused. "I've also got the bad kind. Your brother just told me who torched Jackson's home. You look puzzled." Marks took a step forward and looked Boxley in the eye. "Let me explain. It's good news for me and bad for you. Your brother implicated both of you. He admitted that *you* set the fire."

Boxley laughed.

"You find that funny?" said Marks.

Boxley shook his head. "You're the one who's funny. Even if there wuz somethin' to admit — and there ain't — my brother wouldn't never yap."

Loggin laughed out loud. Hard to believe, but the young upstart was even more naïve than Loggin had previously thought.

Marks pointed his finger into Boxley's face. "Reverend Miller confirmed that Clyde, not you, dished the beans. No jury would take the word of convicted felons over a man of the cloth, especially one with no axe to grind. Clyde knew he was in a jam. That's why he decided to deal."

"Is that so?" said Boxley, a concerned look contradicting his seeming bravado.

Loggin realized Marks must have called the Reverend when he had stepped out of the room. But what new tidbit from the interrogation had enabled the Reverend to identify Clyde Boxley?

Marks eased down into a chair. "Reverend Miller says the fellow who dished the beans had a scar on his right cheek. One of his parishioners noticed it."

"Bull," barked Boxley. "Clyde covered it with makeup and — "

"And what?" said Marks.

Boxley broke eye contact. His silence confirmed the slip-up. Loggin glanced at Marks. The rookie had duped Boxley into revealing that Clyde was the one dishing beans at the church. Orin Boxley had just fingered himself as the arsonist.

"Listen up. And listen good," said Marks. "I'm giving you one chance and one chance only to help yourself. Take it now, or I'll do everything in my power to send you on the big ride."

Boxley raised his head but said nothing.

Marks pointed at Boxley again. "Like I told you before. We want the big fish. Give us his name, and we'll put in a good word with the DA."

"How do I know it's gonna help?"

"You don't," said Marks emphatically. "But rest assured, if you don't cooperate, the DA will hear from us eighty-nine ways to Cucamonga why he should blast your ass. And let me tell you, the DA pays attention to us. Our testimony makes or breaks his cases." Boxley started to open his mouth, but Marks cut him off. "One more promise. If you jerk us around now, come time for sentencing, I'll put in a bad word — and I mean bad — in the sentencing report to the court."

Boxley leaned forward, his head on his chin Loggin studied the suspect. Nine-to-five the weasel was about to crack. Nevertheless, Loggin had mixed feelings. The rookie was showing him up.

Boxley remained motionless. Seconds slowly ticked. Finally, he said, "My brain told me the caper wuz a disaster waitin' to happen. But damn, my brain ain't no match for four G's." Shoulders slumped, he looked at Marks. "I torched the place."

"Who hired you?"

"This skinhead fellow. His name is Jake Brewster. He lives in a dump out on Route 47, just this side of Potterstown."

"Did he say why he wanted the place burned?"

You really need to ask, thought Loggin.

"He didn't say, and I didn't ask." Boxley paused. "Of course, when a skinhead hires you to fry *Sambo's* home, you don't need no sheepskin to figure out why."

Loggin was fed up with playing second fiddle. He said, "A minute ago you told us this Brewster fellow lived in a dump. Didn't you wonder how he came up with the four grand?"

Boxley shrugged. "Tell you the truth — I didn't care. Long as them bills wuz green, they suited me fine. Anyway, I figured him and a bunch of his skinhead buddies probably kicked in the dough."

"Any idea whether Brewster belongs to the *Aryan Alliance*?" said Marks.

"You got me."

"Did he have an *AA* tattoo on his shoulder?" asked Loggin.

Boxley frowned. "I did a deal with the guy. That's as far as it went. He weren't my type, if you get my drift."

"We want a written statement," said Marks. "I'll tell the DA you cooperated." He looked at Loggin. "You'll put a word in for Boxley too. Right?"

"Huh . . . me? Yeah." Loggin bristled. Who did Marks think he was? Bad enough the Chief had put the kid in charge. Did he have to let Boxley know?

Marks prepared a statement. He made certain that every line conformed to Boxley's understanding of the facts. Once finished, he read the whole thing aloud and had Boxley sign it. Orin and Clyde Boxley were booked, and Marks, along with Loggin, headed into the Chief's office.

"How'd you make out?" asked the Chief.

Marks handed him the statement. The Chief read it. When he finished, he said, "Great job. How'd you get him to confess?"

Marks put a hand on Loggin's shoulder. "Frank zigged, and I zagged. I threw the softies, and Frank fired the hard ones. Sure enough, Orin slipped up; let us know that Clyde was at the barbecue." Marks patted Loggin's back. "It was a real team effort."

Loggin did a double take. Maybe the college kid wasn't so bad after all.

———————

"Sorry to keep you waiting," said Lauren, as she approached Jordan in the *Chronicle*'s lobby. She adjusted the zipper on the jogging suit she had just changed into.

Jordan greeted her with a kiss. "How'd your day go?"

"Okay . . . No, make that good." She made sure no one was within earshot. "Nielsen didn't cross my path once. How was yours?"

"Excellent. I settled the *Ferguson* case. He was thrilled. Said he never imagined the insurance company would pay that much. I've got some other news, even better, though it means I'll have to eat humble pie. But first, where should we jog?"

Lauren was more interested in the news, but knowing Jordan, she opted for patience. "Suppose we head over to the park. We can do a couple of loops and circle back to *Flame and Fry*. That way we won't have to change for dinner."

"Ah . . . the gourmet special." He shrugged. "Yeah, I suppose fast food at an outdoor umbrella table fits a sweaty duo." He headed for the door with his step already approaching a jog.

Lauren hurried to catch up. "You plan to leave me in the dark. What's the news?"

"I got a call, about an hour ago, from Loggin. He caught the thugs who torched my house. Twin brothers. Crin and Clyde Boxley."

The names rang no bells. "Who are they?"

"A couple of losers from Potterstown."

"What's their motive?"

"Money. Loggin says they were hired by a skinhead named Jake Brewster."

The name was equally unfamiliar. "Is he from Potterstown too?"

"According to Loggin he lives in a trailer off Route 47, halfway between Cedar Creek and Potterstown."

With her father and Jordan having accused one another, the arson had been a touchy subject. The newest revelation might put that animosity to bed. Of course, other issues still remained. Lauren said, "It looks like a hate crime."

"Apparently." Jordan hesitated. The pace of his jog slowed as well. "But even assuming that's the case, it begs the question — Why?" He waited a moment and then drew to a halt.

She stopped a few steps ahead of him and then eased back. "Isn't this conversation getting a little heavy for a jog?"

"Fine. We can sit over there." He pointed to a bench adjacent to the Broad Street Monument bearing the names of Cedar Creek soldiers killed in the Civil War.

Lauren preferred to continue the run. Not because it was important; rather to evade the issue. But she understood Jordan's underlying point. They needed to talk. In recent weeks they had begun skirting matters of race. When they had first begun dating, it wasn't that way. They had freely discussed the subject numerous times. Neither doubted that the other had no compunctions about dating someone of differing color. That wasn't the rub. Lauren's father was more problematic, and conversations about race inevitably shifted to him. His objections to Jordan and their relationship saddled Lauren with feelings of doubt and guilt. His influence reared itself in other subtler ways as well, as rancor often replaced dialogue. Bright lights of open communication gradually faded behind Roger Worthington's long, dark shadow. Lauren knew that sooner or later the matter needed to be faced, but procrastination was easier. She realized that *sooner-or-later* had arrived. She said, "Let's go talk on the bench."

Jordan took hold of her hand and led the way. Once seated, he said, "Let's return to my earlier question. Why the hate?"

Lauren had thoughts, but one in particular stood out. She said, "Ignorance."

Jordan shook his head.

"You disagree?"

"Not exactly, but chalking it up to *ignorance* is a copout. It's far more complicated."

His point, one with merit, left her searching for an answer. She said, "Fear, economics, self-justification . . . I suppose a wealth of factors play a role."

His blank expression gave no hint as to his reaction. He said, "How would you deal with discrimination?"

His unusually serious manner, as much as the question, had her brain at a momentary standstill. "Education," she said, her response ringing hollow. The grimace that greeted her eyes confirmed the assessment. "I know. That's another copout."

"You said it. Not me."

"But you thought it." She poked him in the side.

He smiled.

The reaction offered the chance to reverse roles. She said, "Wouldn't you agree we're making progress, albeit slow?"

He shrugged. "No doubt we've come a long way from the days of segregation. Public transportation, accommodations, schools, water fountains, etc. are available, but discrimination is alive and well."

"But we're making progress."

"I guess." He glanced off into space and mumbled, "Two steps forward and one in reverse." He looked back at her. "But let an economic downturn occur, and it's apt to be one forward and two back."

"Where do you think we'll be in forty years?"

"Two thousand . . . twenty-three. God, that's a long way off." He heaved a sigh. "I don't know. What do you think?"

An optimistic assessment would likely draw an unwelcome challenge. But Lauren had no desire to play the pessimist when it came to racial relations. She said, "Maybe dinosaurs will be roaming the earth again." The disparaging look that greeted her words prompted her to add, "Maybe not dinosaurs. But given the cold war and the Soviet Union's arsenal of weapons, not to mention our own, people may nuke themselves right off the face of the earth."

Jordan shrugged. "You have a point. But let's assume we don't blow ourselves to kingdom come. What then?"

As a reporter Lauren lived in the world of facts. To her the only thing predictable about the future was its unpredictability. She said, "I don't know. You tell me."

He shook his head. "My heart longs for better days, but my brain is skeptical. It's the subtler forms of racism that frighten me most. Take the job market, for example. There are those who argue affirmative action has leveled the playing field. Opponents go even further. They claim it has tipped the scales in favor of blacks. What do you think?"

Lauren took a deep breath. Affirmative action had appeal, but she had reservations. She said, "Well — to quote a dear friend, it's complicated."

Jordan gave her the evil eye. "That's a sweet dodge." He pecked her on the cheek. "You sure you didn't go to law school?"

She pecked him back. "Newspaper reporters have a trick or two of their own."

"Especially reporters of the fairer sex." He gazed skyward and gestured at the heavens. "When you created women, did you add the feminine wiles just for a few laughs?"

Lauren heaved a sigh. "Give me a break. Now it's men who lack a level playing field." She jabbed him in the side. "We can debate that one in the context of the job market — if you'd like."

Jordan maintained an upward gaze. "I rest my case, Lord." He turned back to her. "Before you completely sidetrack me, let's go back. Let's talk about affirmative action. How do you feel about it?"

Lauren had debated the issue with her father. His dislike of the concept had encouraged her to argue the other side. But mixed feelings, plus the journalist in her — or, perhaps, the gadfly — inveigled her. She said, "Let me put my father's favorite argument on the table. A responsible, white student has studied hard and developed an impressive academic record. He applies to his favorite college. He is rejected. But thanks to affirmative action, a less-qualified, minority applicant from the same high school gets in. How does the white feel?"

"Disappointed." Jordan shook his head. "No, pissed."

"You . . . you believe affirmative action is unfair?"

"In some ways."

The unexpected concession tempted her to play devil's advocate. She said, "I can't believe you agree with my father. Of all people, *you* oppose affirmative action?"

Jordan shook his head again. "God forbid to your first statement, and no to the second." He hesitated. "You look puzzled. Let me explain. You asked if affirmative action is fair. Not entirely. But that's not the point." He eyed her. "I can tell from your face. You think I'm in left field."

His last remark had merit, but she preferred to keep her mouth shut. She shrugged.

"Let me try an analogy. A thief steals a bicycle from the owner. The thief then sells it to a buyer. In good faith the buyer pays the thief a fair price. The owner learns that the buyer has the bicycle and sues to recover it. The law says the owner gets the bicycle. Is that fair? Not to the buyer, an innocent purchaser. But wouldn't it be more inequitable for the owner to lose his bicycle? The law opts for the more equitable outcome, albeit far from perfect. And by the way, the buyer could sue the thief. Unfortunately, too often the thief has taken off or has no assets."

Lauren thought for a moment about the analogy. "Your point, if I understand it, is that the benefits of affirmative action outweigh the harm."

"Well — yes and no." Jordan hesitated. "You're frowning. I can't blame you. But give me a moment, and I'll try to make some sense." A pensive look came over his face. Finally, he said, "Let me modify my earlier example. Suppose our thief was a con man instead. Let's say he buys the owner's bicycle and pays for it with what he claims is a magnificent diamond. In fact, it's cut glass. The con man then sells the bicycle to the buyer who purchases it in good faith paying fair market value. The owner sues the buyer to recover the bicycle."

"You don't have to tell me. Fair or not, the buyer loses again."

Jordan shook his head. "Nope. The buyer gets the bicycle. In the second example the owner voluntarily dealt with the con man and parted with his bicycle. He could have verified that the diamond was a fake. The law says that the owner, not the buyer, must chase the con man."

Lauren contemplated the two examples. "I hear what you're saying, but . . . "

He waited a moment. "I sense you're troubled. Perhaps because I skipped the threshold question — whether affirmative action is justified."

For Lauren, history — slavery, discrimination and disadvantage — provided more than enough reason. She shook her head. "No, my problem is the inequities it causes. How do you deal with them?"

"Not easy. Though sometimes it's just a matter of recognizing potential. Perhaps I can make the point using your earlier example, but with the addition of a few more specifics. Suppose the white student with the impressive academic record . . . "

Lauren's mind diverged. How different Jordan was from her father. Unlike Dad, who relied on increased volume, Jordan stuck to well-reasoned points. And where her father patronized, especially women, Jordan treated her as an equal. Lauren loved her father, but not his narrow-minded inflexibility. For Roger Worthington any black man, no matter his character, was unfit to marry his daughter. The issue had no shades of gray. Lauren felt a knot in her stomach. Too long her father had tried to rule her life. She was an adult and —

"You're not listening."

"I am too," she said instinctively.

"Fine. What did I just say?"

"That . . . that affirmative action . . . "

Jordan frowned. "That affirmative action is like a pecan-filled hockey puck."

"Okay. So my mind wandered. But it just so happens I was thinking what a terrific guy you are."

Jordan reached into one pocket and then another.

"What are you doing?"

"Looking for a pen and paper, so I can make a note of your novel excuse. Next time someone catches me not listening, I'll be sure to use it."

"But that's really what I was thinking." The wry smile on his face convinced Lauren she was fighting a losing battle. She put her hand onto his leg and slid it across his thigh.

He leaned her way as he draped an arm over her shoulder, his hand coming to rest on her breast.

She heaved a sigh. Profound thoughts vaporized.

CHAPTER X

With Marks at his side, Loggin climbed out of the squad car. He still wasn't crazy about working with a rookie, but at least this time there were no advance instructions from the Chief; the kind that made a veteran feel like a junior lackey. As they walked down the dirt driveway that adjoined the road connecting Cedar Creek to Potterstown, Loggin made a mental note. The banged-up, mustard heap parked alongside the dilapidated trailer was a nineteen sixty-seven Mustang. Loggin knew vintage cars better than anyone on the force. The talent was invaluable, but no one, especially the Chief, gave a damn. He climbed the cinder blocks that served as steps to the faded green, single-wide trailer and rapped on the rusty door. He waited a moment and then rapped again.

"Hold your water."

The gruff voice fit the image Loggin had formed. He had run a check on Jake Brewster before they had come out to investigate. The guy had a rap sheet as long as a shotgun, not the sawed-off kind. There were several assaults. They included a bar fight, an unprovoked stoning of an elderly black man who was walking beneath a bridge and a bullwhipping of a young black boy who was picking berries on the land adjoining Brewster's trailer. There was also a petty theft, reckless driving, driving under the influence, menacing, bad checks and a resisting arrest. Loggin took special note of the last one. He also noted that Brewster was only five-feet seven. If the two-bit scumbag made one wrong move, Loggin would let him have it. With his two hundred twenty pounds, he was just the man to do it. Cedar County, suffering from the leniency of coddling judges, begged for his no-nonsense methods.

A fellow in a sleeveless muscle shirt with a beer belly protruding over the top of paint-stained work pants opened the trailer door. His chin, sporting two or three days of bristly growth, bore more hair than his smooth-shaven head. He reached for the handle to the screen door but didn't open it.

Marks, credentials in hand, flashed them. "Police. We're looking for Jake Brewster."

"You found him. Whatd'ya want?"

"We want to talk to you," said Marks.

"So — talk."

"Ain't you gonna ask us in?" said Loggin.

"Ya got a warrant?"

No, but I got a fist I'd like to shove down your fat mouth. Loggin let his expression communicate the thought.

"We're investigating a fire," said Marks, "a suspected arson that occurred last month on Hickory Lane in Cedar Creek."

Brewster shrugged. "So, why ya comin' to me?"

"We thought you might know something about it." Loggin gave Brewster his patented glare.

"Yeah. I heard about it. On TV."

"That the first time?" said Marks.

"Yeah." Brewster folded his arms. "Ya ain't insinuatin' somethin' else?"

Loggin let a moment of silence answer the question. Then he pointed at Brewster and said, "We got two fellows from Potterstown who say you hired them to torch the place."

"Then ya got two fellows who's lyin'."

"You know Clyde and Orin Boxley?" Loggin watched Brewster's face to see if the names produced any change of expression. Brewster showed nothing.

"Can't say I do." He hesitated. "I ain't under arrest, am I?"

Marks pointed at Brewster's tattoo. "I see — "

"Am I under arrest?"

"Not yet," said Marks.

"Then we is done talkin'."

"Don't push us," said Loggin, noting for the first time the *AA* tattoo just off Brewster's right shoulder. The engraved design gave Loggin pause, but only momentary. Brewster's challenge to their authority had killed any possibility of a break. Loggin grabbed the outside handle of the screen door.

"Open it, and you'll be sorry," said Brewster.

Loggin restrained the urge to laugh. How dare the lug threaten his badge. Loggin yanked the screen door open. He stuck his foot into the doorway in anticipation that Brewster might try to shut the main door. Instead he opened it wider.

"Ya blew it, Copper."

Caught between bewilderment and rage, Loggin grabbed Brewster's forearm.

Brewster glanced at Loggin's hand and then looked him in the eye. "You arrestin' me?"

"You bet I am," said Loggin, though the decision was strictly an afterthought. He glanced at his partner. Marks's face revealed little, but Loggin suspected annoyance.

"Ya gonna give me my rights?"

Loggin wished he were there alone. He would have given Brewster those rights. One in his fat midsection. Another in his ugly kisser. Then he would have added a couple of lefts before charging the creep with resisting arrest. A claim that Brewster had tried to push him down the stairs would have done the trick. But with Marks there, Loggin couldn't take the chance. The rookie seemed like a decent sort, but when push came to shove, Marks might let him down. Loggin wished it were the old days. Back then there was loyalty. His partner Billy Bob would have covered for him, just the way he would for Billy Bob. Loggin pulled off his cap and from the card that was taped to the inside read Brewster the *Miranda* warnings.

Brewster pointed at the floor just inside the doorway. "Mind if I put my boots on?"

"Fine. Make it quick." As Brewster slipped on the western-style footwear, Loggin searched his vast experience. A little ingenuity, and Brewster might talk. Loggin clenched a fist off to the side of the door jam where Marks, not Brewster, could see it. He looked over at Marks, hoping for a return message. It didn't come.

Brewster stepped outside the door and then locked it.

Loggin slipped a pair of handcuffs onto Brewster's wrists. "Let's go." Loggin pointed at the squad car.

"Whatever you say." Brewster laughed and then turned to Marks. "Your buddy here didn't need to arrest me. I woulda cooperated if he weren't such a — well, ya get my drift."

Loggin saw Marks's eyes widen. Whose side was the rookie on? Back at the station would he tell the Chief that Brewster might have talked if Loggin had shown more patience? Loggin doubted it, but he wasn't going to take the risk. He said, "Tell you what, hotshot. I'm giving you one more chance."

"Fur what?"

Was Brewster really that dumb? "To cooperate. Tell us what you know and — "

"And then you'll take me down to the station. No thanks." Brewster turned to Marks again. "Two minutes ago I woulda spilled my guts. But now that the big fella slapped the cuffs on, I'm gonna take his advice."

Advice? Loggin had no clue what Brewster was referring to.

"Ya look confused," said Brewster. "Let me set ya straight. A minute ago, when my tongue was ready to wag, ya told me I had a right to remain silent and to talk to a mouthpiece. That's just what I'm gonna do." With his two cuffed hands he gestured toward the squad car. "Shall we take that ride?"

Marks led Brewster to the car. Loggin followed close behind. Like him Brewster was a veteran, though their experience had been gained on opposite sides of the law.

Brewster appeared smug. Odds were he had never intended to talk. Loggin chuckled to himself. They were going for a ride together, and when they reached their destination, Brewster, not he, would be the one behind bars. And that was only the beginning. By the time they were done, Brewster would discover that he had messed with the wrong cop.

Lauren pounded the keys of her computer. Just three months and already her old typewriter was nearly a forgotten relic. She reviewed her notes and slipped in another quote from Loggin. Incredibly the lecherous dimwit had earned her story's plaudits. Orin and Clyde Boxley had confessed to their roles in setting the fire at Jordan's home. They had implicated Jake Brewster, and while he was maintaining his silence, the twins' statements established a strong case against the skinhead with the long rap sheet. His previous violence against innocent blacks, along with his connection to the *Aryan Alliance*, provided motive.

But Jordan had made a number of points that troubled Lauren. Where would Jake Brewster get four thousand dollars, the amount he had allegedly paid to the Boxleys for the arson? And assuming he had that kind of money, would he blow it on a fire at Jordan's house? Lauren had answers. They sounded good when she rattled them off. Brewster was a diehard member of the *Aryan Alliance*. Burning the home of the most influential black in Cedar Creek, the village's pre-eminent progressive, was worth four thousand dollars to a bigot like Brewster. And chances were the four thousand dollars didn't come from his pocket. His comrades at the *Aryan Alliance* probably picked up the tab. The logic was impeccable. Why then, Lauren wondered, did she doubt her own reasoning.

She couched her story carefully. Her experience as a journalist, her respect for the First and Fifth Amendments to the Constitution and, most of all, the ring of Nielsen's caustic tongue in the recesses of her brain, persuaded her to hedge her bets. Once the story appeared in the *Chronicle*, there would be no turning back. True, retractions could be printed, but if that happened, heads, particularly hers, might roll.

———————

Loggin sipped his coffee. It had been more than a year since he had sat in on plea negotiations at the District Attorney's office. Normally the prosecutors handled them alone. Sure, they ran many deals by the police force before finalizing them, but Loggin knew it was lip service; one more facet of his job that stuck in his craw. For a change the District Attorney's office had invited him in on the front end. Assistant

District Attorney Don Smith had arranged the meeting with Brewster's lawyer, Bill Poland. Poland had requested that his client attend. Loggin suspected his own invitation may have been Smith's way of evening up the sides. The prosecutor needed a veteran's help, even if he wouldn't admit it.

If Loggin had his druthers, he would have preferred to be teamed with Poland rather than Smith. Poland was conservative and more like a tough businessman than a lawyer. His talk was straight, rather than legalese, and he was practical. Smith, on the other hand, was a stickler for following the letter of the law; the kind who would sooner see a guilty party go free than use an involuntary confession. That annoyed Loggin. As far as he was concerned, Smith belonged in some legal-aid office defending society's dregs. Nevertheless, Loggin welcomed the assignment. It could have gone to Marks. But for once the Chief had shown good judgment, which only proved a point that Loggin had often made. Even a moron picks a winning pony once in a while.

The parties had been meeting for more than an hour. Brewster's eagerness for a deal was obvious. He claimed he could lead the prosecutor to a bigger fish. Brewster's bluster didn't fool Loggin. To his surprise Smith had remained tough. He had bargained a guilty plea with nine years in prison, subject to two conditions: the first, automatic, was court approval; the second, however, was where he showed some mettle. So long as Brewster's claim of a bigger fish remained unsubstantiated, there would be no deal. As Smith put it, Brewster might be fingering someone with no connection just to shorten his sentence. Unfortunately, Brewster had no way to prove his assertion was not a fabrication. Poland argued that Smith's demand was unreasonable. It required Brewster to prove a negative. According to Poland that was the realm of ivory-towered philosophers from academia, not serious negotiators of criminal cases. Loggin agreed, though, unlike the wordy lawyer, he would have expressed the notion in the kind of earthier terms that common folks used.

Round and round the lawyers went. Poland threatened to walk out. Instead of backing down, Smith pointed at the door.

Poland stayed at the table. Smith made a new proposal, one that Loggin had not expected.

"Tell you what," said Smith. "Have your client take a lie detector test."

The expression on Poland's face suggested the idea was like a body at the morgue — DOA.

"Hear me out," said Smith. "We'll agree on the questions in advance. Apart from baseline inquires such as your client's name and age, they'll be few in number."

Out of the corner of his eye, Loggin watched Poland. He appeared no more receptive than before. Poland appeared ready to comment when Smith cut him off.

"The last few questions will identify the mastermind behind the arson and the terms on which your client was hired. You can stop the test at any time. If you do or if your client fails, we'll treat it as if it never took place. Whatever he said can't be used for any purpose. If, however, your client completes and passes the test, he gets his deal."

The proposal, one Loggin had never heard before, intrigued him. Poland's pensive expression suggested he might be interested too. He whispered back and forth with Brewster. A moment later, he said, "Don't get me wrong. I'm not enthusiastic, but I'm willing to listen. What are the operative questions?"

Smith took a deep breath. "It's not that simple. It . . . it'll be like wording a contract. I write it one way. You make a change. I modify that. Back and forth we go until, finally, we either hit pay dirt or a dead end. Let's go down to my office and see what we can do."

Poland whispered with his client again and then said, "You want to talk. I'll talk. But frankly, I doubt it'll do any good."

For an instant Loggin felt pessimistic, but then he recalled something retired District Attorney Charley Waters had told him years earlier. Negotiations are like life. Actions speak louder than words. Bottom line. Poland was getting up from his seat and heading down the hall to work out language.

Smith stood up. He turned to Loggin. "Keep an eye on our friend." He gestured in Brewster's direction. "Meant me, I'll keep the door locked. If you need anything, give a yell and Harley — he patrols the hallway — will handle it." Smith headed out the door with Poland close behind.

Loggin poured himself a cup of coffee. He looked over at Brewster. "You want one?"

"That'd be good."

"Cream . . . sugar?"

"Nah. I take it black."

Loggin put a cup in front of Brewster.

"Thanks." Brewster took a swig. "You a stock-car fan?"

"Yeah . . . from way back. You?"

"Damn straight. Hell — I wuz at Daytona back when Petty copped his second. Man could he drive."

"Never any better . . . though Earnhardt's my choice."

Brewster held out his cup as if toasting. "Number 8. You gotta love him. It's what this country's about."

"I know what you mean." Loggin sipped his coffee. His eyes remained aimed at his cup, but his focus, the mental one, directed at Brewster. The chunky runt with the *AA* tattoo was a better man than Loggin had assumed. Places like Cedar Creek and Potterstown enjoyed a proud past. Guys like Brewster wanted to preserve it. He was no Boy Scout, but with liberal morons ravaging southern traditions, who could blame him? Hell — if Loggin's uncle hadn't bought him a spot on the force years before, he might have gone the same route as Brewster.

An hour slipped by. Loggin suspected the lawyers were off relaxing in some lounge. Lots of times he had seen so-called adversaries, attired in their three hundred dollar suits, schmoozing in the courthouse halls. A few minutes work intermingled with loads of idle gab. All the while, their high-priced meters ran. Loggin resented the waste of his time. He drank another cup. He got one for Brewster as well. Poland and Smith finally returned. Smith motioned Loggin out into the hallway and locked the door behind them. He said, "I think we've worked it out. We'll know as soon as Poland runs it by his client. Our lie-detector man, Phipps, along with a stenographer, is on the way over."

Minutes later, a rap, together with the sound of Poland's voice, came from the other side of the door. "We're all set."

Smith unlocked the door and said, "We'll get started as soon as Phipps and the stenographer arrive. He glanced down the hall. "Here they come now." Once everyone was seated, Smith read a prepared statement that the stenographer took down.

"We are here today, May 19, 1983, to conduct a lie detector test of Jake S. Brewster. It has been agreed by and between Mr. Brewster and his attorney William Poland and myself, Donald Smith, as representative of the District Attorney's Office, that certain designated questions, and only those questions, will be asked of Mr. Brewster. It is further agreed that provided Mr. Brewster answers all those questions under oath and discloses the identity of the person or persons who hired and paid him to employ Orin and Clyde Boxley to set the fire which, on April 16, 1983, destroyed the home of Jordan Jackson at 74 Hickory Lane, and further provided that Mr. Brewster passes said lie detector test to the satisfaction of Paul Phipps, the test administrator, then Mr. Brewster shall be permitted to plead guilty to Arson in the Second Degree, §16-11-110(B) of Article 3 of the South Carolina Code of Laws, in exchange for which plea he shall receive a sentence of nine years in state prison. It is expressly understood that this plea bargain is conditioned upon Mr. Brewster providing testimony in the prosecution of others responsible for the arson and shall be subject to the approval of the Court having competent jurisdiction. In the event that such plea bargain is not so approved or in the event Mr. Brewster fails said lie detector test, nothing he has said in the course of said test shall be used against him in any court of law or for any other purpose whatsoever, and the record of his answers shall be expunged, and the answers given by him shall be deemed as if never spoken."

Smith turned to Poland. "Are we agreed?"

Poland looked at his client. "You understand the terms, and they're consistent with what I outlined to you a few minutes ago?"

"Yeah."

"And you're satisfied?"

"Yup."

Poland turned to Smith. "We're ready to proceed."

Smith glanced at Phipps. "All set?"

Phipps nodded.

Once again, Loggin reluctantly conceded that Smith had more moxie than he had anticipated. But the concession came with qualifications. Loggin had no doubt that if Smith faced the heat of the hard-knock alleys where Loggin earned his pay, Smith's marshmallow insides would turn to goo.

Smith administered an oath to Brewster and then folded back the top sheet of his yellow legal pad. "I'm going to ask you some questions, the same ones Mr. Poland showed you a short time ago. Smith began reading. "What is your full name?"

"John Shandall Brewster. Folks call me Jake."

"How old are you?"

"Forty-six."

"Where do you live?"

"In a trailer out Route 47, halfway between Cedar Creek and Potterstown."

"You have prior convictions for assault, menacing, DUI and reckless driving, among others, don't you?"

Brewster glanced at Poland.

The lawyer nodded. "As I indicated, they help the tester get your baseline readings. Anyway, they're a matter of public record."

"Yeah, I got them convictions."

Loggin kept his eyes trained on Brewster. Years of experience had developed a sixth sense capable of spotting lies. But good as he was, Loggin, ever objective, conceded the lie detector might be better.

"Did you hire Orin and Clyde Boxley to burn down the home of Jordan Jackson at 74 Hickory Lane in Cedar Creek?"

Brewster hesitated. He looked over at Poland again.

The lawyer nodded once more.

Brewster shrugged. "Yeah, I hired 'em."

"How much did you pay them?"

"Four G's."

"Was the arson your idea?"

"No."

Loggin felt a surge of adrenaline. In another moment Brewster would finger *Mr. Big.*

"Did someone hire you?" said Smith.

"Yup."

"Who was it?"

Brewster hesitated again. He leaned over and whispered to Poland. He looked back at the Assistant District Attorney and, in an unequivocal voice, said, "Roger Worthington."

From the corner of his eye, Loggin saw the stenographer wince. Loggin remained impassive. On the job he used the same poker face he sported in his Friday-night card games. That talent had delivered many a winning hand despite an inordinate share of bad deals.

Smith flipped a page in his pad and scrawled a quick note. He looked up at Brewster. "How much, if anything, did this person — whom you've now identified as Roger Worthington — pay you?"

"Eight grand, including the four I gave to the Boxleys."

"Whose idea was it to hire the Boxleys?"

"Worthington. When he contacted me, I told him I wuzn't interested. He said I didn't have to do the job myself. He — " Brewster glanced at Poland.

"That's fine. You can go on."

"Anyway, like I sez, Worthington suggested I hire the Boxleys. It wuz his idea to have one work at the Church Barbecue. That way, if they got caught — somethin' Worthington said weren't gonna happen — they'd have a cover. He said havin' them set the fire would give me extra insulation. That's what he called it. I asked him why he didn't contact the Boxleys himself. He said he wanted extra insulation too."

"Did he hire you in person?"

"Nah, but it wuz him on the phone. I recognized his drawl. I seen him on TV with that local telethon he does with them news people. The one for them retarded kids."

"Last question," said Smith. "Did he tell you why he wanted to burn down Jackson's home."

"Yeah. He said Jackson wuz the one who was killin' his mall. Said the bastard —that's what he called Jackson — wuz tryin' to drive him outta business. He also said he wuz pissed cause Jackson wuz datin' his daughter. I suspected that like me he didn't have no use fur Jackson's kind. That, along with the money, is what got me to ride his train."

Smith took a few moments, seemingly digesting what he had heard. Then he turned to Phipps. "So, what's the verdict."

"Give me a minute."

Loggin didn't need a minute. Nor did he need the lie detector. Antennae, highly sensitized from years of interrogation, had weighed Brewster's every word and every move. Brewster had told it like it was.

Phipps examined the printout his machine's tracking needles had produced. Up and down, back and forth, he perused the lines. Finally, he said, "Jake Brewster told the truth. No one who was lying could produce these gavalnic skin responses. It doesn't happen."

Loggin leaned back. If he were in his office, his feet would have gone up onto his desk. He had caught the Boxleys, then Brewster, and in a few short hours, he would arrest Roger Worthington, Cedar Creek's richest citizen. Loggin sucked in a satisfying breath. The master was at the top of his game.

———————

Lauren poked her head through the kitchen door making sure her father was no longer in the dining room. He had moved to the living room and settled into his big easy chair to watch the news. Lauren shut the kitchen door. "Bessie," she said, "I can't keep coming here for dinner. My father is driving me nuts. Every time it's the same story. Little hints why I should give up my newspaper job and work for him. And soon enough he moves into one of his tirades why I should stop dating Jordan."

Bessie continued to dry a serving platter. "Well — he believes that you should date someone of your own race."

"You're not taking his side?"

"I'm not taking anyone's side."

Accurate or not, Lauren had anticipated support. Ever since her mother had died, Bessie had served as a buffer whenever communication with her father had begun to break down. In Lauren's teenage years Bessie's knack at negotiating leeway, an extra hour on Lauren's curfew or another inch or two off her hemline, had helped soften her father's strict rules. Even when he had remained intractable, Bessie's patient ear had mitigated distasteful outcomes. With Lauren now an adult and her father's worst side evident, how could Bessie turn a deaf ear? Lauren said, "Of all people I thought you'd stand up for me."

"What — and tell you to defy your father and marry Jordan?"

"Better than allowing Simon Legree to treat you like nineteenth-century chattel."

The platter in one hand and a dishcloth in the other, Bessie turned from the sink and glowered.

The look, an unfamiliar one, had Lauren swallowing hard. How could she attack Bessie. Compounding matters, how could the blow be so low. Let me have it, she thought. I deserve it.

Bessie stood motionless for several seconds and then shook her head ever so slightly. Her voice soft, she said, "I could tell myself to consider the source if someone else had spoken those words. But coming from you, you might as well have called me a — " She halted midstream and then muttered, "Don't say it." She pressed her lips together. Though her face bore a stoic veil, underlying hurt permeated the façade.

Lauren surmised the unspoken word. Labeling Bessie an Uncle Tom was tantamount to calling her that worst of epithets. Had she spat at Bessie, the slight would have been less. If only she hadn't made the remark. Words, the very commodity that day in and day out Lauren selected with utmost care, had rashly streamed from her mouth. A seasoned journalist, at least she thought herself one, she had behaved like a rookie. "I'm sorry," she said. "I didn't mean it."

"Maybe you didn't, but you said it."

Instinct encouraged another apology. Judgment suggested the utterance would be vapid. Lauren said, "You could have blasted me. I deserved it. Instead you contained yourself. I can't imagine how."

A sober-faced Bessie laid the platter and dishcloth onto the sink. "I was born in 1936. I grew up with segregated schools, buses and bathrooms. Dr. King's birthday, whether or not they finally make it a holiday, is important to me." She turned and gazed out the kitchen window. "Earlier you used the word *chattel*. I was never a slave, but my ancestors were. Growing up, I suffered many indignities, but compared to earlier generations, I had it good." She turned back to Lauren. "Like the Bible teaches, like Dr. King preached, I learned to turn the other cheek."

Lauren swallowed hard. For years she had denigrated her father's views. But there in her own home, she had ignored the condescension he had heaped on Bessie. In his own convoluted way he treated Bessie well. He valued her work. He paid her a good wage and even respected her. But underlying their relationship was a haughty premise. He was the master and she, if not the servant, certainly subservient. "Why did you stay all these years?"

"What do you mean?" said Bessie.

Lauren saw beyond Bessie's words. The housekeeper was trying to avoid the question. Lauren wanted to press the issue; however, her earlier lapse demanded discretion. "As far back as I can remember, you were part of our family. But roles were well defined; so well, that I was blind to the incivility. I took you for granted. Never once did you call me on it."

Bessie stepped closer and put her arm on Lauren's shoulder. "You weren't as blind as you suggest."

The pardon, perhaps more generous than underlying thoughts, was welcome. Still Lauren longed for an answer. She hesitated, but yielded, as delicately as possible, to temptation.

"You deserved better. You could have left, but you didn't. Why?"

Bessie turned to the window again. An instant later she walked out of the kitchen into the den.

Lauren chided herself. Wasn't one slight enough? Did she need to compound the *faux pas* with a denigrating question, one posed with knowledge aforethought.

A minute later Bessie returned with a picture frame in hand. She held it out. "This is why I stayed."

"My mother?"

"Yes, your mother." Bessie eyed the photo. "She was a good person. A very good person. When she died, you were too young to recognize the difference between your parents. Your mother treated me with respect. Yes, I was her employee, but first and foremost I was a human being, entitled to dignity and respect. On that score your mother never left any doubt." Bessie looked Lauren in the eye. "You are your mother's daughter."

Lauren gazed at the photograph. Pride, like a balm, soothed an ailing conscience.

"As you surely recall, your mother lived for several days following the accident that took her life. Before she died, she asked me to care for you."

"Out of duty to my mother, you sacrificed your own life?"

Bessie shook her head. "You were like my own child. I had helped raise you from birth. With your mother gone, I couldn't abandon you. Even if she hadn't asked me to stay, I would have."

For years Bessie had been like a mother to Lauren. Little had Lauren realized that Bessie was, indeed, her second mother. "How did my parents get along?"

"Why do you ask?"

Lauren thought the question was self-evident, given her ongoing friction with her father. "You said I'm like my mother. How did she put up with him?"

"Actually she loved him. And don't look surprised. Your father was an excellent provider. And, more important, he put your mother on a pedestal."

"What about their differing views?"

"It was another era. Feminism was barely in its infancy. Few men embraced it. Certainly not your father. He was the man of the house. Your mother accepted that. In fact, she endorsed it." Bessie looked Lauren in the eye again. "No one is perfect. Your mother made allowances for your father. And don't frown. I'm sure you do it as well. We all do."

Though a seeming truism, Lauren had qualms. Before she could pinpoint them, Bessie said, "Martin Luther King and John F. Kennedy. I suspect you admire them both."

"Of course. But so what. My father is hardly Dr. King or JFK."

"That's not the point. Both philandered. That offends us, but we make allowances. Your mother loved your father. She made allowances."

"And you made them also."

"I suppose." Bessie sighed. "It's hard to explain, even to myself. I was a product of an earlier generation. My mother — may she rest in peace — didn't believe in rocking the boat. She accepted her lot. But she valued education, and, thanks to her, I read everything I could get my hands on: Cervantes, Sophicles, Swift, Flaubert — you name it. Books were my escape. Like their characters I was free to dream. But my mother also taught me to accept the world the way it was. Not that it was fair. She wanted to spare me undue pain." Bessie paused; her empty gaze seemingly directed nowhere.

Lauren remained silent suspecting that Bessie preferred to pursue her own thoughts. For all the years that Lauren had confided in Bessie, this was the first time personal disclosures had flowed the other way. The observation, its seeming egocentric implications, sparked guilt. But was it not that way in most mother-daughter relationships? Conscience hinted the rhetorical question might be a rationalization.

"My youngest sister — she was thirteen years my junior — grew up in a different world. *Brown* was decided by the Supreme Court when she was only five. Unlike me, she had a rebellious side. In her teens she saw the possibilities of change, and she pushed the envelope." Bessie heaved a sigh. "Her road was tougher than mine. Much tougher. But praise to her, and those like her, with the courage to stand up."

"But you — " The ring of the doorbell clipped Lauren's tongue. Bessie was on her way to answer it. Lauren followed as far as the dining room just to see who was there. A moment later Bessie opened the door. Detective Loggin stood on the doorstep.

"Mr. Worthington home?"

"Yes, but — "

"That's okay, Bessie," said Lauren's father, as he came into the hallway. "I'll handle it." He approached the door. "What can I do for you, Frank?"

"Sorry 'bout this, Mr. Worthington," said Loggin. "I have to arrest you."

"You what!" said Lauren's father.

"I have to — "

"I heard you the first time. What the hell is this about?"

Lauren watched in disbelief as Loggin held out a pair of handcuffs and started putting them onto her father's wrists. She moved from the dining room into the hallway.

"I'm arresting you for arson, setting the fire which burned the home of Jordan Jackson."

"You gotta be nuts." He pointed the index finger of one of his cuffed hands in Loggin's direction. "I'm gonna have your job."

"It's nothing personal. It's — "

"Sure. And when I sue your ass, it won't be personal either."

Loggin pulled off his cap. "I have to read you your rights." He stared at the inside of his cap and read the *Miranda* warnings. As he did, Lauren walked toward the doorway. "Stay right there, Miss."

"Why are you arresting my father?"

"Like I said — for the arson at Jackson's place."

"What makes you think my father's involved?"

"I'm not at liberty to discuss the details. The Judge, along with the DA, will give the *what fors* at the arraignment tomorrow."

Lauren's father separated his wrists, as far as the cuffs allowed. "Loggin, you've got one last chance to remove these bracelets. If not, you'll be sleeping in the gutter when I'm through with you."

"Can't do that, Mr. Worthington. I gotta take you down to the station."

"You plan to stick me in jail until the arraignment?"

Loggin shrugged. "I gotta take you down for booking." He turned to Lauren. "You might wanna call your dad's lawyer. Maybe he can arrange bail or something. Don't get me wrong though. I ain't telling you what to do." He put his hand on her father's arm and drew him toward the porch. "We gotta go to the station now."

Lauren walked to the doorway and watched as Loggin escorted her father down Worthington Hall's marble walkway to the squad car."

"I'm sure your father is not involved," said Bessie.

"He couldn't be," said Lauren. However, comments from Ward and Laughlin, still fresh in her memory, made her less sanguine. A moment later the squad car drove off. As she watched the vehicle disappear around the bend, she contemplated what to do. Her first thought, call Jordan. He was the one she needed to talk to. And he was a lawyer; just what her father needed. Common sense forced her to acknowledge it was a bad idea. The man whose house was burned could hardly represent the person charged. Regardless, her father would never want Jordan as his attorney, not that Jordan would want her father as a client. Lauren went to the telephone and dialed Chester Harwood, her father's lawyer of many years.

Chapter XI

The moment she walked into her apartment the flashing red light on her telephone answering machine caught Lauren's eye. She pressed the message button.

> *Hi, Sweetie. If it's okay, I'll try to meet you at the theater tonight. My EBT in Columbia is sure to run late. The insurance company deposed my client this morning, but the defendant — he's from Virginia — missed his connecting flight and won't arrive until four. By the time we finish his testimony, it'll be close to six. That's assuming all goes smoothly. No promises. Hope you had a good day. Love you.*

Earlier Lauren had considered canceling their plans to see *Fiddler on the Roof* at the Cedar Creek Community Theater. Less than twenty-four hours had elapsed since her father's arrest. Chester Harwood had arranged bail, $50,000, which her father had posted. Both Harwood and her father had said there was nothing she could do. Because she had the tickets already, she dressed and headed to the theater. She assumed that Jordan was still unaware of her father's arrest since he had driven to Columbia for his deposition the afternoon before.

She arrived at the theater about 7:45, fifteen minutes before show time. The tiny, white chapel, formerly a Methodist Church, had become home to local stage productions. As she waited outside for Jordan, she studied the stained-glass windows that decorated the front: Creation — God, encircled by depictions of the seven days; the Garden of Eden, with its forbidden fruit; Noah, at the entrance to the ark, with the animals marching in two by two; and the Last Supper. As a child in her Episcopalian Sunday school, she had learned those stories well. Three consecutive years she had perfect attendance. But that was long ago. In high school her interest in religion had waned. Once she went to college, services became a thing of the past. Apart from a few weddings and funerals she had not attended church in the better part of a decade. She hadn't missed it either. But standing there, she welcomed the messages of the richly colored windows. She realized that her youthful repetition of the biblical parables and proverbs had helped shape her values. Though never a fan of dogma, she appreciated her religious background. No doubt it had made her a better person, as well as a better journalist. She gazed up at the steeple. It evoked fond memories, but the possibility of going to services, even occasionally, was out of the question; at least for the present. She checked her watch. Four minutes to eight. No sign of Jordan. She hurried into the theater. She gave one ticket to an usher and asked him to watch for Jordan. She took her seat in the tenth row, roughly halfway back. A moment later the overture began.

About ten minutes into the show Jordan arrived. "Sorry, I'm late," he whispered, as he seated himself in the aisle seat adjacent to her.

"Things go well in Columbia?"

"Generally. I'll tell you later."

She refocused on the show, but in the back of her mind concerns stirred how he would react to her father's arrest. Her answer would have to await intermission. Soon enough it came.

"How do you like the show?" he said.

"Excellent. Tevye is so dynamic."

"Plus he has that wonderful baritone voice." Jordan was already on his feet. "I need to use the rest-room."

She concluded he hadn't heard the news. Perhaps it could wait until after the show. Several minutes went by. Soon the flickering house lights announced the commencement of the second act. A moment later Jordan returned to his seat.

"I thought you got lost."

"Believe it or not, the men's room had a longer line than the ladies'. And just as I was leaving, Bill Walker corralled me. Asked me what I thought about your father's arrest. Talk about a blind side."

"I was going to tell you." The house lights went down and the curtain rose. "I . . . I didn't — "

"Shh," came a voice from behind.

"We'll discuss it later," whispered Jordan, and he turned to the stage.

Lauren looked there too, but her attention remained divided. The second act was excellent; even better than the first. As Tevye and his family, displaced from their homes, lugged their few possessions over the muddy roads of the Russian tundra, Lauren brushed back tears. The haunting sound of the fiddler's violin augured a venture into the unknown. The notes faded, the curtain fell, and soon enough the cast took its final bows to a standing ovation. The applause waned. The time for even bigger dramatics had arrived. She debated how to broach the subject. She could go directly to the arrest. Or maybe ease into it with some small talk. Perhaps a question about the show or Jordan's trip. Indecision led to a third option. Give Jordan the first word.

"So?" he said, waiting for the aisle to clear.

So *what*, wondered Lauren, unable to decipher his ambiguous tone.

"Did you enjoy the show?"

"They did a great job. What did you think?"

"Frankly, I was distracted." He stepped out into the aisle and made room for her to follow. "I was surprised you didn't tell me about your father's arrest sooner."

"I didn't — " She cut herself off. Lack of opportunity was not the reason. "I guess I should have."

He looked around. "We'll talk about it outside."

They left the building and descended the cement steps that led to the sidewalk. He pointed across the street to a nearby bench. "Over there. Okay?" They walked to the bench and seated themselves. He said, "Tell me the details."

"You know as much as I do."

Jordan looked her in the eye. "You have no idea why the police charged your father?"

"Not really. They claim he hired some fellow named Brewster who enlisted the Boxleys to do the job. I know you heard about them."

For a moment Jordan seemed to grit his teeth, but then he blurted out, "Well, I can't say I'm surprised."

"At what?"

"That your father's behind it."

"My father! How can you even think that?"

"Wait a second. The police, not me, are pointing the finger. And from what Bill Walker said, that Brewster fellow passed a lie detector test."

"I don't care what he passed. I know my father. He couldn't have done it." The stone face that greeted her words did nothing to alleviate her frustration. "Of all people I can't believe you think my father is guilty."

Jordan heaved a sigh. He gazed skyward and muttered, "Lord, you having fun again?"

Ordinarily, Lauren got a kick out of Jordan's shtick. Not this time. "What's that about?"

"Like Tevye, I'm asking the Lord — Why? And don't give me that look. Not when you're making me out to be the bad guy. In case you forgot, I'm the one who lost his house. Your father, on the other hand, is the alleged firebug."

"Why would he do it?" The instant the spontaneous utterance passed her lips, Lauren kicked herself knowing her words had put her in the crosshairs of a loaded gun.

A smirk sneaked through Jordan's seemingly warm smile. "In case you've forgotten, I'm the fellow blocking his mall. Worse yet, I'm dating his daughter. Me — with dark skin. And him . . . " Jordan's voice trailed off momentarily. "I think you get my drift."

The weight of the evidence had Lauren on the defensive, but she was determined to defend her father. Across the street on the theater marquee the big letters that spelled out *Fiddler on the Roof* caught her eye. "In some respects my Dad is like Tevye."

Jordan nodded slowly. "When you put it that way, I understand. What your saying is your father struggles in abject poverty, and all the while, his God ignores his supplications." Jordan gestured with both arms toward the heavens. "Lord, how canst thee be so cruel to thy child, Roger Worthington? Thou suffer him to dwell in the affliction of his pillared mansion, while others bask in their decrepit hovels. What divine — "

"Save your theatrics for a courtroom. I get your point."

"Terrific. Because I don't get yours."

"What I was referring to," said Lauren, defense of her father becoming secondary, "was the conflict Tevye faced when his daughters rejected his traditional values. First his eldest spurned arranged marriage. The next announced that she was joining her rebel boyfriend in Siberia. Tevye continued to bend until his third daughter wanted to marry outside the faith. That pushed him over the edge."

Exasperation showed on Jordan's face. "So, what are you saying?"

"Like Tevye, change is difficult for my father. His views are steeped in tradition."

"You mean like slavery."

Lauren's gut screamed protest. The facts, her family history, silenced her. She choked on the truth. "What I meant was my father's childhood was etched in an era of segregation. The idea of his daughter marrying an African-American is as hard for him to accept as it was for Tevye when his daughter decided to wed outside the faith."

"Isn't it about time your father adjusts. After all, he's had decades since statutes prohibiting miscegenation were declared unconstitutional."

"It's not — "

Jordan held up his hand. "Let me finish." His tone was uncharacteristically sharp. "The Russians persecuted Tevye and his fellow Jews, seizing their homes and evicting them from their village. Amidst such abuse, his daughter's resolve to marry a Russian understandably angered him. Regardless, in the end, Tevye, in his own way, acquiesced. Your father, on the other hand, is the persecutor, not the persecuted. To suggest past wrongs, especially his own, excuse his current failings is outrageous."

Lauren found it hard to disagree. Emotion, not logic, had prompted her analogy. She had no excuse for her father's racist behavior.

"By the way," said Jordan, "Tevye, unlike your father, never resorted to burning anyone's home."

"You . . . you really believe my father set fire to your house."

"Let me reiterate. The police do. And their case against him reveals motive, plus an implicating co-conspirator. We'll see what a jury says."

Lauren disliked the response, not that it was unfair; only that it underscored how bad her father's situation appeared.

Jordan heaved a sigh and then took her hand. "I don't mean to give you a hard time. I know you're in a tough position." He ran his fingers over hers. "Damn. This mess is making me crazy. I'm sorry."

"Me too," she said, welcoming the olive branch he had extended. In the face of cross words he often found a way to suppress pride. Lauren, on the other hand, was her father's daughter.

Jordan glanced at his watch. "Shall we stop at the *Black Lantern* for dessert and coffee?"

His voice revealed a trace of reticence. Or was she projecting her own frustration onto him. She said, "I'll go if you want, but I'm not very hungry."

"To tell you the truth, I'm really tired. Last night I stayed up until two reviewing my file for the deposition. And today was a marathon. By the time we finished at the courthouse, it was six-thirty. I drove directly here from Columbia."

"Perhaps we should call it a night."

"Maybe so." He gestured off to the left. "I parked in the next block. I'll walk you to your car."

She pointed. "It's right over there."

They walked to her car. He kissed her good night. She climbed in, and he headed off. The abrupt end to the evening left her cold. She was annoyed with Jordan but even more with herself. His home had been burned. At times her words, rather than empathetic, had rubbed the ashes in his face. She gazed out the windshield into the dark space ahead. When she and Jordan had first begun dating, she knew her father would have misgivings, but she assumed that with time the two men would develop mutual respect. Time, however, more than six months, had proved her assumption wrong. To make matters worse, friction between the men was contaminating her relationship with each. Her professional life was faring no better. Nielsen had threatened to fire her. He had labeled her a pretentious know-it-all. He had predicted she would run for cover when things got tough. Maybe — just maybe — Nielsen was right.

———————

Jordan's fingers lumbered over his computer keyboard. He typed several words and then deleted them. The process repeated itself over and over. Drafting a complaint for litigation, most of it boilerplate, was second nature. He could do it in his sleep. Why then was *lawyers' block*, or some such affliction, inhibiting him. Allegation after allegation, the same question nagged. Why not press the insurance company for a settlement? Let them subrogate to his rights. They could go after Worthington and the goons he had hired to set the fire. The logic was impeccable, but Jordan continued to pound the keys. Important as the money was, the matter had become personal. When it went to court, he wanted to look Roger Worthington in the eye and examine him under oath. Watching an insurance company lawyer ask the questions wouldn't cut it.

Jordan drew his hands back from the keys. The old adage, *A lawyer who represents himself has a fool for a client*, popped into his head. He needed to rethink what he was doing. If he let the insurance company handle the matter, his financial loss from the fire might be fully and quickly compensated. The insurance company, not he, would bear the risk of an unfavorable outcome in court. And Worthington, if responsible, would still be called to account. The People, represented by the District Attorney, were prosecuting Worthington for the crimes of arson and conspiracy. The litany of reasons was compelling. The rationale was unimpeachable. Jordan reached for the telephone and began to dial Dick Parks, the attorney for his insurer, *Rockhill Indemnity and Casualty.* Just before he pressed the final digit, Jordan's fingers froze. Arson, an intentional tort, would support a claim for punitive damages, and Jordan wanted to make that argument himself. The image of an insurance company lawyer delivering a summation to the jury left him empty. After what Worthington had done to him, Jordan was entitled to extract his pound of flesh, and extract it he would. He hung up the telephone. His fingers returned to the keyboard. They danced across the keys spelling out the allegations of his complaint.

Lauren pressed the doorbell. As usual, she wasn't carrying the key to Worthington Hall. She glanced at her watch. She was ten minutes late. In recent weeks she had been making excuses, managing to skip her father's Tuesday-evening ritual nearly half the time. If she had it her way, she would have skipped it altogether. But now with her father out on bail with felony charges, he needed her support.

The front door opened. "Hi Bessie," said Lauren.

"Good evening. I like your blouse." Bessie gestured toward the mauve, *Lyonnais* silk that Lauren was wearing.

"Thanks." Her voice lowered to a whisper. "What kind of mood is his nibs in tonight?"

Bessie shook her head and then pointed at Lauren's watch.

"I know," said Lauren. "I was working on a story and lost track of time. I should have called before I left the office."

"Bessie, is that Lauren?" came her father's voice from the dining room.

"Yes, Dad. It's me." She waited a moment anticipating a response.

"You better get in there," said Bessie softly, "before his thermometer gets any higher."

Lauren hurried into the dining room. "Hi Dad."

He looked over toward the far corner at the grandfather clock, a 1790 antique original by Issac Thomas, master clockmaker of Willistown, Pennsylvania. The exquisite

timepiece had been in the family for over a century. "No doubt
Mr. Thomas appreciated time, enough to wrap his bell-strike
movement in a shell-carved door with fluted columns."
Lauren's father shook his head. "Apparently I failed to measure
up to Mr. Thomas' example and teach you the virtue of
punctuality."

"I'm sorry I'm late. I — "

"I wasn't criticizing you. I was scolding myself."

Sure, thought Lauren, aware the evening might be even
more difficult than most. She seated herself in her usual seat.

"But you could have called."

"I know. I lost track of time; not that it's an excuse."

"Certainly not." He gestured toward himself. "Mind you,
I'm not complaining. But Bessie saves her best for Tuesday
evenings when she knows you're coming." He looked over at
Bessie who had just come in from the kitchen. "Isn't that right,
Bessie?"

She said nothing as she placed a shrimp cocktail in front
of Lauren's father. She started toward the other end of the table.

"Even my help ignores me." He smiled.

As Bessie put Lauren's shrimp, her favorite, in front of her,
Lauren marveled how Bessie, as usual, had slipped the jab with
neither confrontation nor damage to her dignity. When needed,
Bessie could tactfully fence with her employer. Esteem, not
venom, filled their exchanges. The distinction reminded Lauren
of a wonderful lesson Professor Warren had taught her in
Psychology 101. He had students act out scenes in which they
exchanged repeated digs. Then he put them on a spectrum; on
the one side, caustic barbs that cut deep, and the other, friendly
digs, laden with affection. Lauren discovered that the same
remark could translate into either *you're a jerk* or *I respect you*,
depending on the context, tone, past relationship of the parties,
etc. Even on those short-tempered occasions when Lauren's
father's remarks tested the line of civility, Bessie coolly
deflected them. Lauren wished that she could be more like
Bessie. She told herself she could if her father treated her like
an adult rather than a schoolgirl. Her objective side, one she
proudly brought to her journalistic career, rejected the
rationalization. Undeniably if she and Bessie had reversed roles,

Lauren would have quit years before. Being Roger Worthington's employee was even tougher than being his daughter.

"You're awfully quiet," said her father, gazing down the length of the table.

Lauren gestured at her mouth, as she finished chewing a shrimp. Her musings, if disclosed, would spark a rancorous response. She welcomed the chance to carefully choose her words. She said, "I was savoring the shrimp. They're excellent."

"You should tell Bessie."

For a change her father had a valid point. She made a mental note to follow it.

"You'll never guess what I received this morning."

Her father's sardonic tone discouraged the appetite to guess, not that she had any idea. "You'll have to tell me."

"A summons and complaint from your dear friend, Jordan Jackson. He's suing me for damages for the destruction of his home. It's not enough that I'm being criminally prosecuted for the fire. My daughter's boyfriend has to compound the outrage."

"Well, considering — " Lauren clipped her tongue. Explaining to her father that presumably the insurance company would have brought the lawsuit in Jordan's name if he hadn't was a bad idea. Asking her father whether he was responsible for the fire was worse yet. Weeks earlier the mere suggestion at the Village Board meeting had enraged him. Even her circuitous attempt to broach the subject shortly after he had posted bail drew his indignation.

He said, "For once you might take my side."

Taking sides. Lauren had already rejected the idea. Telling that to her father was another bad idea.

"Just as I thought. You're siding with Jordan."

"That's not fair. I didn't say a word."

"That's exactly the point. If you didn't agree with him, you would have said so." He turned toward Bessie as she came through the kitchen door. "My daughter is sticking up for that boyfriend of hers. She doesn't care that he wants to put me in prison. Really nice, isn't it?"

Bessie took away the dish that had held his shrimp. "Would you prefer Thousand Island, ranch, blue cheese or balsamic vinaigrette on your salad?"

Lauren observed the frustrated look on her father's face. Bessie went about her business as if unaware of the reaction. Lauren wondered why her own attempts to ignore her father, unlike Bessie's, never worked. Perhaps it was simply a matter of luck. The explanation might have been comforting were it not ridiculous.

Her father threw up his hands and stared at the ceiling. "Does no one around here listen to me?" He turned to Bessie, who was already on her way back to the kitchen. "I'll have Thousand Island for a change." He shook his head and then gazed down to the other end of the table. "So, when the usher asks, *bride or groom?* — What do you plan to say?"

Lauren did a double take; confusion, not avoidance, behind her silence.

"When my case comes to trial, will you be sitting behind Jordan or on the defendant's side with me?"

Clarification, what she was looking for, had been provided. She realized ignorance had its advantages. "You're putting me in an impossible position. I'm not taking sides."

"Sure, ever the objective newspaperwoman."

The label, Lauren's goal since becoming a journalist, had suddenly become insidious. "Can't we change the subject. Something lighter perhaps."

He leaned back and folded his arms. He muttered, but loud enough for her to hear. "I'm facing years in prison — maybe the rest of my life — and my daughter can't be bothered."

Lauren did a slow burn. Better to let her father have the last word than continue the futile exchange. She focused on her salad, which, complete with dressing, had just arrived. Unlike her father, she always opted for the low-fat balsamic vinaigrette. Bessie knew Lauren well enough that asking was superfluous. Indeed, Bessie knew them both inside and out.

Through the remainder of the evening, there were no inquisitions. At no time did her father raise the issue of her moving back home. Reminiscences of earlier days allowed her mind to drift away from thoughts of arson and criminal prosecution. When she left shortly before nine, she was in a good mood considering it was Tuesday. On the way home she stopped at Wilbur's Pharmacy to pick up some toothpaste. Charlie Wilbur, the proprietor, who had taken over the fifty-year old business from his father, was about to close.

"Am I too late?" said Lauren.

Charlie glanced at his watch and shrugged. "Come on in." He locked the door behind them.

"Thanks," she said. "I just need some toothpaste. I'll be quick." She hurried to the dental section where she grabbed a tube of *Gleam*. She brought it to the counter and paid for it. "I appreciate your accommodating me."

He chuckled. "I could pretend I'm doing you a favor, but it wouldn't be true. It's the way my Dad always ran the place. As he put it, we need our customers more than they need us. These days with the chain stores, it's truer than ever." Charlie ushered Lauren to the door and unlocked it. As she started out, he said, "If you don't mind me saying, I hope the Board goes thumbs down on your father's mall. I understand he hopes to bring in a *CVS* or a *Long's*." Charlie heaved a sigh. "An independent like me has a snow cone's chance in an oven against those giants." A reticent look came over his face. "Regardless, I wish him good luck with his newest difficulties."

"Thanks," said Lauren. "Both for the words of support and . . . (she gestured with her bag) the toothpaste."

"And thanks to you." He shut the door.

Before heading to her car, she paused a moment, gazing up and down Broad Street. Forthright, hardworking shopkeepers like Charlie Wilbur were hard to come by. For years they had been the backbone of the Village. Vacant storefronts attested that time had taken its toll. Might Cedar Mall be the death knell? Or was it, as her father claimed, the means for the Village to be reborn? Knowledgeable and objective expertise was needed. What naiveté, what arrogance had convinced her, close as she was to the principals, that she was right for the task. A neon sign on the store's façade went out. She stared into the pharmacy window where her faint image reflected back. Like Broad Street, her image had dulled;

however, in her case the change had been far more rapid. The sound of footsteps turned her head. She recognized the face, though for a moment she couldn't place it. Just as he drew close, it hit her. The passerby was the skinny guy who had solicited money from Jordan. "Excuse me. Aren't you the fellow my friend gave money?"

The shaved-head guy stopped. He peered and then pointed at her. "You're that reporter that's datin' Jackson, ain't ya?"

She nodded. "How do you know him?"

"Hey, it's a small town. Everybody knows everybody. Ain't that so? Anyway, everybody knows your boyfriend. He's a big-shot lawyer. On the Village Board and all."

She studied the fellow. She judged his age around late-twenties, a bit more than she had earlier recalled. "But not everyone slips the next person thirty or forty dollars."

The guy shrugged. "Hey, some do and some don't."

The jabber did little to satisfy her curiosity. But the line between revealing questions and those which would drive him off was fine. She said, "Do you know Jordan well?"

"Well enough." He laughed, the sound as devilish as his eyes.

"Does Jordan represent you?"

He laughed again. This time, more of a snort. "You must be kidding. You think I could afford a high-priced lawyer like him."

"So, how do you know him?"

The guy folded his arms. "What's it to you?"

A skinhead from the *Aryan Alliance* fraternizing with a liberal black man was hardly conventional. Logical though the point was, it left discretion's border far in its wake. She said, "He and I are dating. It's always nice to know his friends."

"Who sez we're friends?"

"He gave you money, didn't he?"

"So — you pay taxes." The guy gave Lauren a mocking look. "Tell me it's cause them government politicians is your friends."

The self-satisfied smirk that accompanied the weak analogy invited a slam, but experience counseled otherwise. "I see your point. But taxes aren't a choice."

"They is for some of us." He glared at Lauren. "Not everyone kowtows to them money grubbers in Washington."

Lauren took a deep breath, giving second thoughts to the judicious approach. "What I was trying to say is that one doesn't normally give money to anyone who asks."

"Speak for yourself, lady. Just yesterday, I gave some homeless panhandler fifty cents. Hadn't never seen him before, but that didn't stop me."

"That was nice of you, but — " Lauren hesitated. Prudence be damned. She wanted an explanation. She snapped, "That's not forty dollars."

The guy pointed at her. "You're awfully nosy. Course it figures. You're a reporter."

"You didn't explain why Jordan gave you the money."

"You're goddamn right. And I ain't gonna. So mind your own business." He started to walk away. He turned back. "By the way, it wuz you, not me, that claimed that me and Jackson is friends. Stick that weed in your column and smoke it." He headed down the street.

She watched him as he disappeared into the night. Who was he? What was his connection to Jordan? Once again, Lauren had questions. And no answers.

Chapter XII

*F*ocus. Lauren chided herself as she stared at her computer. The story she was working on, the after-school program at the youth center, was easy. Well — it should have been. But a distracted mind — preoccupation with her father's troubles, friction with Jordan and other nagging concerns — was making it a chore. Minutes before Nielsen had strolled past her desk without a word. The glower he had directed her way dispelled any possibility that inward thoughts might have been behind his silence.

The ring of her telephone drew her attention. "Worthington speaking."

"It's your favorite radio personality, Jerry Baker. How've you been?"

"Good," she said, his superficiality exceeded only by hers. "What can I do for you?"

"Thought you'd like a return engagement on my show."

The instant she had heard Baker's voice, she had anticipated the invitation. With her father charged with arson, a double root canal would have been more appealing. But telling that to Baker would be a mistake. "Things are rather busy. I'll take a rain check."

"Fine. Suppose we do it in a week or two?"

To deter him, ingenuity was a must. She hesitated. Ingenuity was out of town. "As I said, I've got a lot on my plate."

"Well, I'm sure you can squeeze in an hour for my show. You pick the night. Anything but a weekend. I'm not on then."

"I know." Lauren waited several seconds. "Hello. You still there?"

"You left me speechless. I didn't expect a liberal like you would know my schedule. Next thing you'll tell me you're a regular listener."

"Never miss." Trading quips with him had grown easier since her first appearance.

"Great," said Baker. "Then coming back will be just like home."

She kicked herself. Banter was great, except when you stick your foot into your mouth. "I appreciate the invitation, but . . . "

"But what?"

"But I think I'll pass."

"You wouldn't want to do that."

Wanna bet. And who are you to tell me anyway. She chose her words more carefully. "As I said, I'm going to pass."

"I doubt that."

"Excuse me," she said, tested patience sharpening her tone.

"Let me put it this way. You'd be ill-advised to decline."

An egotistical laugh rang in her ears. Her blood boiling, she waited for an explanation.

"Can I take your silence as a *yes*?"

"No. And what do you want with me anyway?" Another laugh greeted her ears; this one diabolic. "What's so funny?"

"You, of all people — a newspaperwoman — pretending to play dumb. Why does that paper of yours put rapes and homicides on the front page? Cause they sell copy. It's no different with me. My listeners froth at the mouth for a liberal like you. And now with your conservative, white father charged with burning down your black boyfriend's house, what more could I ask for?"

"You're like those damn tabloids."

"C'mon — save your almightier than Thou, left-wing sentiments for the folks who watch PBS. In the meantime, I'll pencil you in for next Wednesday, the 17th."

"Not so fast."

"What — you prefer a different date?"

Damn. The creep refuses to quit. "Look — I'm busy. I'll call you if and when I decide to do the show."

"Well — " There was a long pause. "Have it your way."

The ease with which he had suddenly given in came as a pleasant surprise; one, however, that was only fleeting.

"While we've been talking, I've been taking notes. I've also got the tapes of your past appearances. I doubt my listeners will appreciate you dodging them, especially after you promised to follow through. With a little encouragement — I'll supply that — your editor will be swamped with unflattering mail." Baker lowered his voice. "My dear, you can put that on the record."

"You're threatening me," said Lauren.

"Gosh, you think so?"

She did a slow burn. His earlier arm-twisting had tightened into a hammer lock. Only a cry of *uncle* would release it. "Fine. I'll do your show next Wednesday night."

"Glad you see it my way." He cleared his throat. "You have a nice day."

"Thanks." She halted the urge to slam the receiver just before it hit the cradle. She thought back to the first time he had called. What foolishness had prompted her to accept that first invitation? The rhetorical question had a distasteful answer. Ego.

———

Seated next to her father in the first row of Village Hall, Lauren remained impassive. She would have preferred a seat alone in the rear corner, but her father had asked her to sit with him.

Laughlin had quickly disposed of a series of inconsequential matters. He had saved discussion of the mall for last. "To bring everyone up to speed," he said, "our consultant has begun examining the plethora of issues surrounding the mall. Were it not for tawdry developments, the topic would not be before us tonight. However, a consensus of this Board determined that Mr. Worthington's arrest has raised concerns worthy of immediate advertency."

As Laughlin reached for his water glass, Lauren observed his self-satisfied look. That communication suffered, a victim of verbosity, mattered little when the man of letters enjoyed a chance to display his elocutionary and linguistic skills.

"Lest anyone misconstrue this Board's position," he said, his speech even more affected than usual, "let me elucidate. Our re-evaluation of issues pertaining to the mall casts no aspersions on Mr. Worthington. With utmost respect for his presumption of innocence, we focus exclusively on the needs of Cedar Creek. That said — sound judgment demands that his proposed mall be viewed in the context of potential adverse eventualities. The charges that Mr. Worthington faces are real. Might the mall become a project begun, but one unfinished. Might Cedar Creek be the recipient of a white elephant? Such risks in mind, the question whether to defer the mall must be weighed."

Lauren dared not look to her left. The oscillation of her father's foot, visible from the corner of her eye, hinted that rage was brewing. A check of the back of his neck for the telltale protruding veins would have verified her suspicion. She wondered how long he would keep his cool.

"Mr. Chairman," said Janet Warner, "may I be heard?"

"The floor is yours."

"I see no need to halt our consideration of the mall. The process — "

Of course, thought Lauren. The insurance agent hopes to rake in thousands providing coverage. She wants the project to move forward, wise or not. The jaundiced reaction launched Lauren on a tangent. When she had first become a newspaper reporter, she had quickly discovered the need for skepticism. Public officials, like Warner, soon increased those doubts. Recent days had converted her into a full-blown cynic. Even the persons closest to her were subject to question. The possibility her father had set fire to Jordan's home was real. And Jordan's connection to the skinhead with the *AA* tattoo had stirred questions. If that weren't enough, self-doubts had her re-examining her own credibility. She pushed the vexing thoughts just below the surface as she tried to refocus on the meeting.

"And so, my friends," said Warner, "we need to move full steam ahead with the mall."

Lauren might have regretted the distraction of her own ruminations were she not certain that Warner had contributed nothing more than her usual stream of platitudes.

"Mr. Ward," said Laughlin, "I know you wish to address the issue before us."

"I do. But perhaps we should allow Mr. Worthington to speak first. That way, we can weigh any new arguments he has in support of his proposal."

From his place in the center Laughlin glowered down the long table at Ward. "Your suggestion is noted. Absent objection from your fellow Board members, we'll follow it. But in the future kindly make such recommendations in advance of the meeting." Laughlin turned to Lauren's father. "Should you wish to be heard, the floor is yours."

Roger Worthington straightened his red and black power tie and then strode to the microphone located to the Board's left. He took his time, adjusting the device upward for his six-foot frame. He cleared his throat. "Cedar Creek has been my family's home for a century and a half. Cedar Creek has been good to us . . . and *we* have been good to Cedar Creek." His cadence slowed. "*Very good indeed.* Plaques in the hospital, park and senior center, among others, attest to Worthington generosity. Unfortunately, memories are all too short. Regardless, Cedar Mall stands on its own. It will bring desperately needed new businesses to our suffering economy. Over the past three months I have been quietly negotiating with *Cybertrixon, Inc.*, a systems development company. Their CEO Dennis Shoreman and I were fraternity brothers thirty-odd years ago at the University of South Carolina. Dennis told me of his company's plans to open a new center for their computer operations. He expects it will employ about two hundred fifty people. I suggested the mall. At first he dismissed the idea as if it were preposterous. Gradually, I convinced him. He liked the anchor location at one end of the mall; in particular, the end whose parking area adjoins the village park. There his employees would have plenty of parking and green space. He also liked my plan to have a fitness center, as well as a food court, near his end of the mall. Cedar Creek's low cost-of-living, available housing and access to the interstate increased his enthusiasm. But what probably swung the deal was the availability of reasonably priced labor." Lauren's father cleared his throat again. "Excuse me a moment while I get a drink."

As her father walked to the water cooler, Lauren's eyes followed him. With the possibility of jobs, the audience was salivating. One-on-one, at home in Worthington Hall, he was a difficult man, but given a stage, he had charm and charisma. And from all appearances, he had something good to sell.

He returned to the microphone. "Dennis plans to bring in about thirty of his own people, mostly executives and managers, the kind that earn big salaries. A number of those folks are likely to build new homes. Slow as things have been, some of you here, our local contractors and construction people, wouldn't mind that, would you." He paused. "As for the other jobs *Cybertrixon* would bring, the largest segment would be comprised of good-paying computer operation and programming positions, along with clerical opportunities. Mr. Shoreman would be looking to fill those jobs with local talent. As he put it, *Give me some hard working folks in a town that's down on its luck, and I'll train them.*"

The audience buzzed. Lauren's father had them eating out of his hand. He gestured at the Board, but his eyes remained focused on the audience. He said, "Last month our village leaders demanded I pay for a consultant of their choice to evaluate the advisability of my proposed mall. Now they debate whether to hold the project in abeyance pending the criminal process. Let me assist these learned leaders who have guided our fair village to its current depressed state." He folded his arms. "Never again will the mall clog their agenda should they, in their great wisdom, put the project on hold this evening. Because the moment they do, my plans to build the mall permanently and irrevocably cease." He marched back to his seat.

The announcement, one that stunned Lauren no less than the rest of the audience, ignited a sea of muttering.

Laughlin reached for his gavel. He drew it back but then held it in a cocked position. His eyes moved from one end of the Board to the other. The members exchanged shrugs, whispers and puzzled looks. Laughlin appeared to glare in Lauren's direction, though she suspected the look was directed at her father who was back in his chair next to her. Finally, Laughlin pounded his gavel. "We're taking a recess. The Board is going into Executive Session." The giraffe-like educator got up and exited the hall with the other four members close behind.

Lauren gazed at her father. "That was a shocker."

"They asked for it. Pushing me the way they did." He motioned toward the door at the back. "C'mon outside. We'll talk there."

She followed him into the comfortable night air. "So, what do you plan to do?"

"Just what I said."

Lauren recalled Steve Ward's comments the night she had visited his home. The possibility her father had monetary woes troubled her. Over the years he had never discussed his financial condition with her. She only knew that he lived very well. She looked around making certain no one was within earshot. She said, "You must have lots of money tied up in the project. The land had to be expensive, and architectural fees and the like aren't cheap. Can you really afford to walk away?"

"Hey, you do what you have to."

The cavalier response tempted Lauren to follow up with more pointed questions. That's what she would have done if she were on the heels of a news story. But not with her father. Not with their relationship already strained.

He looked up and down the street. "This town needs me far more than I need them."

He had a point, but, on the other hand, if he were convicted and sent to prison, he would be even worse off than the village. The detail, hardly a minor one, deserved mention. However, Lauren needed to be more circumspect. She said, "If the mall isn't approved, what will you do with the land?"

"Not even gonna think about it."

"But aren't you being a bit — " Her father's grimace clipped her tongue. The look underscored that the question she most wanted answered — whether he was connected to the fire at Jordan's home — would provoke far greater anger.

"People are filing back in. The dimwits must have finished their Executive Session." He motioned her to follow as he re-entered the hall.

"Kindly take your seats," said Laughlin. He waited a few moments. "The Board, dedicated as it is, to bettering our village, has evaluated the potential benefits which Mr. Worthington's negotiations with *Cybertrixon* present. Before polling the Board on what action it wishes to take, certain members desire to express their views on the record. Laughlin looked to his right. "Mr. Ward, the floor is yours."

"Thank you, Mr. Chairman." Ward gazed out at the audience. "Much as I would love to lend my support to the mall — "

Someone in the back emitted a loud groan.

"Hear me out before passing judgment. Mr. Worthington tantalizes us with his plan to bring jobs. What if *Cybertrixon* doesn't materialize? What if he is convicted of arson? Will the town be left with a charred landscape, an eyesore next to its park? Like you, my desire for jobs has me thinking with my heart; however, as your representative, I must vote with my brain. Common sense, as well as my conscience, demands that I withhold approval."

Indignation gritted Lauren's teeth. She was pleased that others were more vocal. A woman off to her right, one row back, barked, "Don't let him fool you. He's trying to protect his dying strip mall." Someone else called out, "Ward's a phony," while others voiced displeasure with catcalls and the like.

Laughlin, normally quick to quell unruliness, allowed the disruption to continue longer than usual. Once the hubbub had largely quieted itself, he looked over at Jordan and said, "Mr. Jackson, I understand you also wish to be heard prior to the vote."

"I do, Mr. Chairman."

For an instant Jordan's eyes met Lauren's. Don't disappoint me, she thought, her progression of pessimism dampening expectations.

"My friends, from day one you all know that I have been the most outspoken critic of the mall. In recent months personal animosities between Roger Worthington and me have grown. Just this week I commenced litigation against him to recover damages as a result of the fire at my home. The last time the Board addressed this issue, we decided to seek the advice of an independent consultant. The possibility of jobs, something this community desperately needs, sheds new light on the project, but don't be misled. Keep in mind that if Roger Worthington is convicted, the project is likely to go by the wayside. Under the circumstances, we must proceed cautiously. Having said that, I concede that pursuit of the consultant's report meets that criterion. Since Roger Worthington has agreed to absorb the costs, it poses no burden on the Village. Accordingly, I believe we should allow the consultant to continue."

Laughlin put his hand on his microphone but hesitated. "Excuse us a moment." He motioned the other members of the Board to come his way and began whispering. A minute later they returned to their seats. Laughlin said, "Earlier Mr. Jackson referenced the report of the independent consultant. While data is yet to be compiled and numbers crunched, the consultant has provided this Board with some preliminary observations. In the interest of keeping you up to date and with the consent of my fellow Board members, I will share that information with you. Understand, however, it is strictly prefatory and, in all respects, subject to modification." He removed a sheet of paper from a folder. "Our consultant indicates the mall has major positive aspects for our community. Among these are jobs, both in the construction phase and long term, as well as increased availability of needed goods and services and a boost to the economy, owing especially to the influx of dollars from nearby locales and people who use the interstate." A tap of his gavel halted a murmur in the audience. "Like every street, there's another side. Our consultant informs us that the magnitude of the project is apt to strain police and fire services, create traffic congestion in the area of the interstate and cast undesirable shadows on our park. Yet to be determined is how the tax breaks and costs of additional services will weigh in vis-à-vis the increase in our tax base. Effects on the aquifer have not been examined either. Like all of you, we eagerly await these results. In the meantime, we will endeavor to keep you advised."

The woman seated next to Lauren whispered, "I'm glad I voted for Medford Laughlin. He's brilliant. And he tells us ordinary folks what's going on."

"Well — " Lauren bit her tongue. It was neither the time nor the place to debate the Chairman's motives.

"Do any of the other Board members wish to be heard?" Laughlin waited a moment. "Then I will poll the Board on the question." A quick tally showed that only Steve Ward wanted the entire project, including the consultant's report, put on hold.

"Mr. Chairman," said Ward, "before we conclude, I'd like to be heard again."

"If you wish," said Laughlin, a frown, however, contradicting his words.

"Earlier I outlined the reasons underlying my opposition to the mall. Nevertheless, I feel the need to speak out on Roger Worthington's behalf."

Lauren, whose attention had drifted to the brass eagle atop the flagpole, instantly focused on Ward.

"I'm not a lawyer and don't pretend to be. But all of us are familiar with the presumption of innocence. In the past few days I have heard comments from people who believe that Roger Worthington is guilty. That may prove to be the case. But unless and until a jury has reached that verdict, none of us should make that assumption. So, please, keep an open mind."

Lauren glanced at her father. For years he had played poker at the country club on Friday nights. He prided himself on his poker face. Doubtless thoughts were racing through his head, but his stoic exterior proved he could hold his cards close to his vest; so close that one might assume he had never looked at them. Lauren suspected her face was more revealing. Steve Ward had surprised her. He had stepped up to the plate. Even Lauren, cynic that she had become, had to give him his due.

CHAPTER XIII

As Jordan readied to argue the motion, once again he questioned his good sense. He could have filed his claim under the insurance policy and let *Rockhill Indemnity and Casualty* sue Roger Worthington under the subrogation clause. That's how he would have advised a client. He tried to convince himself that his discussions with Richard Parks, house counsel for *Rockhill*, allowed him to have it both ways. They had agreed to act as co-counsel, with Jordan as the lead. If and when Parks became dissatisfied with Jordan's handling of the matter, Parks could demand to take over. If Jordan declined, he would forfeit his rights under the policy. Jordan told himself he would not allow that to happen. Still he worried if push came to shove, ego might supersede judgment.

He glanced over at the defense table where Chester Harwood was seated next to Roger Worthington. With his pinstripe suit, silver hair and mustache, Harwood looked distinguished. A capable practitioner, he had represented Worthington for years, but he was far more a business lawyer than a litigator. Jordan hoped that would work to his advantage.

The arrival of Judge William Boston interrupted Jordan's musing. Along with everyone else, he stood up.

"Please be seated," said his Honor, even before he took his seat. Despite his easygoing style, there was never a doubt who was in charge. Judge Boston had an extraordinary knack for tightening slackened reins. "Good morning, Gentlemen." He looked over at the defense table. "Mr. Harwood, I have carefully reviewed your papers, as well as those of the plaintiff.

Why should I grant your motion to hold this case in abeyance pending the outcome of the criminal charges?"

Harwood got up from his seat. "Your Honor, this civil claim for damages does not require proof beyond a reasonable doubt. A mere preponderance of the evidence will entitle Mr. Jackson to recover. Assume hypothetically that my client is found liable to Mr. Jackson for damages. That determination could unfairly influence the jury in the criminal case."

Judge Boston turned to Jordan. "Mr. Jackson, do you disagree?"

Jordan got up and went around to the far side of the plaintiff's table. Judge Boston seemed disposed to grant the motion. And why not. Criminal cases often took precedence over their civil counterparts. "Your Honor," said Jordan, "Mr. Harwood voices concerns, but nothing that would justify the relief he seeks. Let us assume, as my adversary suggests, Mr. Worthington is found liable here. And might I note that such worry may have much to do with Mr. Worthington's responsibility for the fire." The momentary furrow in Judge Boston's brow told Jordan his not-so-subtle hint had not been well received. He said, "In any event, the Court which tries the criminal case could, and certainly would, instruct the jury to disregard any verdict in the civil case. The — "

"Excuse me," said Judge Boston, "but doesn't that beg the point? Telling the jury to ignore information is one thing. Having them do it, quite another."

"Your Honor, with all due respect, you, yourself, on numerous occasions have instructed juries to disregard inadmissible testimony."

"Yes . . . that's true. But asking a jury to ignore a few extra words, often innocuous ones, is very different from telling them to put a verdict of another jury on the same issue out of their minds. Don't you agree?"

"Your Honor," said Jordan, "having observed you many times, I know how adept you are at guiding juries to equitable results." The Judge showed no reaction. Nevertheless, Jordan knew that neither his fawning, nor his sidestep of the loaded question had fooled the jurist. Gentleman that he was, Judge Boston had let the weak argument pass. He had no need to deprecate the messenger. At the appropriate time his decision would serve as the final word. Jordan realized he was on thin ice. "Your Honor," he said, "Mr. Harwood's alleged concerns are premature. His Answer to the Complaint was accompanied by a Demand for a Bill of Particulars. Once the Bill of Particulars is served, there are sure to be depositions, as well as other pre-trial discovery and motions. Only then will the case be placed on the calendar for trial. By that time the criminal case may well have been tried with a verdict rendered and his claims of potential harm moot. As your Honor has often noted, and countless precedents confirm, courts should not rule on issues that may not require judicial intervention."

Judge Boston appeared to nod ever so slightly. He looked over at Harwood. "Mr. Jackson has a point."

"But — " Harwood hesitated. "By granting an immediate stay, the risk of influence on a criminal jury will be obviated."

"I understand, but I can allow this case to proceed and, down the road, should a stay become necessary, grant it then. That way we'll have the best of both worlds." Judge Boston's gaze drifted into space as he seemingly confirmed his own reasoning. "At this time, Mr. Harwood, I'm denying your motion without prejudice to a renewal if and when circumstances merit. Assuming there are no other matters requiring my attention, this Court is adjourned." He got up from the bench and headed toward his chambers.

Jordan stuffed his papers into his attaché case.

"Good job," said Parks.

"Thanks," said Jordan, his exterior cool and calm. Though Parks was his peer, at that moment Jordan treated him like a client. No flaunting or boasts. A matter of fact reaction to victory. Jordan wanted to try the case against Roger Worthington, and what better way to convince Parks and the insurance company that he was the man for the job.

———————

"Chic sweater you're wearing," said Baker, his scrutiny of the form-fitting top far more than a passing glance. "Peach becomes you. Complements your light brown hair."

Lauren nodded, refusing to otherwise acknowledge the purported tribute. Baker was as bad as Loggin. True, the radio talk-show host decorated his lecherous overtures with prose alien to the vulgar cop, but his gawk, the kind that undressed, rendered his genteel words no less unwelcome.

A fellow outside the glass-enclosed studio held up two fingers.

"Two minutes until airtime," said Baker.

Though Lauren preferred to be elsewhere, she felt far less intimidated than earlier appearances. She had come to the studio with a plan of attack. If Baker surprised her and took the high road, fine. If not, she would dish out more than she took. She understood his bullying style. Once he got the upper hand, he would pound away. The only defense was to respond in kind. His leer suggested civility was already becoming a foreign commodity. By the time the show ended, Baker would regret having extended her the invitation. She pointed at the shelf where he kept his team photo of the Baltimore Colts. "Did you play for the Colts?"

He shook his head. "Never got the chance. Knee injuries. I still have bursitis and degenerative joint disease." He turned and pointed at the timeworn pigskin that adjoined the picture. "Game ball. Made eleven tackles for Texas Southern the day we upset Baylor in sixty-three. Back then I had dreams of a pro career; at least until I wrecked my knee a second time. You a football fan?"

"Not really."

"Too rough for the little lady?"

Much as she detested the game's violence, Lauren refused to concede the point. She said, "Let's just say I prefer cerebral activities."

"Like baking cookies." He heaved a sigh. "Football takes a lot more smarts than you think. And more important, it builds men. Shapes character. Take the man in the White House. President Reagan is a football fan from way back. They don't call him the *Gipper* for nothing."

Lauren scratched her head. "Gosh. I thought he earned the nickname as an actor, playing that fellow from Notre Dame."

"Very funny." Baker hesitated. "We'll continue this another time." A moment later the *On the Air* light flashed. "Greetings to all my friends out there in the hill country of South Carolina." He had shifted into his broadcast voice. Words were rolling from his tongue like the hills to which he referred. "Thanks for letting me into your homes and cars this sultry, summer evening. We're in for some lively dialogue. Lauren Worthington, reporter for the *Cedar Creek Chronicle*, is back again. And as you folks, especially those from Cedar Creek, no doubt know, matters related to the proposed mall have turned juicier than a Pickens County peach. But just in case someone out there has been hibernating, I'll fill you in. Roger Worthington, father of my guest and developer of the proposed mall, has been charged with setting fire to the home of Village Board member Jordan Jackson, who just happens to be the boyfriend of my guest." He looked at Lauren. "Tell me, Ms. Worthington, what are your thoughts about the arson?"

Though the bait was not unexpected, it had come sooner than anticipated. "As far as any pending litigation involving either my father or Mr. Jackson, I intend to leave it where it belongs — in the courts."

"Gee, I read the *Chronicle* faithfully. It never mentioned a gag order. Did the Judge issue one?" Baker punctuated the question with a smug look.

"You, the fountainhead of right-wing politics, read . . . (she hesitated, tempted to stop there, but forced herself to finish the sentence) . . . the *Chronicle*?"

"Ooh — the claws are out tonight. Had I known, I would have invited Dr. Wiley, chief vet at the Clarksville Zoo. to join us." Baker ducked his chin and flashed his dukes in a boxer's pose. He winked. "Let me take a call." He pressed a button. "You're on the air with Baker."

"Hi, Jerry. This is Lou."

"Welcome Lou. Can't say I recognize your voice. You a first-time caller?"

"Not really, though it's been a long time. But I'm a regular listener."

"That's what we like. So, tell me Lou, what's on your mind?"

"I wanna say that Roger Worthington is okay in my book. We need his mall and the jobs it's gonna bring."

"You got a question for my guest tonight?"

"No. Just a comment. The way I see it. It'll be her fault if the mall don't go through."

"How do you figure that?"

"Her father wouldn't be in the fix he's in. Hell, if she wuzn't datin' Jackson, her father wouldn't have torched the guy's place. Let me tell you though. I mighta done the same thing if Jackson blocked my mall and then started datin' my daughter."

"I appreciate the thought." Baker trained his eyes on Lauren. "Ms. Worthington, Lou says it'll be your fault if the mall gets the kibosh. He's right, isn't he?"

A *yes* was impossible. But a *no* walked into Baker's ambush. Lauren said, "The suggestion doesn't merit a response."

Baker groaned. "All your big talk about pursuing the issues. The first tough question, and you duck for cover. C'mon."

The bully had struck. Two could play the same game. She said, "Certain talk show hosts have the same reputation. Suppose we try the shoe on your foot. Tell me, are any of the rumors about your womanizing false?" The anger that greeted her eyes made it hard for her to restrain a smile. She suspected a mirror might have shown it to be more of a sneer.

"Had I known you planned to behave like this, I wouldn't have extended the invite."

"Thanks. That's the nicest thing you've ever said to me."

His jaw clenched. "Time we take another call." He pressed a button. "You're on the air with Baker."

"Hi Jerry. This is Angela from Potterstown. First off, I want to say that I'm not a fan of your show."

"Thanks for the encouragement. So, how come you're listening, and why the call?"

"A friend told me Lauren Worthington was your guest tonight. People here in Potterstown are interested in the mall. We could use it, as well as the jobs, and unlike Cedar Creek, we won't bear the freight. You know, the tax breaks and the demands on public services."

"You have a question for Ms. Worthington?"

Just a comment. I want to commend her. I read her piece in the *Chronicle* a couple months back. It was well balanced. That's not easy when you're in the middle of a firestorm. No pun intended."

"Appreciate the call." Baker's expression suggested otherwise. "Let's take another."

Sure, thought Lauren, having become familiar with Baker's *modus operandi*. Sing his praises, and you stay on the line. Turn tough, and you get short shrift. Admittedly Baker had a glib tongue and a decent mind, but a button to command the airwaves and a naïve audience didn't hurt. Like a huckster at a carnival Baker stayed two jumps ahead. And perhaps the similarity didn't end there. Lauren pondered the possibility that his callers included a shill or two.

"You're on the air with Baker," said the host.

"Hi Jer. I ain't gonna take long. Just wanna say that I'm convinced Roger Worthington is guilty."

"Want to tell us why?" Baker waited a moment. "You still there?" He waited again. "That was a quickie." He looked at Lauren. "Care to respond?"

"People shouldn't prejudge. They should wait for the evidence."

"The police believe he's guilty."

"They've been wrong before. In any event, it's premature to draw any conclusions."

"I can if I want." Baker folded his arms. "That's what's great about living in a free country." He gestured at her. "Being a newspaperwoman, you know all about that. But for now, let's see if we can find another caller, one who won't hang up right away." He pushed a button. "You're on the air with Baker."

"You mean I really got through?"

"Yes. And if you turn your radio down, our ears won't get shattered with feedback." He looked at Lauren. "Wanna join me in a chorus of *Yankee Doodle* while the caller adjusts the volume."

"Thanks, but — "

"Hi Jerry. This is Mac. You hear me now?"

"Loud and clear. What's on your mind?"

"I think Roger Worthington is gettin' a raw deal. Don't make no sense that he'd torch Jackson's place. If I were a bettin' man, which I am — and, if I say so myself, a pretty fair handicapper — I'd lay 4-1 they got it ass-backwards. The way I sees it, Jackson's probably behind it. Figured he could collect the insurance, kill the mall and get the filly. On that last point, can't say as I blame him. She's a looker. I seen her dolled up on that telethon with her father last year."

"Well — " said Baker, "when it comes to the fire, I won't speculate. But as for the filly, no arguments here." He winked at Lauren. "Of course, we'll keep that a secret. We wouldn't want to swell Ms. Worthington's liberal head, would we?"

Go to hell. Lauren silently, but distinctly, mouthed the words, so Baker could read her lips.

"Ms. Worthington, did you just swear at me?"

"Me? You must be kidding. I didn't say a word." She looked him in the eye. "Are all conservative talk-show hosts prone to paranoia? Or is it only former football jocks who suffered brain concussions? That's what you told me. Right?"

"Very funny. And just to set the record straight, they were knee injuries."

"Could have fooled me."

"About what? Keeping the record straight. And since when did that concern you?" He glowered. "We've got a caller with an interesting point. He thinks your father is innocent. Suggests he was framed by your boyfriend. Maybe for the insurance. What do you say?"

If Lauren were alone on the street with the caller, she would have given him a piece of her mind. She said, "I know my father. I know Jordan. Neither would resort to arson. Regardless, as I said earlier, the matter should be left to the courts."

"C'mon," said Baker. "You're ducking the issues again." He shook his head. "I can't believe it. You get the chance to go to bat for your father, and what do you do. Damn, if I had a daughter and — " He cleared his throat. "I'll spare you my thoughts and give you another chance to answer Mac."

An inner voice encouraging one last try on the high road contained Lauren's urge to lash out. She said, "Admittedly I'm short on answers. But speculations by me without the facts would serve no purpose."

Baker unleashed another of his patented groans. "Mac, I apologize. You posed an excellent question. Unfortunately, my guest doesn't want the ball." He glanced over his shoulder in the direction of his football memorabilia. "Back in my playing days, Coach used to say: *The ones with the biggest mouths have the smallest hearts.*"

The shot pushed Lauren over the edge. She said, "Your coach was a wise man. But give yourself credit. Chances are, you educated him."

"Come again," said Baker, displaying a rare look of puzzlement.

Lauren pointed at him. "I doubt your coach ever saw a mouth bigger than yours."

Baker glared. "I can invite you to leave now."

Thumb up, index finger pointed, hand like a gun, Lauren aimed at Baker. "*Make my day*, Mr. Cluck."

"That's it!" barked Baker. He gestured at the door. "Close it on your way out."

"With pleasure." Lauren got up from her seat. She unhooked her wireless microphone. She started to put it down, but then raised it to her mouth. "Planted callers with planted questions." She ran one index finger over the other. "Shame on you, Jer."

Baker jerked back but said nothing.

Lauren hesitated, just long enough to savor the exasperation that painted his fat, crimson face. If her memory bank had to include his portrait — and no doubt it would — what better memento than the look he bore.

A few puffy cumulus clouds floated peacefully above in the azure sky. Temperatures hovered in the upper seventies as a soft breeze rustled through the trees. Lauren leaned back against the bench where she and Jordan were seated. His hand caressing her shoulder, like an overpowering aphrodisiac, quickened her heart, sparking the thrill that had personified the first months of their relationship. Burdens lightened. Stress abated. Lauren gazed skyward. Love's incomparable rainbow, superimposed onto nature's canvas, had created a perfect Sunday afternoon.

"What would you like to do?" said Jordan.

"I'm happy just sitting here with you." She breathed deeply inhaling the fragrance of the creamy white blossoms of the *Sweet Bay* magnolias. Some referred to them as *Swamp Magnolias*, but Lauren believed trees that beautified both the landscape and air deep into September deserved better. She ran her hand over Jordan's knee.

He tilted his head against hers and hummed a few bars; the melody, nothing identifiable. He said, "Later we could take a walk and get ice cream over at — " A forward lean interrupted his speech. He pointed off to their left. "Isn't that your father coming up the street?"

The mere possibility, like threatening clouds, darkened Lauren's mood. She hated the lowered threshold that had crept into her personality, but tensions had taken their toll. She peered beneath the branches that overhung the sidewalk. "That's him all right." She turned to Jordan. "Whatever you do, don't start with him."

"Me? He's the one you should talk to."

"Well — it takes two to tango." She took her hand off Jordan's leg. "Regardless, I don't want a scene, especially one where I'm the monkey in the middle."

"Fine, I'll be civil . . . as long as he is."

Lauren took a deep breath as she tried to relax a tightening jaw. Chill, she told herself. Moments later, as her father drew near, she said, "Hi, Dad."

"How's my favorite daughter?"

She skipped her standard comeback: a reminder that she was an only child.

"Good afternoon, Mr. Worthington."

"Jordan, as I've told you before, please, call me Roger."

Jordan nodded, though his expression was equivocal.

"Care to join us?" Lauren's words, reluctantly spoken, rang hollow in her ears. She suspected her father read between the lines.

"No thanks. Third wheel isn't my thing." He looked at Jordan. "I'd like to talk with you. Not now. Maybe we could arrange to meet."

"You . . . and me?" Jordan shook his head. "My discussions should be with your attorney. The canons of ethics prefer it that way."

Rules or not, Lauren was glad Jordan had nixed the idea. A meeting between the two had all the earmarks of trouble. Insults. Maybe even fisticuffs. If by some chance communication did occur, she could picture her father proposing a deal that took Jordan out of her life.

"Suppose my lawyer blesses the get-together?"

Jordan hesitated. "I wouldn't do it without an authorization signed by both of you. Not that I don't trust you. On second thought, let's be candid."

"The feeling is mutual. I assure you." Lauren's father showed a toothy smile, but dagger-laden eyes transformed pearly whites into fangs. "If I get the authorization, you'll meet?"

"That's not what I said."

Lauren's father glanced at her. "Tell me your friend doesn't speak with a forked tongue. Not that it surprises me." He looked back at Jordan. "That's just what I'd expect from a — "

"Don't you dare," said Lauren. Out of the corner of her eye, she tried to catch a glimpse of Jordan, not that it was necessary. She knew the look of a fire-breathing dragon.

"C'mon," said her father. "You don't even know what I was about to say."

"I can imagine," said Jordan. "But just so you don't feel shortchanged, let's hear."

Roger Worthington folded his arms.

Jordan folded his and stared. "Ashamed to say, aren't you?"

"If anyone should be ashamed . . . " Roger Worthington shook his head. "But just to set the record straight, I was about to call you a lawyer and, worse yet, a politician."

Skepticism showed on Jordan's face. Lauren understood why.

"Let's not get sidetracked," said her father. "A minute ago you told me you'd meet if I got the authorizations. You deny that?"

"Absolutely. I told you I wouldn't meet without them. Translation — the authorizations are necessary, not sufficient, for a meeting."

Lauren's father turned to her. "You see what I'm dealing with."

In spite of the comment, she suspected he understood the nicety Jordan had drawn. On the other hand, that begged the question what Jordan had intimated earlier.

"Does your silence mean you're siding with him?" said her father.

How often she had heard him utter that same aggravating phrase. She said, "I'm not siding with anyone."

"Sure." He started to walk away but glanced back at Lauren. "I'll see you for dinner on Tuesday. Right?"

"Uh . . . "

"Good. I'll see you at six." He hurried on his way.

"Thanks for backing me up," said Jordan.

"What did you expect me to say?"

"Something." He waited a moment. "You know what he was insinuating."

"You're misreading his intent. I'm certain."

"Oh yeah?"

A woodpecker rapping his beak against the trunk of a half-dead poplar drew Lauren's attention. "Can't that infernal creature find another place to rat-a-tat-tat?" She glanced up at the beautiful sky. So much for a perfect Sunday afternoon.

———————

Monday mornings were always tough, but a bad night's sleep, owing to the ugly scene between Jordan and her father the afternoon before, made it especially bad. As Lauren entered the *Chronicle*'s lobby, Mary, the receptionist, greeted her. "Nielsen wants to see you in his office. Right away."

"Wonderful," said Lauren. She stepped through the door into the copy room. She glanced in the direction of Nielsen's office. "Let the maggot wait," she muttered under her breath. She went to her desk, grabbed her mug and headed toward the coffeepot. Halfway there, Vic, the office assistant, cut her off.

"The Bastard wants you. On the double."

"So I heard."

Vic looked around and then spoke in a lowered voice. "Someone must have jabbed a hot poker up his ass. He's nastier than usual, if you can imagine that."

Lauren glanced at the coffeepot and heaved a sigh. She walked back to her desk, banged her mug down and headed over to Nielsen's office. She knocked on the door jam as she poked her head into the open doorway. He looked up from his desk.

"Have a seat. I'll be with you in a minute." He picked up the telephone receiver. He studied the mouthpiece for a moment and then grabbed a tissue. Muttering under his breath, he wiped the mouthpiece repeatedly. Finally, as Lauren took a chair, he dialed.

In an effort to be discreet Lauren looked toward the far wall at a wooden plaque, not that it interested her. In the meantime Nielsen arranged a late-afternoon golf date Her thermometer rose when his conversation shifted to the pitching duel in the preceding night's Braves' game. Several more minutes passed. She gave her watch a demonstrative stare. *His Majesty* continued. His strict policies against employees fraternizing at the water cooler or doing personal business on the *Chronicle*'s time didn't apply. He was the boss, and his style of management was fear, not example. At long last, he hung up the receiver.

"You wanted to see me?" she said.

"As a matter of fact, I did." He leaned back, his eyes drifting into space. "People tell me I'm lucky because I've got the top job. Sure, there's the occasional perk, but this is where the buck stops. Decisions, responsibility and, the one everyone forgets, supervision. They're all mine."

She sat expressionless. If he was looking for sympathy, he'd picked the wrong person, as well as the wrong day.

"This morning I've got one of those difficult chores. Personnel matters are always that way." His eyes made contact with Lauren's for the first time. "I'm letting you go. Giving you your two weeks' notice."

Her brain disbelieved her ears. True, he had threatened the possibility, but she had assumed the threats were idle. At the very least, she had expected an unambiguous, final warning. She had no idea what to say.

"I thought you might be upset. Apparently you knew it was coming. Right?"

She shook her head, still unable to find the right words. Begging for her job, especially from Nielsen, was impossible. But walking meekly out the door was equally unacceptable. She said, "Why now?"

"I ought to ignore that question. I don't owe you an explanation. But, be that as it may, I'll give you one." He folded his arms. "Suffice it to say, you're a loose cannon. And don't give me that wide-eyed look." His voice grew louder. "Against my admonitions you went back onto Baker's show. I'm easygoing, but I don't tolerate defiance. The one thing I demand from my team is loyalty."

Give me a break, thought Lauren. His list of demands from his employees outnumbered the pork items the legislators in Columbia stuffed into the State budget. However, debating the point was as futile as attempts to free the system of political favoritism. On the other hand, past discussions with Nielsen had proved her father's influence could make a difference. Trading on Dad's sway was becoming a distasteful habit, but Nielsen had asked for it. She was about to play the trump card, when Nielsen, almost as if clairvoyant, let her know the hand was *no trump*.

He said, "I have to tell you. If it weren't for your father's predicament, you might not have gotten the ax; at least for the time being. When I told the home office that he had been charged with arson, the loss of his advertising became a non-issue. In a syndicate of twenty-two newspapers the *Chronicle*, small as it is, hardly determines the bottom line. On the other hand, if its biggest supporter were a convicted felon, that could be a liability. The boys up north said I used good judgment putting the reputation of the organization ahead of my own operation." He smirked.

Lauren swallowed hard. She should have been better prepared. Her boss was hardly one to make the same mistake twice. And more often than not when he played his cards, he had already stolen a peek at his opponent's.

"You're unusually quiet," he said.

The self-satisfied look that accompanied his quip was more than she could take. Common sense urged her not to burn any bridges, but with her job gone the chance for visceral satisfaction obliterated judgment. She said, "In case you weren't aware, everyone out there refers to you as *The Bastard*." She shook her head. "That's not entirely true. A couple of women in data entry prefer an anatomical epithet." She started to get up.

Nielsen leaped from his seat. "Forget about two weeks. Clean out your desk. Right now!"

———

Lauren's steak knife slid easily through the buttery soft filet mignon. Bessie had prepared the prime beef to a medium-rare perfection, topping it with golden, crisp onion rings. Cheddar-coated broccoli, along with a sprig of parsley and a maroon apple ring, completed the presentation on the Ascot, gold-trimmed Wedgwood. Unfortunately, less palate-pleasing fare seasoned the menu. Dear old Dad was again harping on his familiar theme: why his favorite daughter should move back home. And now that she had neither a job, nor the income it provided, his argument had merit.

"Look at it this way," he said. "If you move back, you can take your time looking for a new position. You won't be in a financial bind. And it's not like you'll be trading down. Instead of that little studio apartment you call home, you'll have your own suite, along with all the amenities."

Sure, thought Lauren, trade my independence for fancy digs. Much as she loved her father, at that moment the utensil he held looked more like a pitchfork. No way would she accede to his devilish offer.

"So, what do you say?"

She jabbed her fork into the filet. Her jaw clenched. She felt her newly acquired temper taking control. And why not. There was friction with her father. Friction with Jordan. His house had been burned. She had just been fired. Her father was constantly pressing her to move home. He was charged with arson. Jordan was suing her father. The list seemed endless.

"Do you plan to ignore me?"

"I'm not moving home. So, forget it." The splenetic expression that greeted her words tightened her grip on her knife.

"C'mon — don't be stubborn."

Stubborn! Of all the bullheaded people, how dare you call me stubborn. "Damn it, Dad! Stop trying to run my life!"

He turned to Bessie who had just come in from the kitchen. "Do you believe that unemployed daughter of mine? I offer her free room and board in a place like this (he extended both arms), and what does she do? Accuses me of meddling."

Without uttering a word, Bessie placed a silver sugar and creamer set on the table. The response mirrored what Lauren had anticipated. She could also predict what would follow; at least she thought she could.

"There you go," he said. "Ignoring me again."

Bessie started back toward the kitchen.

"Damn it!" he snarled. "For once don't hide behind silence."

Bessie halted. She did an about face. "You want a response. Fine. I'll give you one." Her uncharacteristically sharp tone drew a hush. She looked her boss in the eye. "If I were you, and I had one daughter (she gestured at Lauren), one beautiful daughter like this, I would never carp and nitpick the way you do. You're playing with fire." She shook her head. "You're a rich man. A very rich man. But keep it up, and you'll lose your most precious asset." Bessie turned and marched into the kitchen.

Silence, as thunderous as a sonic boom, punctuated her exit. Lauren, her focus directed at her plate, mentally gave Bessie a standing ovation. The housekeeper had served her employer exactly what he had demanded. Whatever his internal reaction, he swallowed the strongly seasoned morsel without a whimper.

Chapter XIV

Seated alone in a booth at Harper's Luncheonette, Lauren moved her coffee cup to the edge of the table making room to unfold her copy of the *Chronicle*. She went directly to the want ads. Of the thirty or so jobs listed, most paid little more than minimum wage. The others, such as auto mechanic, computer programmer, art teacher, dental hygienist and crane operator, demanded skills she lacked. Finding new employment in Cedar Creek wouldn't be easy; impossible if she intended to continue her career as a reporter. Since Nielsen had fired her two days earlier, she had weighed the alternatives and had come to the inescapable conclusion that either she would have to leave Cedar Creek or give up reporting. She had rejected both options.

Her father's push for her to move back home was fast becoming an offer she couldn't refuse. More than once she had run the numbers. Her bank balance would carry her for another two months, provided there were no major, unexpected expenses. Time would not solve her dilemma. Another newspaper in Cedar Creek might, but the chances of that were more remote than her winning a *Pulitzer Prize*.

"Good afternoon, Lauren."

She looked up and saw Detective Loggin standing over her. His slovenly belly was about two feet from her face.

"You don't mind me calling you Lauren?"

"Well — that's my name."

"Would you like some company?"

A search for a diplomatic excuse prompted hesitation.

Loggin motioned to the waitress. "A refill over here for the lady and a coffee for me." He eased down into the seat across from her. "Sorry to hear about your job."

News, especially the bad kind, travels fast, thought Lauren, not that she was surprised. Growing up in Cedar Creek, she had learned how gossip moved in the small town. Her experience as a reporter had made her an expert.

"I hear that boss of yours is a real slave driver. His stupidity is the *Chronicle*'s loss."

Difficult as the past couple of days had been, the kind words were welcome, even from Loggin. She said, "Nielsen isn't the easiest person to please."

Loggin dumped a load of sugar into his coffee, which had just arrived. "If I were your boss, no way would I give a fox like you the boot."

She chided herself. How naïve to think he had complimented her talent as a reporter, rather than her physical attributes.

"So, whatd'ya plan to do now?"

None of your damn business. Her face may have transmitted the thought. She said, "Things are up in the air. I'll have to see."

"You plan to stay in the news reportin' business?"

"I haven't decided but — " She cut herself off. If the nosey flatfoot with the thick skull needed a less subtle hint, she would oblige. "You're awfully inquisitive."

"Comes with the territory, I guess. Being a detective and all. Kinda like being a reporter."

She shook her head. "I confine my prying to news stories." She looked him in the eye. "Other times I respect people's privacy."

Loggin nearly choked on his coffee. "I . . . uh . . . wasn't trying to snoop."

His reaction appeased her irritation enough to re-evaluate the situation. The opportunity to pick his brain was more valuable than the need to vent. An absurdity popped into her head. Picking a vacuum was a contradiction. She restrained a chuckle and said, "I was wondering. What led you to the Boxley brothers?"

"Now who's prying?" Loggin smiled.

"Like I told you, I do it when it relates to work."

"True, but the Boxleys are my work. Can't be yours, not when you ain't got a job."

He had a point. She conceded he wasn't quite the dunce she had labeled him. However, a glimpse of his eyes ogling her breasts reminded her that he was no less the lecher. She was tempted to tell him but curbed the urge. She swallowed pride and said, "Folks around town are very impressed with the way you caught both the Boxleys and Brewster. It's a feather in your cap."

"Especially if we get a conviction of the top dog. Don't mean to rub it in, him being your father and all, but nailing Cedar Creek's leading citizen ain't chopped liver." Loggin appeared to study her face. "Course, you probably think he's innocent."

"Absolutely." She had no intention of debating the point further. She said, "Tell me. What led you to the Boxleys?"

"Good detective work."

Aren't you wonderful. She took a deep breath reloading a sarcastic tongue with judicious words. "What was the key?"

"Persistence . . . Yup, that's what did it. Persistence."

The empty answer magnified her curiosity. "But there must have been something, a particular fact or clue, that pointed you to them."

"Uh . . . I suppose."

"So, what was it?"

"Well — my investigation led me to this fella, and to make a long story short, he fingered the Boxleys."

"Who's the fellow?"

Loggin looked away. "Uh . . . doesn't matter."

Jobless or not, Lauren still had her nose for news, and his response smelled. The situation called for Loggin's technique, the same one used by reporters. Persistence. But to avoid a dead end, she had to be circuitous. "How did you find this fellow?"

"You're asking for my trade secrets."

His repeated dodge made her more determined. A trick she had learned from Nielsen, of all people, came to mind. He called it the *crowbar*. It was specially fitted to narcissistic subjects. An explanation that minimized their importance would pry the truth. "Let me guess," said Lauren. "The fellow called you with a tip." She waited a moment assuming Loggin would counter the speculation that dumb luck, rather than his investigative skills, had led to the arrests.

He shrugged.

She restrained the temptation to laugh. "An anonymous tip led you to the Boxleys."

"Well — folks don't wanna get involved. You know how it is."

"Sure — I know how it is." The sight of him squirming brought a conscious smile to her lips. In the back of her mind questions stirred. Who furnished the tip? How did he get the information? And why did he give it to Loggin?

"You've got something on your mind. I see it on your face."

"You're very perceptive." The fawning turned her stomach.

"I suppose I am. Part of it comes from experience, but mostly, you got it or you don't."

She restrained the urge to roll her eyes. "So, tell me, how did your tipster know the Boxleys started the fire?"

"Easy," he said. "Two-bit thugs love to brag. They got big egos."

Like someone else I know. Once again, she chose discretion. "But the Boxleys aren't Johnny come latelies. Their rap sheets read like a list of Euclid's theorems."

"Who?" Loggin scratched his head. "Is he from around these parts?"

"Not exactly, but — " Lauren cut herself off. Talking to Loggin was like talking to the hard-rock maple table on which his fat elbows rested. On second thought, the table never asked stupid questions. She said, "It doesn't surprise you that career criminals like the Boxleys would shoot their mouths off?"

"Not really. The way I see it, clods like them ain't too bright. That's why they keep gettin' caught." He looked her in the eye. "You follow what I'm saying?"

She silently counted to five. Having Nielsen talk down to her was bad, but Loggin? That transcended the sublime.

"Creeps like the Boxleys make lotsa enemies. Once the word gets around, someone's sure to call the cops. It's just a matter of time." Loggin leaned back. "You folks with the college degrees learn the stuff they put in books. Dates from history and words that ain't got no use except to fill up the dictionary. But us detectives have street smarts, the kind that work in the real world."

"I take it you don't have much use for higher education."

"Not from what I've seen. Young pups come on the force fresh outta college. Right off they're spouting that *socialogy* stuff."

Lauren shot him a jaundiced look.

"Uh . . . whatever they call that ivory-towered garbage. Bottom line — they don't know puppy chow from dog dung."

"Important difference, isn't it?"

"You tell me." His leering eyes moved south once again.

One time too many. She said, "Puppy chow — that's what you eat for breakfast. And the other stuff — that's for . . . " She shrugged.

He pointed at her. "You're just like 'em. Just cause your daddy's rich and you got an education, you think you're Miss Uppity-Do." He stood up. He tossed a buck and two quarters onto the table. "You know. Fifteen minutes ago when I sat down, I felt sorry for you, gettin' fired and all. Not any more." He walked away.

Good riddance, thought Lauren. She sipped her coffee, now cold. An anonymous tip seemed too convenient, even if Loggin had bolstered it with a credible explanation.

———

Books in hand, Lauren came out of the Cedar Creek Public Library. Now that she had no job, she had time for all that reading she had been longing to do. Of course, if she didn't find work, she'd have books and time, but no food or shelter; that is, unless she was prepared to move back home with Dad. That was out of the question. Whether an empty stomach and

no roof over her head might change her thinking remained to
be seen. She had walked about a block from the library —
walking was replacing driving, an effort to save money —
when a young fellow approached.

"Got a minute?"

It was the skinny guy who had solicited the handouts from
Jordan; the same one she had spoken to a week or two before.
"I guess so," she said, her interest far greater than she let on.
Repeated rehashing had yielded no clue why Jordan was giving
money to a member of the *Aryan Alliance*.

"You're a reporter for the *Chronicle*. Right?"

"I'm a reporter, and I was with the *Chronicle* until a few
days ago. What do you want?" If it was money, he was
knocking on the wrong door.

"I got information. The kind that'll gas your tank."

Lauren shrugged. "Such as."

"Let's go over there." He pointed at the alley that ran
adjacent to a vacant storefront. "It's a little more private."

"Suppose we try that cottonwood in front of the building."
The spot would allow them to still be seen though not heard.

"Whatever." He led the way to the tree. Once there, he
said, "I heard you on Baker's show, talkin' about the new mall
and the arsonist."

"And . . . " Lauren waited a moment. "You said you had
information."

"Ain't you the patient one."

Common sense told her not to trust the guy. She inched
back.

"I ain't gonna bite." He waited a moment. "You still
interested in the arson?"

"You know something about it?"

"Maybe."

She eyed his every move. "What does that mean?"

"Let me put it this way. What I got might tie to the arson
and . . . it might not."

"Suppose you tell me, and I'll be the judge."

"You got twenty bucks?"

Intuition suggested a scam. The possibility of information
tempted her to reach into her purse. But for current financial

straits, she would have. She said, "Unlike Jordan, I'm not your meal ticket, not when I don't have a job."

"Suit yourself."

She worried he might walk away. She debated whether to counteroffer, but before she could decide, he began muttering.

"What the hell. I milked the thing for all it's worth." He pointed at her. "You're gettin' a freebie." He hesitated and then began muttering to himself again. From what little Lauren could pick up, he appeared to be chastising himself for going soft. She waited to see what he would do next. Finally, he said, "Case you didn't know, that boyfriend of yours torched a place in Georgia some years back."

Jordan — an arsonist? She eyed her source. She reminded herself a good reporter examines the facts before drawing any conclusions.

"Shook you up, didn't I?" His shoulders pulled back, allowing his bony chest to protrude against the coiled rattlesnake that adorned his T-shirt with cutoff sleeves.

"Why should I believe you?"

"Suit yourself. It don't bother me none."

Once again she was concerned he would leave. "Tell me more about the fire."

"Newspaper lady is nosy." He reached into his back pocket and pulled out a folded piece of paper. "I could use a few bucks." He held up the paper. "A sawbuck and you get a look."

"I thought the information was free."

"Changed my mind. And Jesus, were only talkin' a sawbuck."

"That's ten dollars. Right?"

A scornful laugh blurred his speech as he garbled, "I thought reporters was supposed to be good with words."

"The articles I write aren't filled with slang."

"Touchy critter." He shook his head. "You know, most times it pisses me off when black dudes chase white skirts. But damn, Jackson deserves a bitch like you. And by the way, a sawbuck is ten dollars." He peered briefly off into space and then turned back to her. "Tell you what. I'll show you what I got. If it's hot, pay me the ten bucks. If not, spit in my face."

He pointed at her. "Consider this your lucky day. If Jackson hadn't cut me off the last two times I hit him up for dough, I wouldn't be tellin' you nuttin'."

Lauren read between the lines. The guy had been blackmailing Jordan. Discretion, desire to see the paper, kept her from exploring the theory.

The guy handed her the document. She unfolded it. A photocopy of a seal at the bottom, along with a signature followed by the printed words Juvenile Court Judge, caught her eye. She read the main section. It indicated Jordan Jackson had admitted to an act of delinquency, setting fire to an abandoned shack. It directed that he be committed to the Augusta Youth Development Campus for a period of twenty-four months. "May I keep this?"

The guy snatched the paper.

"How did you get it? Juvenile court records are normally sealed."

"I got my ways. Anyhow, that's *my* business."

"How do you know it's not a different Jordan Jackson?"

"If it was, you think your boyfriend would have been giving me dough?" He gestured at his *AA* tattoo. "You saw him that day in the park." He pointed at the paper. "It says Jordan Jackson was born on April 26, 1953. That's your boyfriend's birthday. Right?"

The verification left her speechless.

"So?" The guy waited a moment. "Do I get my sawbuck?"

She stepped back, opened her pocketbook and took out a ten-dollar bill. Once she had re-closed the purse, she handed him the money.

He stuffed it into his pocket and then looked her in the eye. "What's a chick like you see in a coon like Jackson?"

Her jaw clenched. "Jordan Jackson is a hundred times the person you'll ever be."

The guy, just about her height, 5'5", stepped closer, so his face was within a foot of hers. "Lady," he said, "save the high and mighty crap for your bleeding-heart readers." He pulled the paper out of his pocket again and waved it in front of her. "Your boyfriend ain't nuttin' but a goddamn firebug." He shook his head disdainfully.

"You've been blackmailing Jordan, haven't you?"

The guy shrugged. "You got it all wrong. I asked him for money. Fine fella that I is, he gave it to me. Course, when he started turnin' me down, I figured it was time I flash the paper elsewhere." He pointed at Lauren. "No better place to start than you."

Common sense told her she had wasted enough time on him. But she recalled what Jordan had said and done the night they had dined on the verandah of the *Ale House*. Confrontation had bred opportunity. The method was worth a try. She said, "Why do you hate black people?"

"Damn. If you don't know . . . " He shook his head. "I'll tell you. They got it fixed so everything is ass backwards. They sit on their cans and collect welfare and stuff. And when there's a good job they get that too. That affirmative action crap." He looked Lauren in the eye. "They got it made."

"You don't say. Then how come most are way down on the economic ladder?"

The guy sneered. "That's their problem. And if they don't like it, they oughta go back to the jungle." He ran his fingers under his hairy armpits and howled like a gorilla. "Case you didn't know, white folks founded this country."

"Excuse me," said Lauren, her patience all but exhausted. "I believe Native Americans occupied the continent first and that African-Americans were dragged here on slave ships. You — "

"Blah, blah, blah." His raised voice drowned her out. "Just you wait and see. We're gonna take this country back." He pointed at his *AA* tattoo and marched away.

Blood boiling, Lauren watched him hurry down the street and disappear around the bend. So much for Jordan's method. Her thoughts shifted to the paper the guy had shown her. Disconcerting questions nagged. At the top of the list — Could Jordan have torched his own home?

Chapter XV

Friday morning. Lauren had slept late. The *Today* show, her standard breakfast companion, was nearly over. She was finishing her morning coffee as she read the *Chronicle*. Ordinarily she was familiar with it well before it arrived at her apartment. But since her firing, her first look didn't come until after the paper had hit the newsstands. The sound of footsteps on the front porch drew her attention. She got up and looked out the window, just in time to see the mail truck moving on to the next house. She stepped outside, went to the mailbox and removed the contents: the New Yorker magazine, a postcard addressed to *occupant* offering discounts on vinyl siding and a first-class, business-size envelope with no return address. She took the mail inside and again seated herself at the kitchen table. She opened the envelope and read the enclosed note.

> **Lauren Worthington**
> **Poke your nose where it don't belong and you're gonna wind up like Jordan Jackson's house.**
> **A friend (with no "r")**
> **P.S. I know about cars and how to wire them.**

A knot gripped the pit of her stomach. Nervously she read the note a second time. On plain white paper, it yielded no clues. Her experience as a newspaper reporter enabled her to recognize the font, Bookman Old Style, but the observation proved nothing. She reached for the envelope. Same font. From all appearances both the note and envelope had been printed on a computer or electric typewriter. What to do. Logic said contact Loggin. Her stomach turned at the thought. She decided to call Jordan first. She hurried to the telephone and dialed his number. She read him the note.

"Stay there," he said. "I'll be right over."

Five minutes later, as she watched out the front window, he pulled up. She opened the door.

"Are you okay?" he called out, as he hurried her way.

"I guess." A moment later she felt his warm embrace.

"You're shaking."

She closed her eyes and breathed deeply as she focused on the caress of his hand moving up and down her back. The soothing strokes were welcome. The note had upset her even more than she had first realized. The better part of a minute elapsed before she finally leaned back and pointed in the direction of the kitchen table. "The note is over there."

He took her by the hand and walked the several steps across the small studio apartment to the table. He started to reach for the note but stopped. "It's better I don't touch it. Just in case there are fingerprints."

"Mine must be all over it," she said. "I've read it a half-dozen times."

He eyed the note silently. Then he read it aloud. "Any idea who sent it?"

"Your guess is as good as mine."

He eyed the note again. "You should contact the police."

"Loggin?"

Jordan shrugged. "Unfortunately, he's the one handling the case."

Appealing or not, the point, exactly what she had concluded when the note had arrived, was self-evident. She said, "Fine. I'll call the dunce." She picked up the telephone and dialed. Once connected, she detailed the facts.

"I'll be right out," said Loggin. "I'll have our bomb specialist check your car. In the meantime, let it be. You haven't told anyone else about the note, have you?"

"Only Jordan Jackson. He's here with me now."

Loggin groaned. "Well — all right, I guess. But tell him not to mention it to anyone else. At this point only the sender,

Jackson and the two of us know about it. Let's keep it that way. And one more thing — our discussion should be private. It's best you send Jackson on his way."

Meeting with Loggin alone at her apartment gave Lauren pause. But he was a detective, and this, a police matter. Reluctantly, she agreed. She hung up the telephone and said, "Loggin's on his way over. He wants to meet alone."

"So I surmised. You okay with that?"

She hesitated but, having already agreed, said, "It's fine."

Jordan sighed. "Well — if that's how you want it, I'll call you later." He gave her a hug. "I love you," he said, and he headed out the door.

Lauren quickly tidied up her apartment. Having things out of place when Jordan came was one thing; quite another with anyone else. She folded her futon bed back into its couch position. The last thing she wanted was to give Loggin false impressions. Minutes later the doorbell rang. She pulled back the window curtain, making certain who was there. She opened the door.

"Good day," said Loggin.

"Come on in."

He stepped through the doorway and looked around. "Nice little place." He inhaled slowly. "Nice perfume you're wearing."

Lauren pretended to miss the compliment. She wondered if sending Jordan home had been a mistake. She said, "The note, along with the envelope is over on the kitchen table." Loggin followed her there. "Earlier I handled them both. That was before Jordan mentioned you might want to check them for fingerprints."

Loggin read the note and then nodded slowly.

"What do you think?"

"It's a threat. The question — who sent it?"

No fooling. She made a conscious effort to keep the sarcastic notion off her face.

He re-examined the note. "*No 'r'.*" A perplexed look came over him. "The guy who wrote this likes puzzles. But we'll figure it out."

"I thought that *friend with no 'r'* meant *fiend.*"

Loggin looked at the note again. "Oh . . . uh . . . yeah. That's what I . . . uh . . . was thinkin' too. But we wanna check all the angles."

This time Lauren was less discreet, though she doubted Loggin discerned the ridicule of her deeply furrowing brow.

"Postmarked Cedar Creek." He shook his finger. "Don't let that fool you. The sender could have brought it to a local mailbox just to throw us off."

The possibility had already crossed Lauren's mind. She allowed Loggin, who had a pleased look, to assume the conclusion was original.

"The writer claims he knows cars and how to wire 'em. Course that could be a red herring." He gestured at himself. "That's a term we detectives — "

"I know what a red herring is."

"Just makin' sure." His focus returned to the note. "Someone doesn't want you nosin' around. That someone is afraid you're gonna find something out. But why you? It doesn't make sense."

"Unless . . . " said Lauren, "it's because I'm the only one still nosing around. You've stopped looking. You're convinced my father is behind the arson."

"You bet we are. We've got a solid case against him."

Lauren gestured at the note. "What about this?"

He shrugged. "Wouldn't surprise me if your father sent it just to throw us a curve." Loggin jerked back. "Don't get excited."

"Well — what do you expect when you suggest my father plans to do me in."

"Whoa." Loggin held up his hands. "I'm not saying he plans to carry out the threat. Just that he sent the note."

"You actually think my father would terrorize me?"

"To save himself . . . " Loggin shrugged. "But look — I'm not tryin' to hard time you. I've seen this kinda thing before. We won't take it lightly. Our bomb man is gonna check your car, and I'll have the note dusted for fingerprints and the like. In the meantime, let's think. Do you have any enemies, the kind that might wanna do you harm?"

Lauren racked her brain. "Not really."

"What about people you don't get along with? Maybe they dislike you more than you think."

Nielsen came to mind. There was animosity, but he had no reason to threaten her. He had fired her, not the other way around. She said, "Perhaps someone who doesn't like my liberal views — a skinhead, maybe — sent the note just to scare me."

"Possible, but not likely. They're more apt to go after folks like your boyfriend." Loggin hesitated. "Gotta tell you. Now that we've talked, I'm more convinced than ever your father sent the note."

"Why?"

"It's a matter of induction." Loggin displayed a self-satisfied look. "That's another term we police detectives use. You eliminate all other possibilities and — "

"I know from induction. You needn't talk to me like a third-grader."

Loggin jerked back. "You always this touchy?"

"Only with — " She bit her tongue. "Let's focus on your induction theory. How did you arrive at my father?"

"I invited you to expand my list."

"Who besides my father was on your list?"

"No one."

"One person! You call that a list?"

"Hey, it's one more than yours. And you don't need to raise your voice." Loggin smiled.

Though not the salacious type, it was equally unwelcome. "What you're telling me is that apart from my father your investigation of the note is done."

"You've got it all wrong. Like I told you, we're checkin' your car. Forensics are gonna dust the note for fingerprints. And I'm gonna stay in touch." Loggin smiled again; this time, provocatively.

Enough. If she needed police assistance, she would go over Loggin's head. Straight to the Chief. She got up from her seat. "Thanks for coming."

"My pleasure," he said, as he followed her to the door. "And don't worry." He jabbed the tip of his thumb into his chest. "*I'll* make sure you're well protected." He patted her on the back and then stepped out onto the porch.

She closed the door behind him. Jordan was right. Loggin was a useless boob. She seated herself at the kitchen table with a pen and pad. She examined every aspect of her life, everyone she knew — friends, acquaintances, as well as people who might dislike her. Not one possibility. Not even a remote one. She scribbled the word *Dad*. He had motive for the arson. Worse yet, the evidence clearly pointed his way. Facing a long prison sentence, he might be desperate. As Loggin had suggested, the note would do no real harm, but what an effective way to create reasonable doubt in the minds of a jury. She told herself her father would never use her that way. She reached with her pen to cross out the word *Dad*. Her hand froze, leaving her with the same list as Loggin. She stared at the paper. "Damn!" she snarled, as she hurled the pen across the room.

Lauren could hardly remember the last time she had been in her father's attic. She pulled a small cardboard box down from the top shelf of a bookcase. She took the box over to the window where she rummaged through the old negatives it contained. One by one she held them to the light. A close-up of her mother wearing a warm smile evoked memories of happy times. People often told Lauren how much she resembled her mother. Lauren could see it in the flattering photo. She set it aside and began searching for a family shot. The choices were few since her father was almost always the photographer. Near the bottom of the box, she found a picture of all three taken at Stone Mountain, Georgia, when she was in second grade. Her mother and father stood on either side, their arms draped around her back. She turned the negative over. Her mother and father reversed places, while Lauren stayed in the center. As she contemplated the anomaly, her eyes focused on the backdrop, carvings of the Confederate war heroes who decorated the face of the rock wall. She dug further into the box, but pictures of her with her parents were scant, and closed eyes, overexposure, etc. forced her to stick with her original choices. Eight-by-tens of the two negatives, nicely framed, would be a welcome adornment on the end table in her apartment.

She had just put the box away when she heard the telephone ring. With her father out and Bessie off for the day, Lauren tried to hurry though the attic's clutter. She wended her way around her great-grandfather's hickory rocking chair and then tripped on several suitcases, managing to grab her balance before she went down. She squeezed between her dollhouse and an antique highboy. Down the steep staircase she made her way to the nearest telephone, the one in the second floor den. By the time she arrived, the answering machine had already invited the caller to leave a message. Lauren listened.

"Hello Roger. This is Jordan. Per our discussion, I'll meet you tomorrow evening at *Phelp's Tavern* at seven o'clock."

Lauren stared at the telephone. Jordan — meeting with her father? *Phelp's Tavern*? The name rang no bells. She knew every establishment in Cedar Creek, not that there were many. She took the telephone book out of the top drawer of the desk. She thumbed her way until she found *Phelp's* in the yellow pages. It was located on Route 127 in Beaulin. It had to be nearly fifteen miles away. Why would Jordan and her father be meeting at some out-of-the-way joint?

She pressed the play button on the answering machine. She listened to the message again. It made no more sense than before. She went back up to the attic and got the two negatives. She headed downstairs to her car. Before leaving, she stopped at the telephone and played the message one more time. Sure enough, it was Jordan's voice. What, she wondered, were he and her father up to?

Lauren leaned back in the easy chair that occupied the corner near the front window of her studio apartment. She reached for the telephone and began pressing the headset numbers. Just before she hit the seventh and last digit, she hesitated. She hung up the receiver. The straightforward approach wouldn't do. Like a used-car salesman, she needed some clever patter.

Five minutes later she reached for the telephone and dialed again. Moments after, Jordan answered. "Hi Honey, it's Lauren. Did you have a nice day?"

"Not bad. What's up?"

"I wondered if you'd like to have dinner here tomorrow evening. I plan to make shrimp kabobs. Just the way you like them."

"Uh . . . Thursday . . . That's really nice but . . . "

"But what?" A pang of conscience admonished her to let him off the hook. No way. He and her father had chosen the devious road. She too would take that detour.

"I'd better take a rain check. Loads to do. Stuff at the office, etc."

"You've got to eat."

"I will. I'll grab a burger and fries at the drive through."

"That's a fine how do you do." The feigned indignation came with remarkable ease. "You prefer fast food to my home cooking?"

"C'mon. That's not what I said."

"Not word for word. But I got the gist." She waited a moment. "You still there?"

"I'm here."

"So — you coming for dinner?"

"Suppose we make it Friday?"

Lauren wrestled with the urge to make him explain. She already knew the answer, though the reason behind the *Phelp's Tavern* meeting remained a mystery. For the moment she would keep her distance. "Fine, we'll do it Friday. Should I pick up fast food rather than making kabobs?" The anguished sigh that greeted her ears provided adequate reparations; at least for the moment. "Just teasing. I'll see you on Friday. Six o'clock?"

"I'll be there, Sweetie. And thanks."

As she hung up the receiver, she tried to speculate what was going on between Jordan and her father. Common sense told her the effort was futile. But common sense wasn't calling the shots. Her brain was fixated. Dispelling the perplexing issue was as difficult as spurning an image of the Washington Monument rocketing skyward with huge purple wings. Back in fifth grade, her teacher, Mr. Wilbur, had painted the vivid image and then challenged the class to completely erase it from their minds. When he asked those who were successful to raise their hands, not one arm went up. Certainly not Lauren's.

Barker Nielsen examined the hanging baskets at Llewelyn's Nursery. Non-stop begonias with large crimson blooms would look nice on his front porch. He checked the price tag on the bottom of the container. Not at $7.95. The $2.95 red impatiens he had seen earlier would do fine. He was about to take the basket to the register when he heard someone call his name. He turned and spotted Medford Laughlin. "Fancy meeting you here."

Laughlin shook his head. "It's the other way around. I'm the amateur horticulturist. The question is what brings you here?" He looked at the impatiens. "They prefer shade, you know."

"That's why I chose them. They're for my porch." Nielsen had no idea that impatiens grew well in shade, but no need to let Laughlin know.

"I hear you fired Lauren Worthington. Good move. She's nothing but problems. Most everything she writes bears her scarlet brand."

Nielsen was familiar with the headmaster's predilection to bookish allusions. Still he struggled to make sense of the seeming literary link. "You mean Hawthorne's letter *A*?"

"Not *A*." Laughlin grimaced. "You know — the *L*-word. Liberal. In a town like Cedar Creek most folks prefer things the way they are. They don't appreciate bleeding-heart troublemakers like her."

"The same goes for the *Chronicle*. That's why I got rid of her." Nielsen knew his audience. As editor of a small-town newspaper, he always kept that in mind. Experience had taught him that principles were nice, but circulation paid the bills. He had also learned the importance of maintaining the right contacts, and Medford Laughlin, Chairman of the Village Board, was near the top of that list.

"The *Chronicle* hasn't taken a position on school vouchers," said Laughlin. "It's an idea whose time has come." Laughlin looked him in the eye. "You agree?"

Nielsen welcomed the overture but reminded himself of patience's virtue. He said, "You never know. The concept might merit consideration."

"What does that mean?"

"Just what I said."

Laughlin frowned. "Save your double talk for the retractions and corrections you bury in the hinterlands of your paper. I'd like some support. And the *Chronicle*, being the only paper in town, is the one to give it. An editorial recommending vouchers would go a long way."

"Well — given the right circumstances, we might just print one." Nielsen needed to be subtle, but *not* too subtle. He needed to be careful as well. For several years the *Chronicle* had been trying to get the tax assessment on its building reduced. Pulling it off would be a feather in his cap with the home office. Nielsen also wasn't happy with the real estate taxes on his home. He pointed at his basket of flowers. "We don't want to jump the gun. Plant too soon, and posies can die from a late frost. Unlike death and taxes, weather isn't a sure thing." The frustrated look on Laughlin's face gave Nielsen pause, but the opportunity was too good to miss. "Speaking of taxes, can you believe that my house was tagged at $163,000 when the Village went to full-value assessment? And the *Chronicle* has been getting the shaft for years."

Expression pensive, Laughlin gave a tiny nod.

Nielsen struggled to decipher the reaction. He waited, all the while projecting a stoic exterior.

Finally, Laughlin said, "You know, I need to check those taxes. Maybe talk to the assessor. You and that paper of yours shouldn't be over-assessed. That wouldn't be fair." A wry smile painted his face. He gestured at Nielsen. "And you should take another look at school vouchers. I think you'll find that winter is long past. It's time to plant."

Nielsen put his hand to his chin. "You could be right. Folks ought to have more choices. School vouchers are sounding better all the time."

Chapter XVI

F rom her seat in the last row Lauren surveyed the packed courtroom. Within the dignified backdrop of fine-carved mahogany walls, lined with portraits of aristocratic, robed men, the appetent throng buzzed. Their prurience was better suited to a prizefight or even a sideshow. On one side her father sat with his lawyer, the polished and sartorially splendid Chester Harwood. On the other, there was Jordan, along with Richard Parks, House Counsel to *Rockhill Indemnity and Casualty*.

Lauren wondered if the insurance lawyer might assume control of the case. Theoretically Jordan could turn him down, but, as Jordan had explained, from a practical standpoint it was Park's decision. Under Jordan's homeowner's policy, *Rockhill* could demand to take over the litigation. If Jordan refused, he would forfeit his insurance benefits under the policy.

Lauren ran her eyes over the many spectators seated with her behind the bar. Off to her right, down in the first row, directly behind her father, sat Nielsen. Her former boss may have been there to get the story. Litigation by a Village Board member alleging arson by the town's wealthiest and, arguably, most prominent citizen would certainly merit the personal attention of the *Chronicle*'s Editor. Nevertheless, Lauren suspected that Nielsen's interest was no more professional than most of the others.

Nielsen wasn't the only journalist who caught Lauren's eye. Across the way, in the rear of the courtroom, a team from *Judicial TV* was camped out. At first glance the sight seemed curious, but the reporter in Lauren quickly understood their presence. Arson in a rural town, intertwined with money, politics, romance and racial overtones, provided all the ingredients of a provocative story. Unfortunately, Lauren was caught in the middle. Stay away, she told herself — stay far away — from the predators of *Judicial TV*.

Two rows in front of her sat District Attorney Keena Waite. Her showing up was no surprise given the criminal matters pending as a result of the arson. The Boxley brothers had both pleaded guilty and were awaiting sentencing, and Brewster's plea bargain was conditioned upon his continued cooperation with the prosecutor's office.

Lauren checked the audience looking for the Village Board members. Jordan had subpoenaed them all, hoping examination under oath might reveal things they had kept secret. Lauren spotted Steve Ward in the front row. Jack O'Leary and Janet Warner were seated together at the far end of the back row. Lauren had heard rumors that the two were spending an inordinate amount of time together; far more than Board business would require. Unlike Jordan, who had put little stock in the gossip, Lauren was more skeptical. She scanned the remainder of the audience looking for Medford Laughlin. No sign of him. She was checking the rows one more time when she noticed a skinhead with the all too familiar *AA* tattoo on his upper arm. She had seen him before. But where? And when? The skinny fellow who had solicited money from Jordan? Definitely not. A moment later it clicked. He was the one whom she had helped several months earlier when he was being harassed in the alley by the two black youths. What was his interest in the lawsuit? She was mulling over the question when the Chairman of the Village Board, his nibs, strutted into the courtroom. An instant later her attention was drawn to the bailiff who was commanding them all to rise. Judge Boston was entering from the door behind the bench.

"Please be seated," said the bespectacled jurist. He filled his water glass from a silver pitcher and then shuffled some papers. "On today's docket we have the trial of Jordan Jackson against Roger Worthington. Let the record show that I have reviewed all the pleadings, including, among others, the plaintiff's Complaint seeking compensatory and punitive damages, and the defendant's Answer setting forth a general denial, as well as a counterclaim for abuse of process." The Judge looked over at Jordan. Is the plaintiff ready to proceed?"

"Yes, your Honor."

Judge Boston turned to the defense table. "And the defense, Mr. Harwood?"

"Ready."

"Before we move forward," said Judge Boston, "let the record show that the parties have stipulated that the plaintiff, Jordan Jackson, is the owner of real property located at 74 Hickory Lane in Cedar Creek. The parties have further stipulated his home at said address was destroyed by fire on April 16, 1983." The Judge directed his attention to Jordan. With that bit of housekeeping completed, Mr. Jackson, your opening statement, please."

As Jordan approached the jury and began outlining what he intended to prove, Lauren grew increasingly uncomfortable. Up until then the litigation between her boyfriend and father had seemed remote, but Jordan's deep voice modulating from loud to soft amidst the otherwise hushed courtroom altered that. The battle was joined, and there were sure to be casualties. The list of possibilities included her relationships with Jordan and her father. For twenty minutes according to her watch, though it seemed far longer, Jordan detailed his upcoming evidence. Harwood followed with a somewhat briefer statement. Each fired heavy volleys. Both were eloquent. As Harwood returned to his seat, Lauren wished she could change the channel. Unfortunately, this was not TV.

"Mr. Jackson," said Judge Boston, "please call your first witness."

Jordan got up from his chair. "The plaintiff calls Francis Loggin."

Lauren watched the rotund detective, his stomach hanging over his belt line, as he plodded to the stand and took the oath. Clad in a stretched-out, tweed sport jacket, lavender shirt and multi-colored tie, he contrasted with the smartly dressed attorneys.

"Would you state your full name for the record please?"

"Francis X. Loggin."

"How old are you?"

"Forty-six . . . uh . . . make that forty-seven. God, you need a score card the way the years fly by."

The gratuitous comment drew a chuckle from the audience. A momentary furrow of Judge Boston's brow suggested the jurist was less appreciative of the humor.

"You're a detective with the Cedar Creek Police. Correct?"

"Yup," said Loggin. He leaned back, gradually settling into a pronounced slouch.

Jordan stood motionless, seemingly waiting for Loggin to get comfortable. "How long have you been so employed?"

"Well — twenty-three years with the force. The last thirteen as a detective. Before that I was a patrolman."

"In the course of your duties were you assigned to investigate the fire which destroyed my home at 74 Hickory Lane?"

"Yup."

Lauren glanced at her father. She wondered what was going through his mind. From the time he was a child, born with the proverbial silver spoon, Cedar Creek had been his oyster. For him, a pillar of the community, image was important. Never had he faced hard times. The current civil suit, with criminal charges waiting in the wings, had turned his world upside down. Though he maintained a confident exterior, Lauren sensed what lay beneath the veneer. As a reporter for the *Chronicle*, she had covered other trials, effectively tracing their ebbs and flows while taking copious notes. Now a spectator, but one with a definite interest, her mind wandered. She redirected her attention back to the proceedings.

"Did you investigate the cause of the fire?"

"I did. Right after the fire department put it out."

"And what, if anything, did your investigation reveal?"

"Me and Fire Chief Murray found a gas can with the charred remains of an old rag stickin' out of the spout, right where Chief Murray said the fire started."

"Objection. Move to strike what Chief Murray said."

"Sustained." Judge Boston looked over at the jury. "Please disregard the witness's reference to Chief Murray's comment." He turned to Jordan. "Counselor, proceed."

"Did there come a time when you arrested Jake Brewster for hiring Orin and Clyde Boxley to set fire to my home?"

"Yup, and I helped get Brewster to talk."

"Detective Loggin, did you take steps to verify the information that Jake Brewster gave you regarding the fire?"

"Absolutely. Along with the DA, we gave him a lie detector test."

"Objection," shouted Harwood, as he jumped from his seat. "The witness surely knows that lie detector results are inadmissible."

"I didn't say the result. I — "

"Detective Loggin, I heard what you said." Judge Boston's tone was sharp. "At the moment I have an objection to consider. And I'll rule on it without your assistance." Judge Boston hesitated and then directed himself to the attorneys. "The probative value of knowing that a lie detector test was administered is far outweighed by possible speculation as to the results. Accordingly, I will not permit such testimony." He turned to the jury. "The witness's comment concerning a possible lie detector test is stricken. Please disregard it."

Lauren wondered whether Loggin's reference to the test might have been a ploy. As Harwood had pointed out, Loggin must have known the testimony was inadmissible. Did he hope that knowledge of the test and the defense's desire to hide the outcome would influence the jury. Did Loggin have more guile than his naiveté suggested? The question preoccupied Lauren, and before she resolved it, attorney Harwood was getting up for cross-examination.

"Detective Loggin, you're not a fireman, are you?"

"No."

"And you haven't taken any courses for determining the origin of fires?"

"Nope, but Chief— "

"You've answered my question." Harwood stood silent for a moment. "That's all I have." He returned to his seat.

"Redirect, Mr. Jackson."

"No, your Honor."

"Then call your next witness."

"The plaintiff calls Jake Brewster."

Lauren watched as a stocky, but muscular fellow, accompanied by a sheriff's deputy, entered. His T-shirt, jeans and smooth-shaven head suggested he would have been more at home at a bikers' bar. He walked forward, took the oath and then seated himself in the witness chair.

"Would you state your full name for the record please?"

"John Shandall Brewster, but folks just call me Jake. I even sign my name that way."

"Where do you reside?"

"On Route 47 outside of Potterstown. I got a trailer there."

While Jordan moved through the preliminaries, Lauren focused as much on Brewster's demeanor as his words. Legs spread apart and elbows propped on the arms of his seat, his wide chin seemingly flailed against his short flabby neck as he spoke. Though hardly polished, unlike the typical lay witness, he appeared at ease. Whether it was a product of repeated bouts with the justice system or unmitigated arrogance, Lauren had no idea. How it would play with the jury was equally hard to guess. Regardless, she suspected they too were sizing Brewster up. Her attention was drawn to Jordan who, from his position behind the plaintiff's table, meandered to a spot halfway between the Judge and jury, about ten feet from the witness.

"Prior to the 16th day of April of this year did you hire Orin and Clyde Boxley to set fire to my home?"

Brewster showed nothing, almost as if he were preoccupied.

The courtroom drew silent. All eyes, Lauren's included, transfixed on the witness. Hushed expectation set the stage for Brewster's response. Though Lauren assumed his plea bargain with the District Attorney's office made his answer a foregone conclusion, hearing it from Brewster's lips would have a different aura.

"Mr. Brewster, we're waiting," said Judge Boston.

The witness turned to the Judge. "I'm taking the Fifth Amendment."

"If your Honor please," said Jordan, "the witness has entered a plea bargain in connection with the arson. He has waived his privilege against self-incrimination."

The pique in Jordan's voice suggested to Lauren that the unexpected curve had thrown him off. She wondered how the Judge would rule. His upward gaze gave no hint.

His Honor finally said, "I'm aware that Mr. Brewster negotiated some form of plea bargain before Judge Gardiner in criminal court. Unless that agreement specifically waived his privilege against self-incrimination, he still enjoys it here in this court. That is not to say that its exercise might not jeopardize his plea agreement. But that risk is for Mr. Brewster to weigh. As matters stand, I will not require him to answer the question." The Judge looked at Jordan. "Proceed."

Jordan stood motionless. Like a gunfighter ready to draw, his laser-like stare challenged the witness.

Brewster, equally still, stared back.

On the streets of the old west, Jordan could have forced the issue. But Brewster, armed with the Constitutional protection, wore bulletproof armor. Jordan said, "Mr. Brewster, do you know Orin and Clyde Boxley?"

"Objection," said Harwood. "Your Honor has just ruled that the witness is entitled to take the Fifth Amendment."

"I did, indeed, but he is a witness, not a defendant. This is not a matter where he can refuse to take the stand. Mr. Jackson is free to ask his questions, and Mr. Brewster can assert his privilege, question by question." The Judge turned to the witness. "You heard Mr. Jackson's question?"

Brewster nodded. "And I'm taking the Fifth."

Jordan took a step forward. "Did you ever give any money to Orin or Clyde Boxley?"

"Fifth Amendment."

Jordan pointed in the direction of the defendant and raised his voice. "Did Roger Worthington engage you for the purpose of setting fire to my home?"

"Fifth Amendment."

"Your Honor," said Jordan, "if I may take a few moments."

"You may."

Jordan turned and walked back to the bar. He leaned over where District Attorney Keena Waite was seated. She got up. She and Jordan whispered back and forth. She removed a paper from a file and handed it to Jordan. He took it to the court stenographer and requested that he mark it for identification. Jordan redirected his attention to the witness. "I show you Plaintiff's Exhibit 1, marked for identification, and ask if that's your signature?"

Brewster examined the document. "Yup, that's my signature."

"Is this the plea agreement you entered with the District Attorney's office?"

"Yup."

"I direct your attention to the second paragraph and — "

"Your Honor, counsel is attempting to do by indirection that which you precluded directly. The witness is entitled to exercise his privilege against self-incrimination."

"That he may, Mr. Harwood. But Mr. Jackson is entitled to ask his questions." Judge Boston turned to the witness. "May I see the document." Brewster handed it to the Judge. He read it and then called both attorneys to the bench where he showed the document to Harwood. The Judge said, "There are some evidentiary matters we need to discuss. To avoid potential prejudice, we best consider them in private." He glanced at his watch. "It's ten-thirty. We could use a break. I'll meet with counsel in my chambers in fifteen minutes." He turned to the jury. "I need to meet with the attorneys on some technical issues, plus we could all use a break." He rapped his gavel. "Court is in recess."

Lauren hurried out of the courtroom and down the stairs to the first floor vending machines where she got a coffee. She seated herself on a bench in the hallway and sipped the hot beverage. If Brewster remained mute, her father might win the lawsuit. But what about Jordan? His home had been burned. Neither he, nor *Rockhill* should ultimately bear the costs of the arsonist's acts. And Jordan had a claim for punitive damages. Didn't he deserve justice? And the same held true for the citizens of Cedar Creek. They were entitled to assurances that the person who had masterminded the arson was identified and held responsible. Lauren tried, as she had done many times before, to convince herself that her father couldn't be responsible for the fire. Months earlier she had never anticipated the facts would lead to the current confrontation. Her bravado on Baker's show had come easily. Much as she missed her job at the newspaper, in one respect Nielsen had done her a favor. From all appearances she had relentlessly pursued the issues to the point where it had gotten her fired. Only she knew the truth: she had been hoping for an easy way out. Then again, losing her job was a *way out*, but hardly *easy*. And far from what she had in mind.

Along with Harwood and the District Attorney, Jordan sat waiting for Judge Boston in his chambers. The large office was decorated with finely crafted appointments, the centerpiece of which was a huge, English-walnut desk. Jordan glanced at the beautifully hand-tooled leather surface. How many times he had admired it. Past visits enabled him to picture the antique's triple-banded drawers with inlaid central panels that adorned the opposite side.

"Sorry to keep you waiting," said Judge Boston, as he finally arrived and took a seat behind his desk.

"Your Honor," said Jordan, "since the District Attorney is an integral part of this issue, I invited her to join us."

"That seems to make sense." Judge Boston glanced at Harwood. "Any objection, Chet?"

"No, your Honor."

Judge Boston turned to the District Attorney. "Keena, what's your position?"

"In his plea agreement with my office, Jake Brewster expressly agreed to give his full and unqualified cooperation in any and all matters attendant to the facts and circumstances relating to the arson. I consider his reliance on the Fifth Amendment and his refusal to answer questions here a violation of that agreement. Should he remain mute, I will ask Judge Gardiner to vacate his plea and reinstate the charges against him."

"Is Mr. Brewster aware of your position?"

"No, your Honor. Since he is represented, I felt it would be improper for me to approach him directly."

"Point well-taken." Judge Boston sighed. "Does that mean we're at a standstill?"

"I don't believe so," said Jordan, mentally patting himself on the back. "As soon as your Honor recessed, I phoned Bill Poland, Brewster's attorney. He said he'd come down immediately. I assume he's meeting with Brewster in the prisoners' holding room now."

Judge Boston pushed the button on his intercom. "Mary, would you see if Bill Poland is in the prisoners' holding room? If so, ask him to join us here in my chambers."

Minutes later Poland entered. "Have a seat, Bill. How've you been?"

"Better, your Honor, but — " He chuckled and then exchanged pleasantries with the other attorneys.

"Do you know why I asked you to join us?"

Poland nodded. "My client took the Fifth. He got some brilliant legal advice from his buddies down at the lockup. God, those jailhouse lawyers can drive you nuts. They suggested he play hardball today in order to negotiate a better deal. They told him he could always fall back on the one he had."

"Wanna bet?" said the District Attorney.

Poland looked over at the prosecutor. "Relax, Keena. His head is back on straight. I believe he's ready to testify."

"You're sure?" said Judge Boston.

Poland nodded. His expression, however, lacked the confidence of the gesture.

Jordan appreciated the reaction. Experience representing criminals like Brewster had taught him one could be sure of nothing. Fortunately, on this occasion the thug was someone else's client.

"Well — let's find out," said Judge Boston. "We'll reconvene in the courtroom in five minutes."

The lawyers left his Honor's chambers. As they started down the hall, Poland pulled Jordan aside. "Let me fill you in on a few details. I think they'll help. My client has a stake in your success. He wants his plea bargain." Poland motioned toward a discreet corner of the hallway where the two spoke and then returned to the courtroom.

A minute later Judge Boston returned to the bench. With the jury still out, Brewster was escorted back to the witness stand. The Judge said, "Let the record show that I met in chambers with the attorneys, Messrs. Harwood and Jordan, along with the District Attorney and William Poland, criminal counsel for the witness, Jake Brewster." The Judge turned to the witness stand. "Mr. Brewster, you've had the opportunity to consult with your attorney, Mr. Poland. Correct?"

"Yup."

The Judge looked over at Poland, who was seated in the first row behind the bar. "Counselor, you have no objection to your client waiving his privilege?"

"No objection, your Honor."

Judge Boston redirected his attention to the witness stand. "Mr. Brewster, I understand that after speaking with your attorney, you have decided to testify rather than exercise your privilege against self-incrimination. Correct?"

"Yup."

"And you're doing so voluntarily and without any promises from the court or the parties here?"

"Yeah, but . . . uh . . . "

Jordan's grip on his pen tightened.

"Mr. Brewster," said Judge Boston, "it's your decision whether to answer the questions."

"I wanna, but what if they ask me about other stuff? Ya know, the kind that could git me more charges."

Jordan sensed the understanding reached in chambers was about to unravel. If it did, his case would too. He wanted to jump in, but Brewster wasn't his client.

Judge Boston rocked back, his gaze seemingly upward into empty space. Finally, he looked back at Brewster. "If I understand your position, you're willing to testify. However, later you may decide to resort to the Fifth Amendment."

"Yeah, that's what I wuz tryin' to say."

"Well — I believe we can accommodate you." Judge Boston's face grew stern. "But understand, any questions you answer become water over the dam. Your Fifth Amendment privilege is gone as to those questions. And understand further, that if down the road you opt to exercise your privilege, your plea bargain with the District Attorney's office may again be in jeopardy. Do you follow me?"

"Yup."

"Mr. Poland," said Judge Boston. "With that understanding you're willing to have your client testify?"

"Yes, your Honor."

Jordan exhaled slowly. The roadblock had been removed; at least for the moment.

Judge Boston motioned to the bailiff. "Mr. Lockman, please bring the jury back into the courtroom." Once they were seated, Judge Boston said, "Ladies and Gentlemen, we have had some colloquy and resolved some issues with which you need not concern yourselves. Please focus on the evidence as if the interruption had never occurred." He turned to Jordan. "Mr. Jackson, at long last, I believe you can proceed. How far we go is another matter."

Jordan got up from his seat. "Mr. Brewster, let me return to my earlier question. Prior to the 16th day of April did you hire Orin and Clyde Boxley to set fire to my home?"

Brewster hesitated, appearing to glance at Poland. An instant later, with his gaze redirected at Jordan, he said, "Yeah, I did."

Jordan mentally breathed an invisible sigh of relief. "And when was that?"

"Just a few days before they torched the place."

Jordan eased forward alongside the jury box rail, so that Brewster's gaze would angle further away from Roger Worthington. "And why did you hire the Boxleys?"

A puzzled look appeared on Brewster's face. "To burn your house down. Is that what you're askin'."

"Well — I understand. But you must have had a reason or purpose."

"Yeah, money. Roger Worthington paid me eight thousand dollars. Half I gave to the Boxleys, just like he told me to."

"And when you say Roger Worthington, you're referring to the defendant, the gentlemen seated at the table off to my left. Correct?"

"Yeah." Brewster extended his arm toward Worthington.

"Let the record show that the witness pointed at the defendant," said Judge Boston.

Jordan leaned against the jury-box rail. A huge barrier had finally been broken. "Did Mr. Worthington pay you the eight thousand dollars all at once?"

"Nah, he gave me half when he hired me and half when the job was done."

"Whose idea was it to hire the Boxleys?"

"His."

"Did he tell you why?"

"Objection," said Harwood.

"Overrruled. The question calls for the defendant's statement. He's here in court." Judge Boston turned to the witness. "Did Roger Worthington tell you why he wanted you to hire the Boxleys, rather than do the job yourself?"

"Yeah. He said it would give us *insulation*. That's what he called it. He said he wanted the Boxleys, cause they wuz identical twins. If one wuz caught, they'd be able to jerk the cops around. Like Worthington said, the cops ain't gonna know which one done it."

"What payments did you make to the Boxleys?"

"I gave 'em two thousand when I hired 'em, and two more after they done the job."

Jordan eyed his yellow pad. His mind, however, looked beyond the page. Delving too far could allow Harwood to make hay on cross-examination, but motive could not be ignored. He said, "When Roger Worthington hired you, did he indicate why he wanted to burn my house down?"

"Yeah, he said you wuz a thorn in his ass." Brewster glanced at the Judge. "'Scuse my lingo, but that's what he said." Brewster looked back at Jordan. "He said you wuz killin' his mall while datin' his daughter, both at the same time."

Jordan took another moment, as much to let the slurs sink in as weigh the need for more questions. Guilding the lily would only sharpen Harwood's pitchfork. "No further questions," he said.

The bespectacled Harwood got up from his seat. He moved forward, his bearing indicative of the confidence, experience and skill gained over more than thirty years. Jordan caught a glimpse of the smile that Harwood appeared to be giving the witness. Warm as the expression seemed, Jordan suspected it masked a dagger-laden tongue.

"Mr. Brewster," said Harwood, "you have a trailer out on Route 47. Right?"

"Yup."

"How long have you lived there?"

"About two years."

"And where did you live before that?"

The question, which drew a startled look from Brewster, came as no surprise to Jordan. He could object, but, ultimately, Harwood would be allowed to make his point. He had a right to attack Brewster's credibility.

"Mr. Brewster," said Judge Boston, "kindly answer the question."

"I was in the Watenee River Correctional Facility in Rembert, South Carolina."

Harwood looked over at the jury as he asked his next question. "As a matter of fact you were serving a three-year sentence for aggravated assault. Right?"

"Yeah."

"You've also been convicted of two other assaults, as well as petit larceny and issuing bad checks, haven't you?"

Brewster nodded.

"I'm sorry," said Harwood, "the court stenographer needs an audible answer."

"Yeah, I wuz convicted of that stuff."

"Tell this jury how many years you've spent in prison altogether."

"Objection," said Jordan.

"Overruled. Like the convictions the punishment bears on the witness's credibility." Judge Boston glanced at Harwood. "I'm allowing it, but we'll not make this a trial of Mr.

Brewster's criminal history." His Honor turned to the witness. "Please answer the question."

Brewster appeared to count on his fingers. Finally, he said, "About nine, maybe ten years."

Harwood's face bore a disparaging look. "Mr. Brewster, you've entered a plea agreement with the District Attorney's office as a result of the arson of Mr. Jackson's home. True?"

"Yeah."

"Under that agreement you'll spend another nine years in prison."

"Yeah."

"You're becoming a regular jailbird."

"Objection!" Jordan leaped from his seat. "Counsel is — "

"Question withdrawn." Harwood folded his arms. "With your prior felony convictions, you were facing much more time, weren't you?"

"Yeah. Twenty-five years or something like that."

"By implicating Roger Worthington, you're saving yourself years behind bars."

"I suppose."

"You suppose?" Harwood walked forward and handed a piece of paper to the witness. "Perhaps this will make you more certain." He waited while the witness read the document. Then he said, "In your plea bargain, you agreed, among other things, to testify that Roger Worthington hired you to burn Jordan Jackson's house down. Isn't that true?"

"Yeah."

"That deal got you a greatly reduced sentence, didn't it?"

Brewster shrugged. "Yeah."

Harwood gestured toward the jury. "Give these folks one reason why they shouldn't conclude that you, a convicted felon, a repeat offender, aren't lying in order to avoid a much longer prison sentence."

"Well — I . . . uh . . . passed a lie detector test."

Harwood lurched back and then barked, "Move to strike. Such tests are inadmissible."

"If your Honor please," said Jordan. "Counsel opened the door. He demanded a reason why the jury shouldn't disbelieve the witness. The witness gave him exactly what he asked for."

Judge Boston tapped his pen against an open palm. "I'm going to allow it."

"But your Honor, the very — "

"No, Mr. Harwood. As Mr. Jackson said, you opened the door, and not with a harmless question; rather a rhetorical one that was calculated to allow no possible answer. That's hardly cricket. However . . . " The Judge turned to the jury. "Ladies and gentlemen, I want you to understand that lie detector results are generally inadmissible; their reliability subject to question. That being so, in weighing Mr. Brewster's credibility, you're free, if you wish, to completely disregard the test, including his claim that he passed it. It's strictly up to you." He looked back at Harwood. "Proceed."

Jordan eyed his adversary. No surprise. The dapper lawyer was jotting a note. If the roles had been reversed, Jordan would have scrawled *lie detector* on his yellow pad with a big *A* next to it; a reminder to consider the issue in the event of an appeal.

"Mr. Brewster," said Harwood, "you claim that you were hired by the defendant Roger Worthington. As a matter of fact, you were hired on the telephone by someone who said he was Roger Worthington. Isn't that true?"

"Well . . . I guess."

"You never met Roger Worthington face to face, did you?"

"Uh . . . no. But I seen and heard him on that teletlon last year."

"This telephone conversation you referred to — how long did it last?"

Brewster gazed off into space. "Maybe ten minutes. I ain't too good at judgin' time."

"Maybe you weren't any better at judging who was on the phone." Harwood folded his arms.

Brewster looked at the attorney but said nothing.

"Earlier you told Mr. Jackson that Roger Worthington paid you eight thousand dollars in cash. But a minute ago you admitted you never met Roger Worthington face to face. Isn't that inconsistent?"

"Uh . . . not really. On the phone he said he wuz gonna put the money in my mailbox in twenty minutes, and sure enough the money wuz there, just like he promised."

"Excuse me," said Harwood. "The money was there, but whether you were dealing with Roger Worthington is another matter."

Brewster again said nothing.

"As a matter of fact, you had never spoken with Roger Worthington either in person or by phone prior to that occasion, had you?"

"Uh . . . no."

Harwood stepped closer to the witness. "And you don't know him personally."

"No."

"For all you know (Harwood gestured toward the bailiff who stood in the far corner of the room) that was Mr. Lockman on the telephone the day you were hired."

A blurt of air shot through Brewster's lips. "I doubt that."

"But bottom line, you don't know for sure who was on the phone, do you?"

Brewster opened his mouth part way but remained frozen for several seconds. He glanced at the bench, only to be greeted by a stern face. Finally, he looked back at Harwood and said, "I guess not."

Exterior impassive, Jordan stayed focused on his legal pad. His stomach knotted.

"That's all I have," said Harwood.

Brewster started to get up from the witness chair.

"Excuse me," said Jordan. "I have a few more questions."

Brewster sighed and then re-seated himself.

Jordan took his time as he got up from his chair and came around from behind the plaintiff's table. He said, "A minute ago you told Mr. Harwood the person who hired you for the arson said the money would be in your mailbox. As best as you can recall, what, specifically, did that person say?"

"Objection, hearsay."

Jordan was about to counter, but his Honor was quicker. "Mr. Harwood, assuming we have an out-of-court statement from a third party, and that's debatable, your examination regarding the telephone call opened the door to the balance." Judge Boston turned to the witness. "You may answer the question."

"He said he wuz gonna drop the dough off in about a half-hour. He said to stay where I wuz and wait."

"Where were you at that time?"

"My trailer."

"And do you know the date?"

Brewster shrugged. "I know it wuz a Saturday, but I ain't sure of the date. It wuz (he counted on his fingers) five days before the Boxleys torched your place. They done it the next Thursday."

"If I told you that the fire occurred on April 16th, could we agree that the telephone call in question occurred on April 11th?"

Brewster mumbled to himself as he again went to his fingers. "Uh . . . yup."

"And about what time was it when you received that telephone call?"

"Let's see. It uh . . . had to be real close to two in the afternoon."

"And what did you do next?"

"I waited."

"And what happened?"

"Some twenty, maybe thirty minutes later, I was watching out the window when I seen this shiny, black Mercedes pull up and an arm stick somethin' in my mailbox. I wuz about to go out there when my phone rang. It was Worthington again. He said he had just put the cash in my mailbox. That I should get it right away, before someone else snatched it. I hurried out. Just as I did, the Mercedes pulled away. I went to the mailbox where I found a brown envelope stuffed with four thousand dollars, all in crisp hundred-dollar bills."

Jordan strolled back toward the plaintiff's table. The hiatus provided a chance to strategize upcoming inquiries. He said, "You indicated you saw a black Mercedes pull away. How can you be sure?"

"I know my cars pretty good. And around these parts, ya don't see many pricey wheels like them."

"Were you able to see the driver?"

"Not really. The car had dark tinted glass."

Jordan gestured to his right. "Tell the jury what you did once you got the money."

Brewster turned to the jury. "First off I hid the dough. But I wuz nervous. Crossed my mind that this could be a police set up. Me and the cops don't get along, if you know what I mean. So, later that day I drove out where Roger Worthington lives. Sure enough, there wuz the big, black Mercedes parked in the driveway. Just like the one I seen. That convinced me it really wuz Worthington that hired me."

"You say you went to his home. How did you know where he lived?"

Brewster furrowed his brow. "C'mon, ya must be kiddin'. Round these parts everyone knows Roger Worthington and his mansion."

The smiles that appeared on several faces of the jurors told Jordan he could move on. He gestured at Brewster's right shoulder. "Would you mind rolling up your sleeve?"

Brewster did a double take but then pulled up the sleeve.

Jordan pointed at the large *AA* tattoo emblazoned there. "What does that stand for?"

"*Aryan Alliance.*"

Brewster's resolute voice, grating though it was, played dulcet notes in Jordan's ears. "What type of organization is that?"

"White supremacist."

"I see," said Jordan matter of factly. "Would it be fair to say that members of the *Aryan Alliance* believe in segregation of the races?"

"You bet. This is a white country, and it should stay that way."

Jordan gestured at the jury. "Tell these folks how you feel about people of color."

Brewster shrugged. "You asked, so here it is. I ain't got no use fur 'em."

"Objection," called out Harwood. "Mr. Jackson is impeaching his own witness."

"Excuse me," said Jordan. "I simply asked the witness for his view. In no way have I challenged that view."

"Objection overruled."

Jordan refocused on the witness. "Earlier, in response to Mr. Harwood's questions, you admitted serving three years for assault. What were the circumstances of that assault?"

Brewster sat up taller and looked straight at Jordan. "Me and a buddy stoned and bull-whipped this colored guy cause we caught him dancing at the *Crooked Horseshoe* with this chick — a white chick — that my buddy used to date."

Jordan, a smile on his face, stepped closer to Brewster. "How do you feel about me?"

"Well — like I said, I ain't got no use fur your kind. But you, one of them black, bleeding-heart activists . . . you make me sick."

"You feel the same way about Roger Worthington?"

Brewster shook his head. "Not at all. He's a straight shooter."

"Plus he's white."

"Objection."

"Withdrawn," said Jordan. "So, when you testified earlier that Roger Worthington hired you to burn my house down, it wasn't because you wanted to help me prove my lawsuit against him."

"Objection . . . leading."

"Sustained."

Jordan eyed the jury. No doubt they understood that Brewster's testimony had not been motivated by a desire to help Jordan and his case. "Mr. Brewster, what's the telephone number at your trailer?"

Brewster furrowed his brow. "My telephone number?"

"Yes, please."

"555-3004."

"No further questions."

Brewster shrugged and then started to get up.

"Excuse me," said Harwood, still in his seat. "Recross. I assure you that I'll be brief." He stood up but remained between his chair and the defense table. "Mr. Brewster, you're not sure who delivered the arson payment in the black Mercedes, are you?"

"Uh . . . not exactly."

"For all you know it could have been anyone." Harwood pointed at the defense table. "Maybe it was the plaintiff, Mr. Jackson."

"I believe he drives a Maxima." Brewster smirked.

"He might have rented a black Mercedes just to make you think it was Roger Worthington. Did you ever think of that?"

Brewster's eyes were wide. "Uh . . . no."

Harwood pointed at the witness. "Bottom line, you don't know who was in that car."

"I guess not."

Harwood leaned against the defense table. "Just one last question. You said you have no desire to help Mr. Jackson, but isn't it true that more than anything, you want to preserve that plea agreement you made with the District Attorney?"

"Wouldn't you, if you were me?"

Harwood nodded. "I sure would." He glanced at the jury and then looked back at the witness. "That's all I have."

Judge Boston had the bailiff escort Brewster from the witness stand back into the custody of the Deputy Sheriff. The Judge glanced at his watch. "The noon hour fast approaches. Perhaps it is best we break for lunch." He rapped his gavel. "Court is recessed until two o'clock this afternoon."

Seated in a side hallway with an edition of the *Chronicle*, Lauren checked the clock on the far wall. It reminded her of the one that decorated the rear of her tenth grade geometry class. Both had big Roman numerals, as well as a seemingly sluggish pace. A half-hour remained until court reconvened. She flipped to the *Word Jumble* and began filling in the blanks. A minute later Harwood stepped out of a conference room a short distance down the corridor. A skinny guy followed. It was the same fellow who had solicited money from Jordan and showed her the paper about the Georgia fire. Lauren doubted the duo noticed her as they headed off in the opposite direction.

Harwood must plan to call the guy as a witness, she thought. Jordan would want to know. The Georgia blaze could blind side him. But how could she take sides; meddle in a way that would hurt her father, especially when a criminal prosecution, one that could send him to prison, was on the horizon. She got up. She needed to think and some fresh air to do it. She hurried out of the courthouse lobby, down the marble steps to the street. Telling one side what she saw, but not the other, was unfair. But if she told both, each would accuse her of disloyalty. Back and forth she debated. Just minutes prior to two o'clock she returned to the courthouse. She went directly to the courtroom, taking the same seat she had occupied during the morning session. Procrastination, the path of least resistance, had made her decision. No one knew she had seen Harwood with the skinny guy.

———

His witness sworn, Jordan eyed his own left hand. His fingers were tightly wrapped around the barrel of his pen. He laid it down and then adjusted the knot of his silk tie as he got up from his seat. The satiny feel of the delicate fabric reminded him of the quaint shop along the beautiful Cayman Island beach where Lauren had bought it for him. How nice if they could be there strolling hand-in-hand along the sun-drenched Caribbean shore. He imagined the ebbing flow of the clear, aqua waters breaking against his ankles with fine, white sands underfoot. He breathed a tiny sigh and strolled in the direction of the jury-box rail. The thump of his heels on the marble floor directed his thoughts back to reality. "Would you state your name for the record, please?"

"Janet Estelle Warner." Her clearly enunciated name suggested center stage did not upset her. Not surprising, given her experience on the Village Board.

"You run an insurance agency, don't you?"

"Yes, the Warner Insurance Agency."

"Among other things, you write liability and casualty policies on real estate."

"Yes."

"You're also a member of the Cedar Creek Village Board, aren't you?"

"I am."

"In the course of that position you've had occasion to consider the proposed mall the defendant wants to build just outside of town. Right?"

"Yes."

"How do you feel about the mall?"

Warner shrugged. "My views are an open book. I've repeatedly spoken out in favor of it at Village Board meetings."

"Have you ever discussed it with the defendant outside of public meetings?"

"Well — I suppose."

"During those discussions has the defendant ever pressured you to approve the mall?"

Warner turned to the Judge. "Your Honor, aren't my conversations regarding matters pending before the Board confidential?"

Judge Boston shook his head. "Ms. Warner, while certain matters conducted in executive session may be shielded from the statutory mandates requiring open meetings, that's entirely different from litigation. In any event, day-to-day conversations enjoy no such protection. Accordingly, please answer the question."

Warner hesitated and then turned back to Jordan. "Mr. Worthington has asked me to support the mall from time to time."

"Is it a fair statement that he wanted it approved very badly?"

"I suppose."

Jordan moved a bit closer to the witness. "What, if any, insurance do you write for the defendant?"

Warner squirmed in her seat. "Uh . . . his home . . . car and business."

"Did you and he ever discuss the possibility of writing insurance for the mall if and when it was approved?" Jordan waited a moment. "Ms. Warner, do you want me to repeat the question?"

Several more seconds of silence. Finally, she said, "It may have come up, but I'm not sure."

Jordan folded his arms. "The possibility of huge fees, and you're not sure?"

"Objection. Argumentative and intended to impeach his own witness."

"Sustained."

Jordan debated whether to rephrase the inquiry but quickly opted to let the matter be. He said, "Just a couple more questions. Do you own a mobile telephone?"

"Yes."

"And what carrier provides your service?"

"*AT&T.*"

"Thank you. That's all I have." He turned to his adversary. "Your witness."

"Ms. Warner," said Harwood, still in his seat, "regardless whether you discussed insurance for the proposed mall, Mr. Worthington never promised that you would get the insurance business if the mall was approved. True?"

"Absolutely."

"That's all I have."

Judge Boston excused Janet Warner. Jordan called Medford Laughlin as his next witness. Attired in a herringbone, three-piece suit, the lanky educator with the long neck paraded to the stand where he seated himself. Halfway between bushy eyebrows and the top rim of reading glasses that sat low on his Roman nose, Laughlin's eyes peered out over the courtroom. He glanced at the jury and then placed his right hand on the Bible. At *Cedar Academy* or a Village Board meeting, Laughlin was the man in charge and free to talk down to everyone. Whether he was foolish enough to behave that way in Judge Boston's courtroom remained to be seen. Apart from an aloof air, Laughlin responded with minimal fanfare as Jordan took him through the preliminaries — his name, address, employment, etc.

"Mr. Laughlin," said Jordan, "among the issues currently pending before the Village Board is Mr. Worthington's proposal to construct a mall. Is that correct?"

"Yes."

"Outside of regular Board meetings, has Roger Worthington ever approached you regarding that proposal?"

Laughlin eyes widened. "You must be kidding. As a matter of fact, he answered Cervantes' great question."

"Pardon me," said Jordan. Out of the corner of his eye, he caught Judge Boston's grimace. Apparently the jurist appreciated the odd response even less than Jordan.

"What I alluded to," said Laughlin, his speech more affected than usual, "is that Roger Worthington proved you can have too much of a good thing. He was constantly pestering me."

The theatrics were no surprise to Jordan. Whether he could turn them to his advantage was another matter. "How many times would you estimate he approached you about the mall?"

His angular face contorted, Laughlin gazed into space. Finally, he said, "At least twenty. Probably more."

"So, he was really on your back."

"Objection — leading."

"I'll rephrase," said Jordan, his purpose already accomplished. "How would you characterize the defendant's interest?"

"Intense."

"In the course of your discussions, did the defendant ever express any views about me?"

Laughlin groaned. "Did he ever."

"What did he say?"

"That you're a pain in the ass." Laughlin turned to the jury. "Excuse my French." He looked back at Jordan. "He also called you the *goddamn gadfly of Cedar Creek*."

A smile on his face, Jordan turned to the defendant and gave him a long, hard look. Like Laughlin, he too could employ theatrics. He strolled over to the plaintiff's table. As he seated himself, he said, "Your witness, Mr. Harwood." Despite his cool exterior, Jordan had misgivings. A pompous intellectual like Laughlin might be fodder for cross-examination.

Harwood got up from his seat and eased his way toward the stand. "Mr. Laughlin, to date you've taken no position pro or con regarding the mall, have you?"

"I'm waiting for all the facts. We've hired an independent consultant, you know."

"You're the only member of the Board yet to take a position. Right?"

"Yes."

"The Board is otherwise split, two and two."

"That's right."

"Isn't it true that you've lobbied both factions to support your school voucher program?"

Laughlin sat up tall. "Cedar Creek needs that program. And yes, I have encouraged my fellow board members to support it."

"Isn't it true," said Harwood, "that you've offered to trade your vote on the mall with either side if they'll support your voucher program?"

Laughlin scowled. "That's a misrepresentation. I have labored long and hard to improve our Village."

"Is it your testimony that you've never linked your vote on the mall to your voucher program? And before you answer, let me remind you that I can call your fellow Board members as witnesses."

Jordan watched the witness slowly exhale. His indignant expression failed to mask concern. A part of Jordan relished the sight, but his more judicious side knew that Laughlin's comeuppance, though long overdue, would be preferable on some other occasion.

"Mr. Laughlin, we're waiting," said Judge Boston.

"Doubtless," said Laughlin, "the two issues came up in the same conversation, along with other Board business." His voice grew louder. "But never . . . absolutely never did I offer to trade my vote on the mall for approval of the voucher program."

Jordan thought back to the numerous times when Laughlin had broached the subject with him. Not once had he ever proposed a tit-for-tat trade; at least in so many words. Sure, the hint was there, but the master of words had managed to say one thing while communicating another. Chances were he had done the same when speaking to the other Board members.

Harwood inched closer. He too raised his voice. "But you pushed vouchers every chance you got, didn't you?"

"You bet I did. I represent a constituency that demands higher quality education, and I intend to pursue it."

Sure, thought Jordan, translating the headmaster's words. You represent a bunch of wealthy whites who want segregated private education, complete with a public subsidy. And most of all, you represent your own interests.

Harwood gestured towards the defense table. "You don't like Roger Worthington, do you?"

"Not especially."

"You're biased against him. You'd like to see him lose this lawsuit, wouldn't you?"

Laughlin peered disdainfully over the top of his narrow-rimmed glasses. "My good Sir — and I use the term *quite advisedly* — to quote the Duke of Wellington, *I care not one two-penny damn.*"

A ripple of laughter from the audience drew the rap of Judge Boston's gavel. He glared at the spectators just long enough to insure decorum and then refocused on the witness. "Mr. Laughlin, spare us your erudite references."

"Whatever pleases your Honor, though some well-chosen prose would surely enhance — "

"Mr. Laughlin, this is a courtroom. *My courtroom.*" Judge Boston's booming voice echoed off the marble floor. "Save your tutorials for your academy." The Judge gestured toward Harwood.

The polished advocate nodded but took his time, appearing to study his notes. Jordan suspected his adversary enjoyed letting Laughlin stew. Finally, Harwood said, "Mr. Laughlin, you were here earlier when Jake Brewster testified. Right?"

"Yes."

"He used to work for you as a handyman, didn't he?"

"As a matter of fact, he did."

The disclosure caught Jordan off guard. Harwood had done his homework. He knew things Jordan didn't. The question remained, what other surprises, perhaps more problematic, were waiting in the wings.

"You fired him, didn't you?"

"Yes, because he was unreliable."

"Can you amplify . . . explain exactly what you mean?"

Laughlin eyes moved to the jury. "Brewster often showed up late. Other times he failed to show up at all. Then there were the times he came in drunk. I run an exemplary facility. I expect no less from my staff."

"Prior to the time that you fired Jake Brewster, you loaned him some money, didn't you?"

His attention redirected to Harwood, Laughlin heaved a sigh. "I did, though with hindsight my generosity was, doubtless, ill-advised."

"How much was the loan?" said Harwood.

"Thirteen hundred dollars, and nearly a thousand remains unpaid."

"But you have a lien on his trailer, don't you?"

A surprised look appeared on Laughlin's face. "My lawyer had him sign some papers. One of them was a lien."

Harwood hesitated. Finally, he said, "No further questions." He returned to his seat.

Laughlin started to get up from the witness chair.

"Excuse me. I have a few questions on redirect," said Jordan, conscious that the rare chance to make the pompous headmaster continue playing on his terms had influenced the decision.

Laughlin frowned and then reseated himself. As he did, he reached down and pulled a pocket watch out of his vest. He eyed the timepiece and shook his head.

Jordan glanced at the jury. He suspected they had little sympathy for the witness, not when they were giving far more of their time to civic duty. Jordan refocused on Laughlin. "Earlier you indicated to Mr. Harwood that you don't like Roger Worthington. Isn't it true that you dislike me as well?"

"Absolutely."

"Are you hoping I win this lawsuit?"

Laughlin's eyes drifted upward. "Need I quote the Duke of Wellington a second time?"

"You'd better not!" barked Judge Boston.

Laughter again filled the courtroom. Jordan restrained the urge to join in. "Did you come here today voluntarily?"

"I assure you I have better things to do." He reached into his inside jacket pocket and pulled out a paper. "And I'd be doing them if you hadn't served me with this subpoena."

"That's all I have," said Jordan.

Harwood immediately got up. "A few more questions."

A glare on his face, Laughlin muttered under his breath.

Harwood moved around from behind the defendant's table. He gestured at Jordan. "Mr. Jackson is a thorn in your side, isn't he?"

Laughlin's affirmative response was no surprise to Jordan. Exactly where Harwood was headed was less clear.

"From what you've told us, you dislike both the plaintiff and the defendant."

"You've got that right." Laughlin glanced at the jury. "If I weren't under oath, I might be more diplomatic." He redirected his gaze to Harwood. "Anyway the feelings are mutual. And it's not as if I'm saying something these gentlemen — and I use that term loosely — don't already know."

"Whom do you dislike more?"

Laughlin stuck his thumbs into the vest pockets of his three-piece suit. "That's a tough one. Like choosing between the *Cyclops* and *Medusa*." Out of the corner of his eye he appeared to catch Judge Boston's glower. "Let me rephrase that in plebeian terms. It's like choosing between vermin and lice."

"Why do you dislike my client?"

"He's the most influential person in town, and education hardly tops his list of priorities. If it weren't for him, I believe we would have had school vouchers years ago."

"Mr. Laughlin," said Harwood, "you drove here today. Right?"

"I wouldn't walk. Not the better part of two miles."

Jordan swallowed hard as he suddenly realized where Harwood was going. Laughlin's aplomb suggested he was less astute.

Expression inquisitive and tone amiable, Harwood said, "What kind of car do you drive?"

Laughlin pulled back.

"Mr. Laughlin, I didn't hear your answer."

"A . . . uh . . . Mercedes."

"As a matter of fact, a black one."

"Uh . . . yes . . . it's black." Laughlin's voice had suddenly become subdued.

"With dark, tinted windows."

"Yes."

Harwood folded his arms. "It's like the defendant's car, isn't it?"

"You're not insinuating — "

"Kindly answer the question."

"Uh . . . I guess it's like the defendant's."

"And it's like the car which Mr. Brewster testified was used to deliver the arson payment to his trailer, isn't it?"

"I resent the aspersion." Laughlin's jaw clenched.

Harwood glared at the witness. "Resent or not, your car is like the one used to deliver the arson payment, isn't it?"

Laughlin glared back. "Yes."

"Brewster worked for you, didn't he?"

"Yes . . . but I fired him."

"You knew he had a criminal record when you hired him, didn't you?"

"I suppose."

Harwood's voice grew louder. "You've acknowledged that you despise both the plaintiff and the defendant."

"Yes, but — "

"No buts. Just answer the question."

"Objection," said Jordan. "Counsel is badgering the witness. Not giving him a chance to answer."

"Overruled. This is cross-examination. The question called for a *yes* or *no*, and the witness said *yes*."

Harwood walked back to the defense table. He took a paper out of his file. "Mr. Laughlin, you own *Cedar Academy*, don't you?"

"Yes."

"*River Valley Bank* holds a mortgage on your school, doesn't it?"

Laughlin hesitated. "Yes."

"How much do you owe?"

Laughlin turned to Judge Boston. "My personal affairs are nobody's business."

"I'll decide that," said a stone-faced Judge Boston. "Answer the question."

Laughlin muttered inaudibly. He looked back at Harwood and growled, "Offhand, I don't know the exact amount."

Harwood looked at his notes. "Would three hundred fifty thousand be a fair approximation?"

Laughlin appeared to sulk.

"Your answer," said Judge Boston.

"Something like that."

"You're behind in your payments. True?"

"A little."

"A little!" Harwood banged his hand on the table. He marched forward and stuck a paper in front of Laughlin. "As a matter of fact, *River Valley Bank* has threatened to foreclose, haven't they?"

Laughlin's gaze lowered. "Well — " His normally decisive voice was barely audible. "Yes."

Harwood yanked the paper away from Laughlin. "No further questions." He headed back to the defense table, along the way giving the document to Jordan. "Keep it," he said. "It's only a copy."

Jordan eyed the paper; his mind, however, was elsewhere. Earlier better judgment had urged him to excuse the witness. Unfortunately, Jordan had ignored the wisdom. He had gone ahead and, in so doing, given his adversary another shot. Though the damage appeared minor, Jordan suspected that down the road more serious consequences might ensue. Little did he realize how soon the repercussions would come. "No questions," he said.

"The witness is excused." Judge Boston checked his watch. "This is a good time to call it a day." He rapped his gavel. "Court is adjourned until nine a.m. tomorrow."

Jordan began stuffing his papers into his file when Parks, his co-counsel from *Rockhill Indemnity and Casualty*, who had been silent most of the day, said, "Too bad you gave Harwood another bite at the apple. He put his teeth marks into Laughlin, not to mention our case."

Jordan studied Parks's face, trying to get a read on the insurance company lawyer's thinking. Might he demand to take over the case? Jordan begrudgingly decided to concede his miscalculation. He said, "If I had it to do over, I might choose a different approach. Of course, hindsight always makes us wiser."

"You've put us behind the eight ball." Parks knocked the back of one hand against the palm of the other. "The jury may refuse to hold Worthington liable, given what they heard from Laughlin."

"Do you think Laughlin is behind the arson?"

Parks pulled at his chin, as his eyes appeared to drift along the row of portraits that lined the far wall. "Not really. But I wouldn't stake money on it. Especially my insurance coverage."

Jordan swallowed hard. Parks had a point, and this time Jordan was reluctant to admit it. He said, "Even if I had excused Laughlin earlier, Harwood could have re-called him as part of the defense."

"Maybe he would . . . and, then again, maybe he wouldn't. Regardless, he couldn't impeach his own witness. You would have been the one cross-examining; the one asking leading questions."

Once again, Parks had a point. "What do you plan to do?" said Jordan, anticipating Parks was about to take over the case.

Parks shrugged. "Nothing, really. Just go with the flow."

Jordan breathed a sigh. "I appreciate that."

"Hey, don't mention it. As far as I'm concerned, it's your game to win or lose. Of course, if you lose, we won't know who's responsible for the fire. We'd have to include you on our short list of possibilities. In that case I doubt the company would pay your claim. I'd certainly discourage it; at least until a jury rules otherwise."

You son of a bitch. You were hoping I'd stab myself. Jordan glared at Parks. He wanted to blast the insurance company lawyer, and he would have if candor had not cast guilt's shadow the opposite way. Reluctantly Jordan admitted that self-indulgence, his choice to handle the case, had created his problem. He resumed the process of stuffing his papers into his file. His brain reverberated with the old adage: *A lawyer who represents himself has a fool for a client.* How apropos, he thought, as he trudged out of the courtroom.

———

Lauren lingered in the hallway outside the courtroom. She would have made her usual quick getaway, but the night before Jordan had left a message on her answering machine asking her to wait.

"Hi," she said, as he approached.

"What did you think of today's proceedings?"

"Interesting."

"That's an evasive answer."

"What do — " She stopped herself. Defensive instincts were useless when they both knew he was right. Out of the corner of her eye she saw her father approach. The new dilemma, exactly the reason she desired a quick getaway, eclipsed the need to duck Jordan's question.

"Am I interrupting something?" said her father. "A strategy session, perhaps?"

Jordan chuckled.

Though the laugh seemed amiable, Lauren suspected it masked a lawyer's shrewdness.

Her father slapped Jordan on the back. "Laughlin gave you some funny answers on the stand today. Might be because he's behind the arson. You oughta check him out. Then again, maybe that's unnecessary. If you arranged the burn yourself, you already know all the details."

Jordan shrugged. "My money is still on you, Rog."

Though the two were exchanging jabs, Lauren detected a strange undercurrent of seeming affability. Even in moments of sarcasm Jordan would never refer to her father as *Rog*. The subtlety might have escaped Lauren had she not heard the telephone message Jordan had left at her father's home several days earlier. The question, however, remained: What was going on?

Jordan turned to her. "What do you think?"

Playing dumb seemed the wise course, plus she preferred to be a listener. Indeed she preferred to be elsewhere. Unfortunately, both men were looking her way. "Uh . . . hard to say." The inane remark echoed in her ears. Her father's frown, a familiar one, aroused a bad memory. As a youngster she hated Sunday school, especially the religious homework. On one occasion when she had let it slide, her father had confronted her. A straightforward explanation, telling him the biblical readings were boring, backfired. As she grew older and learned the art of subtlety, she tried to dance around his questioning. That worked no better. The recollection convinced her that she was merely delaying the inevitable.

"You didn't answer the question," said her father. "I'm sure you have opinions. So share them."

She eyed the two men, their impatient stares demanding. Each wanted her to point an incriminating finger at the other. She said, "You can't rule Laughlin out."

Jordan rolled his eyes. "That's obviously not where you're putting your money."

She hesitated.

"We're waiting," said her father.

"You're placing me in an unfair position."

Her father turned to Jordan. "I could have sworn she was the one who went on the radio and promised to pursue answers."

You would have too, she thought, if you had Baker on your back. Legitimate or not, the argument had as much chance as one of Laughlin's literary references in Judge Boston's courtroom. She said, "Back then, we were talking about a mall. I never expected arson." Frustrated looks had her squirming. "What do you want from me?"

"A little support would be nice."

"I could use some of that too," said Jordan.

"We've got something in common." Her father put an arm over Jordan's shoulder. "Got a minute?"

"I suppose. But remember, the chips fall where they may."

Her father nodded and then gestured toward a bench at the end of the hallway. "You'll excuse us," he said. "We have things to discuss. Meantime, you can search for those answers." The two started to walk away. Her father glanced back. "We'll be waiting with bated breath."

She watched them stroll down the corridor. How dare they gang up on her. Sure, Baker had drawn her boast, but . . . but what was going on? Her father and Jordan, long-time adversaries, embroiled in bitter litigation, were acting like old friends. And now they had the gall to make her the butt of their jokes. Enough. She wanted answers, and she was going after them. But how? Her mind began racing. She headed out of the courthouse and down the marble stairs that led to the street. She was almost to the bottom when the sight of an old telephone booth sparked an inspiration. The yellow pages might yield a clue. Common sense told her the idea was a long shot. Experience as a reporter dictated that she re-examine all the facts before going off half-cocked. She hurried to a bench and pulled a pen and pad out of her purse. In a stream of consciousness she began listing what she knew.

1. Her father owned a black Mercedes identical to the car that had delivered the payoff to Brewster.
2. Jordan had been giving money to a member of the Aryan Alliance.
3. Jordan had a juvenile record relating to a fire in Georgia.
4. Her father was apparently in a financial bind.
5. Jordan and her father, courtroom adversaries, had become far too friendly.

She was about to write the number 6 but stopped. Making the list was a bad idea. Too much suggested that Jordan or her father might be responsible for the fire. And recent events had added a previously absurd possibility. Both.

Jordan welcomed the two-minute respite that Judge Boston had granted him. For nearly two hours he had bored the jury with meaningless testimony. Chief Murray had provided technical details about the fire, but nothing that linked it to Roger Worthington. Jordan glanced at his list of remaining witnesses. Not one would offer compelling testimony. He was playing *Blind Man's Bluff*. How could he possibly sustain his burden of proof? Up until that moment wishful thinking had kept him positive, but the dose of reality forced him to confront the likelihood of defeat. Identifying the arsonist, even if it wasn't Worthington, might have been a sufficient consolation. Unfortunately, that too was pie in the sky.

Jordan knew his mind was drifting. He began silently counting to ten in an effort to recapture focus. Less than halfway through, the unwelcome image of another lawyer interrupted the enumerative process. He visualized a scowling Richard Nixon, a decade earlier, telling his constituents he was not a crook. Soon enough an irate nation made Nixon eat his words. Jordan feared the jury might have a similar fate in store for him. Counting, even to a million, wouldn't change the outcome. Regardless, like Nixon, Jordan had to appear steadfast. Starting on his own initiative, rather than Judge Boston's impatience, would be a step in that direction. Jordan took a deep breath as he got up from his seat. He said, "I call Steven Ward to the stand."

The tall witness, his slicked-back hair in perfect place, strode forward. Attired in his well-tailored blue suit, he displayed the confidence Jordan needed to convey. However, unlike Jordan's, Ward's was genuine. He seated himself in the witness chair, placed his hand on the Bible and in a deep and resonant voice took the oath.

"Please state your full name for the record," said Jordan.

"Steven Alfred Ward."

"Where do you reside?"

"27 Millbrook Lane, here in Cedar Creek."

Jordan glanced at the jury, in particular, the females. All of them, the elderly seamstress included, were focused on the witness. Whether their attention was owing to something other than his words — physical attributes, perhaps — was an open question. "You're a member of the Village Board. Right?"

"Yes."

"Among the matters pending before you is the defendant's application to build a shopping mall in Cedar Creek. Correct?"

"Yes."

"At any time has the defendant pressured you with regard to that application?"

"Well — he . . . uh has been persistent. Lots of phone calls, and he stopped me on the street several times looking for support." Ward hesitated. "But I understand. He's got a lot at stake. From what I've heard, if it doesn't go through, he'll be in deep financial weeds."

"Objection," shouted Harwood. "Move to strike as hearsay anything the witness claims he heard."

"Sustained. The jury is directed to disregard the remark." Judge Boston gestured Jordan to proceed.

"Please tell the jury how many times the defendant has spoken to you about the mall."

Ward gazed off into space. Finally, he said, "Well — I don't mean to make him sound like a nuisance, but it must be fifteen or twenty."

Jordan studied the witness. Might his reluctance to cast Worthington in an unfavorable light be more show than real? In Village Board executive sessions, closed to the public, Ward had often badmouthed Worthington. Regardless, the engaging witness had served the purpose for which Jordan had called him. "No further questions," he said.

Harwood got up from his chair. "Mr. Ward, you own a strip mall on Broad Street, don't you?"

"I do."

"You make your living from the rents you collect there. Right?"

"Yes."

Harwood walked halfway to the witness, a distance of about ten feet. "If the defendant's mall is approved, you're likely to lose some tenants, aren't you?"

"Objection," said Jordan. "Speculation."

"No, it's cross. I'll allow it." Judge Boston turned to the witness. "Please answer the question."

Ward, as smooth as his glossy oxfords, shrugged. "Personally, I doubt it, but one never knows."

An impassive exterior camouflaging reactions, Jordan's eyes remained focused on his legal pad. In back rooms Ward had a sharp bite, but in public forums he was the consummate politician.

"You have some vacancies now. Two, I believe," said Harwood.

"Yes."

"You oppose the defendant's mall because it's a threat to your livelihood." Harwood's tone sharpened. "Isn't that true?"

"Not really." Ward paused. "Don't get me wrong. The mall won't help me, but that's not why I'm against it. Very simply, it's bad for Cedar Creek. Traffic, the aquifer, damage to green space. I could go on and on."

"Are you asking this jury to believe that the threat of competition doesn't color your views?"

"Well, I have to admit . . . " Ward heaved a sigh. "If the proposed mall were a close call, I'd have a hard time ignoring my interests. But that just isn't the case." He turned to the jury. "A big shopping mall next to our park would turn Cedar Creek — this village we call home — into an unsightly, congested facsimile of anywhere America."

A smattering of applause from the rear of the courtroom drew a stern look from Judge Boston, along with a rap of his gavel. A seemingly imperturbable Ward sat motionless. The courtroom may have been foreign territory, but experience in Village Hall suggested otherwise.

Harwood walked back to his seat. "No further questions," he said.

Jordan debated for an instant about redirect. With a past blunder still fresh in his mind, he concluded that Ward had given him what little mileage he could. Jordan glanced at his watch — 11:30. He could request a recess for lunch. If so, should he excuse the two telephone company employees he had subpoenaed? They were in the audience waiting. He had spoken to them before court but had no idea what either would say. Each, asserting privacy, refused to discuss the documents he had brought. Disclosure required that Jordan call them to the stand. If he did, he would be shooting craps. Maybe with loaded dice. Under other circumstances he might have sent them home, but with his case failing, why not take the gamble. With a little luck he might be able to prove that Roger Worthington had made the telephone calls to Jake Brewster arranging the payoff for the arson. Even if that didn't pan out, he might discover who did. He said, "I call Robert Thomas to the stand."

A man in his thirties, medium build, stepped forward and was sworn. Preliminaries done, Jordan said, "By whom are you employed?"

"*Sprint*, the communications company."

"What are your duties?"

"I'm the manager of the area office."

"And that area includes Cedar Creek?"

"Yes, Sir."

"You're here in response to a subpoena *duces tecum* that I served on your office."

"Uh . . . yes, we got a subpoena."

"And that subpoena required you to bring some records. Right?"

"Yes, I brought them."

"And these are records which your *Sprint* office keeps in the regular course of its business?"

"They are."

Jordan quickly mapped strategy, deciding to jump ahead. If necessary, he could always backtrack and lay a further foundation. He said, "Referring to the records, is Roger Worthington a customer of your company?"

"Yes."

Jordan was halfway home. The next question might yield a jackpot. "What, if any, calls were made from his mobile telephone on the afternoon of April 11th of this year to the telephone of one Jake Brewster; that is, 555-3004."

The witness slowly reviewed his records. "I'm sorry, Sir. There were none."

"That's fine," said Jordan, careful to hide disappo ntment. "Tell me," he said, "do any of the other five persons listed in the subpoena, those on our Village Board, including myself, have mobile-phone accounts with *Sprint*."

"Two. You and Medford Laughlin."

With shortened odds on a jackpot, but also boxcars, Jordan prepared to roll the dice again. He said, "Were any calls made on those mobile telephones to 555-3004 on Apr l 11th?"

"There were no such calls."

"Thank you," said Jordan. "No further questions "

Harwood had no cross-examination. Jordan called his next witness, Charles Townsend, an employee cf *AT&T*. Preliminaries completed, he tossed the dice again. "Is Roger Worthington a customer of *AT&T*."

"No."

"Has he ever been a customer?"

"No."

"Are any members of the Cedar Creek Village Board, the other five persons named in the body of your subpoena, customers of *AT&T*?"

"Two. Janet Warner and Steven Ward."

"Did either of them make any calls on their mobile telephones to 555-3004 on the afternoon of April 1th?"

"No."

"Thank you," said Jordan. He nodded appreciatively. Whom was he fooling? The jurors weren't stupid. They had watched him shoot craps without making a single point. "No further questions," he said.

"I have nothing," said Harwood.

Judge Boston excused the witness and recessed for lunch.

As the courtroom emptied, Jordan sat alone with his file. His complaint, like his opening statement was replete with definitive allegations against Roger Worthington. Unfortunately, his proof was more like the Swiss cheese sandwich he planned to order for lunch at the nearby café.

Alone in her studio apartment, seated at the kitchen table, Lauren was happy to be away from the case during the lunch break. Why then, she wondered, did she choose to read about it in the *Chronicle*, especially a front-page article that bore all the earmarks of Nielsen's tabloid style.

> *Like the flames that raged at the home of Cedar Creek Village Board member Jordan Jackson this past April 16th, questions are ablaze in the courtroom of Judge William Boston. Who is the arsonist? Will he strike again? Rumors abound that the fire may have been racially motivated and the Aryan Alliance behind it. When interviewed, fellow Board member Steven Ward, who recently received a threat, characterized the perpetrator "as a craven terrorist who must be stopped."*
>
> *In his lawsuit papers Jackson has alleged that prominent Cedar Creek real estate developer Roger Worthington is responsible. Worthington has countered with an answer demanding damages for abuse of process and suggesting Jackson set the fire himself to recover the insurance. Against this backdrop, Jackson, who is black, has been dating Roger Worthington's daughter, Lauren Worthington. Sources close to the parties say that the interracial relationship fueled bad blood between the two men. Sordid allegations of arson, sex and bigotry are turning the litigation —*

The ring of the telephone drew Lauren's attention from the article. She picked up the receiver. "Hello."

"Is this Lauren Worthington?"

"Yes. Who's this?"

"You work for the *Chronicle*?"

"Who's calling?"

"The *Aryan Alliance* member you talked to on the street a few months back."

Lauren immediately thought of the skinny guy with the *AA* tattoo. "Jordan Jackson gave you money in the park. Right?"

"Are you nuts?"

"Aren't you the fellow with the document from Georgia? The one I gave ten dollars."

"You didn't give me nuttin'."

Lauren was about to close down. "You must have the wrong number."

"Ain't you that reporter who helped get them two black guys off my ass. It wuz in the alley next to the antique place, the one that used to be a theater."

The information jogged her brain. She recalled the incident and the stocky youth she had helped. He bore the *AA* tattoo, the same as the skinny fellow who had solicited money. "Yes. Now I know who you are. What do you want?"

"I got some information that I think you'll find interesting."

"I'm listening." She grabbed a pen.

"First things first. You'll keep me out of this. Okay?"

Lauren hesitated. She said, "I'll try, but — "

"What's that mean?"

"I don't work for the *Chronicle* anymore. I'm currently unemployed. Unlike a reporter, one who's working, my sources aren't protected." Silence greeted her ears. Curiosity cajoled her to promise confidentiality. Better judgment curbed the temptation. Information on an unknown subject from a dubious source didn't justify the risk. The way her luck had been going, a court would hold her in contempt and put her in jail for refusing to disclose. She said, "I'll promise you this. I won't tell unless a court orders me."

"Not what I wanted." There was a long pause. "Ah, what the hell."

Lauren cradled the telephone receiver between her ear and shoulder so she could take notes.

"I been followin' the arson case. Course everyone has. I work at the Cedar Creek office of *Sprint*, sortin' mail and stuff. What with *Sprint* being the top mobile-phone carrier round these parts, I wondered if any of our customers called that

Brewster guy on the afternoon of April 11th. I took a gander in the files. Guess what I found?"

"Got me," she said. Her interest was far greater than she let on.

"Sure enough, there were two calls to Brewster's trailer, just over twenty minutes apart. The customer who made 'em don't mean nuttin' to me. Corporate line — *Blue Sky Realty Corporation.*"

The name, though only vaguely familiar, knotted Lauren's stomach. "I appreciate the information," she said, as she jotted it down.

"Don't mention it."

"Why'd you call me?"

"I figured you'd wanna know, seein' as how it's your father and your boyfriend that's involved. I told myself, what the hell, she helped me when I wuz in a jam."

"I appreciate that."

"By the way, back when you wuz on Baker's show, I almost talked to you. I tried to call, but I couldn't get through. That Baker is one cool dude. Talks my language."

Discretion kept Lauren from debating the point.

"You don't hafta say nuttin'. I know there ain't no love lost between you and him. Gotta go." An instant later the telephone clicked.

Lauren hung up the receiver. She stared at the pad where she had written *Blue Sky Realty Corporation.* Before moving out of her father's house, she had seen the name on business envelopes there. She had no idea what connection her father had to the company. Minor, perhaps, but he could just as well be an officer or even the owner. Earlier that morning when Brewster had testified that her father had made the two calls arranging payment for the arson, Lauren had her doubts. The newest revelation whittled away at them. More and more, evidence pointed in her father's direction. She tried to dismiss the logic. She told herself that Brewster was an ex-con who couldn't be trusted. Unfortunately, the platitude failed to explain how he had passed a lie detector test.

Lauren stared at the salad she had made for lunch. Suddenly, it looked less appetizing. She checked her watch.

Court would be back in session in another hour. What to do with the new information. The problem smacked of *déjà vu*. Last time she had kept quiet, but this time she had something concrete. Should she call her father? What about Jordan? Or even Loggin, the DA or Judge Boston? She could investigate on her own and then make a decision. She grabbed a large chunk of cucumber and stuffed it into her mouth. She chewed it, along with a whole lot more.

———

Lauren handed Jordan a folded note. She had given an identical one to Harwood only moments before when he had entered the courtroom. The note read:

> During the lunch recess a confidential source informed me that on the afternoon of April 11th, *Sprint* customer *Blue Sky Realty Corporation* made two mobile-telephone calls to Jake Brewster's trailer (555-3004).
>
> I am giving a copy of this note to both sides of the case. Do not ask me any questions, including the name of my source.

Lauren took her usual seat in the rear of the courtroom. She watched as Jordan, who was standing alongside the plaintiff's table, read the note. He turned her way. She lowered her gaze just enough to break eye contact. A minute later, out of the corner of her eye, she caught a glimpse of Jordan rushing out of the courtroom. A member of the crew from *Judicial TV* followed. The sight of the pursuing vulture ignited disparaging thoughts. Reflection altered her perspective. If she had been there on assignment for the *Chronicle* and one of the principals had dashed for the door, she would have been at his heels. Activity was the harbinger of the unexpected, and the unexpected, often adorned with lurid details, was the foundation of a good story. Anything for a good story.

———

Jordan hurried back down the center aisle of the courtroom. Judge Boston had just taken his seat. "Your Honor, may I approach the bench?"

"Permission granted." The Judge gestured Harwood to join them.

Jordan handed Lauren's note to the Judge. "I received this only minutes ago." Jordan waited while the Judge read.

"Very interesting." Judge Boston glanced over at Harwood. "You have a copy, I assume."

Harwood nodded.

"Who is the note from?"

"Lauren Worthington," said Jordan. "She's the daughter of the defendant, as well as my girlfriend."

A telling look appeared on the Judge's face. "She's a reporter with the *Chronicle*, isn't she?"

"She was," said Jordan, "until a few weeks ago."

"Let me guess." The Judge breathed a sigh. "You want her source."

"I'm hoping that won't be necessary. As soon as I received the note, I called Robert Thomas, the gentleman from *Sprint* who testified this morning. He agreed to return and should be here any minute. His office is just a few blocks up the street."

Judge Boston eyed the note again. "This could be significant." He looked over at Harwood. "Any objection to a brief delay." Before Harwood could respond, the Judge pointed at the rear of the courtroom. "That won't be necessary. Here comes Mr. Thomas now." The Judge motioned him forward to the witness stand. "We appreciate your coming back." As Thomas took his seat, the Judge said, "You're still under oath." He turned to Jordan. "Counselor, please proceed."

"Mr. Thomas, earlier when you were here, I asked you about certain individuals and whether *Sprint's* records showed they had made any mobile-telephone calls to 555-3004 on the afternoon of April 11th. A short time ago I requested that you return with the bill, if any, listing the April, mobile-telephone calls of *Blue Sky Realty Corporation*."

"Yes."

"Does *Sprint* have a customer by the name of *Blue Sky Realty Corporation*?"

"It does."

"You have in your hand a document. Is that the bill of *Blue Sky Realty Corporation* which includes April 11ᵗʰ of this year?"

"It is."

"May I see it?"

Thomas handed it to Jordan. He flipped to the second page and ran his finger down to April 11ᵗʰ. A pair of entries had him struggling to contain an outward reaction. He took the bill to the court stenographer and had it marked for identification. Then he took it to the witness and said, "I show you Plaintiff's Exhibit 2 marked for identification and ask if it was made in the regular course of *Sprint's* business?"

"Yes, Sir."

"And was it the regular course of business to keep the information it contains?"

"It was."

"I offer it in evidence."

Harwood went over to the witness stand and examined the document for several moments. "No objection."

"Received," said Judge Boston.

Jordan took a deep breath. He said, "Referring to the bill, please tell the jury what, if any, calls were made on the mobile telephone of *Blue Sky Realty Corporation* to 555-3004 on the 11ᵗʰ of April."

Thomas looked at the second page. "There were two. One at 1:52 p.m. and the other at 2:16 p.m."

"Do you know the identity of the person or persons who made those calls?"

"No."

"Do you know who owns *Blue Sky Realty Corporation*?"

"I don't."

"Do you know the name of the representative of *Blue Sky Realty Corporation* with whom Sprint deals? You may refer to the bill if you wish."

Thomas looked at the document. "I'm sorry. Not offhand. We might have that information at the office, but after I got your call, in my rush to get here, I simply grabbed the bill."

"I understand," said Jordan. "If possible, I'll try to avoid the need for a third trip." He looked at Harwood. "Your witness."

"No questions."

"Mr. Thomas, you're excused," said Judge Boston. "Thank you for coming." As Thomas left the stand, the Judge turned to Jordan. "Call your next witness."

"If I may take a moment, your Honor." Jordan leaned over to Parks and whispered. "Would you have someone from *Rockhill* contact the Secretary of State and get the lowdown on *Blue Sky Realty Corporation*?"

"Will do." The insurance company lawyer got up and left the courtroom through the rear door.

As Jordan prepared to call his next witness, common sense told him his desire to question the defendant under oath — emotion, rather than judgment — was influencing his decision-making process. For an instant he debated whether he should toss the dice. Shooting craps was not what trial attorneys were supposed to do. They owed their clients a fiduciary obligation. But Jordan was his own client. He could play fast, loose and however he pleased with the fool's case. He said, "The plaintiff calls Roger Worthington."

Dressed in a charcoal gray suit, the six-foot defendant, a distinguished hint of gray around the temples, walked forward intrepidly. He took the oath and then seated himself on the stand.

Jordan studied the defendant as they went through the basics. There were no signs of defensiveness. That might have come as a surprise, were it not for their recent private exchanges. The otherwise arrogant entrepreneur had shown another side. Jordan moved to the jury-box rail and said, "Mr. Worthington, what, if any, interest do you have in *Blue Sky Realty Corporation*?"

"I own forty percent of the stock."

Adrenaline surged. Jordan contained any outward reaction, even as he caught a glimpse of a tiny lurch from juror number three. It crossed Jordan's mind that Lauren must have known where her note was apt to lead. He refocused on Roger Worthington. "On the afternoon of April 11th, using *Blue Sky's* mobile telephone, did you call Jake Brewster at his trailer?"

"No."

"Did someone else do so at your request or direction?"

"No."

Worthington's responses were crisp and unwavering. Piercing holes in his testimony would not be easy. But circumstantial evidence might work. "Do you own a black Mercedes?"

"Yes."

"You were here the other day when Jake Brewster testified that you hired him to engage the Boxley brothers to burn my house down?"

"Yes, I was here."

The terse answers suggested that Harwood had his client well prepared. Jordan said, "You heard Jake Brewster testify that on the afternoon of April 11th he received two calls from you; the second when you dropped off a cash payment of four thousand dollars at his trailer."

"Objection. Counsel is leading his own witness."

"Overruled. The defendant is an adverse party." The Judge turned to the witness. "Please answer the question."

"Yes, I was here when Brewster said that. But it's not true."

"Was Mr. Brewster mistaken when he said he saw your Mercedes?"

"I don't know what he saw, but I wasn't driving it."

Jordan walked forward, closer to the witness. He was making headway, but he assumed the defendant would never admit he had arranged the arson. He said, "Does anyone else have a key to your Mercedes?"

"Not that I know of."

"Did you loan or otherwise authorize anyone else to operate that vehicle?"

"No."

"Your Mercedes is equipped with one of those electronic anti-theft security keys, isn't it?"

"So they tell me."

Jordan watched for non-verbal cues. The defendant appeared as self-assured as when he had first arrived at the stand. "Was your Mercedes stolen or otherwise out of your control at any time during this past April?"

"Not to my knowledge."

The chance for headway had come, but the necessary questions were a double-edged sword. Would victory in the courtroom cost him his relationship with Lauren? The thought gave Jordan pause. He had given the jury food for thought, and he needed time for exactly that. He turned to Judge Boston. "At this time I have no further questions of this witness, but I would like to reserve the right to recall him later."

"We'll cross that bridge if and when it becomes necessary." Judge Boston gestured to the defense lawyer.

Harwood got up and walked around the defense table. "Mr. Worthington," he said, "how did you acquire your stock in *Blue Sky Realty Corporation*?"

"Payment of a debt."

"Can you be more specific?"

"I loaned fifty thousand dollars to *Blue Sky*. They pledged forty percent of their stock as security. When they couldn't pay — uh, let me rephrase that. They gave me a check drawn on *Blue Sky's* account at *Cooperative Trust*. It bounced. That's how I got the stock, not that it's worth a helluva lot."

"Do you know who owns the other sixty percent?"

"Medford Laughlin and Steve Ward."

"Do you know their respective shares?"

"I'm not sure."

"Are you or have you ever been an officer, director or employee of *Blue Sky Realty Corporation*?"

"No."

"Have you ever used *Blue Sky's* mobile telephone?"

"No. I didn't even know they had one."

Harwood walked toward his seat and then turned back toward his client. "On April 11th, did you call Jake Brewster?"

"No."

"Did you ever hire him to set fire to Jordan Jackson's home?"

"No."

"Just one last question. Do you know who did?"

"I don't."

Harwood turned toward the bench. "Your Honor, lest there be any confusion, I wish to emphasize that my questions, though purposely direct rather than leading, were only intended as cross-examination. If and when the defense proceeds with its case in chief, I may call my client for more comprehensive testimony. But given the plaintiff's failure to present a *prima facie* case, I believe dismissal may be in order without the need of a defense. In any event, I have no further questions at this time."

Jordan, whose eyes were focused on his notes, could feel those of the entire courtroom aimed at him. The ball was in his court. The case had taken on a whole new light. The possibility that he had jeopardized his insurance coverage while engaging in a losing battle was growing. He glanced at his watch — 3:49. "Your Honor," he said, "no redirect." He took a deep breath. "I realize it's early, but I request that we break for the weekend."

Judge Boston hesitated and then glanced over at the defense table.

"No objection."

"One last item, your Honor," said Jordan. "On Monday I anticipate recalling Jake Brewster. I would appreciate the sheriff's office arranging to bring him here from the county jail again."

"Mr. Jackson, it seems you've put the cart before the horse. Had I known you planned to recall Mr. Brewster, I would have been reluctant to suspend for the weekend. If by chance Mr. Brewster is still in the holding room, would it not make more sense to have him testify now?"

"It would, your Honor, under ordinary circumstances." Jordan hesitated, well aware the ice under foot was thin. "I anticipate calling other witnesses whose testimony may be a necessary foundation to my further examination of Mr. Brewster. Accordingly, I am requesting the Court's indulgence."

Judge Boston sat stone-faced, his eyes still trained on Jordan. "Okay," he said. He looked over at the deputy who stood next to the American flag. "Mr. Crane, please have Mr. Brewster here on Monday."

Jordan breathed a sigh, but it was hardly one of relief. He had just traded on future good will; a practice he scrupulously tried to avoid. Come Monday, if he failed to justify his request, Judge Boston would view him like the boy who cried wolf. During future visits to the court in other cases, and there would be many, a distrusting ear was apt to greet Jordan.

The Judge surveyed the courtroom and then turned to the jury. "Ladies and gentlemen, we have had a most interesting series of witnesses today. An early break will allow us all a chance to digest what we have heard. Regardless, I doubt that anyone will object to an early start to the weekend. I understand the weatherman forecasts a ten. Of course, with *his* record it wouldn't be admissible in this court." His Honor smiled. "Enjoy your weekend. And please remember: Do not discuss the case with anyone, your fellow jurors included." He tapped his gavel. "Court is adjourned until nine o'clock Monday."

The moment the Judge's gavel struck, Lauren was on her way out the door. All too recently after court had recessed, her father and Jordan had ganged up on her before strolling off like old buddies. Lauren was not about to invite a replay of that scene. And too, she was in a hurry. Moments before court had concluded, she had an idea. To pursue it, she needed to call business offices before they closed for the weekend. It was nearly four o'clock. She hurried down the courthouse steps and went directly to her apartment. She took out the telephone book and looked up the number for the Department of Motor Vehicles. She dialed hoping to find the names of those in the surrounding area who owned black Mercedes. Her call was shuffled about, and she was repeatedly put on hold. The clerk to whom she was finally transferred put up a bureaucratic wall of questions: the license plate number of the Mercedes about which she was calling; if more than one, all plate numbers; if an accident was involved, where and when. Lauren tried to explain her problem. The clerk suggested she make a written request. Lauren hung up.

She reached for the telephone book and flipped to the letter *R* in the yellow pages. She quickly counted the twenty or so rental-car agencies listed in the surrounding area. One-by-one she began dialing them. Halfway through the alphabet, she had drawn blanks. At the letter *N* she hit a possibility. *Newland Luxury Rentals* had two Mercedes. But one was white and the other, silver.

She was about to dial the next number when her mother's rainbow magnet caught her eye. What was it doing on the floor? It could have fallen when closing the refrigerator, or maybe she brushed against it, knocking it off. But wouldn't she have heard it land? She picked it up from the vinyl floor and placed it back onto the refrigerator. For a few moments her thoughts drifted to her mother and the drunk driver who cut her life short. Timing was everything. A superstitious person might have considered the fallen magnet a sign. Lauren rejected the possibility. But a more sinister explanation was harder to dismiss. Could someone have been in her apartment while she was in court? Thoughts of the threatening note she had received quickened her heart. Her palms grew sweaty. She gazed all around the apartment. Nothing seemed amiss. She checked her dresser and nightstand where she kept a few valuables. No signs there. She returned to the refrigerator and stared at the magnet. Perhaps she had knocked it off. Her standard morning company, the *Today* show, may have drowned out the sound of its fall. A month earlier, before she had received the threatening note, if she had come home and found the magnet on the floor, she would have picked it up without a second thought. The idea of an intruder was fanciful. Paranoid, as well. No way would she give in to such foolishness.

She refocused on the list of rental car agencies in the yellow pages and again began dialing one after another. Third from the last, the voice on the other end of line answered, "*Top-Notch Car Rentals*. Rick Wilson speaking. How can I help you?"

"Do you have any Mercedes?"

"One, but it's rented through next Wednesday."

"That's okay," she said. "Is it black by any chance?"

"Just so happens it is."

Possibilities loomed. She jotted Wilson's name. "I live in Cedar Creek, about twenty miles away. Is that a problem?"

"Not as long as you pick it up." Wilson chuckled.

"I think I might have seen the car." Her experience as a newspaper reporter had schooled her in the art of ferreting information. "Did you rent it to someone in Cedar Creek back on April 11^(th)?"

"Who is this?"

"Lauren Worthington. But you didn't answer my question?"

There was a moment of silence. "Was our rental car involved in an accident or something back in April?"

"You still didn't answer my question."

"No fooling. And you didn't answer mine either."

Touché. "I'll make you a deal. Tell me whether it was rented to someone in Cedar Creek, and I'll tell you if it was involved in an accident."

Several seconds passed before Wilson finally responded. "A man from Cedar Creek rented it, but don't ask his name. So, was there an accident?"

"None that I know of." The growl that Lauren heard from the other end prompted her to add, "But it may have been used to commit a crime."

"Are you a police officer?"

"No."

"Insurance investigator?"

"No."

"So, what's your angle?"

Lauren hesitated. Wilson was hardly a pushover. "I'm a reporter, but I'm not — "

"Reporter? And you said your name is Worthington." An utterance, half chuckle and half grunt, followed. "You're the daughter of that rich fellow from Cedar Creek, the one I've been reading about in the papers. He supposedly hired a couple of thugs to burn down the house of some black politician. I think he was town supervisor or something like that. You think our Mercedes had something to do with the arson?"

"Well — " Her mind raced. The hole in the doughnut strategy popped into her head. Trade empty nothings, public information from the courtroom, for what she wanted to know. "I'll make you another deal. Tell me who rented the car, and I'll tell you more about the crime."

"I'd love to hear, but no thanks. As I said, we don't give out customers' names."

"Can't you make an exception?"

"Nope. And I've got a call on the other line. Gotta go." The telephone clicked.

She told herself — *Good Try*. Unfortunately, she had heard that complimentary, two-word phrase too many times from her Bridge partner. And never after making a bid. Only after coming up short once the hand had been played. On the bright side, unlike a failed Bridge hand, the conversation with Wilson had yielded something valuable. She hung up and immediately dialed Jordan. "Hi. It's Lauren."

"Lauren who?"

"What's that supposed to mean?"

"That I hardly know you the way you disappear after court."

"I know, but something important pulled me away. To make a long story short, on April 11th someone in Cedar Creek leased a black Mercedes from an agency called *Top-Notch Car Rentals*."

"Interesting . . . very interesting."

Lauren visualized Jordan seated in the back room of his office gazing pensively out the one small window not far from the telephone. Whether her supposition was accurate was another matter.

"Any idea as to the lessee?"

"No. The agent wouldn't say." She glanced at the note she had jotted earlier. "His name is Rick Wilson. His office is over in Beaulin."

"Beaulin . . . of all places."

"What about it?"

"That's where Reverend Miller's parish is located. Clyde Boxley worked there the night of the fire. That's how he and his brother created their alibi."

"Might be a coincidence."

"True . . . but it might not. And I intend to find out, as well as the identity of the person who rented that black Mercedes."

"How? I doubt Rick Wilson will tell you."

"Oh, I think he will . . . once he gets the right invitation. It's called a subpoena."

Jordan ran his eyes over the rear of the courtroom. The cameramen from *Judicial TV*, along with a journalist from the show, were in their usual spots. There were many familiar faces but also loads of strangers; too many for Jordan to identify the individuals he had subpoenaed. The brief descriptions contained in his process server's affidavits of service gave hints, but discovering who was who would have to wait until the witnesses took the stand. The announcement of Judge Boston's arrival had Jordan up on his feet.

Once Judge Boston completed his usual housekeeping, he said, "Mr. Jackson, please call your next witness."

"The plaintiff calls Kirby Osgood, Vice-president of *Cooperative Trust Company*." Jordan had subpoenaed the bank officer as a result of Roger Worthington's testimony about *Blue Sky Realty Corporation*. Worthington's responses regarding the transfer of stock in lieu of the bounced check and the links to Laughlin and Ward had posed a wealth of questions. Manila folder in hand, a short fellow with thinning hair and a blue polka-dot bow tie came forward and took the oath.

"Would you state your full name for the record, please?"

"Kirby Alvin Osgood." His nasal voice grated like fingernails on a chalkboard.

Out of the corner of his eye Jordan saw juror number one cringe. Jordan complimented himself for spotting the non-verbal cue. If only he were that astute, and better yet clairvoyant, during summation and *voir dire*. He refocused on the witness. "How old are you?"

"Forty-two, plus a couple of days. My birthday was Saturday."

"A belated happy birthday," said Jordan. "Please tell us where you work and your title."

"I'm Vice-president of *Cooperative Trust Company.*"

Bookkeeper or actuary seemed more appropriate, even if banks were notorious for giving out titles rather than money. "You're here in response to a subpoena. Correct?"

"A subpoena *duces tecum.*" Osgood took a paper out of his folder and pointed at the Latin words."

Jordan restrained the urge to roll his eyes. "Yes. a subpoena requiring the production of documents. And I assume you brought those documents regarding the account of *Blue Sky Realty Corporation.*"

"Right here." The witness held up his folder. "We keep them in the regular course of business." He straightened what had been rounded shoulders. "I've testified before."

"I can see that," said Jordan, thinking what fun it would be to cross-examine the fastidious weasel. Unfortunately, he was Jordan's own witness. "What type of account does *Blue Sky* have at the bank?"

"Corporate checking."

"Let me direct your attention back to the first eleven days of April of this year." Jordan waited while the witness thumbed through his records. "What, if any, cash withdrawals were made from *Blue Sky 's* account during that period?"

The witness took a pair of wire-rimmed spectacles from a case in his pocket and carefully put them on. "Uh . . . fifty-three hundred dollars was withdrawn on April 10th."

Jordan hadn't laid a complete foundation as would entitle the witness to testify from the records, but Harwood wasn't objecting. And why should he? The evidence would do nothing to incriminate his client, assuming Worthington had testified truthfully regarding his interest in and connection to *Blue Sky.* Jordan said, "Do you know who signed the withdrawal slip?"

"Yes, I have it right here." He looked through his folder again. "Steven Ward, as President of *Blue Sky Realty Corporation.*"

"Did he make any more withdrawals that month?"

The witness ran his finger down the page. "On April 15th he took out thirty-eight hundred dollars and another nine hundred dollars on April 27th. Both times cash." The witness popped his hand to his mouth. "Oops. I should only answer the question you asked. Isn't that right?"

"Yes, but you're doing fine," said Jordan. "Did anyone else make any withdrawals from *Blue Sky's* account during the month of April?"

"No."

"Does *Blue Sky* have any outstanding loans from your bank?"

"One."

"Tell the jury the balance."

He looked through his records. "As of the end of last month, including late payments, $253,345.68."

"Is any individual personally liable on that loan?"

"Yes. Steven Ward."

"When, if ever, did he last apply for additional credit?"

Osgood refocused on his file. "March 2nd of this year. But we turned him down. I'll tell you why, if you'd like."

"Please do," said Jordan, struggling to keep derision from his face.

"Well — it's like this. His income, after expenses, you know, the rents from his strip mall, barely covered the payments on what he owed, let alone the additional ninety-five thousand he wanted." Osgood looked over at the jury. "If we had given him the new loan, we would have thrown our good money after his bad." He shook his head. "You can't do that in the banking business, not if you want to . . . uh . . . stay in the banking business. You know what I mean." He peered at the jury, appearing to measure their understanding. "Anyway — when we told Mr. Ward, *no,* he blew his top. He called me a scrawny staple saver and a couple of other names I'd rather not repeat, not with ladies present." Osgood glanced at Jordan, as if asking whether to continue.

Jordan hesitated. His open-ended question had invited an open-ended answer. The approach was risky. But like a compulsive gambler, Jordan was finding it easier to pick up the dice. Despite the odds, there was always the chance he'd make a tough point on the next roll. He said, "Mr. Osgood, what else did Steven Ward say?"

"He said it was dirt bags like you and me that had wrecked Cedar Creek. He said that you with your so-called progressive ideas had screwed the folks who oughta run the village." Osgood adjusted his bow tie. "He said some other nasty stuff about you, if you want me to tell."

"Uh . . . no thank you." Jordan swallowed hard. "That's all I have."

"No questions," said Harwood.

Osgood glanced at Judge Boston.

"You're excused."

"Thank you, your Honor. I'm always glad to do my civic duty." He got up from his seat, smiled at the jury and left the courtroom.

"May I see both counsel at the bench," said Judge Boston.

As he walked forward, Jordan tried to speculate what the Judge had on his mind. A moment later, as he and Harwood arrived, Judge Boston said softly, "It seems this case has taken a peculiar fork. Mr. Jackson, you have offered evidence which, unless I'm mistaken, fails to prove that which you allege in your complaint. Ordinarily I would expect that Mr. Harwood would object. However, his silence is understandable since the evidence, if anything, exculpates his client." Judge Boston looked at Jordan. "This is your lawsuit, and far be it from me to try it for you, but am I missing something?"

Jordan hesitated. He had repeatedly asked himself similar questions over the weekend. Calling witnesses who disproved his case made no legal sense. Nevertheless, it made sense to him. At times he was the intrepid lawyer, determined to win his lawsuit against the defendant, Roger Worthington. At others he was a victim who needed to identify the person responsible for the arson of his home. Superimposed on these inconsistent roles was his personal life. And judgment had gradually enabled him to remove the blinders of pride. Success in the courtroom at the expense of his relationship with Lauren would be a disaster. "Your Honor," he said, "I realize my tactics are unorthodox, but — "

"Unorthodox — that's an understatement. Action inconsistent with your client's interests is a breach of fiduciary duty. But (the Judge shook his head) . . . you represent yourself. Breach of duty to oneself is a legal impossibility."

"Your Honor, the client in me took some gambles in an effort to get to the bottom of this mess." The hollow ring of his words forced Jordan to rethink them. Rather than the client, the *fool* in him was calling the shots.

"Interesting explanation," said Judge Boston.

"How so," said Jordan, unable to decipher the Judge's comment.

"Well — you describe your tactics as a gamble." He gestured around the courtroom. "It struck me more like an experiment."

"Pardon me," said Jordan.

"Your method — it appears to be *trial and error*. And instead of proving your case, you're proving the obvious. *Error* has no place in the courtroom."

Jordan tried to remain stoic. He suspected, however, the knot in his stomach reached his face.

The Judge glanced out over the courtroom. "We have a lot of people waiting. So, let's get on with it." The attorneys returned to their respective tables.

"Mr. Jackson, please call your next witness."

"The plaintiff re-calls Jake Brewster."

From the side door next to the jury box, a deputy sheriff escorted Brewster to the stand.

"Mr. Brewster," said Judge Boston, "I remind you that you're still under oath." He gestured for Jordan to proceed.

"Mr. Brewster, when you testified last Friday, you indicated the vehicle that dropped off your arson payment was a black Mercedes. Do you know the model year?"

"Not fur sure, but it wuz pretty new."

"Could it have been either a 1982 or 1983?"

"Yup, that's 'bout what it wuz."

"Anything else you can tell us about the car?"

"Just that it had four doors and wuz black and real shiny and . . . oh yeah, it had dark, tinted windows."

"Did you see the driver?"

"Not really. I was watchin' out the window of my trailer. But mainly I just seen the guy's arm when he stuffed the envelope — the one with the cash — in my mailbox. He didn't lower the window down none too far."

Jordan took a few steps backward. He needed a moment to think. The nagging questions, compounded by Judge Boston's admonitions, were again rearing their odious head. Subordinating his case against the defendant in favor of a blind pursuit of truth was not part of his legal training. Within the canons of ethics he represented his clients with undivided loyalty. But representing himself, lines had blurred and roles confused. And his relationship with Lauren had put a premium on other interests. He said, "Could the driver have been someone other than Roger Worthington?"

Brewster thought for moment. "Uh . . . I guess."

"Could Mr. Ward — the gentleman seated back there in the next to last row, third seat from the end (Jordan pointed) — have been the driver?"

Brewster squinted as he peered in the direction where Jordan pointed. "Could have, I guess. Like I sez, I couldn't really see who was at the wheel."

Jordan gazed at Ward and then back at Brewster. His career as a trial attorney had included many unusual experiences. But never had he been so unsure where he was headed or what he was trying to accomplish. He said, "No further questions."

"No questions," said Harwood.

Judge Boston had the deputy escort Brewster out of the courtroom and then directed Jordan to call his next witness.

"The plaintiff re-calls Steven Ward."

The urbane businessman, dressed in a green blazer and yellow sport shirt with an open, button-down collar, walked to the stand. Though his outfit was far more casual than the previous Friday, it bore the trim look of fine tailoring. He seated himself with folded arms.

"You're still under oath," said Judge Boston.

"I know," said Ward, his steely eyes trained on Jordan.

Jordan caught himself, just before a wry smile appeared on his face. If it had been a boxing ring, Ward would have been a hell of an opponent. But in the current arena, mental, not physical, attributes counted, and strict rules treated trash talk as exactly that — garbage. "Tell me," said Jordan, "where were you on the afternoon of April 11th?"

"At my office, I suspect. Keeping track of my whereabouts on random days many months ago is not my thing."

"How about the night of April 16th."

Ward chuckled. "That one I remember cause that's the night your house went up in flames. I recall they interrupted the Braves' game with a local news bulletin. They said there was a fire at the home of an area politician. Turned out to be yours."

That Ward had an alibi came as no surprise, not when Orin Boxley had set the fire. "You don't like me, do you?" said Jordan.

"Since you asked — no."

"It's because I won't let you manipulate the Village Board."

"I didn't say that."

Jordan folded his arms. "But you're not denying it."

"Objection," said Harwood. "Counsel is being argumentative and cross-examining his own witness."

"I'll withdraw the question," said Jordan. The possibility that he might enjoy a free hand with inquiries not inculpating Harwood's client had disappeared. Still there had been latitude. Soon enough Jordan planned to test the waters again. He took a couple of steps toward the witness. "Whom do you dislike more — Roger Worthington or me?"

Ward rubbed his chin. "That . . . that's a tough one."

"Anyway, you dislike us both."

"No argument there."

Jordan studied the witness. Might he be responsible for the fire? There was admitted animosity. But animosity hardly translated into arson. Jordan disliked Ward as much as vice versa. That hardly implied Jordan would set fire to Ward's home. Jordan said, "You were here earlier when Mr. Osgood testified that you withdrew fifty-three hundred dollars from the account of *Blue Sky Realty Corporation* on April 10th."

"Yeah . . . so?"

"What did you do with the money?"

"I spent it. You know, for groceries, gas, clothes, a trip to Asheville and you name it. Oh — and one more thing — I lost a bundle at the track. I'll bet that last tidbit brightens your day."

Jordan glanced casually at his notes. "What kind of car do you drive?"

"A Cadillac." Ward pointed to the first row behind the bar. "You might better ask Medford Laughlin that question. He drives a black Mercedes, a lot like the defendant's, even if it isn't quite as new."

A request to have the non-responsive remark stricken would surely have been granted, but the possibility it might prove useful down the road kept Jordan silent. "May I take a moment, your Honor?" He walked back to the plaintiff's table as he reflected upon the mishmash of information he had acquired. He recalled Laughlin's veiled threat to Lauren; his reference to the line from the Bayard Taylor stanza — *Ignorance like a fire doth burn*. Might Laughlin be behind the arson? The cocksure witness on the stand, Steve Ward, had become a possibility as well. Jordan glanced over at the defendant. Roger Worthington could not be ruled out. Nor could the Aryan Alliance. But maybe it was someone else altogether. The quick analysis convinced Jordan he was playing a guessing game. It also convinced him that the Judge's earlier criticism had merit. He said, "At one time you were the sole owner of *Blue Sky Realty Corporation*, weren't you?"

"Yeah."

"How did Medford Laughlin acquire his interest?"

"I needed some money."

"Did you try the bank before you sold part of your stock?"

Ward failed to respond.

Jordan used the hiatus to steal a peek at Parks. The insurance company lawyer was leaning back comfortably in his seat. And why not. Every time Jordan rolled the dice, Parks, though he never put up his ante, had a chance to make hay. Jordan refocused on the witness. "We can bring Mr. Osgood back, if you prefer."

Ward glared. "You having fun parading my personal finances in front of the world."

"Mr. Ward," said Judge Boston, "you will confine yourself to answering the questions. Now tell us, did you or did you not apply to the bank for a loan?"

"Yeah, I did."

"And they turned you down," said Jordan. "Didn't they?"

"Yeah."

"How many storefronts do you have in your strip mall?"

"Six."

Jordan held up a pair of fingers. "Two are vacant, aren't they?"

"At the moment."

"For the moment, you say." Jordan eyed the witness. From his slicked-back hair to his glossy oxfords he was smooth. But well-chosen questions could scrape away the unctuous veneer. "When was the last time either storefront was occupied?"

Ward hesitated. "Offhand I couldn't say."

"Couldn't or — " Out of the corner of his eye, Jordan caught a glimpse of Judge Boston's frown. "I'll withdraw that," said Jordan. "Would it be fair to say that both storefronts have been vacant for over a year?"

"No. The repair shop only closed last winter."

"But the other has been vacant more than a year."

Ward scowled.

"I'm sorry," said Jordan. "I didn't hear your answer."

"Yeah, it's more than a year."

From the corner of his eye Jordan checked his adversary. So long as leading questions pointed incriminating fingers away from his client, Harwood seemed willing to allow them. But like before, he could change in an instant. Jordan said, "Earlier we heard testimony that Roger Worthington and Medford Laughlin both own part of your business. But they're just stockholders, aren't they?"

"Yeah . . . so?"

"So, they don't have any involvement with the operation of the business, do they?"

"No, and they shouldn't."

"What percentage of the stock do you still own?"

"Forty-five percent."

"Less than half." Jordan pointed at the witness. "If Roger Worthington and Medford Laughlin decide to team up, they could take control of your business, couldn't they?"

"They'd be fools to try." Ward's posture stiffened. "Anyway, they haven't."

"You mean *not yet.*" The glower that greeted Jordan's eyes hinted that Ward was growing testier. Juries often distrusted flaring tempers, and anger deposited many a foot in a witness's mouth. "You were in dire straits," said Jordan. "The bank had turned you down. Your head was barely above water. Approval of Roger Worthington's mall would drown you. Isn't that how it was?"

Ward's jaw clenched. Five . . . ten . . . fifteen seconds passed.

"Who besides you has access to the mobile telephone of *Blue Sky Realty Corporation*, the one that was used to arrange the delivery of the payment to Jake Brewster?"

Ward sat motionless, appearing to stew. Finally he said, "Think you're pretty smart, don't you?" He pointed at Jordan. "I'll bet the folks on the jury would love to hear how you did time for torching a farm in Georgia."

Jordan grabbed hold of the jury-box rail. Spectators behind him gasped. His heart pounded. The din grew louder. Judge Boston hammered his gavel. The noise resounded in Jordan's ears. Harsher echoes from a buried past rattled within his brain. He looked toward the witness stand where Ward, with a snake's eyes, was glaring his way. Jordan tried to get a grip on surging emotions. Perhaps he had rolled the dice one time too many.

Judge Boston rapped his gavel again. The courtroom hushed. He turned to the witness. "Mr. Ward, I admonish you one last time. Direct your responses to the questions asked. And only the questions asked." The Judge turned to Jordan and gestured him to proceed. However, his Honor's eyes hinted at what were ordinarily impenetrable thoughts.

Jordan was certain Judge Boston was preoccupied with the truth of Ward's claim about the Georgia fire. No doubt the jury, as well as everyone else in the courtroom, was asking the same question. Jordan debated whether to ignore Ward's allegation.

But what would it accomplish. Harwood was sure to bring it out later, and when he did, it would appear as if Jordan had been trying to conceal the damning information. Harwood might even save it for the very end of the trial. Jordan envisioned the impact of testimony just before the jury began deliberations that he, the plaintiff, suing for arson, had pleaded guilty to that very offense. The oft-repeated advice of Jordan's law-school evidence professor rang in his head. *Don't be an ostrich. Grab the forceps, and pull the rotten teeth yourself. Because if you don't, your adversary will use a giant pair of pliers and yank your head off.* Jordan said, "If your Honor, please, I'd like to respond to the witness's allegations concerning my past."

"This is no time for speeches."

"But they need an explanation. I — "

Judge Boston held up his hand. In a rare moment of exasperation, he said, "Mr. Jackson, we have rules of evidence, though unfortunately both you and your adversary, for reasons only known to the two of you, have often declined to employ them. Our record is replete with kitchen sinks." The Judge turned toward the defendant's table. "Mr. Harwood, your position, please."

"May I take a moment to speak with my client?" said Harwood.

"You may," said Judge Boston, appearing to welcome the respite. He poured himself a fresh glass of water and took a drink.

A murmur draped the courtroom as the better part of two minutes elapsed. Finally, Harwood got up from his seat and circled around to the center of the arena. "Your Honor, these proceedings are not only clearing my client, but perhaps leading us toward the person who, with both threats and arson, has spread fear in our community." He gestured at the stand. "I remind the Court that my client's answer contains an abuse of process counterclaim. It alleges that the plaintiff brought this action in bad faith for the purpose of impugning my client's character and undermining his proposed mall." Harwood gestured toward Jordan. "If and when my adversary wishes to offer evidence disputing the counterclaim, he should do so under oath from the stand, not with a speech."

"Point well taken," said Judge Boston. "However, we currently have another witness there."

"I understand," said Harwood. "If Mr. Jackson wishes to testify, I have no objection to interrupting Mr. Ward's testimony, subject to recall, including my right to cross-examination."

Judge Boston looked over at Jordan. "You seemed anxious before to respond to the allegation. Do you wish to take the stand now, or would you prefer to continue with your examination of Mr. Ward?"

Common sense told Jordan he was stepping into a minefield. More and more he understood the folly of representing himself. But he was too far down the road for hindsight, and the urge to immediately address the slur against him colored his thinking. "Yes, I'd like to testify."

Judge Boston excused Steve Ward, who returned to his seat in the audience. Jordan stepped forward. He went directly to the Bible and put his right hand there.

"Do you swear to tell the truth, the whole truth and nothing but the truth?" said Judge Boston.

"I do." Jordan took his seat in the witness chair

"As you know," said Judge Boston, "there are two ways for you to proceed. You may either use the narrative, or you can ask yourself questions and then answer them. In any event, Mr. Harwood may voice objections at any time. He will also have the right to cross-examine."

Jordan thought for a moment. "I'll try the narrative. It should move more quickly."

"Fine. Proceed."

Jordan took a deep breath as he tried to collect his thoughts. Thanks to an ill-conceived strategy, his words, rather than well planned, would come off the cuff. He looked at the jury. "My name is Jordan Jackson. My home is at 74 Hickory Lane, but, thanks to the fire that you've heard so much about here, I currently reside at 138 Broad Street, in the back room of my law office. I'm thirty-one years old. I grew up in Georgia. I am the attorney for the plaintiff, as well as the plaintiff in this case." A frown on the face of a female juror in the second row, an elementary school teacher, momentarily halted Jordan's speech. He suspected that the jury observed his discomfort. Try not to be long-winded, he told himself. "I never knew my father. My mother died when I was three. I bounced around from one foster home to another. By the time I was fifteen I was running with a bad crowd. One June evening, along with two other fellows, I made a bonfire in an old, abandoned barn. It got out of control. The barn was destroyed. The fire nearly spread to the adjacent farmhouse. Fortunately, the fire department got it under control. I was taken into juvenile court in Statesboro, Georgia and charged with juvenile delinquency. The Judge sent me to a facility for troubled youths in Augusta." Jordan took a moment to catch his breath. He glanced out at the audience. Their penetrating eyes, as if armed with voices, seemed to be shouting *pyromaniac*. "I . . . I spent more than two years in the institution. It was there that I came under the wing of a very fine counselor who redirected my energies toward self-discipline and education. He helped me get a scholarship to Grambling College. From there I went on to law school at the University of South Carolina. From the moment I graduated law school, I tried to bury my past. And much to my surprise, it was easy. A résumé starting with my college education rarely raised questions. When it did, I simply said I grew up in foster homes. If anything, people were sympathetic." Jordan cleared his throat. He glanced at Harwood. The attorney could have made the difficult job tougher, but he was allowing the narrative to proceed uninterrupted. "I came to Cedar Creek to practice law about six years ago. My past was ancient history until last fall when a young fellow, several years my junior — he had arrived at the juvenile detention center just before I was released — approached me here on the street. I didn't recognize him, but he knew me. He reminded me of my ugly past; the fire I had set years earlier. He asked if I could spare twenty dollars. I told myself I was helping a fellow down on his luck. The rationalization grew harder to deny as the frequency and amount of his demands increased. Harder yet when warmer weather and a sleeveless shirt revealed an *AA* tattoo on his shoulder. I was giving in to a blackmailer. Why else would I be giving money to a member of the *Aryan Alliance*. I had to put a stop to it. So, recently when he made his demands, I told him to get lost. Chances are he let my secret out; maybe even sold it for a few bucks." Jordan gestured toward Steve Ward. "When my fellow Village Board member told you that I served time for setting a fire, he told you the truth." Jordan swallowed hard as his words echoed in his head. The admission was painful, but it was also liberating. No longer did he need to live in fear that his sordid past would be found out. Repercussions, immediate ones, were possible, but perhaps they would be less than the endless evil borne of secrecy. He forced himself to make direct eye contact with the jury. "However you judge me, I will understand. But I assure you, I had nothing to do with the fire that destroyed my home." Utter silence filled the courtroom. Jordan gazed down at the marble floor in front of the witness stand. Still he sensed the laser stares that no doubt were aimed his way from all directions.

Mere seconds elapsed, though, like the slow motion of an impending auto accident, it seemed far longer. Finally Judge Boston said, "Mr. Harwood, you may cross-examine."

Yellow pad in hand, the defense attorney got up. He walked slowly forward, about halfway to the witness stand. He studied his notes. "Your Honor," he said, "I have no questions at this time." He returned to his seat.

Judge Boston turned to Jordan. "You may step down from the witness chair." Once Jordan arrived at the plaintiff's table, Judge Boston said, "No doubt this has been draining. It's almost eleven. We can take a short recess if you'd like."

Jordan thought for a moment. Back in law school a two-part exam had always seemed worse than an exam with just one, no matter how long. He said, "I'm ready to proceed."

"Then call your next witness."

"The plaintiff calls Rick Wilson."

A man about thirty of medium build, attired in slacks and a blue and yellow striped polo shirt stepped forward and took the oath. The basics quickly covered, Jordan said, "Mr. Wilson, what do you do for a living?"

"I own and operate *Top-Notch Car Rentals* in Beaulin."

"Among the automobiles that you have for rent at your establishment, are there any Mercedes?"

"Just one."

"Would you describe it, please?"

"It's a 1982, black, four-door sedan."

"How different would that be from the 1983, black, four-door Mercedes sedan?"

"Apart from perhaps the taillights and some trim, as best I know, they're pretty much identical."

Jordan took a couple of steps back as he mentally prepared for the critical questions. "On April 11th of this year was your agency's 1982 Mercedes rented?"

"May I refer to my records to be certain?"

"You need them to refresh and verify your recollection?" said Judge Boston.

"Yes, Sir."

"Go ahead."

The witness looked down at a binder he had brought. "Yes, the vehicle was rented on April 11th."

Jordan glanced at the jury. They were fully engaged. Jordan said, "Mr. Wilson, would you kindly tell us to whom you rented the Mercedes on that date?"

The witness turned to the jury. "Steven Ward of Cedar Creek. It was a two-day rental. April 11th and 12th."

Jordan looked toward the rear of the courtroom where Ward was seated. All eyes, with the exception of Ward's, which were aimed downward, were directed Ward's way."

"Do you see the person to whom you rented that vehicle here in the courtroom?"

Wilson nodded. "Yes. It's the fellow who testified a little while earlier. He's sitting over there with his head down, two seats from the far aisle in the next to last row."

"Let the record show that the witness has identified Steven Ward," said Jordan. He turned to Harwood. "Your witness."

"No questions."

Judge Boston excused Wilson. As Jordan watched him depart the courtroom, he saw Ward get up from his seat and walk toward the rear door. He was about to ask Judge Boston to halt Ward's exit, but His Honor was a step ahead.

"Mr. Ward, you're not leaving us, are you?"

Ward turned and looked at the Judge but said nothing.

The Judge motioned him back to his seat.

"Your Honor," said Jordan, "I wish to recall Mr. Ward to the stand."

"I don't have to," barked Ward.

"Pardon me," said Judge Boston, his glare less cordial than his words.

"Like Brewster, the other day, I'm taking the Fifth."

"That may be," said Judge Boston, "but you'll do it on the stand." The Judge waited a moment. "Come forward now." He pointed at the witness chair as Ward drew near. "I remind you that you're still under oath." He turned to Jordan. "Counselor, proceed."

Jordan walked over by the jury box about fifteen feet from the witness stand. He leaned casually against the rail. He anticipated Ward would give him few substantive responses, but that didn't matter. The hard work had been done. He said, "Mr. Ward, you were here just a few minutes ago when Mr. Wilson from *Top-Notch Car Rentals* testified, weren't you?"

"Fifth Amendment," snarled Ward.

"Excuse me," said Judge Boston. "You believe a question whether you were here in the courtroom could incriminate you?"

"Yeah, I was here."

"Did you rent a black Mercedes from Mr. Wilson's agency for the days of April 11th and 12th of this year?"

Ward glanced at the Judge. "Fifth Amendment."

"Prior to April 16th did you hire Jake Brewster to set fire to my home?"

"Fifth Amendment."

"When you spoke to Mr. Brewster, did you identify yourself as Roger Worthington and instruct him to hire the Boxley brothers to carry out the arson?"

"Fifth Amendment."

"The reason you rented the black Mercedes was to make Mr. Brewster believe you were Roger Worthington. Isn't that true?"

"Fifth Amendment."

"On April 11th, using a black Mercedes, did you deliver cash withdrawn from the account of *Blue Sky Realty Corporation* to Jake Brewster as a down payment for setting the fire?"

Elbows on the arms of his chair, Ward pressed a fist against the palm of his other hand.

"Mr. Ward," said Judge Boston. "We're waiting."

"Fifth Amendment," he growled.

"Isn't it true that no one besides you had access to the *Sprint* mobile telephone from which the two calls were made on April 11th to Jake Brewster arranging payment for the arson?"

"Fifth Amendment."

Jordan looked at the jury. They were focused on the witness. He could continue to bombard Ward, but what purpose would it serve? The witness would face his consequences another day. "No further questions," said Jordan. He looked over at Harwood.

The defense attorney hesitated and then got up from his seat. "Just a couple of questions, Mr. Ward. Isn't it a fact that you framed my client with the arson in an effort to block the construction of his mall?"

Ward glared at Harwood and muttered under his breath.

"The witness will respond," snapped Judge Boston.

"Fifth Amendment."

"As a member of Cedar Creek's Village Board you opposed my client's proposed mall, not for the good of the community, but because you feared it would kill your strip mall."

"I think the project is a lousy idea."

Jordan, who had anticipated another cry of *Fifth Amendment*, welcomed the answer. He suspected it caught Harwood by surprise. Regardless, the defense lawyer remained impassive.

"Just one last question," said Harwood. "Who do you hate more, my client or Mr. Jackson?"

Ward hesitated. "That's like comparing two dinner plates, one with slop and the other, slime. Take your pick."

"Thank you," said Harwood. "That's all I have."

Ward got up from his seat.

"Mr. Ward," said Judge Boston. "Please stay right there."

A scowl on his face, Ward turned away from the Judge and muttered under his breath. Jordan was unable to discern the remark.

"Pardon me," said Judge Boston. He waited a moment, but then turned to the deputy sheriff. Mr. Peterkin, please take Mr. Ward into custody. Your office can proffer appropriate charges and arrange for arraignment before Judge Gardiner."

The deputy sheriff walked over to the witness, snapped handcuffs onto his wrists and ushered him out of the courtroom.

A murmur persisted in the audience. Rather than quelling it, Judge Boston rocked back and waited until quiet returned of its own accord. "Gentlemen," he said, "pleased as I am at the light shed on the criminal shadow recently plaguing our community, let us not lose sight that we are here trying a civil case, such as it is." He gestured at Jordan. "Mr. Jackson, you have sued Mr. Worthington for damages resulting from a fire at your home." His Honor turned to the defense table. "And Mr. Worthington, you have counterclaimed for abuse of process. One way or another, these issues need to be resolved. That being so, Mr. Jackson, proceed."

Jordan got up from his seat. "Your Honor, with all due respect — not necessarily to myself — I believe I have successfully disproved the allegations in my complaint." The ring of the absurd comment erased all doubts, if any remained, as to the folly of Jordan's self-representation. Nevertheless, he felt no regret. He said, "Under the circumstances I move to dismiss my complaint."

The wide-eyed Judge nodded. "If that's what you wish to do, so be it." He turned to Harwood. "I assume you have no objection."

"None whatsoever, your Honor. Moreover, it . . . " His voice trailed off, his gaze drifting into space. A moment later he redirected himself to the bench. "May I take a minute." He leaned down and whispered back and forth with his client. Finally, he stood up straight and said, "Your Honor, proof of the defendant's counterclaim would be problematic at best, and, regardless, he has no desire to pursue it. Accordingly, I move to dismiss that counterclaim."

Judge Boston scratched his head and then looked at Jordan. "No objection, your Honor."

A wry smile appeared on Judge Boston's face as he rocked his chair back and forth two or three times. "The motions to dismiss the plaintiff's complaint and the defendant's counterclaim are both granted. The . . . " Judge Boston hesitated. His expression turned pensive.

Jordan suspected His Honor was struggling with the bizarre scenario. Indeed, Jordan himself found it hard to fathom.

"Mr. Jackson," said Judge Boston, "under the rules of practice I believe the defendant is entitled to court costs."

Amidst the unusual turn of events, the minor matter hadn't crossed Jordan's mind. A quick assessment convinced him. There was no denying that he had initiated the unsuccessful lawsuit. "I understand, your Honor."

"Excuse me," said Harwood. "If I may take another moment." He turned and once again whispered to his client. "Your Honor, my client is satisfied that this difficult litigation has reached an appropriate conclusion. He wishes to waive costs."

Judge Boston shrugged. "Given the illogic of everything that has preceded, it makes perfect sense." He chuckled and then turned to the jury. "Ladies and Gentlemen, I'm sorry that after your long and devoted attention you will not have the opportunity to deliberate this case. But lest you think your services were for naught, think again. Without these proceedings, of which you were an integral part, the issues of this case would remain unresolved. Perhaps even more important is that together we may have ended the arson and threats that have plagued our community in recent months. I submit that your services far exceed those we could have anticipated when we embarked on this extraordinary trial. On behalf of the parties and myself, I thank you for your time and attention. You are excused." Judge Boston picked up his gavel. He gave it a momentary glance but then laid it back down. "This court is adjourned."

Chapter XVII

or once with no need to duck out fast, Lauren waited at the rear of the courtroom. With both her father and Jordan cleared and their animosity seemingly tempered, she was eager to speak with them. But both were preoccupied. Her father was seated at the defense table talking with Harwood, and Jordan was at the bench laughing with Judge Boston.

A tap on the shoulder caused her to turn.

"You're Lauren Worthington, aren't you?"

"Yes," she said, defensive antennae shooting up, as she recognized the man in the blue sharkskin suit as a reporter from *Judicial TV*.

"Your father is the defendant, and your boyfriend, the plaintiff. Right?"

"Yes." His questions, phrased like the cross-examinations she had been hearing in the courtroom, suggested he was as slick as his attire.

"You're a reporter for the *Chronicle*."

"I was until a few weeks ago. And you're a reporter with *Judicial TV*."

"Actually, a combination — reporter and lawyer. My name is George Acker."

Lauren reached out and shook the hand he extended. "What can I do for you?"

"We're doing a show about the trial."

"So I've heard, though I can't imagine why."

Acker gave her a skeptical look. "C'mon. We've got arson, politics and romance, complete with racial overtones, converging in a rural southern town. You have to admit it's a fascinating story."

"To an outsider like you, maybe. But for someone like me, it's — " Lauren bit her tongue. Exchanging more than pleasantries with the smooth-talking newsman was as imprudent as a ghost-town rendezvous with a serial rapist. She said, "You didn't answer my question." The puzzled look on his face prompted her to add, "What do you want with me?"

"We understand you were instrumental in solving the case."

Lauren shook her head. "You've come to the wrong place."

"I don't understand. The case is over. And from what I've heard, back when things were a lot more controversial, you were very outspoken."

"Well . . . " The possibility an interview might help her sagging career tempted Lauren. Were it not for her experience on Baker's show, she might have bitten into the forbidden fruit.

"C'mon. I'm sure you have some fascinating thoughts. You should share them."

"Why?"

"Because . . . uh . . . folks will be interested."

The justification, one that hardly benefited Lauren, confirmed the need to be judicious. But as a member of the news media, she could at least extend him professional courtesy. She said, "Off the record, I'll tell you why I'm reluctant. A few months back I found myself in the eye of a hurricane. As a reporter, I considered it a challenge. Being personally involved, I should have known better. The storm was brewing all around me, but from my vantage point in the center, everything seemed crystal clear." She chuckled. "Big problem. The only way out of a hurricane's eye is through the teeth of the storm." Thoughts of the difficult path, one that had cost her job, served as a stern reminder. She said, "When it comes to the middle of a storm (she gestured toward herself) — *Been there, done that.*"

"I understand," said Acker with a warm smile.

His agreeable response might have caused her to drop her guard, but she had lost only her job, not the skills acquired as a reporter. As early as her first week at the *Chronicle*, Nielsen had taught her the congenial trick. She smiled, anticipating Acker's next ploy.

"I've only been in Cedar Creek for a few days, but from what I've learned, your investigative work solved the case. Didn't you — "

"What have you learned?" she said, determined that she, not he, would make the inquiries.

"Oh — a bit of this and a bit of that. But I was wondering, did — "

"Excuse me. You ignored my question."

"Touché," he said, heaving a sigh. "I doubt you'll comment, but what the hell. My sources tell me you discovered that the two calls to Jake Brewster's trailer were made on *Blue Sky's* mobile telephone. They also tell me you found out that someone from *Blue Sky* rented a black Mercedes the same day those calls were made. Seems you cracked the case." He waited a moment, as if looking for a reaction. "I listened to the tapes of the Jerry Baker show. You stuck your neck out. Of course, anyone can do that. Difference is, you backed it up." He waited again. "Aren't you going to say anything?"

She had already given him professional courtesy. He was pressing his luck. "You want an answer. I'll give you one. And this one's for the record. *No comment*."

For an instant Acker looked annoyed, but then he shrugged. "Damn. You're good." He smiled and walked away.

A rush of adrenaline quickened Lauren's heartbeat. It made no difference that Acker, the seasoned pro, had given her little information. She had given him less. She turned and looked to the front of the courtroom. Deserted. Jordan, her father, Harwood, the Judge — they all must have left through the door behind the bench. The one time that she was glad to see them, they had all gone the other way.

She headed out of the courthouse. Next to one of the pillars at the top of the granite staircase Acker was speaking into a hand-held microphone while his associate stood with a camera on his shoulder just a few feet away. Lauren veered to her right and quickly descended the staircase. Odds were Acker wasn't looking for a second chance, but, in any event, she wasn't about to find out. She went directly to her apartment. When she arrived, the blink of her telephone answering machine beckoned her. She pressed the flashing button.

> *Hi Lauren. It's Dad. I'm at Harwood's office. Sorry I missed you after court today. We had some loose ends that needed to be addressed. Tomorrow is Tuesday. I'd like you to come for dinner. We've missed too many lately. I'll see you at six.*

Lauren glared at the telephone. Yes, she would blame the messenger. If the device didn't come with a damn answering machine, her father would have needed to confront her directly. With her eyes still focused on the infernal contraption, she reached for the receiver. Two can play the same game. She started to dial his number when she realized it wouldn't be right. Chances were, Bessie would answer and inherit the unenviable task of passing on the message that she was skipping dinner. Putting Bessie in the middle, a position all too familiar to Lauren, was unfair. She slammed the receiver into its cradle. Her father's manipulation had to cease.

Tuesday morning. Lauren slept in until nine. Rising late was becoming a habit since Nielsen had fired her. She had spoken with Jordan the night before, but only briefly. He had called from his office, having gone directly there from the courthouse. One of his best clients had just been arrested in Columbia, about a hundred miles away, and was being arraigned the following morning. Anticipating a late night, followed by a busy day, Jordan expected it might be well into the evening before he returned to Cedar Creek. He had lovingly apologized and promised that Wednesday evening, plus the entire weekend, would be theirs to share. Lauren appreciated Jordan's dilemma. She might have been less understanding had not her work as a reporter often forced her to cancel plans.

She poured herself a bowl of raisin bran, heated a pot of coffee and sat down with the *Chronicle*. In recent weeks her usual routine, a businesslike critique of the morning daily, had been replaced by a cursory check of world news and then on to more salient matters, the TV schedule and the crossword puzzle. She had nearly finished the puzzle — at least as much as she could — when the telephone rang. She reached for the receiver. "Hello."

"Hi Lauren. It's Barker Nielsen. How've you been?"

You must be kidding. You fire me, and then ask how I've been. "Excellent," she said. Whether he expected her to inquire in kind, she refused.

"That was quite a trial over at the courthouse."

So what, she thought, unwilling to make small talk. She pictured him pompously seated in his sumptuous leather chair. Then again, perhaps the fastidious tyrant was hunched over his desk searching for specks of dust with a magnifying glass.

"First thing this morning Larry Sunfield called me from the home office. You'll never guess who called him yesterday. George Acker from *Judicial TV*."

Don't tell me that creep put words in my mouth. "What did he want?"

"Well — Larry says Acker was raving how you did one hell of an investigation, solving the arson and all. Of course, you know how Larry tends to exaggerate."

"Not really. Remember — I was only a reporter. I didn't rub shoulders with the big boys from the syndicate's home office."

"Anyway, Larry claims *Judicial TV* plans to give you some very positive national exposure. They want you to do a network interview. Larry says it'll be a real coup for a tiny local like the *Chronicle*."

Suddenly Lauren suspected why Nielsen was calling. The worm had turned. Nielsen was caught in the middle, and it was his turn to come crawling. "What's Larry's number? I'll give him a call."

"What are you talking about?"

"I want to make arrangements with *Judicial TV*. You told Larry that you fired me, didn't you?"

"Well — not exactly."

"Gosh. He may be upset when I clue him in."

"Slow down. You're getting this all wrong. I want you back at the *Chronicle*."

Common sense urged her to jump at the opportunity. But the chance to eradicate its major drawback was too good to pass up. She said, "That's nice, but I've been looking at other possibilities."

"You . . . you haven't committed yet?"

"Well — nothing firm." Fortunately, the smile that covered her face didn't travel the telephone lines.

"Larry asked about your salary. When I told him, he suggested a twenty-percent raise. He said excellent reporters, the kind you can trust with independence, are hard to come by."

"I assume you told him I'm very difficult."

"Oh . . . can't we let bygones be bygones?"

She greeted the question with silence.

"C'mon, tell me what I need to do to bring you back into the fold."

She had him where she wanted. Her ego, rarely so large, seduced her to make him beg. Better judgment, perhaps even a touch of sympathy, prevailed. She said, "Treat me like a professional."

"Fine, I — "

"Wait a second. I haven't finished." She punctuated her words with a long pause. "If you expect me to come back and keep the firing our little secret, you'll have to deal with me as a colleague." The remark, its distasteful hint of blackmail, made her think twice. But it was now or never. "I understand that you're the boss, and you make the decisions, but from now on, treat me with respect."

"No problem. You've got it."

Sure, thought Lauren, doubting his glib reply.

"So, we all set?"

"Hardly. I didn't mean lip service."

"I wasn't — "

"Maybe my coming back is a bad idea."

"C'mon, don't think that way. I'll do better. I mean it."

Lauren debated with herself. A minute before she wanted to make him beg. He was doing just that. But stooping to his level would produce only visceral gratification. What she needed was a substantive change in their relationship.

"Please, tell me what you want."

He was ready to listen. True — his driving force was self-interest. But for once he was ready to listen. She said, "First off, I expect common courtesy. That includes a friendly greeting, but it's a whole lot more. If you need to discuss something with me, fine. But don't make me sit like a dummy while you make other phone calls."

"I understand, but sometimes there's an emergency. You know, a major breaking story or the home office wants me."

"That's not what I'm referring to. I mean conversations about your weekend golf match or yesterday's ball game; the kind of arrogance that says to a waiting employee she doesn't matter." Lauren anticipated a reaction, but there was none. "You disagree?"

"Uh . . . just the opposite. I get the picture. Ugly, but accurate."

The self-condemning words, something Lauren had never heard from Nielsen, might have evoked compassion were the context different and he, someone else. She said, "You know, you do it to everyone, not just me."

He heaved a deep sigh. "Something you said the day I fired you has been — " He stopped midstream. "I'm sorry. I should be listening now."

She wondered what he was thinking, but a more important point, one that had stuck in her craw for a long time, needed mention. She said, "When a decision has to be made, you put those involved, myself included, in an impossible position. You ask for our opinion. If you disagree, you do the opposite. On the other hand, if you like the recommendation, you pretend to go along. But always with a warning that it's against your better judgment and there will be a price to pay if it doesn't work out."

A chuckle came from the other end of the line.

"You find that funny?"

"Not at all. I'm laughing at myself. You knew my game all along."

"Everyone did."

"I guess . . . " His fading voice grew briefly inaudible. "I need to know." He hesitated again. "The day I fired you . . . uh . . . you said that everyone calls me *The Bastard*. Is that really true?"

The pain in his voice made it hard for Lauren to reply. He had treated her badly, and she had longed to get even. *An eye for an eye*. That's what the Bible said. The thought summoned recollections of younger days when she had perfect attendance at Sunday school. Her fifth-grade teacher had encouraged forgiveness. The momentary dilemma curbed Lauren's desire for retribution.

"You've answered my question." Nielsen began mumbling, almost as if he were speaking to himself. "*The Bastard*. God, that's how my employees think of me."

"Well, not everyone — "

"No need to explain. I get the message. As a matter of fact, it's been ringing in my ears for several weeks. Night after sleepless night." There was an uncomfortable moment of silence. "With no family, apart from a cousin in St. Louis, the *Chronicle* is my life. And to think, my people hate me." He heaved another sigh. "All along I've told myself my employees respect me. Fear, not respect — that's what I command. Just like my high school history teacher, *Dolan the Despot*." Nielsen sighed yet again. "How easy it is to delude oneself until finally, like the morning headline, the truth is there in big, bold print."

Lauren swallowed hard. It made no sense. Of all people she was empathizing with Nielsen.

"Well — I guess if I want a better name, I'll have to earn it. But that's my problem, and not why I called. As Larry said, you're a fine reporter. You deserve independence, as well as a twenty-percent raise. Assuming you decide to come back, they're yours, along with respect. I'm determined to do better." He hesitated. "I need to do better with a lot of people."

Nielsen's contrition was disarming. Even knowing that promises and action were as different as hopes and reality, Lauren gave credence to his words. Assurances, less than he had given, would have sufficed. She wanted her job. "I'm back on board," she said.

"Music . . . sweet music in my ears." The effervescence in his tone matched his words. A moment later his voice turned resolute. "Ms. Worthington, I apologize for my long pattern of rude conduct. It was uncalled for. I will try to do better."

"Apology accepted," she said, amazed that a telephone line connecting them could be carrying such harmonious sounds.

"Beginning tomorrow this editor intends to make some changes. Tops on that list are more understanding and patience."

His words struck hard at her cynical side. "That will mean a lot," she said. Whether his behavior would change was an open question, but Lauren was convinced he intended to try.

"The weatherman forecasts a beautiful week. Why don't you take the rest of it off . . . with pay of course. We'll see you next Monday."

"I appreciate that, but first I want to put together the story on the arson trial. That's one I want to do myself. I'll drop it off tomorrow morning."

"That's my girl. I — " There was a momentary silence. "Sorry. Poor choice of words. What I meant was that's my colleague, my very capable colleague. Have a good week."

"You too." Lauren hung up the receiver. She pumped a fist high into the air. She loved being a reporter. She also loved Cedar Creek. The *Chronicle* was the only way to have both. It had been good to her in spite of her boss. Perhaps he had turned a new leaf. If so, her job at the *Chronicle* was about to get a whole lot better.

She stared off into space and began contemplating the bizarre chain of events comprising the past year of her life. As if someone had unlocked her subconscious, disjointed recollections, many laced with unresolved issues, poured forth. She took several deep breaths and then suddenly, for the first time in years, burst into tears. Why — she wasn't sure, but two . . . five . . . ten minutes she continued to sob. Gradually the crying subsided, replaced by breathless gasps for air. Physically spent, she laid her head on her arms as her mind drifted somewhere between fantasy and reality. Little by little, she regained a semblance of normalcy. She raised her head and looked all around her apartment. Her eyes moved to the *Chronicle*, which lay before her on the kitchen table. She stared blankly at the newspaper, its printed words all but invisible. Month after month, amidst constant stress, she had played the part of the indomitable reporter, the energetic, modern woman who, whatever the challenges, could do it all. It had taken its toll. Only now, after the floodgates had lifted and emotions surged, did she begin to comprehend the magnitude of that toll. Was it worth it? *Yes* was an easy answer. However, candor, the kind worthy of a quality journalist, left her unsure. If she could turn back time, would she chart the same course knowing what it would entail? Maybe. But maybe not. She had taken tough positions, not that they were altogether right. But on balance she felt proud. The possibility her roughest times were behind her was a welcome thought. Standing tall was nice, but coasting awhile — perhaps recapturing her easygoing reputation — would be a welcome change.

With the litigation between her father and Jordan over, her job back and time off, the upcoming evening would have offered the perfect opportunity for Jordan and her to celebrate. Unfortunately his legal emergency had taken him out of town. Regardless, it was Tuesday and dear old Dad expected her for dinner. She loved her father and would not have minded the ritual were it not for his constant meddling and pressure, especially his move-back-home spiel. Anticipation of the inevitable scene momentarily dipped her mood, but then a conscious smile came over her face. The time had come to tell him *no,* once and for all. No longer unemployed, she had her job back, plus a twenty-percent raise. She could pay her own rent.

Lauren climbed out of her Dodge Neon and walked up the driveway of Worthington Hall. With its Ionic white pillars rising from the curved, granite portico, it contrasted with her Spartan studio apartment. On either side well-kept gardens, each a mirror image of the other, created a vision of perfect symmetry. Just before she ascended the porch, Lauren paused on the tapestry-brick walkway. Behind the façade of every fine edifice anomalies lurked; more often than not, the grander the palace, the greater the contradictions. She glanced in the direction of the freshly painted gazebo that adjoined the pond at the west end of the house. On the nearly placid water a rippled reflection of the latticed retreat painted an impressionistic image. Pastel recollections of charming childhood days camouflaged antilogies; some patent, others subtle.

Lauren slowly climbed the porch's seven stairs, counting them one by one. Her thoughts turned to her mother. Lauren gazed upward at the late afternoon sky. The Big Dipper lay hidden behind a bright veil. Soon enough when nighttime fell, the constellation would reveal itself. She rang the doorbell.

Within moments Bessie opened it. She glanced at her watch. "You're fifteen minutes early. Your father hasn't even come down yet."

"Thought I'd shock him. She took note of Bessie's form-fitting black dress, complimented by a pearl necklace. "That's a sleek number you're wearing. You planning to hit the clubs tonight?"

"What — at my age?"

"You talk like your prehistoric."

Bessie turned toward the hall mirror, an ornate, gold-trimmed antique. "Well — come next March, I hit the big five-0."

"Big deal." Lauren pointed at the mirror. "Most women my age would kill for a figure like yours."

"Sure . . . and coal tastes better than candy." Bessie shook her head and headed through the dining room.

"Here, let me help you in the kitchen."

"Everything's done already."

"Well — I'll go in there and sit with you." As Lauren passed through the dining room, she noticed that four places, rather than the usual two, were set around the long table. And the silver champagne bucket stood ready with an iced bottle of the bubbly. "What's going on?" she said.

"Pardon me?"

"Why the four settings?"

Bessie shrugged. "Always good to be prepared. You never know when company may drop by."

Lauren was about to question the curious response, but Bessie, who had already passed through the kitchen door, didn't give her a chance. "I made a new hors d'oeuvre that I want you to try." She removed a cheese-stuffed mushroom from the oven and handed it to Lauren on a small plate. "Careful, it's hot."

Lauren nibbled the tidbit. "Delicious. I could make a meal of these." She was about to reach for another when she heard her father's voice.

"Bessie, is company here already?"

"Only me, Dad." She headed into the dining room, with Bessie close behind.

"What's this *only-me* stuff?" he said, as he came in from the hall and gave her a hug.

"I'm hardly company."

He frowned and then turned to Bessie. "Set the young lady straight."

Lauren chuckled to herself. Her father never learned.

"Lauren," said Bessie, with a chiding finger, "here at Worthington Hall, there is no company more special than you. And you don't need to look surprised."

"Wait a second. You're taking his side?"

Bessie nodded. "For once, your father happens to be right."

"So what." The absurdity of Lauren's comeback echoed in her ears. "You don't need to acknowledge it."

Both Bessie and her father started to laugh.

"You two are in a festive mood."

"Why not?" said her father. "It's a holiday."

"Holiday? What are you talking about?"

"It's . . . it's the first day after yesterday." He looked over at Bessie. "Isn't that right?"

Bessie rolled her eyes. "You're pushing your luck."

Lauren gazed at Bessie and then her father. Something was going on. Something very strange. She was about to press the issue when the doorbell chimes interrupted.

"Excuse me," said Bessie, as she headed to the door.

The distraction forked Lauren's brain back to another curiosity. She said, "Why is the table set for four?"

"Be patient, and soon enough you'll see." A smug expression punctuated her father's words.

A moment later Bessie returned with Jordan alongside. Lauren immediately raced his way and hugged him. She was eager to give him the good news about her job, but first she wanted her explanation, including the identity of the last guest. She whispered, "You were invited, I assume."

"I heard that," said her father. "And yes, he was."

Emotions surged. But years of conditioning curbed the urge to celebrate. A reporter always verified the facts before going off half-cocked; a tendency that Lauren had discovered was not all bad. Gratification delayed was not gratification denied. And it left one better prepared in the event of disappointment. She looked into Jordan's eyes and said, "*What* is going on?"

"Nothing." His attention immediately turned to Lauren's father who was extending a handshake.

As the two men seemingly ignored her, Lauren thought better of trying to get a straight answer from them. She turned to Bessie. "What's this all about?"

"What's what about?" Bessie's puzzled look was plainly contrived.

"You too?"

Bessie shrugged.

Lauren waited a moment until her father and Jordan had completed their greetings. She said, "Okay — enough. What's going on?"

Her father looked at Jordan, who gestured back. "I yield to my host."

"How extraordinarily thoughtful." He smiled and then turned to Lauren. "Jordan and I have been talking of late."

"So I've noticed. And I must say, it seemed strange." The contrary expression on her father's face prompted her to add, "All of a sudden you two have become very chummy, just when you were busy battling in the courtroom. Rather odd. Wouldn't you say?"

"Lawyers do it all the time." He slipped an arm over Jordan's shoulder. "Isn't that right, Counselor?"

"Absolutely. I knock heads with my adversaries all morning, bark at their every word, and then have lunch with them in the courthouse cafeteria."

"Not with Bernie Raxson," said Lauren.

"Of course not," said Jordan. "That moron is a double-dealing dimwit. But what's he got to do with anything?"

Lauren suspected Jordan was playing dumb again. "My point is that after you leave the courtroom, you're only pals with people you like."

Jordan nodded. "And I happen to like your father."

"The feeling is quite mutual." He gestured toward Bessie who had just come in with a platter of her cheese-stuffed mushrooms. The two men each took one.

Bessie started to offer one to Lauren. "In a moment," she said. "First, I want some straight answers. How did you two get so friendly?" She gestured at her father.

He motioned at his full mouth and continued chewing. He started to reach for another mushroom.

Lauren grabbed his hand. "Not until I get an explanation."

Her father glanced at Jordan. "Impatient, isn't she?" He looked back at Lauren. "You don't need to scowl. I'm glad to cooperate." He took a deep breath. "It's like this. Jordan was talking to Chester Harwood after the consultant's initial report on the mall came out. Jordan liked the scaled-down version. It had lots of green space adjoining the park. It protected the aquifer and all but eliminated the traffic concerns." He turned to Jordan. "Isn't that right?"

Jordan nodded. "There were enough positive aspects that I quietly began a dialogue with your father. What appealed to me most was the cost/benefit analysis for the Village. With the scaled-down version, Cedar Creek will have a positive payback on the tax breaks in less than five years. And *Cybertrixon*, unlike a retail anchor, was the clincher. Instead of jobs just over minimum wage, it means two-hundred fifty quality positions, most of them professional, the kind that will help keep our best and brightest young people from moving away."

As Jordan spoke, Lauren felt his contagious enthusiasm. She recalled the consultant's preliminary report, which Village Board Chairman Laughlin had briefly shared with the community the night the Board opted to allow continued consideration of the project. Though the consultant was far from finished then, his early findings suggested the scaled-down mall had many pluses for Cedar Creek.

"The revised plan," continued Jordan, "also reduces the Village's costs. Demands on police, fire, water and sewer services will be less. And unlike a big department store that would generate a constant flow of people coming and going, *Cybertrixon* employees are there for the whole day. And on weekends, the time when our park gets its most use, *Cybertrixon's* end of the mall will be closed. Plus we've got extra green space and — "

"You know," said Lauren's father, "you've convinced me the new proposal is even better than I thought." He nodded slowly, his expression pensive. "Maybe I should ask the Village for additional tax breaks." As fast as Jordan could open his mouth, Lauren's father added, "I'm only kidding. I like the revised proposal exactly as it is."

"And as a member of the Village Board," said Jordan, "it will be my pleasure to break the logjam and become the third member to support that proposal." He looked at Lauren. "What do you think?"

She eyed the two men, one as effervescent as the other. After jerking her around, they expected dispensation. She folded her arms. "The whole thing is balderdash. Pure, unadulterated balderdash."

Her father bore a look of disbelief.

"You don't like it?" said Jordan.

She shook her head defiantly. "What — you expect me to like a plan that will make Cedar Creek a better place to live." She hesitated just long enough to savor their perplexed expressions. "Of course, I like it. But I wasn't about to say so without a little retribution. And wipe those indignant expressions off your faces because you'll get no sympathy here. You may, however, get a nice piece in the *Chronicle* supporting the project."

Jordan shook his head. "That last tidbit is hardly funny." He raised a clenched fist. "I'd like to give that former boss of yours a taste of this. He had some nerve firing you."

Lauren smiled broadly.

"From the look on your face," said Jordan, "you'd like to see me do it. Or, perhaps, you'd prefer to clock him yourself."

She shook her head. "That's not why I'm smiling. Nielsen and I had a little talk. I've got my job back, along with a twenty-percent raise and his promise to treat me with respect."

"Sure," said her father. "And I'm Leonardo da Vinci." He turned to Jordan. "Have you met my daughter, Moaning Lisa?"

Jordan sighed. "You mean the moody one with the enigmatic smile?"

Lauren folded her arms once again. "Whenever you boys have finished prattling, I'll continue." She waited a moment, refusing to acknowledge her father's piqued expression. Finally, she said, "You may have noticed that *Judicial TV* followed the trial. They're doing a segment, and they were impressed with my investigative work. To make a long story short, after they contacted the *Chronicle's* home office, Nielsen had to beg me to come back. Those terms I mentioned a minute ago are for real."

Jordan's eyes widened. He hugged Lauren.

Her father slapped Jordan on the back. "You know, now that she's got a good job — what with a raise and all — maybe she's not such a bad catch. You might want to think about it."

Lauren studied her father's face. Was he mocking her again, or, in his inimitable way, had he hinted at something else?

Jordan pulled back from his embrace with Lauren and looked at her father. "You've got a point, Rog. I'll have to give that some consideration."

Whatever her father had intended, Jordan had gone too far. "Well, haven't you two become the best of chums."

Her father slapped Jordan on the back again. "Over the past few weeks my buddy and I have gotten to know each other a whole lot better. The counselor here is okay. He's intelligent. He's honest. Good-looking. Charming and . . . " He glanced at Jordan. "Any more adjectives and you're apt to get a swelled head. Can't let that happen." He turned back to Lauren. "Watch out. He can be stubborn." Her father jammed his thumb into his own chest. "I know. I'm an expert at that."

Lauren's brain raced down divergent paths; one trying to fathom her father's apparent shift in attitude and the other reacting to the pair of male chauvinists. The latter reminded her of the production of *Fiddler on the Roof* that she and Jordan had recently seen. She looked at him. "Is this Anatevka?"

"*Ana what!*" said Jordan, his eyes wide.

"You know, that imaginary place from *Fiddler* where Tevye, the papa, and that butcher fellow, the slovenly, old guy in the blood-stained apron, made an agreement for Tevye's daughter to marry the butcher."

"You're comparing me to that meat cutter?"

Lauren shrugged. "If the apron fits, tie a bow in the back."

Jordan turned to her father. "Can you believe she said that?"

"Don't look at me. I never saw the show." He gestured at Lauren. "The father, this Tevye fellow. He's a nice guy. Right?"

"Sure — if you like mules." Lauren sensed her father was ready with a comeback, but she had another matter on her mind. "Since when do you approve of my dating Jordan?"

Her father gestured toward the kitchen. "Your friend in there got me to thinking. It all started that night at dinner when she jumped down my throat."

Lauren recalled the evening when Bessie, ever passive, had shocked them both.

"She made me realize I was risking the most important thing in my life — my daughter. I was forcing you to choose between Jordan and me. I realized I was playing Russian Roulette, and, worst of all, the kind where suicide is inevitable. You pull that trigger often enough, and sooner or later it's the chamber with the bullet." He paused, but his thoughtful look suggested he had more to say. He shook his head. "Ironic."

Lauren waited a moment. "What's ironic?"

"Years ago, when I wanted to marry your mother — she was the light of my life — her father tried to drive a wedge between us because she was Catholic and I was Protestant. Instead he drove her away. I almost did the same thing." He shook his head again. "My logic — it always seemed sound — was no better than that of my father-in-law. I focused on the pigment of a man's skin. The things that mattered — his character, his intelligence, his decency and, most of all, the way he treated my daughter — didn't count." He stretched out both hands taking hold of Lauren's with one and Jordan's with the other.

With his free hand Jordan grasped Lauren's connecting the three in a circle. They stood there in silence. A minute, maybe more, elapsed, as Lauren basked in what would have seemed inconceivable only a day earlier. When finally they separated their hands, Lauren turned to Jordan. "Just a few short weeks ago you were reluctant to meet with my father. Why the change of heart?"

"My reasons weren't all that different from your father's. That day in the park when he first suggested we should talk, I gave him the cold shoulder. Later that night, after I had time to think, I realized I was cutting off my nose to spite my face. The last thing I wanted was to lose you. Everything else became secondary. So, I decided to listen. I could always ignore what he said. Much to my surprise, there were areas of common ground. Doubts began to develop whether he was the arsonist. By the time we went to court, my brain was schizophrenic. The rational side, equipped with legal training, dwelled on evidence that pointed to your father. But the emotional side, guided by my heart, hoped he was innocent. I had to know the truth. We agreed to let the chips fall where they may. But the bottom line — neither of us wanted to lose you."

A conscious smile came over Lauren's face as she gazed at Jordan. Her eyes moved to her father. She was proud of them both. When push had come to shove, they had cared enough about her to give one another a chance. All along she had loved them both. But they had frustrated her. No longer. Their conduct had earned her respect. As an added bonus her father's problems might be resolved as well. She said, "Once the new mall is approved, will that take care of your financial difficulties?"

"Financial difficulties? What are you talking about?"

"Uh . . . I know you never shared your money matters with me, but I . . . I heard you had problems."

"And just where did you hear that?"

She tried to recall. *Was it from Laughlin? No . . . He wasn't the source. Ward?* An instant later her memory clicked. She said, "Forget the whole thing. It doesn't matter." She swallowed hard. With the power of suggestion the man behind the arson had provided bait to cast suspicion onto her father. And bite, she had. Thank goodness she had kept the information to herself. *Judicial TV* might have had second thoughts about her crack investigative skills had they known how credulous she had been. The kitchen door opened drawing her attention.

"If you all don't sit down," said Bessie, "dinner will be cold."

Lauren eyed the dining-room table. She gestured at the four place settings, each now bearing a shrimp cocktail. "Aren't we still waiting for another guest?"

Her father shook his head and seated himself at the head of the table. Lauren hesitated but took her usual seat at the opposite end, while Jordan took the chair off to her left. A moment later Bessie sat down to Lauren's right. Lauren did a double take and then looked down the table's broad expanse at her father.

"Something the matter?"

"Nothing . . . Nothing at all," she said, savoring that which, with the artistry of a journalistic masterpiece, had rewritten the tabloid she had lived for months. She gazed up at the crystal chandelier that hung above the center of the table. One of its many prism-cut glasses refracted the light of the setting sun into a multi-colored spectrum. The rainbowed effect shifted her thoughts to her mother. The possibility that the kaleidoscopic display might be a sign crossed Lauren's mind. Her rational side, ordinarily the final arbiter, rejected the sentiment. Lauren gave the rainbow another look. That a piece of glass could separate a ray of light into such an amazing array of colors was magical. It defied logic. The paradox encouraged reason to yield to emotion. She felt a glow, a surge of unmitigated joy. Like a vista revealed upon reaching a mountain peak, a simple notion, one that had long escaped Lauren, manifested itself. What more would her mother have wished for her than happiness. What greater tribute could she pay to her mother's memory than to live a rich, fulfilling life. A huge burden stretching to the heavens lifted from Lauren's shoulders. The grieving process, for years stifled, could be laid to rest. Lauren looked over at Jordan. His loving smile warmed her heart. Her eyes moved around the rest of the table and then back to Jordan. She whispered to him. "The next thing you know my Dad will be asking Bessie for a date."

"I heard that," said her father. With a tilt of his head and a protracted gaze at Bessie, he added, "I might just do that."

Lauren laughed. Obviously her father wasn't serious. She looked around the table. Maybe . . . maybe he was.